Mademoiselle Revolution

ZOE SIVAK

Mademoiselle Revolution

BERKLEY

New York

BERKLEY
An imprint of Penguin Random House LLC
penguinrandomhouse.com

Copyright © 2022 by Zoe Sivak

Library of Congress Cataloging-in-Publication Data

Names: Sivak, Zoe, author.
Title: Mademoiselle revolution / Zoe Sivak.
Description: New York : Berkley, [2022]
Identifiers: LCCN 2021059088 (print) | LCCN 2021059089 (ebook) |
ISBN 9780593336038 (hardcover) | ISBN 9780593336052 (ebook)
Subjects: LCSH: France—History—Revolution, 1789–1799—Fiction. |
Robespierre, Maximilien, 1758–1794—Fiction. | Haiti—History—
Revolution, 1791–1804—Fiction. | LCGFT: Historical fiction. | Novels.
Classification: LCC PS3619.I944 M33 2022 (print) |
LCC PS3619.I944 (ebook) | DDC 813/.6—dc23/eng/20211210
LC record available at https://lccn.loc.gov/2021059088
LC ebook record available at https://lccn.loc.gov/2021059089

Printed in the United States of America
1   3   5   7   9   10   8   6   4   2

BOOK DESIGN BY KATY RIEGEL

For Amanda, my best friend and lighthouse

The language and opinions described in this novel express the problematic beliefs held by many in the eighteenth century and beyond, even by those who themselves are victims of racism. Words like *mulatto, negro, slave,* and *master*—instead of *biracial, Black, enslaved person,* and *enslaver*—were terribly commonplace.

To depict history is not to condone it: we must face our past with clear eyes so we may continue down our long road toward dismantling racism.

Mademoiselle Revolution

Part I

Saint-Domingue,
Hispaniola

Chapter One

If we fall asleep for an instant on the edge of the abyss, we will tremble upon awakening! . . . France will receive a mortal wound, and a multitude of honest citizens will be impoverished and ruined; we will lose everything.

—*Vincent Ogé, Address on the Abolition of Slavery*

janvier 1791

By the age of eighteen, Sylvie de Rosiers had mastered fractions. She lounged on the sofa, feet neatly tucked beneath her, maintaining a primness even *en repos*. Her gown encircled her in a pool of white muslin; the *chemise à la reine* had come into fashion a few years prior, but its airiness made it ubiquitous among the wealthy women's wardrobes on Saint-Domingue. And the thin fabric showed off her legs to their ultimate advantage.

But the new house slave disrupted the pleasantness of her morning. She knew the girl was a recent addition to the household staff because Sylvie noticed *all* fractions, and this servant presented a challenge.

On the French colony of Saint-Domingue, fractions were not innocuous numbers separated by lines of dark ink (though she knew those, too). Here, fractions had faces. *Mulatto, quadroon, octoroon*— these terms divided the blood into halves and quarters and eighths, Black and white and whiter still.

Sylvie regarded the newcomer from under her thick fan of lashes. The girl was pretty enough, as many house slaves were, though clearly inexperienced at household tasks. House slaves, as a rule, needed to be attractive; no wealthy family wanted an ugly girl serving tea.

Most often, *Creoles*, those who survived on the island long enough to know the language of the colonists, worked in the house. *Bossales*, African-born slaves, worked fields.

Her father's wife, Madame Catherine de Rosiers, chose maids like she chose rugs: pretty ornaments that served a purpose, but that mustn't distract.

Too thin to be truly beautiful, this girl could not match Sylvie's loveliness.

The servant had dark skin, though not dark like the coffee Sylvie's father grew. Her *tignon*, or hair wrap, was a plain handkerchief tied close to her head. Sylvie's tignon, like that of other free mulattas, towered high in a mass of bright colors and intricate folds. Her lady's maid, Alice, wrapped the best tignons of any of the house servants, hence why Sylvie valued her most of all of her father's slaves.

A true mulatta? she mused. White fathers normally freed their children according to island custom, but even so, the occasional planter ended up with suspiciously light-skinned slaves generations down the line.

But she is too dark. A third, perhaps? She almost shook her head and thought with no little pride, *No, she is not as fair as me.* Sylvie's face was prettier, paler, and had a better nose.

White masters and their wandering hands left more than one slave heavy with child. Sylvie's mother had been one of them. So no matter how many house slaves came and went, she saw her own shameful pedigree in every face. But she never saw divisions when she beheld her own reflection each morning; no marks partitioned Blackness on her skin, only the smooth expanse of bronze marred by a dusting of freckles across her nose.

Few eligible men on Saint-Domingue had yet to meet Mademoiselle de Rosiers, and fewer still left the introduction without their heads swimming with hazel eyes and twinkling pearls—she was a Venus of Saint-Domingue, Caribbean sea-foam come to life.

But she did not have to see those divisions in order to feel them.

Thus, her understanding of fractions became more than simple arithmetic and rather a lesson in her very identity. Those lines kept Sylvie, and all other *affranchis* like her, from the fields their mothers worked and died on.

Sylvie decided that the girl was simply a fair-skinned Creole—thus comfortably lesser—and commenced to stir her tea now that the equation had been solved.

Les Affiches américaines, the only newspaper on Saint-Domingue, lay on the silver tray beside a fashion journal. She ran a disinterested eye over the tiny print. The press always wrote articles advocating for the complete independence of the island from France, especially after the United States managed to do it with its leaders' heads still attached. They made freedom look so messy, with two constitutions and a tacky striped flag.

She pushed it aside, favoring the *Magasin des modes* instead. It took months for new editions to make it to the island, and she absorbed every page for hat trimmings and changing silhouettes.

But the new slave disturbed the morning quiet. Her trembling hands made the cups rattle. The china was not built to endure such rough handling, and Sylvie grimaced at the thought of drinking broken porcelain as well as tea.

"Do go and fetch a fruit platter," she said. Wide-eyed, the servant scurried out of the room to do her bidding.

Finally able to relax, Sylvie settled more deeply into the cushions. She had not even finished with the third page of the journal when Gaspard burst through the breakfast parlor doors, and she spilled tea onto her magazine.

Gaspard, her blond, cherubic brother, plopped onto the chaise in indolent splendor. He shrugged a shoulder at her glare—only one, as both would have required too much energy.

"I've still got a bloody splitting headache from last night," he moaned, brandishing a personalized silver flask. He dressed in bright, showy fabrics and a sloppily tied cravat. He'd probably locked out his valet to ensure a quiet morning. But it never mattered what he wore; he was the prettiest of the three de Rosiers siblings and reveled in his foppishness. "I was as drunk as Davy's sow. And you're the only person in this blasted house who doesn't make it worse with mindless chatter."

"Yes," she crooned with a smirk, dabbing the tea before it smudged the print. "I'm extremely supportive of you becoming a regular brandy-face." He never treated her as less than a full-blooded sister despite their only sharing a father, and she loved him for it.

He wrinkled his nose. "I'm no brandy-face, more like a connoisseur of fine spirits."

"I just wish you'd drink something less"—she glowered at his flask—"*plebeian*."

He sipped from his favored blend of black tea and rum. Gaspard had discovered the drink, aptly named "gunfire," from a visiting British sea captain the previous year. The only time he had been on a ship was during the crossing from France as a little boy—which he hardly remembered—but he enjoyed the affectations of the foreign sailors.

She was not so reckless as to drink gunfire this early in the day, but she would steal a nip or two before dinner.

He unscrewed his flask and took another drink, smiling broadly. She tried not to laugh while she poured more tea.

"I don't know why you insist on always having tea here," he continued, sneering at the drapes and worn rugs. "The room is in desperate need of a renovation."

The salon hadn't been updated since their papa built the estate twenty-odd years prior. Yet, she preferred this room—not for its dated furnishings or size, but rather the windows. They faced north, protecting her from the afternoon sun that threatened to darken her skin. Vanity did not dictate she live in shadows, but her future did.

Dark-skinned girls worked in fields; light-skinned girls got husbands.

"It's quiet here," she replied. "I don't have to endure Madame's screeching while I pretend to do needlepoint."

Gaspard wiped the drops of gunfire at the corners of his mouth. "And I don't have to endure Edmond's morning sermon."

She snickered. Of all of their father's children, only Edmond showed any real interest in slaving and coffee. Sylvie's interest in either extended only so far as the comforts she could buy with their profits, and Gaspard had no interest at all.

As the eldest and the heir, Edmond felt it his duty to tolerate their father's morning routine of angry muttering, complaining about gout, and reading the newspaper. Gaspard argued his brother simply liked playing the martyr.

"Wherever he is"—she stirred a lump of pristine white sugar into her cup and took a sip—"I'm grateful. I hate watching Papa work himself into a fit. The doctor says he must rest, but he insists on reading the paper or writing to his friends in the Assembly. Much good *that* does." Despite her earlier judgment, she poured a splash of rum into her own tea. "So what was so urgent that you're out of your chambers before noon?"

Leaning back, he folded his arms behind his head. "I know something you don't."

"I'm surprised"—she glanced at the slave in the corner and at the archway connecting the room to the corridor—"you hear anything with your head so far up your—"

He slapped his thighs and popped up from the chaise. "A shame, and I was *so* eager to share the secret with you. But now you'll have to wait until Father decides to tell."

She sniffed and resumed her reading. "A terrible shame."

Indulging him only meant he would string her along until he'd confess some absurd rumor that had perhaps a whisper of truth.

"Oh," he said, tapping his chin in mock consideration. "I *was* going to recommend wearing blue next week—he is an indigo planter, after all—but since you're disinterested . . ."

She dropped the magazine like cold ashes into a pan: *he* was a rather critical pronoun. "What? Who is?"

"No, no." He backed away with his hands raised. "I've over-burdened you already."

"Gaspard." She crept toward him. "*Gaspard.*" He grinned, know-ing and wicked, before giving in.

"I think you ought to explore Father's study today before he comes back from town."

"Explore? You mean go prying into his affairs?"

"Me? Advise you to burgle our father's study? Come now, I com-port myself with dignity."

"Indeed, if dignity charged you by the hour." His blue eyes glis-tened with memories unfit for repeating. Sylvie rolled her eyes.

"As witty as your remarks are"—he pulled out their grandfather's pocket watch, which had been too "ostentatious" for Edmond's dreary taste—"I declare you only have perhaps a half hour for reconnaissance."

She hurried toward the study with singular focus, the feather in her tignon bobbing with each step. Servants carrying clean linens hugged the wall to avoid a collision. Sylvie was grateful that skirts had narrowed quite a bit, or she would have bent a pannier.

She approached the mahogany double doors of Papa's study—cut and carved on this very island. Fashion plates and cartoons exag-gerate the constraints of stays; she couldn't blame her breathlessness on any undergarment.

She slipped inside the familiar room filled with the scent of coffee and paper, past the regularly dusted books lining the walls. Her fa-ther and his wife were not particularly well-read, but Sylvie's gov-erness, a similarly situated mulatta like herself but without her extraordinary beauty, had tried in vain to introduce Sylvie to the broader world of reading.

You would enjoy Rousseau, she had said with feeling. *His* Julie *captures your very soul with the struggle between our private hopes and morality.* Sylvie preferred the copy of *Dangerous Liaisons* she hid under her mattress.

She moved toward the desk at the center of the study, which featured a promising dark box.

Curious, and heartily tempted by the gold and mother-of-pearl calling her to the hidden treasure within, she gently opened the small chest.

In a bed of ocean-blue velvet sat a double strand of pearls with a matching pair of fat teardrop pearl earrings. They were well maintained, though clearly in the baroque style, with small sapphires joining the two strands at several points.

Sylvie had her share of pearls. Her father called her "my pearl," and Saint-Domingue had long been called the Pearl of the Antilles for its wealth and beauty. She considered them her signature, like the Medici women of old.

But this set was beyond the delicate elegance littering her vanity— it was the sort of opulence only *grand blanc* money could buy. Even if they needed to be reset and updated a tad.

She reflexively touched her throat, imagining the pleasant weight of them during a dinner party. Anyone would want her with a face like hers and a necklace worth a dowry dangling between her ample breasts.

Her skin may not be pearl white, but that hardly mattered when you were dripping in them.

She pinched an earring between her fingers, watching the sapphires splash light like the oceans they had crossed to be in her hands.

The glint of blue fell across the array of papers beneath the jewelry box. Some of the documents were simple accounts or valuations of coffee shipments, the usual fare of her father's office. But the most striking pages said *Articles of Sale*, featuring the purchase of fifteen articles—slaves.

Half of the world's coffee came from Saint-Domingue, and they lived in the interior, more mountainous region of the island—ideal for coffee growing. Most windows in her house faced the coffee fields and the slaves who worked them.

Sylvie knew where their wealth came from—knew where *she* came from.

And yet, pearl in her fist, she scrolled through the list of numbers and receipts of purchase. Fifteen numbers, twelve men and three women, with their ports of origin and insurance claims.

Some slaves had notes scribbled in the margins in her father's hand: *strong legs*, *nimble*, and *superstitious*. No doubt referring to vodou, the religious practices she heard Edmond grumble about.

The women, however, had different sorts of comments. One said *fine figure* and another referred to the whiteness of her teeth. But one number, one slave, had an asterisk and comment beside her row in another man's writing saying *private use*. She only recognized it as not Gaspard's.

Did her mother start her own life here on such a document? What notes did Papa write in the margins? Did she have white teeth or a shapely figure? Was she for private use, promised for the house and not for the field?

She searched through a gallery of dark faces in her mind—the chambermaids and scullery girls and laundresses. Who had written what in their margins?

She threw the pearl back into its chest and closed the lid, eyes trained on that ambiguous asterisk.

"You shouldn't be in here." Edmond stood in the doorway, frowning. Twenty-four-year-old Edmond had less of his father's handsome looks but all of his self-importance. And, like always, he was more fastidious in his dress than Gaspard, his cravat tied in a practical knot. But he did not fill his wardrobe with the colors of the tropics or the shimmer of gilt—just the white iciness of sterile cotton.

She pushed away from the desk. "How long have you been lurking there? I didn't hear you knock."

He scoffed. "This isn't your study; you can't demand privacy. Get out. You shouldn't be in here."

She swallowed her unease and crossed her arms. "Honestly, I have more right than you. Papa lets me serve as his secretary; maybe he would give you the honor if you weren't so insufferable."

He stood over her in front of the desk, staring down at the paper she still gripped in her hand. A little smile danced on his face. "Enjoying some light reading?"

She dropped the sheet like it had bitten her. "There is such a thing as loving one's work too much."

"I take my pleasure where it's owed."

She did not understand him, and the voice of her father stripped her of the opportunity to ask. A dog barked in the hall, and her father's voice followed: "Sylvie, dearest."

"Papa," she greeted as she stood up, her eyes moving between the box and him.

Papa's chestnut hound, Richelieu, sat by his feet. His tail twitched excitedly behind him upon seeing Sylvie. He was one of many, seeing as his master always enjoyed companionship.

"I'm glad to see you, my pearl," Papa said. He held out his hands, and Sylvie dutifully came out from behind the desk, feeling a small part guilty and uncomfortable from Edmond's words, and took them in hers. "It seems Edmond has found you."

"Indeed he has," she said as she kissed Papa's cheeks.

Edmond rolled his eyes and checked his silver fob watch. "Well, now that you have her, I'll be leaving to finish surveying the western fields." He brushed by them and out the door—the whip he kept in his coat poked out from the hem, following behind him like a tail.

Chapter Two

None are so hopelessly enslaved as those who falsely believe they are free.

—*Johann Wolfgang von Goethe*

To what do I owe this honor?" Sylvie asked with a pinched mouth. She sat down in a guest chair opposite the desk. "Has someone died?" Perhaps the pearls were some inheritance from family in France.

"Does someone have to die for me to spend time with my dearest and only daughter? You've been in my study a thousand times." Richelieu scurried over to sit beside her feet. "Traitor," he scolded at the panting beast.

She laughed, shifting her skirt to avoid muddy paws. "True, but I have never seen you quite so nervous." His underarms had darkened with sweat, though Papa had never really acclimated to the island climate.

"You have always had such a keen eye. It made you quite a terror when you were in leading strings."

"I prefer *precocious*." She pointed to the jewelry box peeking from behind his figure. "And what is that lurking on your desk there?"

He patted the lid with a wry smile. "I shall choose to believe that you were in my study and did not look inside." He clasped his hands together. "Madame has made it clear that a lady in your . . . *position* is at a most unfortunate disadvantage and quite vulnerable to the thorns of society."

Sylvie restrained a snort. *Position* made it sound like her role as an illegitimate daughter was transitory rather than permanent. She had no choice regarding her *position*. "Papa," she started, "I'm not quite certain—"

A series of light knocks preceded Madame—or Catherine de Rosiers—flurrying into the room with a butterfly spaniel in her arms. She did not wear her irritation well.

She had never been a handsome woman, her golden hair her only truly lovely feature. Her white skin had a propensity toward redness rather than the delicate flush most ladies desired. But what she lacked in attractiveness she made up for in wealth: her bloated dowry had brought much to the de Rosiers estate—specifically more slaves and more jewels.

"I told you I wanted to be present when you told her, Julien."

"Do not worry, Madame," Sylvie said with the docility of a cat who licks your hand before biting. "Dearest Father has yet to tell me anything, though I am most eager to hear."

Despite not having a mother of her own, Sylvie preferred the company of Gaspard or Papa to Catherine.

It was not that she disliked Madame—she couldn't hate a woman who'd cared for her to some degree since birth—but she had no respect for a wife who so clearly did not keep her husband's interest.

When *she* married, her husband would not so much as breathe in another woman's direction—least of all a slave's.

Papa shuffled and picked up the box. "Indeed, I have not. I was just saying that, er, the thorns of society and whatnot . . ."

"What your father means," Madame said from her perch on the other overstuffed chair, "is that you have become a most charming and accomplished young lady. I declare it is time for you to wed." And from Madame's eager little grin, she was more than happy to get her mulatto interloper out of this home and into another.

Though Sylvie didn't exactly mind the idea of seducing a rich foreign captain into marriage. Or being courted by a dashing mulatto like herself.

Her father, box in hand, came around the front of the desk and presented it to Sylvie with misty eyes. She opened the box again, but for some reason the Articles of Sale seemed to dull the luster of the pearls. Still, she smiled and touched the necklace with the appropriate reverence.

Julien nodded. "We do not intermingle with the *affranchi* class, of course, but for your sake, we have invited a Monsieur Blanchard to come dine with us when his business allows. You must wear them then."

Sylvie whirled toward her father, shocked by his cavalier declaration. "My intended has *already been chosen*?" she gasped. "These are an engagement gift?"

The appeal of landing a husband was the chase—disarming him with wit and sweetness until he went mad with longing. By all accounts, marriage was the capstone of a woman's existence, and Sylvie wanted a modicum of control over her own future.

Misreading her distress, her papa patted her hand and assured her, "He is a decent man, uninvolved with all of that rebellion nonsense—I've had Edmond be sure of that." She didn't understand what he meant, so she made a note to ask Gaspard about it later. "A quite wealthy quadroon from what I understand, a very civilized fellow. He owns a large and successful indigo plantation; I've been hoping to dabble in the indigo trade—"

She looked back into the blue abyss of the sapphires.

She could be a proper wife to an influential and rich man of her station. They'd share a lifestyle and a skin color. *Affranchis* had their own balls, soirees, fashion, and entertainment; she could finally circulate and thrive in a society in which she'd be considered an equal.

"An excellent match by all counts," Madame interjected, knowing that Sylvie had different concerns over the charm of her intended, economics of indigo not being one of them. Madame's lapdog chewed on the ribbons dangling from her stomacher.

"I've heard of the Blanchard family, but I didn't realize we were acquainted," Sylvie said.

"Well, we weren't," Madame explained. "But Gaspard introduced us through a friendship with Blanchard's eldest legitimate daughter, I believe."

Gaspard probably concluded that if he enjoyed bedding a Blanchard, Sylvie would as well. Genteel white women were few on the island, save for a scant number of lingering prostitutes shipped over years ago. Trust Gaspard to know every one.

Their gazes rested heavily on her face, and she took in a deep, steadying breath and brushed aside her disappointment. Even the dog watched the necklace with interest.

"Well, if he's an indigo planter," she said, letting herself be distracted by the glisten of the pearls, "then I'll have to wear blue."

JANUARY KEPT THE stifling heat and humidity away with strong breezes off the ocean, making Sylvie and Gaspard's stroll within Le Cap more pleasant.

Short for "Le Cap Français," Le Cap was the cultural and economic hub of Saint-Domingue—so much so that most referred to it as the Paris of the Antilles. Most of the large public parties for white families were held there, and Sylvie only went for the occasional shopping trip.

She had asked Gaspard to bring her into town to have the pearls assessed by a jeweler as a guise: she wanted to know more about Papa's grumbling about rebellion.

Sylvie and the family didn't often travel into the capital given the roads, weather, and distance. But in the months since she'd last visited, the city—usually a shining twin of Paris on a smaller scale if her father was to be believed—crackled and hissed like coals doused in water. Militiamen moved in packs throughout the square with the same skittish eyes as stray hounds, and the usual stares her color invited felt wary rather than intrigued.

A footman led their horses from behind the pair at a respectable distance—she didn't want any servants to hear about her curiosity.

"Brother, why are there so many soldiers lurking about?" She teetered around puddles of horse piss: she needed to watch both her tongue and her feet. "Has there been some trouble?"

They crossed the town square, where a group of slaves were expanding a wooden platform under the supervision of militia. Sylvie only noticed because she followed Gaspard's gaze.

"Do you remember Vincent Ogé?" he asked, squinting into the afternoon light.

She vaguely recalled some scuffle last fall that had Edmond particularly hostile. "The mulatto fellow Edmond wouldn't stop sneering about in October? He was some mutineer, I think."

But the occasional rebel wasn't anything new, and Father did not let Edmond speak about it much when she was around. She didn't try to discover more—not that her eldest brother would ever be forthcoming.

Gaspard nodded, reaching for the flask in his pocket. "It was a bit more than a scuffle. The mainland would be more proactive about the whole affair if the king weren't practically under house arrest." Between the march on Versailles and the Storming of the Bastille, Sylvie and Gaspard reached their majority in an age of unrest. But France was far away, and it hardly disturbed the well-entrenched and wealthy ways of Saint-Domingue. Power may shift and wane, but money was invariable. "Though that's the gist of it. He's quite popular."

"With who?"

He laughed. "Anyone unlike Edmond: progressives, mulattoes, free Blacks. People who think color should not be a bar to citizenship."

"So he wants freedom for everyone." She couldn't imagine a Saint-Domingue where she could marry whom she liked, go where she liked, and wear what she liked. The idea of a person like her descending from the hills to demand equality at the end of a bayonet gave her an unexpected thrill.

Gaspard guided them away from the sound of work and hammers. "No, not everyone. He was quite clear on his stance that only free men were included."

She felt a bit silly for thinking of marriage first. She supposed freedom was a smaller concept then.

But she was not surprised by Ogé's reticence to include slaves in his crusade. All of those mulatto bachelors wealthy enough to court her, like Blanchard, made their money one way.

There was no bonding between mulattoes and slaves—mulattoes like Sylvie built their success on distancing themselves from their African roots. To them, whiteness was a way of life.

"Was he—"

A gray cloud of ash caught in her throat. A white woman had emptied a hearth out of a window right beside Sylvie. It thankfully did not land on her but beside—filling the air around them.

She jumped away, coughing and smacking her pale skirts to free them of ash.

Gaspard shouted up at her, "Watch where you are pouring your waste, you ill-begotten fishwife!" The haggard woman must not have seen Sylvie's clearly wealthy white escort, and her gaping mouth and rounded eyes were similar to the fish his insult implied. She scurried away from the window and out of sight. "*Mon Dieu*, are you all right?"

The left side of Sylvie's gown had a gray cast, and her throat tickled. She whacked away his helping hand as she tried to shake off what she could. The dress wouldn't be permanently ruined, at least.

This altercation was one of many. The unpleasant menagerie of Sylvie's childhood memories was made up of such offenses: some from family, some from strangers, some at the hands of her government.

But this act, so cruel in its randomness and physical in nature, brought out such a burning in her chest, she thought her ribs would blacken.

She crumpled the fine muslin—now no better than the raw, unbleached cotton of a field hand—between her ringed fingers. Its beauty spoiled, its craftmanship unappreciated.

"Has he been captured?" she asked.

"What?" He wiped some ash off her tignon. "Who? Ogé?"

"Yes. Was he captured?"

Gaspard looked up at the window, frowning at the closed shutters. "He was handed over by the Spanish, yes."

Sometimes Sylvie wondered if all her efforts would ever amount to happiness. Whiteness is a fantasy promised but never realized.

She plowed on toward home, leaving Gaspard by the little pile of ashes, pretending the burn in her eyes was from their dust and not the truth.

Chapter Three

We have the wolf by the ears, and we can neither hold him, nor safely let him go. Justice is in one scale, and self-preservation in the other.

—*Thomas Jefferson*

février 1791

Their laundresses had returned her petticoats to their former glory, but Sylvie swore she saw a gray smudge every now and then.

The entire issue of Ogé and the uneasiness his ideology stirred in her had Sylvie shying away from most of the family—with no little help from her father.

"Vincent Ogé," her father had roared, "has the impudence to return here with American weapons. I cannot believe the gall of him. It does not matter that he's captured. The damage has already been done!" More details had trickled in about Ogé's efforts, and soon even Sylvie's presence couldn't keep her father from expressing his fury.

Her papa would fume over his breakfast, so annoyed by his correspondence that he hardly ate his food—his cheeks burning red like they'd been touched by flame. The cook complained to Sylvie on more than one occasion, saying that he made breakfast to be eaten, not shouted at.

She hated these choleric episodes, not only because of her own conflicted feelings, but because of the attention they drew to her—and not the kind she enjoyed. Ever since Ogé's capture, Edmond's dark eyes fixed on her like a fox's on a hare.

She skipped the morning meal for this very reason. Her father would only utter a few articulate sentences before a servant brought him his letters and he descended into furious sputters.

So she lounged in a minor parlor surrounded by sheet music with an untouched tray between her and Gaspard: she never ate before one, and he barely ate at all. She wanted to pick the ideal pianoforte pieces for Blanchard's scheduled visit at the end of the month. Gaspard mentioned she may want to use the opportunity for meaningful discussion; she tartly reminded him that sirens used song and not conversation to lure in prey.

Half of the importance of cleverness is knowing when not to use it.

Haydn and Handel littered the table with a dash of old folk chansons—but the familiar scraping of chairs and their father's muffled shouts from the nearby dining room disturbed the sonatas she ran through her head.

Sylvie cringed. Her father was causing more unnecessary trouble, certainly.

The shouting continued on for a few minutes, and she wiped imaginary ash from her skirts until she needed to distract herself. "Bet you a piece of eight that Madame's first words to us shall be something about 'poor Papa' and his suffering."

Ever a gambling man, her brother replied, "I'll take that wager."

The woman in question arrived moments later, fiddling with the lace on her sleeves and waving her ivory handkerchief about like a white flag of surrender.

They chose their morning hideaway randomly, yet she found them with a tracking hound's ease.

"Oh," Madame sighed. "How your poor papa suffers. The situation in France vexes him like nothing else."

Sylvie muffled her laugh in a handkerchief, while Gaspard groaned. "Do you accept IOUs?" he asked his amused sister.

"Gaspard!" Catherine exclaimed.

"Do not worry," he said. "'Twas only for one silver piece, not the family fortune. Fair sister has won it honorably."

The lady clicked her tongue, ready to scold her troublesome son. A useless endeavor, but Sylvie was always amused watching her try.

"I do, in fact," she teased, "accept IOUs. But if you fail to come up with the funds, I will be forced to set Edmond on you. I will have him sermonizing about Christian duty for an hour at least."

Gaspard feigned terror, shuddering in his seat. "Oh, how *fearsome.*"

Two bright spots of color formed on Madame's cheeks, and she twisted her handkerchief. "I will not pretend to understand an inkling of what nonsense you two are speaking," she chided. "Honestly, Sylvie, you are getting much too old for Gaspard's games. You will be a married woman soon."

Sylvie laughed. "He's older than me by two years! And I should hope my intended shares my respectable enjoyment of vice."

Madame pursed her lips, pouring herself a cup of coffee as her ward grimaced; Sylvie could never bring herself to drink the bitter stuff, even if it was the precious foundation on which Papa built his wealth. Madame added enough sugar, however, that the drink looked more like cane syrup than coffee. Even the smell gave Sylvie a bad taste in her mouth.

"Perhaps," Madame said, "but I have indulged this behavior for far too long. When the lady of a house enters a room, you ought to at least greet her formally."

Sylvie arched her brows, then nodded. "*Oui,* Madame," she intoned, shooting Gaspard a wry glance. "Forgive my impertinence."

A quarter of Saint-Domingue was made up of infidelity that rich wives were well trained to tolerate, if not ignore: Madame Catherine treated her somewhere between a poor relation and sentient furniture.

"And you ought to show more concern for Monsieur de Rosiers's health," Madame continued. "He provides everything for you out of the goodness of his heart. I do not know of a more generous soul."

Sylvie had been sensible enough to squash any familial love between them, even if Catherine's naturally affectionate nature had sometimes made that difficult in childhood. The maze of divisions between whites, Blacks, and mulattoes—both tacit and overt—was too treacherous to navigate.

Sylvie smoothed her stack of music, her eyes narrowing in warning. "I worry endlessly over *Father's* health." Though that didn't stop her from testing the limits of Catherine's nerves.

"Do not bully her, Mama," Gaspard interrupted. "It's not her fault he languishes over some impotent king and his whore wife—"

"Gaspard!"

"—or practically swoons in horror at the thought of a slave rebellion. She worries about Father more than anyone. Certainly, more than I do."

"Slave rebellions aren't nonsense, Gaspard." Edmond strode into the sitting room, newspaper neatly tucked under one arm and a coffee plant cutting in his hand. He must've visited the fields. "What Ogé did on the coast could just as well happen here. And the sooner you understand that, the sooner—"

Gaspard sank deeper into the cushions and avoided Sylvie's punishing glare. She didn't want such talk breaching her peace.

"I understand plenty, sweet brother," he said. "I simply do not care."

Though given Gaspard's awareness of the rising tensions on the island, Sylvie doubted that his indifference was genuine.

"Well, you should," Edmond sniffed. Sylvie stiffened in her seat, as she did now whenever he came seeking out confrontation. He was a cantankerous plow horse—always eager to curl his lip and spit on someone. He made himself his own cup of coffee, adding hardly any sugar at all. "For we depend upon those wretched creatures for everything."

Gaspard poured the contents of his flask into a teacup and took a loud gulp. "The White Man sleeps at the foot of Vesuvius," he muttered into his cup. He couldn't help but poke at the wasp's nest.

Sylvie fidgeted, pulling at the tassels hanging from her chair. She imagined plumes of smoke rising out of a waking mountain—the white pillars of her château slowly darkening to black under the onslaught of hot ash.

Ogé's revolt had been small and easily crushed, but Edmond presented their circumstances as much more precarious than she previously thought. Her eldest brother was many things, but stupid was not one of them.

The more Edmond saw her and himself on opposite sides of the battlefield, the more appealing Ogé's camp became.

"Out!" barked Edmond to the maid in the corner. She curtsied and left quickly. Sylvie hadn't even noticed her: the various slaves that provided the comforts of domestic life were as much a part of Château de Rosiers as its bricks or walls. "Lord knows what they conspire about when they're alone."

"No more politics," said Catherine. "It's indelicate."

Gaspard sipped his tea, then spoke over the porcelain rim: "I've never known uprisings to be delicate."

"Since you've put down so many?" sneered Edmond. "You are not the type to die for king and country, *mon frère*."

"What 'king and country'?" Sylvie scoffed. She motioned to the newspaper resting on her tray. "We seem to have little of either, as of late. Our sovereign is more prisoner than king to his own people, and the country is a collection of squabbling hens in a roost."

Edmond's cheek twitched in anger. "That is exactly the sort of blatant disregard for order and authority that has led us to this point."

She raised an eyebrow, wearing a haughty mask to irk Edmond. "The people are unhappy, and the unrest spread to Saint-Domingue." *Her* people were unhappy—which, for once, did not include him.

He slammed his newspaper down on the silver tray that divided them. "*The people*? You defend those negroes? You compare fair France to our property?"

"I do not defend *slaves*, only free men." But she *would* if Edmond kept on this way. His open disdain blurred the lines of her loyalty.

"You sound like Ogé." The name rang out like the lowest of insults. She needed to refrain from provoking him to true anger, but his arrogance begged for a jab or two.

"Why not give free Blacks the vote?" she pressed. "It will bring an end to all of this fuss. What could possibly make you so afraid that—"

"They are all the same! These negroes would not hesitate to join ranks, kill our father, and then defile you on his bleeding corpse."

Her hauteur crumpled, and Gaspard's gaze went from humor to rage.

She had never known Edmond to raise his voice, nor did she care about most topics enough to carry on a debate to such a point. But now her stays, normally a reassuring sensation, were the only thing keeping her heart in her chest.

She looked down—not out of deference, but to avoid the blatant and blaring hatred burning in her brother's stare.

Gaspard stood in an instant. "That is *enough*."

Edmond whirled on his brother and jabbed his finger into his waistcoat. "You would defend such a speech? She speaks like those other mulattoes demanding *equality*. You pretend to be ignorant, but you read the papers same as I. Men like Ogé claim they want peace and rights, but they would murder every white master on this island before the ink was dry on the ballot. You know what will happen if we budge even an inch."

Gaspard's lip curled. "I do not know; no one does. But I *do* know that if you say one more word about the matter, I will run you through for upsetting our sister and mother. The man is in prison; let him plague you no more."

Madame was close to tears; whenever her equally beloved sons fought, she dissolved into hysterics, hoping her distress would end the conflict.

"I know you are fond of Sylvie, but she sounds like Ogé," Edmond said, his tone softening into condescension. Madame sobbed loudly into a lace handkerchief.

Gaspard shook his head. "She is no radical."

Sylvie did not consider voting rights for free men to be radical, but now was not the time to correct Gaspard. Men could be incredibly stupid, and so were their laws.

"She is *Black*—"

"She is our *sister*, first and foremost," Gaspard said.

Behind him, Madame fluttered her handkerchief and postured like she was going to faint, always keeping an eye on her sons to assess if her theatrics were effective. Sylvie made a small smile, grateful for the one brother she could count on, even if she hated being forced into silence. At least now she did not use total ignorance as a shield, instead arming herself with the truth of the political landscape.

"How can you doubt her loyalty? Do you think she sneaks out at night to cavort with rebels? I can barely get her to read something other than gothic romances. She wants a husband and Chantilly lace, not rebellion."

Gaspard concealed her shifting views from Edmond to protect her from his wrath, but his words stung.

This seemed like more than politics to Edmond; it felt personal. His resentment of Papa—or rather Papa's decision to treat her as a daughter—had hardened over these years into something ugly. A dalliance resulting in a bastard was of no consequence—everyone allowed men such natural pleasures as a mistress—but to sully their family house with that of a slave woman was an injustice Edmond could not ignore.

Maybe he believed that since she could never be wholly white she could never be wholly trusted, despite Sylvie's constant strides to be the very picture of French loveliness. As long as her kind wanted to be treated like something closer to human, he would hate her. Once out of the gentle shades of childhood, Edmond had let youthful jealousies manifest into resentment. And with the pressure of politics and the weakness of his character, they hardened into an unshakable bitterness he carried like a rosary.

Madame's braying sobs wore on their tempers. Gaspard sighed when Edmond made another wary glance at Sylvie. "What will it take to satisfy you?" Gaspard asked, exasperated and easily worn down.

Edmond's gaze hardened as he locked eyes with her. She didn't think that he deserved to be satisfied—or that he ever would be—but she would not be seen as weak. She did not look away; Sylvie would not bend, wilt, or break under the weight of his bitterness.

"It is not about my *satisfaction*," he hissed, finally ending their silent duel of wills, "but assurance that the child understands the evil surrounding men like Ogé. She ought to see what happens to men who seek to defy the natural order."

A girl is a child whenever it is convenient for her to be, thought Sylvie, *but when you want a piece of my dowry, I'm suddenly a woman grown.*

Edmond didn't want to educate her—he wanted to punish her. Punish her for closeness to her family, punish her for refusing to bow to him. Punish her for her existence.

"Fine," Gaspard said. "We'll have Sylvie watch a hanging. If that will convince you she's no threat." Execution was a common enough result of arrest, but knowing that the man who fought so hard for her freedoms was doomed to die in a public square like a common thief?

Sylvie had often complained as a little girl to Gaspard that so much about her life was unfair. Unfair that she couldn't have the white husband she wanted. Unfair that she couldn't wear certain clothes. Unfair how her hair didn't grow long and glossy with a gentle curl. The injustices that irked her, the constraints written into her skin, never approached the grandiose things Ogé was prepared to kill for.

And he would die while she was happy to marry whom she ought, wear what she ought, and keep her complaints to the minimum. Was he the mad one, or was she?

Edmond nodded, satisfied with the plan. His happiness so often led to misfortune on Sylvie's behalf, and she flinched at his unnerving smile.

With an unsteady peace established, Madame made a quick recovery. But Sylvie was still obligated to wave a fan on her face and keep offering smelling salts.

Edmond finished off his coffee and turned to leave. He strode out to the fields with a worn cowskin whip at his side—scrutinizing the dark faces plucking the red berries from the green undergrowth. To him, Sylvie imagined, there was no happier sight.

One by one, her family left her in peace. Her parlor once again became a sanctuary for Sylvie and the music.

The slave girl returned to tidy up the coffee and crumbs her siblings had left behind. Warily pushing the altercation from her mind, Sylvie embroidered a sampler with an orchid border swirling with delicate pinks and purples.

Crash.

Sylvie stabbed her finger in surprise. The serving girl froze with her hands outstretched as a half-shattered teacup lolled on its side next to Sylvie's slipper.

If her father had been present, he'd snap at the servant. Other masters, like Edmond, often damaged the slave as penance for damaged goods.

Outside the door, the heavy footsteps of another de Rosiers family member plodded down the corridor, but the precious porcelain still lay on the ground. The girl clutched a hand to her mouth and stared at Sylvie with wide eyes, the skin around her temples pulled tight against her skull.

Instead of chastising the servant or exposing her clumsiness to her family, Sylvie mutinied. Using her foot, she pushed the broken porcelain under her seat.

The girl, in a panicked voice lilting with the accent of West Africa, asked, "Mademoiselle? I don't understand. Forgive me—" She wrung her apron into a twisted mess. Sylvie raised her hand, and the girl stopped stuttering, staring shamefaced down at the floor.

"That'll be all, girl," Sylvie chirped. The maid, confused, returned to arranging tea with a painful slowness.

Sylvie resumed her progress on the sampler with random stabs of the needle. If Ogé were mad, then perhaps she should be a little mad, too.

If Edmond saw her as a traitor, then she'd *be* a traitor. Even in an act of rebellion as insignificant as this.

She offered a delicate smile over the edge of her sampler, and the girl calmed. Their moment of connection, of alliance, of a shared secret, filled her in a way no amount of wealth ever had.

Perhaps later she would scoff at such a tiny act, but in that moment she enjoyed that flush of courage fueling her needle.

Sylvie resumed her sewing—ignoring the tiny drop of blood stained onto one of the freshly sewn orchids, leaving it a vibrant red.

Chapter Four

You may choose to look the other way but you can never say again that you did not know.

—*William Wilberforce*

Sylvie wandered the halls hours later with sore fingertips and a ruined sampler.

Edmond's coldness and Ogé's looming execution left her unsettled. She wanted the comfort of the familiar, so she sought out Papa.

He stood on the veranda on the side of the estate, his expression relaxed and pleasant, with his steward. Gaspard lay on the bench behind their father with his arm tossed across his face—most likely to shield himself against the heat of the late-afternoon sun.

Papa dismissed his steward as Sylvie approached. "I'm sorry you were in poor spirits this morning," she said as her father kissed her forehead. She pushed Gaspard's feet off one side of the bench so she could sit, and he grumbled in response. "Though I'm glad your mood seems to have improved."

She leaned against the white brick of the château, the stone cooling her skin through the thin cotton of her dress. Papa was the indulgent parent, and neither child felt the same pressure to perform under his affectionate eye.

He patted her hand. "Don't trouble yourself over it, my pearl."

"So there's nothing you ought to share?" she pressed. Gaspard kicked her shin.

Papa sank down into his rocking chair and grabbed the newspaper tucked beneath it. "Just the ill-conceived mutterings of men. It shall pass." She tried to hide her disappointment. He had failed her small test, and so she pressed on into more familiar territory.

"Papa, I thought I might order some new trimmings and such. I found a very fine needle lace in town last week—ribbons as well."

He chuckled, his eyes crinkling at the corners, so much like Gaspard's. "My pearl, you have enough lace to open your own shop."

"You should be pleased, dear Father, that I only ask for lace: I may easily ask for a whole new dress. Imagine the cost, the expense! But instead, I ask only for trim to refit old gowns. If I am to run my own household one day, I must learn to economize."

He laughed loudly then, his newspaper forgotten and resting on his knees. "Only you could request a swath of lace and make it sound like an exercise in frugality."

"Perhaps I should become the barrister and Gaspard the mistress of a grand house."

Gaspard spoke from underneath his arm. "I'd look dashing in a mobcap."

"Indeed," Papa said. "A shame you weren't born a boy—not that I love you any less, of course."

"And had I been?" she asked.

"I would have sent you to France for your education, only the best." His eyes misted with fond memories. "The Paris of my school days was unlike anything else in the world. Your uncle Rohmer, may he rest in peace, and I were rather wild then. He hadn't married my sister yet, and, well"—he scratched under his wig with a rueful smile—"a man got drunk off ideas as well as wine and women."

"Easy there, Father," Gaspard said as he sat up with a grin. "There's a lady present." She elbowed him in the ribs. She wanted to hear about the Paris she might have known in another life.

Papa reopened his paper, still smiling at his bygone youth. "Ah well, perhaps Blanchard shall show you Paris. Politics aside, it's a city that leaves a mark on your soul."

6 février 1791

Sylvie stood between her brothers, staring down at her gown in the public square of Le Cap.

The city sat nestled in front of the mountainous paradise of Saint-Domingue. On less grim days, Sylvie loved coming to the city center.

But the streets did not bustle with commerce and activity today. The crowds thrummed with anticipation; the well-to-do white families crowded the space as the Black faces looked on from the outskirts of the plaza. Like most days in February, clouds hid the sun from the town square with the constant possibility of rain.

Some *affranchis* dared to view the execution as well and ignored the jeers and whispers among the whites. She wondered if Blanchard would come as a supporter. But given her father's approval of him, she doubted he sympathized with Ogé, let alone the slaves themselves.

Sylvie fidgeted next to Gaspard and fiddled with her lace sleeves. She'd fussed that morning while Alice, her lady's maid, picked out her clothes. She prided herself on her elegant manner of dress, but her governess had never explored clothing etiquette regarding a public execution.

Once she explained to her maid where they were going, Alice set out her dark purple gown and gray petticoat; they were practical and plain, precisely why she never wore them otherwise. But Alice, her mouth set in a grim line, said that a darker style of dress would be best.

Sylvie stopped toying with the sleeves when Gaspard's voice cut through the silence.

"Where's the gallows?" he asked. A great wooden platform stood at the front of the crowd—she recognized the stage as what the slaves had been building weeks prior—but no telltale noose loomed overhead.

Instead, two enormous carriage wheels, each large enough for a child to run between its spokes, stood tall in the heart of the plaza. Each one was supported by a beam as thick as her torso, and many in the crowd of onlookers were encased in their shadows.

"*Edmond*," rasped Gaspard, an uncharacteristic fury upsetting the languid blue of his eyes as he took in the wheel. "She cannot see this!"

Edmond rolled back his shoulders. "How could I have known they would break him?" He shrugged. "Not that it is not a fitting punishment. Too good, one might say." She didn't understand Gaspard's fear or Edmond's smug pleasure.

"Is it bloody?" she asked. She had never seen death before, or any significant bloodshed beyond a pricked finger or scraped knee.

"Oh no." Edmond smiled. "There shan't be any blood at all."

The crowd's relative stillness shifted into a low roar when the executioner brought forth Ogé, his ankles and wrists shackled. Despite his three-month imprisonment, the revolutionary's eyes radiated defiance.

As the highly lucrative exports of coffee, indigo, and sugar continued, Saint-Domingue enjoyed different imports from France—albeit significantly more dangerous ones: the language of revolution, liberation, and enfranchisement. Sylvie did not pretend to understand them, but as a well-bred child of privilege, she did pretend to be above them.

Yet now, feeling the raging fury of the crowd buzz through her bones, she feared the tenuous prestige she relished as daughter of a wealthy master was built on a faulty foundation—with each clatter of Ogé's shackles driving the cracks deeper and deeper.

Sylvie may have stood with her family in the white portion of the crowd, but she *saw* herself in the eyes of the *affranchis* bound on the platform and those who walked free. How many were there to see vengeance meted out or in somber support?

The executioner tied Ogé and a coconspirator to the two enormous wheels, their limbs stretched in between spokes. Onlookers shouted their approval while Edmond watched in silence, his expression almost smug.

Ogé's arms pulled at his restraints; his muscles and tendons flexed angrily against their bindings. His torn shirt revealed the deep purple and red bruises from weeks of beatings.

"Look away," whispered Gaspard to Sylvie. "I do not care what Edmond says. No one should watch this, let alone endure it." She didn't understand what was going to happen, but by Gaspard's disgusted face, clearly something horrendous. A mix of duty and morbid curiosity kept her gaze on the platform.

The official listed all crimes, prompting more shouts from the crowd.

The executioner lifted the mallet.

Sylvie found some assurance in Edmond's promise that it would be bloodless; to her, bloodless meant humane, painless. Ogé did not deserve death, let alone public torture. But when the executioner lifted his hammer—an instrument meant for forging steel rather than distributing justice—Sylvie realized Edmond's duplicity. She would have preferred the blood.

The hammer struck Ogé's arm first while the white faces in the crowd screamed in approval. The resulting limb hung limp where it was once taut. No justice, just misshapen flesh.

Then the hammer swung again, the other arm its next target.

"Sylvie, please, do not look." Then left hip. "Sister, close your eyes." Then right hip. Left leg. "*Sylvie*." Right leg. His joints pointed in the wrong directions like those of a crushed spider.

Ogé screeched in agony and thrashed to avoid the impending impact. But the executioner always struck true. The echoing *crack* from his bones resonated in the square.

She stood immobile, her pupils blown wide in shock, staring at the fleshy bag of splintered bones that remained of Ogé. His head lolled to the side, and the only hint of life came from the tiny spasms of his useless limbs.

The division between justice and revenge sat as shattered as Ogé's body.

Guards turned the wheel on its side so that he faced the sky. The spectacle of his suffering over, most people scattered into the streets that led away from the square. Unfazed, Edmond left to call for their carriage, with Gaspard and Sylvie the only people in the plaza beside the punished and the punishers.

Sylvie did not dare move any closer. A tiny rivulet of blood had made its way from the beam holding up the wheel to the white cobblestones beneath. Ogé had bitten his tongue to keep from screaming, but he could only hold in his agony for so long, leaving bloody drool to run down from his open mouth.

"Edmond lied," she murmured. "He said it would be bloodless."

The offending stream of red stopped just in front of their feet.

The final portion of his punishment was not death; it was life. He would remain tied to the wheel and be doomed to die days later from dehydration and pain. But until then, his body would loom over the square, trapping Sylvie in its shadow.

She looked at the surrounding buildings and noticed that some of the other free Blacks still lurked, their eyes focused on Ogé's twitching fingers suspended more than a dozen feet above them. Their eyes rested on her, too, and their gazes felt like an accusation.

The White Man sleeps at the foot of Vesuvius, Gaspard had said the day before, recited like a prayer but with the leaden weight of a curse.

Sylvie shivered, pulling her bergère hat lower to conceal herself from the sun and judging eyes. Edmond called for them from the waiting carriage, and the pair turned away from the dying men.

Vengeance intended to rain down upon them on Saint-Domingue, as scalding as the fiery tempest that brought Pompeii to its end. But staring at the tiny stream of red, Sylvie knew that—unlike the ash-coated ancient city—Saint-Domingue would be buried in blood.

Chapter Five

And by what strange overturning of reason was it shameful for a white to wed a woman of color, when there was no dishonor in living with her in the crudest libertinage? . . . The thinking man sometimes blushes at being a man when he sees his like blinded by such a delirium.

—*Abbé Grégoire*

None of the children told Papa or his wife where they'd gone, so the sudden altered atmosphere at the château must have baffled them both.

The morning after the execution, Sylvie went to the family breakfast parlor. She'd slept poorly the previous night; she'd heard Ogé's screams in every silence, seen that same rivulet of blood drip from every surface.

Gaspard avoided any teasing or verbal sparring in those next couple of days, treating Sylvie only with brotherly concern and consideration.

She wanted to punch him.

"Why are you treating me so . . . politely?" she asked, catching him in the foyer before he could head into the city. "I'm your sister, for God's sake—not one of Madame's friends from church!"

He wore the same grim visage from the carriage ride back home after the execution; it had only left his face when he drank gunfire or slept. "I shouldn't have let you see that."

She bristled and spoke with more boldness than she felt. "It's not for you to decide what I may or may not see."

He seemed unconvinced, but he had always played the role of her protector well. Now she wondered if his protection did more harm than good.

She sat in the garden late that night watching the fireflies flicker. The native orchids surrounded her under the cover of the small rotunda. They were her favorites; they preferred shade to direct sunlight, so she could enjoy them without browning her skin. Their vibrant violet petals trumpeted outward like a gown.

She used to pretend she was two inches tall and wore the bulbs as a dress—back when she believed that if she avoided sunlight, she'd become white enough to marry one of the Allard brothers. She didn't see the sun or her orchids once that summer, walking along the far wall of every hallway to avoid the light streaming through the windows.

Even now, she sat under the cover of the domed building in the darkness of night out of habit. She hoped Blanchard would let her keep all the orchids she wanted.

She did not return to the sanctuary of her rooms until four in the morning.

Her lady's maid combed the castor oil through her hair and wrapped it for bed. Her deft hands moved slowly after her interrupted sleep.

"Alice," Sylvie said as her maid pinned the silk tignon. "Does the name Vincent Ogé mean anything to you?" Alice's eyes went wide and uncertain in the reflection of the vanity. "I do not mean to trick you; I want you to be honest."

Alice set down the pins and smoothed her apron. "Yes, I know 'im. He led the revolts in the north."

Sylvie turned on her stool to face her. "So you must support him, then?"

Alice's features set into a disdainful grimace, but she pulled her lips back into a neutral line. "No, Mademoiselle. We do not support 'im, as he does not support us."

Sylvie leaned forward, searching for more. "Please, speak freely." She knew asking for her maid's trust was unfair, but she hoped for it nonetheless. "Who does he support?"

Alice kept her eyes downcast, but she did continue. "Only the *affranchis*, not the Bossales or Creoles. They t'ink they are not like us."

Sylvie stared at Alice's hands: bitten nails short and jagged, and a few scattered scars crisscrossed near her knuckles from past lashings. Alice's skin was darker than hers, but only because Sylvie wore gloves and carried parasols.

"I didn't know," Sylvie said, mostly to herself. Alice wrung her apron, warily watching her mistress with guarded suspicion. After wiping her sweating palms on her chemise, Sylvie dismissed her maid. "You don't need to attend me in the morning, since I came in so late."

Alice thanked her softly and shut the door.

Sylvie crawled into bed. She normally loved her mountains of pillows and downy comforters—all surrounded by a gauzy ivory canopy. The linens glowed in the darkness.

After an hour or so of tossing and turning, Sylvie de Rosiers finally fell asleep in her sea of white.

OGÉ'S BRUTAL EXECUTION incited conflict outside the Château de Rosiers as well as inside; his death created an ever-expanding crack in the hull that threatened to swallow the ship under the waves.

And Edmond's fury-filled eyes would not leave her.

His dark stare rested on her face whenever their father spoke of the opposing factions, searching Sylvie for any sign of sympathy. She presented a pretty target for his ire, and every day she endured his hateful scowl over tea, knowing that her own kin made her an enemy. He never said an inflammatory word to her directly, but the poison lurked in the silences.

When rumors of awarding a handful of *affranchis* voting rights trickled in, his mood toward her only soured more.

On one late morning that past week, Sylvie could stand it no longer and said, "Edmond, *mon chou*, perhaps you could convince Julien to commission a portrait of me."

He'd snorted. "Now, why would I have my father waste silver on something so trivial?"

"So you could glare at *it*," she said. "Instead of *me*." Gaspard laughed, open and unrestrained, while Edmond's eyes narrowed into slits.

Her vindictive brother wanted her reminded of the difference between them, reminded of the certain end that befell people like her if they attempted to overreach their lot in life.

When the day came for Blanchard's arrival, nightmares and doubt had darkened the skin under her eyes to an unacceptable degree.

"More powder, Alice," she said, stretching the thin skin with her finger. Her round face had more definition, which she hoped looked elegant as opposed to ghoulish.

Her belly quaked, and she resolved to only pick at her food to avoid untimely exits to a chamber pot.

As planned, Sylvie wore a deep-blue brocade gown with paler rosettes along the bust and the updated pearl and sapphire earrings to enhance the color of the skirts. They also had the added benefit of parading the de Rosiers's wealth, which had lured Blanchard there in the first place.

After the initial introductions, Madame hurried everyone into the dining room. Blanchard had a gentle voice that matched his almost angelic face. He was undeniably lovely on first impression—he and Sylvie shared the same coiled curls, but his mouth was shapelier and his eyes a lighter brown. He kissed her gloved hand with a light, uncalloused hand.

Divided from him by brothers and platters of roasted meat, Sylvie couldn't get much interaction with her almost-betrothed during dinner. He glanced at her once or twice, but he mostly spoke to Papa and Gaspard; Madame knew the economics of running a household, but not a plantation, and Edmond loathed anyone with skin darker than raw linen.

She hoped that with cards and liquor Blanchard might reveal his true colors. She thought less of the music she might play for Blanchard and more of the sounds of Ogé's femurs cracking.

Blanchard offered to escort her into the salon with a polite smile. He dressed as well as a man of their kind was allowed; he wore a fine green frock coat with a pink damask lining that showed when he walked, and his cravat sat high and heavily starched on his throat. His sharp cheekbones reflected the glow of the candelabras, making his tan skin even more golden. Despite what the courts or men like Edmond said, enough money could make any man powerful—and Blanchard clearly had silver and all the power that came with it.

And he is gorgeous.

Frankly, Sylvie wasn't sure if she should admire his beauty or envy it. Regardless, they'd make a striking pair.

The servants arranged the card tables and chairs. Decanters of rum sparkled on the settee beside the assorted French and Spanish wines with after-dinner coffee.

Papa settled into a chair with a glass of brandy, his eyes already falling shut.

She didn't want to lose her chance to speak with Blanchard, and if Madame forced everyone to play quadrille for hours while Gaspard cheated, then that's exactly what would happen.

"Madame, do you think we might play *piquet au cent*?" Sylvie asked.

Every good Frenchman and Frenchwoman learned piquet early; it was practically the national card game of France and its territories. More importantly, one only played it in pairs.

Madame glanced at Julien, who now snored softly. "Your father is indisposed, and you need an even number—"

Gaspard placed a gentle arm on Madame's shoulder. "Edmond hates cards. He thinks it's the devil's game." Edmond didn't correct him. He just sat in an armchair and opened his copy of the Count of Buffon's *Histoire naturelle*. "So there, we are even once more. Come, *Maman*, you shall be my partner." He guided her a touch too quickly to their seats, leaving Sylvie to thank her lucky stars for one ally in this house.

"Well"—Blanchard pulled out a chair for her—"shall we?"

They settled a good distance from her family; she was sure they both appreciated the privacy. "Forgive my delay in accepting the invitation to dine," he said. "Indigo can be a fastidious crop: we must harvest the leaves before they bloom, and never more than a few cuttings."

Sylvie took the deck before he reached for it—she despised sloppy dealing. With a practiced hand, she removed the twos through the sixes from each suit until they had a thirty-two-card deck. She shuffled the remaining cards while she spoke. "No apologies needed, Monsieur. I have heard that Indigo can be a very particular mistress."

He smiled at her joke before asking, "Do you like cards?" He spun the fine ruby ring on his pinkie finger. Mulattoes, in an effort to appease white aristocrats, were often excessively devout—like enough Hail Marys could lighten their skin. But he asked it without judgment, which Sylvie appreciated.

"Probably too much for a genteel woman," she said with a laugh. "Gaspard adores cards, so I was often tortured with endless games from bouillotte to Pope Joan."

Blanchard chuckled. "I'm afraid I'll embarrass myself tonight, then. I only learned the basics from my father and had few people to perfect the art with."

"You're an only son, yes? Natural-born or otherwise?" Sylvie glanced again at his ring—gold, initialed, and with a single finely cut ruby winking in the candlelight.

He raised a neatly groomed eyebrow. "I am. Your father's spies must be well paid."

Sylvie dealt the first of the six rounds—collectively called a *partie*. A sequence, meaning consecutive cards in a suit, or a set of same-ranked cards had the potential to earn points. The goal of the game was to reach *cent*, or one hundred.

"No need for espionage: your signet ring is a tad too large for you. I assumed it belonged to the elder Monsieur Blanchard? I doubt if he had any trueborn sons he would've given such a gift." Sylvie lowered her voice after ensuring that Gaspard kept Madame distracted. "I'm the only daughter. Madame would not tolerate my presence half so well if she had precious girls of her own."

Madame had indulged in feminine finery and motherly attention when Sylvie was a girl, without the inconvenient reminder of a living slave mistress. Even Madame could not resist the instincts to play house, dressing her up like a little doll.

Once she was old enough to ask questions—to challenge or to want—Madame slinked away behind a wall of discomfort.

Blanchard smirked. "Your observational skills are sharp, Mademoiselle. I admire that. My father has daughters, but I'm the only one of my sex—a truth from which I've benefited all my life, as you have."

Her interactions with other mulattoes had been limited growing up. She enjoyed the mild thrill of speaking to someone with whom she could bond over a shared identity.

Lowering her head in insincere piety, she said, "I count my blessings." She finished distributing the cards. They had twelve cards in a hand and a remaining talon of eight facedown cards from which the players could draw. "I feel that it would bode poorly for our potential marital felicity to have my bridegroom owe me a debt," she said. "Shall we keep this a moneyless game?"

Blanchard made a startled laugh. "So certain of a victory, are we?"

She dropped her cards and caught his eye, her gaze not wavering. "I don't like to gamble, Monsieur; life is already uncertain enough. I only enjoy games that ensure a positive outcome."

"Then allow me to reassure you," he said, brushing her fingers with his equally soft ones. "This game will be successful for both of us."

She smiled warmly, and they played the game in earnest while the conversation remained witty and light. Sylvie admired his elegance in manners and dress and made a mental note to thank Gaspard for his underhanded matchmaking.

"When you come to the estate"—he picked up two cards from the talon—"you'll love the rose garden. All of my sisters adore it when they visit."

"Do you have orchids, by chance? I'm very fond of them."

"Indigo needs a great deal of sunlight, so we haven't got much shade to keep them happy."

Sylvie imagined the scene: the two of them, arm in arm, with rose petals softening their footsteps. And slaves would dot the fields behind them collecting the indigo leaves, fuchsia flowers surrounding her from every angle.

"You have a great deal of responsibility. Your indigo must keep you busy for such a little plant."

He chuckled. "I am not overly devoted to business. I should like to keep a balance as your father has."

"Given our existence, it appears our fathers enjoyed business a bit too much." She covered her mouth as if to restrain it, but the words were out. But he did not flinch, and she hurried to move past it. "Well, you clearly enjoy cards. Do you have other hobbies?"

"I quite enjoy riding—and dancing as well."

"So you like to partake in society?" She envisioned balls and parties and soirees, the stuff of girlish fantasies unfulfilled.

"You have been rather sheltered by your circumstances, but if I may be so bold, marriage provides more opportunities to socialize."

He spoke of their future like it already existed, which should have thrilled her. Yet more than once did she wonder what Blanchard, a powerful mulatto like Ogé, thought of his rights and freedoms. "You are quite active in our circle." The sherry she sipped again loosened her tongue and hopefully his drink loosened his as well. "Surely, you must keep an ear to the Assembly." All the provinces of Saint-Domingue had assemblies, or local governments, like that of France.

He fiddled with his cards. "I like to think I stay informed."

"You are a man of influence and intelligence. My father," she said, and Blanchard's eyes glanced at the snoozing man in question, "seems certain you have no aspirations for—" She paused to think of the tamest word. "*More*."

He laid down his cards. "I want what all free men want."

She put down two kings: one of hearts and one of diamonds. They had the same power only in different suits. "Equality?" Her stomach gurgled from stress and two glasses of sherry.

He glanced over at her family, though they were focused on their game or the backs of their eyelids. "What we want"—Blanchard then pushed forward the queen of hearts beside her matching king—"is not so far out of reach."

After that, he kept all discussion to libertine novels and fashionable fabric colors. Regardless, *equality* had such a bold flavor on her tongue that it lingered for the rest of the evening. She promised him she'd come to see the gardens at her earliest convenience, even if she was indifferent to roses.

"We'd best say our goodbyes," he said. She had won their card game twice that night and felt satisfied with her triumph.

Papa snored loudly now, and Edmond had long since gone to bed. Madame made little braids in her ever-patient butterfly spaniel's fur while Gaspard did card tricks on the table.

"How about you both see Monsieur Blanchard out?" Madame whispered to her and Gaspard, so as not to wake Papa.

They went to the main foyer, and Gaspard gave the pair distance like any decent chaperone should.

"I hope this will be one of many evenings spent together," Blanchard said.

"I pray the next one will have less snoring."

"I'll endure hours of snores if it means I'm in the company of the Pearl of Saint-Domingue." Gaspard snorted into his hand, and Sylvie gave a fierce glare over her shoulder. A dark-skinned slave dressed in livery entered the room, his clothing a similar shade of indigo to Sylvie's gown. Blanchard turned to him and said, "Is the carriage ready, boy?"

The slave looked no more than ten. But Bossales were always notoriously malnourished, so he could have been older than he appeared. The child ran off to fetch the carriage.

Blanchard happily wore his father's ring, while his mother probably wore a shackle like Sylvie's own mother had.

He kissed her hand, lingering for as long as propriety would allow—and then a bit longer than that. Sylvie marveled again at how soft his hands were. He pressed the queen of hearts into her hand before he let go, his signet ring glinting.

Catherine joined them on the steps as Blanchard took his leave. He smiled brightly and waved from the coach window. The little boy in blue hung on to the back of the carriage as it pulled away.

She would be a queen. A queen of an indigo kingdom and little slave boys.

The family waved goodbye as his coach was eaten by the darkness. Sylvie had already headed inside, leaving behind shimmering shreds of the gilded card on the steps of the château.

Chapter Six

I pity them greatly, but I must be mum,
For how could we do without sugar and rum?
—*William Cowper, "Pity for Poor Africans"*

avril 1791

Sylvie avoided both Madame and her father for the next weeks—they would only ask her thoughts on Blanchard. And when an invitation to tour Blanchard's house came, she claimed a headache.

She tried music and more needlework to numb her mind and fingers. But weary with embroidery bloodstained from one too many mistakes and in need of more meaningful distraction, she went off in search of Gaspard. She resolved to return to some level of normalcy and social interaction that didn't involve a needle.

She checked his bed first; he often spent afternoons sleeping off late nights and heavy luncheons. But the only sign of him languished in the embers of the fireplace.

Many hearths in great houses outside of the kitchen solely existed for aesthetic purposes—though some rooms could grow a bit cold on winter nights. However, the unseasonable heat meant none of the fires should've been lit.

Sylvie bent down to the fire-eaten logs to examine the remains clinging to ashen bark. Bits of paper that had escaped the flames hid in the corners of the hearth. He'd been burning letters. And the ink in the inkwell on his desk looked low for a man who claimed to never write.

She left the room in the same state in which she found it so as not to arouse suspicion. Thinking that Gaspard could be feeling bookish, given all his now-burnt correspondence, Sylvie headed toward the library.

Instead, she came upon her other brother walking down the corridor in the opposite direction.

"Edmond," she called. He kept walking with his eyes focused on a bundle of papers he held. His dark hair stuck out in various places, and his cheeks bloomed red.

"Edmond," she called again, hurrying to catch him. Surely, he heard her. "Edmond . . ." She caught his sleeve.

He whirled toward her—his eyes hard and cold. "*What?*"

Sylvie took a reflexive step backward. "You didn't respond when I called for you. I'm looking for Gaspard."

"And how does that involve me?"

She narrowed her eyes. "I hoped you might know where he is."

"Courtyard." He tapped his boot. "Anything else I can assist you with?"

"No." Perhaps Gaspard could enlighten her as to why Edmond seemed so particularly cross. "That's all." He didn't wait for her to finish before stalking off.

As Sylvie approached the courtyard, she heard the hiss of metal cutting through air. She peeked around the corner of a stone pillar and spotted Gaspard wielding his smallsword at an invisible opponent. The golden hilt glinted in the sun.

The sword, a shiny, pointy thing that attended more soirees than battles, moved as an extension of his arm. She'd assumed he couldn't even use the damned thing—he wore a sword like she wore a necklace. Decoration.

Gaspard danced from foot to foot as he pivoted away from his phantom enemy. All gentlemen knew how to fence, but he looked like he wanted to *fight*.

She left her hiding place and crept behind him so as to get a better view. Her heel caught on a loose stone and made a small rattling
noise.

Gaspard turned on his heel with his sword pointed toward her.

Swallowing thickly, Sylvie pushed the blade aside with the back
of her hand. "A hello would suffice, Gaspard."

"God," he breathed. "You startled me. I haven't seen you in days."

"Which warrants an attack?" she asked, gesturing to the offending weapon.

Gaspard continued to catch his breath. "You could've said my
name instead of sneaking up behind me. Most girls have the good
sense not to spy on a man brandishing a blade."

"Neither of us are overly burdened with good sense, brother mine."

He chuckled ruefully. "That's fair."

She took the sword from him and made some practice swings.
"Why are you fencing? It's damned hot." The sword did not weigh
as much as she anticipated, and it looked rather pretty in the sunlight. Guns, on the other hand, dark and hidden in holsters or trousers, did not have the elegance or beauty of a well-balanced blade.

Gaspard crossed his arms and watched his sister's dueling style
with amusement. "A man can't choose the weather. You must be
able to fight in snow or sun."

She thrust forward, enjoying the foreign sensation of power.
"Fight what?"

"Duels over my honor, of course," he said with a grin.

She didn't expect to feel wounded by his dishonesty, but between
her father, Edmond, and now her closest ally, the world she knew
crumbled under her feet. But she just smiled.

She paused to examine the gold filigree inlaid on the pommel.
"Do you know why Edmond's so churlish lately? Did I miss something while I was . . . convalescing?" She could still smell the burning lace: what a fine perfume its smoke would make.

He narrowed his eyes. "What did he say?"

She focused on cleaning a smudge on the blade. "He just seems more unpleasant than usual toward me. I don't understand why—I went to the execution like he wanted. I've had nightmares for weeks because of him."

And now I can't look my father in the eye, or stomach the idea of marriage to a planter, or stare at the château walls without feeling ill.

He took the sword away and put it back into its wooden case. "Ignore Edmond. Keep away from him for now."

"I know you two quarrel, but has something happened?"

"Just leave him be. He's a lobcock."

He went to pick up the sword case, but Sylvie put her foot on the lid. "Stop lying to me. You're horrid at it. And why has your bed not been slept in? And why do you look like you haven't rested in days?"

With a forceful tug, he pulled the case out from under her. "Sylvie, leave it. I look wretched because I've caught a cold, and my bed is made because I preferred another's last night. Does that explanation satisfy you?"

She raised an eyebrow. "No, but I'll find the truth eventually. You hold your drink better than your secrets."

AFTER HER CONVERSATION that afternoon confronting Gaspard proved unsuccessful, Sylvie resorted to amateur espionage.

Most days, she was early to bed and late to rise, but her determination to prove herself right kept her awake. Not *wide*-awake, of course; she yawned several times before the clock struck eleven.

She sat on the chaise nearest the basement servants' entrance, knowing her brother wouldn't dare exit out of the formal foyer. The servants flitted back and forth trying to investigate why their drowsy mistress camped belowstairs close to midnight.

Sure enough, Gaspard appeared down the steps shortly after.

Her sleepiness well forgotten, she channeled her energy into a triumphant expression at having caught him in the act.

He'd limited his sumptuous dress to woolen breeches and a waist-coat devoid of elaborate design or gold thread. Of all the sins, Gaspard favored vanity, and yet there he stood looking like the miller's boy.

"Tell me where you've been going," she said as he squirmed under her narrow-eyed glare. He refused to speak, so she went on. "I *knew* you'd been sneaking out, but you told me I spoke nonsense. Lie all you like, but not to me. Never to me."

"I cannot tell you." He may as well have slapped her. He was her partner, the only person to whom she revealed her true face. To exile her from his confidence was to isolate her completely.

Bristling at his reluctance, she pressed him with more questions. "Whyever not? Is it a woman?" He scoffed, and she dropped her voice an octave. "A man?"

He laughed, but it sounded brittle. "Why do you assume I'm out whoring?"

"You're practically the patron saint of syphilis."

"I wish it were a lover, but no."

Her already-thin thread of patience snapped. "Then *tell* me, Gaspard. When have I ever revealed your secrets? I did not tell Madame about Caroline, Marie, Jeanne, or any of your girls! Not to mention the gambling, that pitiful excuse for a duel—"

"Heaven and Earth," he hissed, gripping her elbow. "Keep your voice low."

Sylvie flinched, moving away from this man so unlike her brother.

If her ire did not wring out the truth from him, then perhaps sweetness would. She adopted a wounded tone, lowering her chin to make her moss-colored eyes appear round and pleading. "You know I would not reveal your secrets to anyone."

He pulled her into the shadows by the door. "They are not my secrets to share, sister."

"But they burden you all the same."

Whatever demons clung to her brother, they were winning. "My burdens are nothing compared to those of most men who call Saint-Domingue home," he said. "I debauched my life away in this god-forsaken house, never once caring about the bodies that built it. Even you, the one who should care most . . ." Sylvie flinched at his accusatory tone—if he only knew what dark thoughts and phantom faces haunted her—but he stopped himself before elaborating. "I should go. You must sleep, or else you'll have dark circles for days."

Sylvie reflexively touched the thin skin under her eyes before frowning. "Fine. *Go*," she snapped. "I hope your burdens are marvelous company."

"Sylvie, I'm sorry, but telling you risks Edmond finding out—"

She rushed past, muttering a bitter *bonne nuit*. Once upstairs, she slammed her door hard, so Gaspard would feel her frustration from downstairs.

He acted like such a martyr, she mused with a scowl, *with his burdens and precious secrets.*

What did he want from her? She was no midnight crusader for abolition. He ate from the same table she did, drank the same wine, wore the same cotton. Gaspard could go on acting like a saint, but at least Sylvie didn't put on airs.

Or maybe he was the only de Rosiers with a spine.

SHE RIPPED A brush through frizzing curls at her mirror the next morning, her blood boiling and her heart a little broken by the future she thought she wanted.

Papa sat in an armchair drinking his sugar-coffee mixture and reading the paper with Edmond on his left. Watching her father sip his morning coffee gave her the same cloying nausea as watching Ogé's execution. Catherine sat on her usual emerald-green chaise.

"Sylvie!" her father greeted warmly. "How are you, my love?" She kissed her father's cheek, holding her breath against the bitter-smelling drink that seemed to cling to him. "Feeling better?"

"A slight headache, unlikely to go away, I think."

He patted her hand. "It seems like this spring just doesn't agree with your constitution."

"It certainly does not." She sat down on her chaise and reached for the fruit tray. Upon looking up, she locked eyes with their head maid.

The house slave who broke the teacup months before—and who had been assigned this room since winter—had been replaced with their head maid, Marion.

Sylvie stood and marched to Catherine. "Where is the maid?" she asked.

Catherine sputtered at her expression. "Wh-which maid?"

Sylvie checked every corner of the salon. "The other maid." She hated that it only occurred to her now to wonder at her name. "Where is she?"

"Lucie, you mean?" Catherine clicked her tongue in disapproval. "She's a bit useless at the moment."

"Why?" Sylvie asked.

Edmond frowned lightly and cut in, "That little negress stole a cup. I thought acquainting her with the cowskin would serve her well."

"How do you know she stole a cup? What in God's name would she do with a *cup*?"

Catherine huffed. "We've been missing one of my grandmother's teacups, the lovely ones with the darling indigo flowers! Who knows what she wants with it? Perhaps some vodou superstition."

Sylvie held Edmond's gaze, chin raised, avoiding the menacing sway of the whip he kept glued to his side. She thought of the girl's back, the split flesh and dark blood from Edmond's gleeful application. "And Edmond kindly meted out punishment when you realized it was her."

Months ago, in a moment of panic, she'd tried to help the girl— out of guilt, solidarity, pity—but instead, she'd condemned her to deforming scars over an insipid teacup. The young, hopeful girl could already be facedown in a mass grave at the side of the château.

Her papa sighed and folded down his newspaper in a huff. "I've told that boy again and again," he started. "Whipping them until they're lame is a waste of money and energy. By God, that's what the overseers are for."

Edmond rolled his eyes.

"And now I'm short a servant," fussed Catherine. "I'd be morti-fied if I had to host a dinner. Why, I'd need to melt the butter myself."

The rage and burning that had been curled in Sylvie's belly since she was left covered in ashes in the town square uncoiled like a strik-ing snake. "You let him whip her half to death because of a scrap of porcelain?"

"You know your brother is overzealous at times," Catherine said, raising a hand when Edmond opened his mouth. "If it were me, I wouldn't have—"

"She could die!" Sylvie yelled, gripping the arms of her seat to keep from slapping the smug look from Edmond's face. He only scoffed.

Their father put down his coffee with a *clink*. "That is enough, Sylvie," he chastised. "Your sympathy commends you, but you must calm yourself." She stared at her father, incredulous that this man could oversee these atrocities and demand calm.

The pain and anguish of the past months welled in her heart, and she threw a teacup on the floor hard enough for it to shatter into dozens of pale-blue pieces. She thrilled when Edmond flinched.

"Are you going to whip me, Papa? Are you going to string me up by my wrists and take the flesh from my back?" she asked, each word louder than the last. "I am a mulatta, am I not? As in a mule? Stubborn livestock that needs to be brought to heel?"

Edmond went to restrain her, but she twisted out of his hold.

"Don't touch me," she screamed. "Don't *ever* touch me!" He jumped back like she was a rearing horse. But he balled his fists and squared his stance, ready to use force to break her.

Papa didn't give him the chance. "Edmond and Catherine, go to your rooms." Edmond looked ready to argue, but Catherine shooed him out. "Marion, find Master Gaspard—wherever that wretched boy may be. He's the only one who can make her see sense," he said to the replacement servant, who fled to fetch Gaspard. Madame, white-faced and frantic, left without argument.

Sylvie slipped down onto her knees and heaved. She trembled like a cornered animal, too sick with the realization that she was not only a victim but a perpetrator.

The damask wallpaper, yellow like the eyes of a drunkard, swirled and contorted around her. She dug her fingers into the plush carpet so she did not float away into the ether. Her father kept at a safe distance, white-knuckling the back of the armchair while he watched Sylvie with wary eyes.

Her father and his ilk condemned Ogé to die in Le Cap—but well before any talk of rebellion, he had condemned *her* to a life of gray, a life of in-between, of almost and not quite. Out of selfishness and lust, he'd made a gray stain on a sheet of white silk, killing her mother and damning Sylvie to a life of public and private shame.

"Would you like something sweet?" he asked slowly. "I know when you were little, a sweet could calm you."

Sylvie remembered her father feeding her sugared figs to keep her from crying. Her face twisted to keep her from sobbing harder. She shook her head and brushed over the fractured porcelain with shaking fingers. "Catherine doesn't understand you, but I know you have a fragile heart. I must admit you get it from me. Try as we might to conceal them, we have sensitive souls." He truly believed what he was saying. And she loved him, which broke her heart.

The damaged cup in her hands, she looked up at Papa.

"You know I would never let anyone hurt you, Sylvie. Not with a whip nor anything else."

For as long as she could remember, he never shied from his role as her father. He did not hesitate to take his little mulatto daughter into his arms, to dress her in the finest cotton fresh from American fields, to listen to her woes and dreams, to feed her well-loved lies of her complicated existence.

He shared not only all the wealth and comforts of his kingdom but all the shame as well.

It was too difficult to speak louder than a ragged whisper. "I know, Julien." He flinched at the sound of his name. She could call him *Papa* no more.

She let the cup ground her as she reined in her breathing. The colors had been so lovely—swirls of blue with blooming pink roses—the cup one of a set the family had had for as long as she could remember. And judging from his concerned, confused, and frustrated face, Sylvie knew he didn't understand how she could suddenly be so hysterical.

When she was very small, he would sit her in his study while she practiced her Spanish—in case a wealthy Spaniard ever showed interest—and would open Diderot's encyclopedia up to random pages and make her translate the topics. The Tree of Knowledge was *El árbol del conocimiento*. Political Authority was *Autoridad política*. He didn't care if his child wanted to study an encyclopedia on the natural sciences and political theory, only that she could speak a language well enough to marry.

And now that she voiced an opinion nurtured by her education, wanted to fight for a cause that meant something, he could hardly recognize her. Angry tears blurred her vision.

"Sylvie?" Gaspard probed softly. She hadn't heard him come in. He didn't barricade himself behind furniture like Julien did. He stood close with his hand outstretched for her to take. Gaspard had a worried line in his forehead, but no judgment or discomfort lurked in his open expression.

Sylvie cleared her throat and rose without his help.

"It seems my headache has gotten worse," she said. "May I take to my rooms?" Marion's curious face peeked from behind Gaspard, but Sylvie couldn't meet her gaze.

Sylvie, like any good woman, knew when she should and shouldn't ask questions. Women made an art of silence. But the burdens of the past weeks made the consequences of ignorance more unbearable than the consequences of truth. They might see her as a radical for demanding answers, but she would break the chain of lies that bound her to this place.

Later that day, after hours of contemplation and frustrated tears to fuel her courage, she marched up to her father's office. "Why did you keep me?" she asked.

Her voice startled Julien, his eyes comically large behind a magnifying glass. He had several coffee beans lined up on his desk, some still encased in the red fruit. Little metal instruments for plant dissection glinted in the candlelight. He must not have heard her knock.

"Sylvie? How do you mean?" he asked. He spoke gently so as not to provoke her.

Sylvie kept her back to him as she perused a print of the anatomy of a coffee plant. She did not have the courage to look him in the eye. "Why did you keep me after my mother died? You could have given me to any of the other slaves to manage."

He sputtered for a moment before saying, "It was so lonely on this island. Especially once your mother passed. As you know, Catherine stayed with your brothers in France for years before I deemed it time for them to travel." He played with the white parchment shells of the coffee beans. "Your mother offered some companionship. And I treated her well." Sylvie tried not to snort.

Her father left a beloved Black mistress with child; she died in childbirth as she pushed infant Sylvie into the world to join the ranks of thousands of mulattoes who followed the loins of white planters. Sylvie was freed the day she was born, and her mother left the world the same way she came into it—as property.

"More than companionship." She flipped through one of his many encyclopedias.

"As much as a slave can offer."

She restrained herself from hurling the book at him. "Then what am I?" she snapped, turning her neck just enough to catch a bit of his expression.

Freedom could not be piecemeal—either you had it or you didn't. Sylvie couldn't be mostly free because she was mostly white.

He paused his examination and finally put the magnifying glass down. "My daughter," he said. "You are my *daughter.*"

"And Ogé was someone's son."

He stood up in anger. "He was amassing an army of rebels—"

"An army of *men like you made!*" She snapped the book shut. "An army of half bloods. An army of people told they are part human—one foot always in the field. An army born of selfish desire and hypocrisy. You grumble over coffee beans and wonder why they fight? You care more about those little black seeds than the Black hands that made them." His expression softened from choler to bewilderment. She knelt in front of him and gripped his hands in hers. "You cannot claim to love me while condemning *them,*" she said. "My humanity—" Her throat tightened around a sob.

"My pearl," he said, cupping her cheek.

She brushed his hand away. Tears clung to her lashes, but she persevered. "My humanity is not merely an extension of your own. I don't want my freedom built on the backs of millions. I do not dare speak for those people in your fields, but I know that their lives are worth more than . . ." She grabbed a coffee cherry from his desk and pinched it between her fingers. The red pulp ran down to her wrist. "Worth more than *this*."

She threw the remnants of the fruit on the floor, some of its juice staining the toe of Julien's shoe.

"And please know," she said as she stood up again, "know that I am grateful for the food on your table and the clothes on my back— for the luxuries I've enjoyed and for the brother I adore. But I only stay here because I am a coward; I will not join a band of rebels and live in the foothills. I have nowhere else to go or means to support myself that doesn't involve a life spent on my back." He flinched. "And I do not think you will cast me out, because you are a coward, too."

They stared at each other, feeling the threads of kinship strain and break. Julien opened his mouth and closed it several times, but he never said anything. She bobbed a curtsy and left his study, resting on the door once it closed to release a shuddering breath.

She was not the daughter he knew anymore.

Thank God.

But in her closure she found a great grief—Sylvie could both revel in her enlightenment and mourn the simple life she had lost.

Chapter Seven

I took up arms for the freedom of my color . . . We will defend it or perish.

—*Toussaint-Louverture*

22 août 1791

Night served as the only bearable time of day on this steaming island—promising soothing midnight breezes and pleasant dreams.

A tropical storm had raged the night before, stealing the clouds and leaving noisy winds to rattle her windows. The hills finally swallowed the sun in a flash of orange flame, taking the withering heat with it.

After two hours of tossing in her tangle of white sheets, Sylvie stared at the ceiling. In spite of the dark relief of eventide, she could not find sleep's embrace.

But under the suffocating blanket of night, there was no golden Gaspard to soothe her with his humor and wit, just the thrum of mosquitoes she hoped the bed's canopy could keep at bay.

Several loud cracks sent the birds by her window shrieking in terror.

Sylvie bolted up in her bed, sheet held up to her throat. She tried to rationalize the blast of a rifle—that perhaps someone was tracking game—but it was too dark for hunting.

Several more shots rang out, and the château came alive with crashes and screams. The clamor outside her door grew louder, and she threw on her dressing robe, haphazardly tying the silken ribbons across her middle.

Thunderous footsteps barely preceded Gaspard striding through the doors covered in muck and sweat. "Sylvie!"

Indignant at his blatant disregard for her modesty, she cried, "Do not burst into my rooms! What if I hadn't been *decent*—"

He paid her no mind, throwing an armful of gowns into her largest valise. He pulled open her drawers, scouring through petticoats and ribbons until the floors became a sea of white lace and muslin.

"What's going on?" she asked. A succession of closer musket shots made the glass vials on her vanity rattle.

Gaspard waited for a moment until the bullets stopped firing, then resumed his pillaging.

"We need to flee," he said as he tore through her things. "*Now.*" He ran to her toilette to grab her various creams and jewelry. He ransacked the crystal and silver trays, and the air went sickly sweet from the spilled oils and perfumes. Chains and pearls dangled from his stuffed pockets. "Pack whatever valuables you have."

Her hands shook. She went to her largest window and counted five dots of orange smoke plumes. Fires, large ones.

He moved to the lower drawers and tore through her stockings and gloves, tossing them into traveling chests. Dresses haphazardly hung out of the trunk, memories and treasures thrown about like sacks of rice.

"Gaspard," she said in a small voice. But he paid her no mind, continuing to dismantle her glass world piece by piece. "Gaspard, please, tell me."

He gripped the sides of the oaken chest, his eyes screwed shut against whatever words he was about to speak. "They've had this planned for weeks, and they took the storm last night as a good omen to begin. Slaves have rebelled all over the island. Plantations are marked for burning, and we're one of them. It's only a matter of time before the people here get the message." Sylvie shook her head, backing away from her brother and the information he carried. "It's true—a band of rebels is going plantation to plantation. A dozen masters and their families have already been slaughtered. It's a revolution, Sylvie."

The past months buzzed with insurrections and mobilizations. She had taken comfort in the idea of the liberation of Saint-Domingue as an eventuality, a distant battlefield to read about in the weekly papers. But nothing on this scale, nothing this *close*, nothing this *soon*.

Madame's screams rang out across the house as her husband and Edmond bellowed orders to their attendants downstairs. Sylvie wondered if this was how the people of Pompeii felt when the ash rained down upon them—the inevitability of their destruction.

Gaspard's swift shake of her shoulders jolted Sylvie from her shock.

"We only have minutes, an hour at most. I've told the family, and the militia has been roused, but pray the plantation does not yet know our plans."

She released a shuddering breath, running her hands over the carved mahogany of her bed. Gaspard rested his palm on her back as her shoulders heaved from sobs.

"We're going to die, Gaspard," she whimpered. "They hate us. They *should* hate us."

She had heard of the cruelties performed by the more violent masters on the island, heard the lewd talk of rape of the womenfolk, the mutilation of limbs, the death of children. This "Pearl of the Antilles" was proud of its particular brand of barbarism.

But she'd liked the wealth slavery afforded and willfully ignored the Black faces in those coffee fields until it was too late.

But they saw *her*.

They saw her father's lovely mulatto daughter. They saw her fine clothes and the pretty cross dangling from her throat, all while humanity's worst sins fertilized the soil that grew her father's coffee. Her mother was a product of this system, but Sylvie pretended she could marry Blanchard and harden her heart against the corrupt origins of their riches. Even though she had realized the truth of her crimes, it came on the eve of the abyss.

If she were a slave, she'd want to kill her, too.

"You are not dying today," Gaspard said. He held her against him, but the comfort was fleeting. "Pack now; I need to prepare the horses."

Richelieu and the other hounds barked from downstairs, their fearful whines shrill and sharp.

She nodded, pulling her robe tighter around her. The mild August night went cold.

Sylvie packed as lightly as her heart allowed, leaving behind her treasured horse statuette and rose perfumes. Her diamonds and other jewels rattled in her valise, interspersed with her underthings and gowns. She snatched the pearl necklace and earring set from one of her many jewelry boxes and shoved them into her pocket.

"Are you ready?" asked Gaspard upon his return.

She stared at her beautiful room. The sky-blue quatrefoil walls, the ivory molding on the ceiling, the delicate lace on her pillows—all would be ransacked and burned by the end of the week, the precious kindling to feed the revolution's ravenous flames.

"Edmond says that soldiers should arrive in a few days," he offered. "He told me we'll be able to come back."

The slaves outnumbered white people one hundred to one. Men like Julien and Edmond could not win. "He is wrong."

Gaspard said nothing and grabbed her valise—but dropped it with a *thump*. "*Mon Dieu*, little sister! What did you pack? All of France?" He sighed and picked it up once more, better prepared for its weight.

They rushed down the corridor that led to the stairs. But Sylvie stopped halfway down the steps, transfixed in horror by the sight that greeted her in the foyer.

Edmond directed his pistol at their house slaves, all of whom looked terrified—some with wounds on their faces from recent abuse. She recognized Marion shuddering in fear. Bloodstains dotted her brother's waistcoat, his eyes lit from within by curdling ire.

"Edmond!" Sylvie shrieked as she ran down the steps. "What are you doing?"

He never took his eyes off Alice. Blood ran down her mouth and jaw. The red droplets decorated the white marble floors. Alice's gaze did not waver from Edmond's, either, nothing in her dark eyes except calm truth. The eyes of a woman who knew the future. Who foresaw the White Man's demise.

"If I allow them to leave, they'll tell the others," he said, stalking closer to bring the pistol into point-blank range. Several servants flinched, but Alice just raised her chin higher.

Sylvie looked helplessly for Gaspard, but he had gone on to load their chests into the carriage. She rushed out to follow him.

Fires still dotted the hillside, and their pillars of smoke rose out of the horizon, only visible due to the dim glow of faraway flames. The air choked her with smoke and humidity; palms burned like grass, quickly and with more fumes than actual heat.

The birds and mosquitoes either kept quiet or had long fled. Had Sylvie not seen the burning plantations in the hills, she wouldn't have known anything was amiss.

Gaspard stood beside their black phaeton, moonlight shining through the spokes of the wheels. A lantern swayed in the restless breeze.

Light and quick, the phaeton only held two to three people.

Sylvie hurried to his side. "Gaspard, we cannot fit everyone—"

He continued loading the carriage with the few trunks they had

packed. "Mama and Papa already left for the docks; we are to follow." He opened the door. "Now get inside."

She wiped her face; fatigue and smoke made her eyes water. "I'm
getting Edmond."

Gaspard sighed and finally looked at her. "He is not coming."

He offered his hand to help her into the phaeton, but Sylvie
couldn't bring herself to move.

She darted back into the foyer—unsure if she meant to save the
hostage servants or her mad brother—as Gaspard shouted after her.
The sooner she pulled Edmond into the carriage, the sooner they
could leave this doomed relic and its liberated people.

Edmond, pale and trembling, still held the pistol. Sweat poured
down his cheeks. The slaves no longer stood; he had forced them all
onto their knees before him with his gun aimed at their terrified
faces.

She rested her hands gently on the extended forearm pointing the
weapon. "Edmond, we're leaving; you can let them go." Alice's eyes
flashed to hers.

He shrugged off her touch and seethed, "I will not be forced out
of my home by my own property!"

To Edmond, slavery was the natural result of racial inferiority as
well as economics, and mixing blood a nasty result of weak men and
poor restraint. Sylvie embodied everything that threatened to tear
his world apart. He cocked his pistol, gesturing to the house. "This
is my birthright, and I would sooner let us all go up in smoke before
these negroes see my back as I flee."

Alice looked almost saintly in her raw linen nightgown, hands
clasped in front of her. She was not a coward, and Sylvie would not
let her die on her knees like one.

The most energetic thing Sylvie had ever done was play croquet on
a particularly warm day, but with all the mindless speed and strength
she could muster, she barreled into Edmond's outstretched arm.

"Run, *run*," she shouted to the hostages as she wrestled for control of the pistol. These people would not die the same night they earned their freedom. They stumbled in their fear, but Alice dragged them to the exit. "Go!"

Edmond outmatched Sylvie's strength by leagues, but she only needed to distract him long enough for the slaves—now ex-slaves—to escape beyond the main gate.

When the last of them fled, she released her stubborn hold on his wrist; he triumphed just in time to see the deserted room. Enraged, he gave her a backhanded slap across the face.

"What have you *done*?" he screeched. "Now the entire plantation will know!"

She gripped her burning cheek, trying to find her voice in the shock and indignity. She could and would forgive the slap. Sylvie could tell herself it was fear or madness that had provoked him, but she knew that terror revealed one's true nature, not concealed it. She swiped her lip with her tongue, and the metallic taste of blood tingled in her mouth.

"Let them go," she shouted. Flame and blood surrounded them, but his pride replaced any sense of self-preservation. "The war is lost. The war has *been* lost, from the moment men like you thought they could own—"

"Things like you?"

She preferred the slap to his malice.

But no matter what he thought of her, they were blood; she could not abandon him here to his own hubris. Sylvie had only just begun to understand the true nature of Saint-Domingue, but she knew what horrors would befall her sibling if he stayed—deserved or not, she did not want him mutilated. On paper, they were not so different, and she hoped that he, too, could learn the truth of his transgressions.

"Come *with* us, Edmond," she pleaded in a hoarse voice. Instead, he hit her on the side of the head with the butt of the pistol. Bright light flashed behind her eyes, and the world became a fuzzy blur of orange and black.

"It is your fault that we are ruined," he said, the frenzied shouting replaced by eerie calm. Sylvie tried to push herself up from the ground, but her head refused to cooperate. Edmond grabbed her hair and pulled her up to face him. Her neck arched away from his grip, muscles resisting against the painful angle. His face was a hair's breadth away from hers, and his bloodshot eyes mirrored the madness within.

"Even before tonight. Father went soft when you were born. The negroes no longer feared him. He fucked one slave and suddenly he forgot who he was, what they are, and what *you* are."

Despite her fear, she spat in his face. A small thrill sparked in her chest when the trail of red saliva ran down his chin.

He threw her to the ground with a snarl. "You vicious little whore." He pointed the weapon at her head, his face shiny from sweat and the glow of candles. "You've doomed us all. But"—he chuckled, showing his bloodstained teeth—"at least you'll die how you should've lived—on your knees."

In all his anger, in all his bitterness, Sylvie never foresaw her death in the barrel of Edmond's gun.

"Edmond," she moaned in dread. She raised her shaking hands in surrender as she stared at this hateful creature so ruined by contempt.

He dragged the gun along her cheek and down her throat like a lover's caress until it came to rest over her heart. "You can teach a dog to sit, to speak—put the bloody thing in a dress—but it will always be a bitch." He brought the pistol closer, shoving the muzzle so close that the cold metal dug into her skin. "That is what you are. And this"—he motioned at himself and then at the general grandeur of the foyer—"is what *I am.*"

The conviction in his own madness broke her. "Edmond, I am your sister. *Please.*"

He looked wild and cruel, more animal than man. She should have seen this coming, should've seen him for what he was. Yet her ignorance had been indiscriminate.

"You are *not* my sister! You are a Black whore, just like your mother—" His poisonous tirade ended when Alice struck his head with the butt of a rifle. The force of the blow sent him reeling into the banister. He moaned in a curled-up heap, bits of blood dribbling from the wound on his scalp.

Time was suspended in the de Rosiers foyer—the world limited to her brother's twitching body and the burning in her lungs. Sylvie could not move from her huddled position on the floor, entranced by the rivulets of blood seeping into the grout of the tile and toward her clenching hands.

Alice broke the spell when she kicked Edmond in his gut and spat at him. He whimpered and trembled, like a dying dog.

Alice pulled Sylvie to her feet and shoved her out the door onto the portico.

Gaspard, stricken with fear, stood at the bottom of the steps. The glow from lit torches made his eyes luminous and glistening like a haunting beacon.

Sylvie squinted into the lining of trees encircling the château. The group of slaves—ex-slaves—had gathered outside the house.

"We have to leave," her brother called. The horses nickered and stomped their hooves in agitation.

Sylvie grabbed a single pearl earring from her pocket and shoved it into Alice's hand. Alice kept her hand extended with the pearl in her palm, watching the facets of the sapphires glint.

"I'm sorry," Sylvie said. The screaming had left her voice hoarse, but she hoped her sincerity shone through—though it hardly mattered in the face of so much pain.

Alice let her fingers close around the gem.

Sylvie knew that the Creoles would raid the château for anything of value—everything in it was the product of their sacrifice, after all—but she hoped that the act of giving the earring freely might mean something more. There weren't enough years in a lifetime to apologize for what they had done.

Alice looked toward the Creoles waiting by the gate, many of them now armed. Gaspard called Sylvie's name again. "If you do not escape now, I cannot promise that others will not kill you or worse," Alice warned. With Sylvie's gait unsteady from the pain in her head, Alice led her down the pebbled pathway to the phaeton.

Gaspard pulled Sylvie into the carriage before she could respond. He snapped the reins, and the horses flew down the road into the night.

Sylvie watched Alice and said a silent curse for the brother who had lit the fire of his own destruction.

She kept her eyes on the flickering of the lanterns lighting the main gate until the darkness devoured the last image she'd ever have of her first home, and they left Vesuvius to consume Château de Rosiers and its last champion.

THE PALM TREES whirred into one dark-green blur as they fled down toward the docks. Sylvie's sweat felt like ice against the stagnant heat. She kept seeing Edmond's face in the shadows of the jungle, his eyes in the moonlight through the branches.

Gaspard couldn't stop the horses in their haste, so she had to vomit over the side of the carriage. The bile made her split lip sting.

The jostling of the horses masked her trembling. Gaspard had run them at full speed for the past two hours, the narrow wheels of the phaeton ill-equipped to soften the rocks and bumps in the road. She prayed the carriage could hold.

Once the horses fell into a steady rhythm and sensation returned to her limbs, she winced from the bruises that littered her chest and sides, from the crescent-moon cuts that dotted her arms from Edmond's nails. She tentatively touched the swelling flesh of her cheek and hissed when a throb shot down her jaw.

"What happened?" Gaspard asked over the thud of the horses. The jostling mostly concealed the waver in his voice.

He did not look over. Her throat hurt—Edmond must have choked her at some point—though it was more than pain that kept her silent. She shook her head. Slowly, he took the fabric of her blood-splattered robe into his fist. "What did he do?" She shook her head again, and only then did he turn to face her.

It must have been her own expression—Lord knows what a traumatized picture she made—that broke him. His face contorted into one of abject misery, and he sobbed into the silence of the empty road.

"Gaspard," she croaked. She wrapped a hand around his right arm—stiff from holding the reins.

"I should have killed him," he cried, tears and sweat beading on his cheeks. "God above, I should have run in there with you. I should have known he'd try and . . ." He let the words die in the space between them. The lantern attached to the phaeton's hood swung wildly, its clanging joining the roar of the hooves. She rested her head against him, letting his shirtsleeves absorb her tears.

SMOKE AND ASH created a false fog over the roads, stifling the meager light from the lanterns. The dark haze had begun to conceal the stars, and only the occasional flashes of lightning assured her that they were indeed on Saint-Domingue and not trapped in the abyss of Tartarus.

Lightning flashed again, revealing the closeness of the docks in the burst of white light.

The illuminated coast glowed under the moon, the soft light reflecting off the sails of ships now that they had put enough distance between them and the burning plantations.

The docks were almost deserted, save for random sailors too drunk for even the most generous of taverns to endure. But the de Rosiers family was one of the few who'd received word of the revolution so early, and their parents' faces were ashen and trembling under swaying lanterns. Gaspard signaled for her to get out.

"Sylvie!" Julien encased her within his shaking arms. "My pearl! Are you unhurt?" She did not trust herself to speak and allowed herself to be held. "Edmond is to stay with the estate until this matter is straightened out," he said. "We shall go to Charleston to stay with my contacts. I had the foresight to do most of my banking in the Carolinas. Everything will be all right, *ma bichette*."

Weariness and shock kept her from correcting him; Edmond would not be joining them.

"We shall be safe in Charleston," Catherine said, her words dripping in false courage. She stood with Gaspard and a man Sylvie presumed to be the captain of the ship.

The low light made it difficult to see her father properly, but he was both wigless and in some state of undress—what little hair he had stuck out in various directions. "We will be safe," he said after he released her. "And we will enjoy the same comforts as at home." The handful of mariners began loading the family's and other emigrants' baggage onto the ship.

She pulled out of his stifling embrace and moved closer to Gaspard, feeling his dissent. But her brother had the strength to voice it. "Father, we cannot go to Charleston."

"What are you on about, boy?"

Gaspard pointed to the plumes of smoke rising out of the northern side of Saint-Domingue. "Look at what you've wrought! Have you learned nothing? You would flee the consequences of slavery by going to *Charleston*?" Madame fluttered by her irate husband's side.

Julien barked, "This lapse in order will be rectified! Edmond will—"

"Edmond is as good as dead!" Sylvie rasped. Madame moaned in agony and collapsed into Julien's shoulder. Sylvie couldn't speak anymore between her raw throat and the burning smoke in the air.

"He is a fool," Gaspard said, soft but insistent. "A cruel, proud fool. The Blacks have organized this for weeks if not months, and do not think for a moment that the British will not capitalize on our disorder."

France was not the only empire gleaning wealth from these islands; Spain and Britain would be on Saint-Domingue's doorstep within days. Julien's cheeks wobbled in rage, but Gaspard continued. "Saint-Domingue has hundreds of thousands of men determined to reap justice—if not revenge. Edmond and his ilk will be the first to fall."

And Blanchard, thought Sylvie.

Soon his pretty indigo flowers would be destroyed—taking their vibrant blue, his money, and most likely his life with them. In one night, her future had burned away into ash. The slave owners might flee to the capital of Le Cap, but no one—Black, white, or mulatto; man or woman—would be spared the fiery storm of vengeance.

Gaspard lowered his head and continued, "I promise you, his end will not be merciful. It may take years, but the liberation of Saint-Domingue is upon us. And as the son of a white master . . ." He lifted his gaze to Julien, pain and regret simmering in his azure eyes. "I would go anywhere but Charleston."

Madame wailed for him to reconsider as people pushed onto the ship, her tears for both Edmond and Gaspard spilling down her mottled cheeks. Julien revealed no more than stony silence, both of his sons and his legacy ripped from him within hours. He looked to Sylvie, his eyes glassy and faraway, but she stared at the salt-eaten wood of the dock—the United States promised the same deeply entrenched roots of slavery, only gilded with the shiny veneer of equality. No society under God's eye could escape the same end as her island.

Where Gaspard went, she would follow.

They boarded the ship, aptly named *Liberté*, and Sylvie watched the only world she had ever known fade into the black sea.

To Mme. Euphémie Rohmer, on Rue Saint-Honoré, Paris

Dearest Aunt Euphémie,

I write without pretense or embellishment on behalf of both my brother Gaspard and myself, requesting your support. As you may not have yet heard, the gens de couleur *have risen up against white masters—and they are masters no more. In anticipation of greater violence, we fled to Charleston due to M. de Rosiers's connections in the city. However, my brother and I disagree with our father's decision to remain in the United States, leading to an irreparable rift. And while M. de Rosiers has not stated an intent to disown Gaspard, we assume such a dissolution of the relationship is imminent.*

Hence, we are resolved to continue on to Paris. Given our desperate straits, we humbly beg for your assistance. I have heard of your liberal attitudes and compassionate nature, and we hope for both in abundance.

~~If my color~~

~~My parentage~~

If for whatever reason you find my presence, but not my brother's, intolerable or otherwise unpleasant—I will find accommodation elsewhere.

We plan to sail the first week of September with the intention of joining you in France. I pray this letter greets you before we do, and that we find your hospitality at the end of our journey.

Your Most Obedient Servant,
Sylvie Euphémie Henriette de Rosiers
Charleston, North Carolina, le 1er 7bre 1791

Part II

Paris, France

Chapter Eight

Paris is not a city; it's a world.
—*King Francis I of France*

The billowing white sails and roaring ocean made Sylvie shrivel in distaste. She thrived on gleaming hardwood floors under crystal chandeliers, not seagull shit and leering sailors.

But she could tell Gaspard enjoyed his temporary life at sea; his fair complexion had darkened from his hours on deck, and he allowed a laughable amount of peach fuzz to grow on his chin. She rarely spotted him without a flask full of gunfire and a grin. They had been on their France-bound ship for about five weeks, and how differently she felt now than those first hours after leaving Saint-Domingue.

"How did you know about the revolt?" she asked in a whisper; the purging made her throat raw. The waters had since calmed as they continued north, and Sylvie and Gaspard huddled portside and away from the other distressed passengers.

His flask was long empty, so he twiddled it in his hands. "I was in a tavern, and a man from a nearby plantation burst in, covered in blood. He told us of the danger; they spared him because he was a mulatto and didn't own any slaves."

"But why did he warn the tavern? Why were you there?"

"After Ogé, I felt this burn—this pressure. I needed answers." He wiped a line of sweat from his brow. "I read Voltaire, Locke, Rousseau—and they revealed the full injustice of that day. I recognized my life for what it was. Slave blood lurked in every cup of coffee, every meal, every jewel. I realized I did not want to be my father." With his free hand, he touched the swelling bruise on Sylvie's jaw. Her entire body ached. "Edmond reacted differently. Ogé's execution, in one way or another, made radicals of us all."

Gaspard had struggled in silence, same as she—two siblings in opposing castes but united by blood. "So you started going to meetings at the local tavern?" She imagined her soft blond brother banding with hardened radicals, sharing rum and ideas, supplying rebels with firearms, but the concept seemed absurd.

He nodded. "At first I was just curious. But I began to see how much dignity so many Black leaders commanded. We treat them like chattel, yet a single man in that tavern had more honor than Father, Edmond, and me put together. And to take away a man's birthright—the right to freedom, to prosperity—is nothing short of evil."

Her brother had waded into the waters of this dark, gruesome world of rebellion and escaped whole. She shuddered and squeezed his arm reflexively.

"Gaspard de Rosiers: revolutionary," she said, letting the idea linger in her mind. It contrasted with her usual impression of her wild, carefree brother. But if tonight revealed anything, it showed that her world was not as it appeared.

"You jest, but I was known as quite the orator after my second flagon. Drink made the guilt lessen"—he smirked—"or worsen. I was never sure."

She pressed her face into his shoulder again, wishing the sun would rise on this endless night. "You are not evil, Gaspard." She had seen evil that day, but in a different brother's eyes.

Disgust flittered over his face. "But is it not evil to see injustice—to partake in the profits of that injustice—and do nothing?"

She could not parley on justice and rights; she did not pretend to be a philosophe. Perhaps because she did not see a place for herself in that world.

Gaspard just wore a cloak and could walk into a tavern without pause or consequences. To refuse her father's charity was to choose destitution. "I'm not sure I'm the best person to ask."

DESPITE BEING RAISED on an island, Sylvie had never been on a ship before the uprising.

Ships held the precious rice from the Carolinas, fine silk from abroad, fresh slaves from West Africa. And now they held Sylvie, a relic from a world Saint-Domingue would never know again.

The Charleston harbor had reeked of the odor she recognized as the scent of human bondage. No amount of perfume could mask it: sweat, blood, sick, and feces. But it was more than the miasma of despair—it was the posters advertising the sale of negroes, and the dirty stares of South Carolinians who didn't know what to make of the finely dressed mulatta walking arm in arm with a white gentleman.

Only Madame chose to see them off from the docks, as Julien refused to even look at Sylvie when her letter to Euphémie left on a silver serving tray.

Their six-week-long voyage had only days remaining, the port in Nantes ready to welcome the shaken travelers.

Sylvie stood behind Gaspard, using his back to block the blustering sea winds. Her petticoats fluttered about like their own set of floral cotton sails. She asked if this journey compared to the first time he'd crossed the Atlantic.

He squinted into the horizon and said, "Well, we left France when I was four—so I do not recall much. Though"—he pinched her cheek—"I *do* recall seeing you and Saint-Domingue for the first time. I hardly knew Father then; he'd been on the island almost all of my life. But he wrote to Edmond about you, and I forced him to read it aloud so I could hear about my new sister."

She smacked his arm. "If *I* recall, you liked to torment me. You always asked if I had dirt on my face." Sylvie wrinkled her nose, touching the smattering of freckles as she pulled down her hat. Too much sun meant more detestable little brown spots on her cheeks. Why could Gaspard not enjoy her company belowdecks and out of the sun? She preferred the somber darkness of their cabins, except the smell below reminded her of the docks in Charleston. So she endured his company above.

At least she knew Paris would have more clouds than the Caribbean.

"I wanted to look like you," she continued. "Blond and blue-eyed, like in the paintings. I hated that I favored no one in the family."

"Mulatta or not," he said, "*Maman* says you favor Aunt Euphémie."

As Sylvie grew up, both Madame and Papa commented on how her manner and features resembled the widowed Madame Euphémie Rohmer, née de Rosiers; her aunt had been known as a great beauty. She had married a very wealthy barrister, the late Monsieur Rohmer, who'd died a decade previously and left behind an independently rich woman.

They had no other family, and until either of them married up or Gaspard could support them, residing with Euphémie might last years.

There was a good chance that their current ship would outpace the missive. But Christian values and hospitality demanded their aunt let them stay for a few months at least—though if she proved disinclined to let a suspiciously brown niece board permanently with her, then Sylvie was out of respectable options.

"I hope I do not favor her too much. I struggled to stay civil with your mother, and most regard her as the most obliging woman on Saint-Domingue."

"Well, *stay* civil. If she proves unwilling to host us"—he took another sip of his bitter drink—"then you shall have more to worry about than freckles."

novembre 1791

Sylvie decided she infinitely preferred sea travel to stagecoach. The journey to Paris from Nantes was filled with broken wheels, miserable weather, unfortunate companions, and poor roads.

Gaspard took all of their trials with good humor, while Sylvie cursed the ungenerous landscape and muddy roads of rural France. And even though the streets of Paris were kinder to the carriage, Sylvie knew she would all but throw herself from the cramped box when they reached their aunt's house.

However, the absence of enslaved people toiling in acres and acres of fields certainly increased its appeal; there was something undoubtedly foreign about a white man working his own land. Not every white person on the island could afford slaves, but Black people made up the overwhelming majority of laborers.

Knowing that the rebels were overthrowing their sugar despots and that mainland France did not maintain an ever-present mass of slaves gave her some relief.

Even the land itself told a different story than the island. Saint-Domingue as a colony had just seen its 132nd birthday. The infrastructure and buildings were all modern—her family's plantation was only a little older than Edmond—whereas France was an ancient kingdom, and the wizened land itself revealed the many millennia of human settlement. It showed its age in the eroded cliffs and soaring hardwoods that dotted the countryside—the Roman roads, the lazy rivers, the stripped woodland.

But nothing could have prepared her for the wonders of Paris.

They rode through the city limits and under the main gates into the heart of the capital. Pushing back the velvet curtains of the carriage window, she pressed her face to the glass. The sea of grass bled into a forest of stone. The entire city had a gray cast, the tops of the buildings blurring into the darkening sky. And surrounding them was a crush of begging children, university students, ladies and their chaperones—she had never seen so many *people*.

"Over half a million residents," said Gaspard, guessing the source of her awe. She could not fathom such a number.

Coats and hoods and hats of all cuts and fabrics flitted by. There was no true winter on the island, only wet and drier seasons. And most people wore light colors if not white to keep cool, where in Paris, dark, conservative colors and heavier cloth draped over pale figures. Sylvie realized she'd need several new additions to her wardrobe if she were to be both fashionable and warm.

However, France differed from its colony in one more obvious way.

The moment she stepped off the ship, a sea of white faces replaced the blue waves that greeted her every morning on her voyage to Nantes—and she had never felt so ugly, brown, and foreign. And that feeling did not leave her, not even in the exciting world of the French capital.

Gaspard caught his sister's surly expression. "Why do you pout? We'll be out of this damned coach and at Aunt's house in five minutes." She frowned deeper. "This journey has turned you into a regular curmudgeon."

"I am not," she sniffed. "It's just that everyone will know I'm a mulatta."

He looked skyward. Sylvie knew that expression. *Lord give me the strength to endure my little sister.*

"You know you aren't the only mulatto in France. Every other planter in Saint-Domingue sends his mulatto son to a French school."

She fluttered her fan anxiously. "But I am not his son. People make allowances for boys. I'm a girl. It's different." She angrily gestured toward the ivory-faced ladies walking arm in arm dressed in patriotic colors. "Look at them! And look at *me*. I'm dark and coarse and—"

He ran a palm over his face. "*Mon Dieu*. I won't stroke your vanity, Sylvie. You were the Pearl of Saint-Domingue, and you shall be the Pearl of Paris."

"The people here do not like pearls," she grumbled. "They prefer liberty bonnets to panniers." *Gaspard does not understand*, she thought, *and how could he?* "Or how about marriage, hmm? Did you think of that? I assume my betrothed isn't in any position to marry." *Since he's very likely dead, not that I'd marry him alive.*

She spoke with a lot more conviction than she felt. Blanchard and other mixed sons were her only real option for a legally recognized marriage on the island. She was just as French as the next girl in Paris, but that didn't mean she knew the ins and outs of the capital's flavor of flirtation and courtship.

"Have you forgotten your pedigree, dear sister? You may have an ample coin purse, but—"

"Men here will be no different from the men on Saint-Domingue," she snapped. "A fine dowry is enough to make any man tolerant."

While they would probably lose much to the rebellion, her father dispersed much of his wealth between the Americas and France— her precious dowry impervious to the violent upheaval that would ruin other masters. She shuddered at the thought of a bride-price bloodied from slave labor, but there was nothing to be done now.

Gaspard snatched her fan and waved it with an effeminate flourish. "Why, yes," he said in a falsetto. "Let me arrange a fortuitous marriage. I know hundreds of dashing, wealthy young men in Paris, after all." She grabbed the fan and smacked him soundly.

Legally, Sylvie was now in her brother's care in the absence of her father. The idea of Gaspard being responsible for her future was laughable. But now she relied on him for everything.

If he could not overcome his selfishness, then she had little immediate hope of marriage. She also harbored little hope regarding Aunt Euphémie, as by all accounts she was an eccentric, private woman who could hardly be depended upon to lure in suitable husbands-to-be.

Sylvie's success must stem from her own efforts; she refused to die a spinster.

Gaspard slouched deeper into the carriage pillows, frustrated and uncomfortable, while she daydreamed of court and husband hunting until the carriage turned onto Aunt Euphémie's street. "Rue Saint-Honoré," she read off the sign engraved into one of the buildings.

She could not have imagined a more idyllic French neighborhood; Rue Saint-Honoré seemed a lovely, bourgeois Parisian street. Elegant town houses lined the road, each one with the same intricate molding and even number of windows—worlds away from the palm trees and blistering sun of Saint-Domingue. White stone replaced tropical plants; busy paved streets replaced empty dirt roads.

Their coach stopped at their new address, and Gaspard squeezed her hand. They had fled to this new world—or, rather, the Old World—in search of sanctuary.

Sylvie prayed that Paris was their tabula rasa: a new start, a new identity free of old sins. And more importantly, she prayed the horrors of their past would not breach the city's ancient walls.

EUPHÉMIE, GASPARD, AND Sylvie sat in the salon in the front of the Rohmer house.

The decorations were dated; most furnishings favored the whimsy and opulence of the ancien régime rather than the solid simplicity of this new France.

A handsome, well-rouged lady of some fifty years, Madame

Rohmer enjoyed a comfortable living at her brother's and dead husband's expense.

Based on her constant chattering, Sylvie had learned that Euphémie's interests included comfits, Rousseau, gossip, and inviting her neighbor's pretty daughters over for tea—even if the girls seemed a bit radical for her tastes.

Heavy, rich fabrics covered the window treatments and chairs, while gold leaf–encrusted surfaces reflected the glow of every candle. Floral motifs and cherubs made their way onto all available surfaces, with their little aunt nestled in the middle of her bourgeois Eden.

Sylvie preferred the pastels and delicate porcelain of the bygone era, but Gaspard made no effort to contain his amusement as he took in the overstuffed pink damask cushions and his aunt's ramblings over sugared tea.

He could afford to be amused—but while their aunt seemed kind enough, Sylvie still feared expulsion after the novelty of their arrival wore off.

"I only just received Julien's note about the rebellion three days ago, did I not, Charles?" asked Madame Rohmer to her stoic butler. "How I wailed! I could scarcely eat more than half of my dinner. And my first words were, 'Oh, how shall my poor niece and nephews bear it?' Did I not say that, Charles?"

Sylvie was surprised by how few servants her aunt kept in spite of her wealth, but she supposed such expenditures were now considered gauche. Grand displays of wealth could be interpreted as anti-revolutionary.

Sylvie pitied the man. She swore another streak of gray bloomed by his temples. "Indeed, Madame."

Gaspard used her distraction to pour rum into his tea for the fourth time in an hour.

"Yes, yes," she went on. "Dearest Julien told me what happened on

Saint-Domingue. I could hardly sleep, hardly eat! Paris is aflutter—not that it needs more to worry about. After that awful massacre on the Champ de Mars this past July, the last thing the city needs is more blood in the streets . . ."

She explained that following the French government's decree that Louis XVI could keep his crown—and a constitution would be drawn up—the poor of Paris rallied on the Champ de Mars. After they threw stones and insults at the National Guard, the soldiers opened fire into the crowd.

Sylvie set her teacup down with some force, looking at Gaspard in poorly disguised panic. As Aunt Euphémie went on, she developed the impression that they had exchanged one revolution for another.

"And now poor Lafayette's reputation is in tatters, and Mayor Bailly declared martial law. Even dear Maximilien had the good sense to move in with the Duplays across the street."

Martial law? Sylvie's color drained from her face. From Euphémie's description, Paris more closely resembled a battlefield than the safe haven they'd prayed for. She needed this woman to stop talking before either Sylvie fainted or Gaspard added so much rum to his tea that he became a human distillery.

"Aunt Euphémie," she interrupted none too gently. "Brother and I have had a long journey . . ."

Euphémie dropped her sugared profiterole in shock. "But of course! I am such a goose; you must be exhausted. Let Charles take your things, while I shall take you to your rooms."

Sylvie didn't move from her seat. "So you received my letter, Madame?"

"Right before Julien's! A sorry state of affairs if the first time I hear from my own niece is after a rebellion drives her to the United States, of all places!"

"Madame—"

"And with hardly a pair of gloves to call your own! Julien should be ashamed, but he was never a man who saw sense in anything besides his account books. We'll have to get you a whole new wardrobe. Ha! I haven't gotten to visit the modiste this much since I was fitted for my trousseau—"

Sylvie stood up, hands balled at her sides and bile in her throat. "*Madame.*"

"Yes, dearest?"

Gaspard glanced up blearily from his drink in surprise.

"Then"—she reached out to grasp her aunt's soft white fingers—"then *I* may stay?"

The woman looked down at their joined hands, and her face softened into something warm but a little sad. "The de Beauvaus have an adopted daughter darker than you, and I daresay Hell hasn't come to Paris yet."

Sylvie curtsied as deeply as she ever had and smiled out of relief rather than politeness. Charles began ushering their limited belongings upstairs. "Thank you, dear Aunt Euphémie."

"Nonsense, and Aunt Fifi will do just fine."

Gaspard just offered a glassy-eyed nod.

IN SPITE OF the violence of the massacre of Champ de Mars months ago, blood did not coat the streets of this quiet Parisian neighborhood. In fact, Sylvie struggled to find anything more exciting than litter or the occasional stray dog.

After sleeping for two days and sitting with her aunt for another, she longed for more diverse company.

Gaspard remained in his own rooms or the old Monsieur Rohmer's study, digesting months of republican newspapers in a single sitting. While in Saint-Domingue, he had planned to attend school to study law within the year, but the University of Paris had been whittled down to insignificance due to the unrest. So, instead, he let the newspapers be his teacher.

When Sylvie truly could not bear her aunt's chatter, she sat with Gaspard and skimmed through the most recent articles. But there were no noble marriage announcements or renderings of scandalous fashions, only political cartoons and talk of bread prices. While she had kept somewhat abreast of local politics on Saint-Domingue out of self-preservation, she did not intend to continue the dull habit here.

The few times she preferred Fifi's attentions were when her aunt fitted her for new gowns and two coats.

"We want only light colors, but no yellow! It makes her look too brown. All that island sun, you know. And nothing too fine, mind you," Fifi had said while the seamstress's assistant measured Sylvie's shapely waist with a suspicious glance. The assistant narrowed her eyes at Sylvie's face, but a fistful of assignats dared her to contradict her aunt.

She had only been in Paris a week, but Sylvie quickly discovered that rich fabrics and jewel-tone colors no longer ruled the fashion scene. Waistlines rose, patterns simplified, and necklines dropped dramatically.

"And wear nothing more extravagant than a string of pearls when you're out," Fifi added. Sylvie's expression pinched into a moue, and the elder lady laughed. "I know, *chérie*. I have a greater penchant for finery than the queen herself. But then my dear Rohmer would say that I never needed gems, for my lips were red as rubies and my eyes sparkled like diamonds. Romantic fool, he was."

Sylvie touched the small strand of pearls around her throat, more a noose than fine jewelry. Julien had called her his pearl, like the island of her birth, for as long as she could remember. She could not shake the association between the pretty baubles and the island. All the soap in the world couldn't wipe the taint of slavery away.

Fifi received enough correspondence to fill a novel every few days, but even if Sylvie *were* to receive any letters, they wouldn't arrive for weeks at least. Aunt or no aunt, she was in desperate need of fresh company.

Aunt Fifi went out later that morning to visit with friends in a nearby neighborhood, and Gaspard spent his day with his face so pressed into Jean-Paul Marat's *L'Ami du peuple* that Sylvie was sure he'd get ink on his forehead.

Sylvie slouched on the chaise as she nibbled on brioche. Aunt Fifi kept a well-stocked kitchen despite the fluctuating costs of bread, and she could see how boredom could lead a lady to overindulgence.

The butler walked in, arms clasped behind his back. "A Mademoiselle Élisabeth Duplay is at the door, Mademoiselle," he intoned. "Shall I tell her that Madame is out?"

She wiped away the crumbs on her cheek and sat up straighter. Aunt Fifi had mentioned the Duplay family when they first arrived—something about handsome daughters. And while Sylvie may have preferred a handsome son, her ennui made the idea of female companionship giddying.

"No, do send her in," she told him.

"Very good, Mademoiselle."

Élisabeth skipped into the salon sporting an enormous grin. "Oh, so it is true!" She turned toward Charles and offered her coat. "Thank you, Charles. Now, I heard my mother go on about Madame Fifi's new stowaways, but *Maman*'s hearing is not what it used to be. I am so very glad her intelligence proved true."

Sylvie stood and curtsied, taking in the exuberant creature in yellow.

Élisabeth appeared to be around Sylvie's age and of similar height. The lady looked stylish but modest, sporting a *robe à l'anglaise* in a subtle floral print under her caraco jacket. Her hair was a warm brown, though partially covered by a turban. She had a natural grace in her movements and a strange habit of biting the tip of her tongue between her teeth when she laughed.

"Forgive us for not greeting you sooner; we did not wish to accost you after such a long journey." Élisabeth stared a bit too intently at Sylvie's face, and she had to remind herself that mixed-race women were hardly commonplace in Parisian sitting rooms.

"There is nothing to forgive—I was grateful for the solitude. Though now I am grateful for the company. I'm Sylvie de Rosiers."

Élisabeth leaned in with her hand guarding her mouth despite the two of them being quite alone. "If I may advise, I would abandon the 'de' in your name. It's considered rather gauche here—no need for such aristocratic folly."

Her sincerity hardly softened the impact of the *advice*: This rift between the de Rosiers family, both physical and emotional, was painfully recent. Now France intended to literally cut off syllables from her very name. "Your recommendation is duly noted, Miss . . . ?"

"Forgive me, I am Élisabeth Duplay," she said. "We are your neighbors, number three ninety-eight!" The girl had unhooked her gaze from Sylvie's face and moved on to marvel at her gown, an emerald-green jacquard affair tailored to fit her from one of Madame's old dresses. Her new wardrobe would take two weeks to arrive, meaning she'd look like the wealthy and foreign woman she was until then. Élisabeth ran forward and touched the fabric with wide eyes. "It's so *decadent*. Do all women dress this way on Saint-Domingue? Do you speak Spanish, too? Is it remarkably hot there?"

Sylvie extracted her dress from Élisabeth's grip and smoothed out the wrinkles. "The women who can afford to. *Sí, por supuesto*. And, yes, it's quite warm."

Élisabeth smiled and clapped in delight, well pleased with the answers. But then her face turned sheepish. "Can you tell me about the slave uprisings? Paris is wild to know about the revolt."

Sylvie sat and tried to push down the nauseating foulness festering in her belly. The chaos and political upheaval happening on Saint-Domingue deserved to be more than teatime gossip.

Not waiting for an answer, Élisabeth went on, "It's only that we feel quite sympathetic for the negroes. We're all fighting for freedom, for our rights as citizens."

Alice's face flashed in Sylvie's mind, the dark pleasure in her eyes as she reduced her enslaver to a quivering heap of bruises and blood. Sylvie doubted that any bourgeois girl in Paris could know true bondage—but then again, nor could she. "We left before the worst of it," she answered. "I'm sure the newspapers will be more useful to you."

But could the newspapers describe the smell of burning coffee fields? The blood caked into the grout of Le Cap's streets? They might write of freedom, but they would never note the sacrifice.

Élisabeth slouched in disappointment—a wasted visit. "My sister would have joined me," she said, "but she is in a lesson."

Sylvie smiled without teeth. "I'm sure your company will suffice my need for entertainment." Élisabeth's enthusiasm and questions had already left her feeling worn, so a half hour with her could satisfy Sylvie's desire for company for days. "Do you have many siblings?" She hoped for handsome brothers, and at least in Paris she could do that much. There were no actual laws—just acts and proclamations that weren't enforceable—banning interracial marriage in France, only in the colonies. And Élisabeth's gown was stylish and fine enough to imply some wealth.

The girl nodded with enthusiasm as she finally took a seat. "Four other than myself. My brother Jacques-Maurice is the youngest and still away at school, then me, Victoire, and Sophie. Éléonore, or Cornélie as we call her, is the oldest."

"Three other sisters?" Sylvie wrinkled her nose. A shame, no marriageable brothers and a horde of women. "That sounds torturous. I would hate to share my parents with so many."

Élisabeth shook her head, a wistful twinkle in her eye. "Oh, no, it was wonderful. But Sophie and Victoire are already wed, and Jacques is in Luxembourg." Her guileless gray eyes turned sad. "I miss them so."

Sylvie called for tea and arranged a cup for Élisabeth—no sugar, only cream—while her companion asked, "Do you have brothers or sisters?"

Sylvie immediately thought of Edmond's pistol pressed into her sternum and wondered if she did indeed have two brothers who still breathed.

"*Oui*, two older brothers. Gaspard is twenty and Edmond is twenty-four. But only Gaspard lives with Aunt Fifi and me in Paris."

Élisabeth grabbed a few almond comfits. "I am envious; I always wanted older brothers. Though I cannot imagine they would have protected me any better than Cornélie." Her eyes sparkled with un-spoken memories. "She always frightened the other girls; she's quite a formidable creature. You remind me of her, actually."

Sylvie leaned forward, her voice adopting a sinister timbre. "Do I inspire fear?"

Mademoiselle Duplay giggled. "I am impervious to intimidation. Once you meet Cornélie you shall see why." Sylvie scowled, and her new acquaintance laughed harder.

Gaspard strolled downstairs into the salon dressed only in shirt-sleeves and breeches, a crinkled newspaper tucked under one arm and a book under the other. Blond fuzz speckled his jaw, and his curls stood up in every which way as he hummed an atonal tune.

He made it halfway through the room before Sylvie cleared her throat and said through gritted teeth, "Dearest, we have company." Her brother glanced up lazily at her from his passage, and she nar-rowed her eyes in annoyance. "*Gaspard*." She gestured to the smiling Élisabeth standing between them, clearly admiring her rakish brother in unrestrained glee.

His expression transformed into the one from before the uprising—

full of indolent charm and open perusal. "Who's this angelic creature?" He took her hand and brushed her knuckles with his lips.

The lady's pink tongue made another appearance between her teeth.

"No angels here, brother," said Sylvie. "Just Mademoiselle Élisabeth Duplay. Has your eyesight gone as well as your sense?"

Before he could make a smart retort, Élisabeth said, "I fear Mademoiselle Sylvie is correct. I'm only an angel when my sister uses me as a model for classical paintings. An angel on canvas, but not in life. Far from it."

He lazily dragged his thumb over her knuckles, and their guest dipped her head in bashful modesty. "I respectfully disagree, Mademoiselle."

Gaspard had yet to release her hand, and Sylvie was prepared to do it for him. She loathed to see him already infatuated while she lay awake at night with Edmond's choke hold on her mind. Gaspard's charm and beauty had no burden attached to weigh him down. He could woo and jilt at will without the ever-present force of self-preservation spurring him on. His future was guaranteed.

"Well," Sylvie said. "Perhaps while Gaspard dresses for the day, you and I could—"

"Is that *L'Ami du peuple* I see?" asked Élisabeth. The gentleman looked under his arm in surprise, having forgotten it was there at all. "We all *adore* Monsieur Marat. We've sheltered him a few times, though he's gone off to London for the time being."

"You *know* Marat?" he asked, incredulous.

Pride colored her cheeks. "Of course. I was younger then when he needed refuge, but my sister still reads his work religiously. He's a bit coarse, but his influence is immense."

Sylvie knew nothing of this discussion, only that she was accustomed to being the center of attention. She forcibly interjected, "You said your sister paints?"

Engaged with Gaspard, the brunette startled at her voice but re-
covered with a smile. "She does—and quite well. Cornélie studies
under Regnault in his shop just north of the district." For the first
time in their short acquaintance, the girl frowned. "She is very private about her art. But sometimes she'll sketch portraits of strangers
in the Tuileries Garden and let me watch."

Sylvie's education required tangible benefits: speaking Spanish,
French, and English to broaden her prospects; mastering the pianoforte and the harp to entertain; memorizing innumerable dances
from every represented country in the West Indies so she would
never fail her partner.

Painting under a master was customary for younger girls in the
schoolroom, but to continue to pursue the art after reaching majority? Sylvie had never encountered such a wanton disregard for one's
own marriageability. "Is she any good?"

Gaspard threw her a withering look, but Élisabeth chuckled.
"You may decide for yourself. Monsieur Regnault and his students
are hosting a small exhibition next week, and I demand that you
both attend."

Saint-Domingue did not lend itself well to patronage or fine art-
istry on a scale like Paris, and Sylvie had been starved of culture for
the past two months at sea.

She accepted the invitation and asked what she might wear, but
Élisabeth heard not—too lost in the eyes of Sylvie's golden brother.

Chapter Nine

A true friend is the greatest of all blessings, and that which we take the least care of all to acquire.

—*François de La Rochefoucauld*

The exhibition could be considered Sylvie's foray into Parisian society, and she did not intend to squander a first impression.

She forwent a tignon, given the lack of sumptuary laws on the mainland, though she struggled to use the curling tongs. Louise, the maid, did her best—but she combed through Sylvie's unfamiliar locks with the same fearful expression as a hare caught in a trap. She handled the coconut oil like it was corrosive.

Sylvie's yellow silk gown, a refitted secondhand dress from Fifi, reminiscent of Old-World wealth, brought out the golden glow of the diamonds swaying from her ears. A muslin fichu draped around her décolletage, pulled down enough to ensure ample view of her considerable chest. White roses trimmed the bustline and wrists as well. She always enjoyed a certain fastidiousness in regard to her dress, tonight especially so.

Once she excused Louise—much to her obvious relief—Sylvie struggled to apply her powder without the brush trembling. She valued control, and the past months had stripped her of it.

Élisabeth did not seem to notice anything odd about her tan skin and black mane, but perhaps others would be more discerning. Though slaves were illegal to own and it was frowned upon by some, pockets of slavery persisted in France. Someone was bound to see through her manners and fine address to the Black blood beneath. She assumed Aunt Fifi only accepted her out of the belief that Sylvie was Gaspard's full sister. Why, her aunt had even commented that Julien himself had always been quite brown—and Saint-Domingue's sun must have done little to help.

Gaspard called for her from downstairs, impatient to see his new ladylove despite his complete disinterest in the arts. He and Élisabeth—whom he called Lise, much to Sylvie's chagrin and Élisabeth's delight—had formed a ridiculous and inappropriate attachment. He did not need marriage for safety or for purpose: love and flirtation were diversions rather than the hammer and chisel of survival.

He gave a nod of approval when Sylvie emerged at the bottom of the stairs. His breeches and dark-gray evening coat sat like a second skin, and he had his own curls tied back with a black velvet ribbon.

With an affectionate smile, he adjusted a feather in her hair that had gone askew. "They will be absolutely overcome, *ma sœur.*"

She preened, powdered, and pinned until every inch of her person met her expectations. But no matter how much effort she exerted on perfecting her appearance, she had no control over this foreign society to which she was alien. Never before had she faced an event in which everyone would be a stranger. The community of wealthy whites on Saint-Domingue was a static one, and the pool of events where she would be welcome shrank those numbers further— regardless of her father's wealth.

But Sylvie knew the social landscape of the island well; there was never an instance where she was caught off guard by hostility or whispers or flirtatious smiles at a party. On Saint-Domingue, mulattoes grew as plentifully as the sugarcane their mothers worked. And if the recent months were any indication, they were just as difficult to dismantle.

Élisabeth met them by the hackney coach, ready with a bright smile for them both. Gaspard fell into step with his new flirtation, and Sylvie lagged behind the new pair as they climbed into the carriage. She envied Gaspard his little distraction; he could swim in Élisabeth's sparkling gray eyes, while Sylvie saw Edmond's black stare every time she closed hers.

The ride to the event was blessedly brief. A rented coach did not offer the style of a phaeton, but she supposed that luxury was more of a social hindrance than anything.

The exhibition was private and arranged outside of the watchful eyes of the Académie as such regulated and elitist institutions went out of vogue. When Madame de Rosiers discussed the salons she attended as a maiden, Sylvie admired them for their sacred exclusivity as well as for the art. But when they arrived at the address—a large and handsome home but not as wealthy as Sylvie expected—it was clear that the exhibitions, at first glance, had become a rather plebeian affair. Much like the government.

The Rosiers siblings were among the better dressed of the attendees. *But*, Sylvie thought with a sigh of relief, *not outrageously so*. As much as she valued being the center of attention, she understood that now was not the time to stand out.

"Monsieur et Mademoiselle Rosiers," said the hostess, almost bounding over to the new arrivals at the entrance. "I'm delighted you've come."

Lise introduced them both, but she only had eyes for Gaspard—leaving Sylvie to answer all the mundane questions about the journey from Rue Saint-Honoré ("Very quick, Madame") and how well the weather cooperated for the evening ("Quite warm for November, wouldn't you say?"). The hostess finally finished the conversation, with Sylvie and Lise expressing the same happy overtures that they had come.

Once the hostess made her excuses, the press of bodies and strangeness of the atmosphere made Sylvie yearn for the dark respite of her room. She used her fan to conceal the hurried little pants she made as she gasped for air. Gaspard did not see her, too focused on wooing the Duplay girl.

Unable to stand still any longer, she wandered the rooms and assessed fellow guests.

The various rooms were equally populated by men and women, some old but mostly young, with numerous tableaux, sketches, and the like framed wall-to-wall. Sylvie concentrated on keeping her chin up and eyes straight ahead—she did not have to ignore white stares with demure grace here, but it would take ages to unlearn a lifetime of polite public subservience.

A large oil painting by Regnault himself, the main attraction no doubt, stood just ahead. It loomed dark and ominous at the end of the corridor, framed by the bewigged heads of viewers. Sylvie strolled closer to the bustling heart of the salon.

She observed the painting just behind the cluster of viewers; refocusing her thoughts on the art cooled her skin and calmed her mind.

However, she was unimpressed. She supposed it was nice in the dull, allegorical way that everyone seemed so mad about these days: neoclassical, austere, and burdened with some profound meaning that escaped her. A few couples whispered and pointed at her, but she just feigned extreme interest in the dreary painting.

Named *Le Déluge*, it depicted a white-skinned youth carrying an elderly man through a flood, a woman beside them holding her pudgy babe above the waters. The elderly man's features were contorted by worry and fear, much like the rest of the characters except the innocent youth.

She assumed it was technically pleasing, but she missed the airy lightness of the decor back home.

A young man with a crown of brown hair approached from her left. He wore a fashionably cut blue coat and held two fresh cups of wine. He didn't have the burnt cheeks and freckles of most men on

Saint-Domingue; Sylvie doubted he spent too many days riding his horse among sun-drenched palms. But she smiled demurely and peeked at him from beneath her lashes. This was a dance she knew.

"Might I offer you some refreshment?" he asked. He spoke slowly, tentatively, like he was either unsure of his own decision to speak to her or of her knowledge of French. White men were either wary in their interest or conspicuous in their prejudice. This man seemed the former.

"A refreshing drink"—she took the cup—"or refreshing company?"

The painting held no appeal, but this handsome face did. She admired his daring—approaching her despite the mumblings and stares showed fortitude.

His shoulders relaxed, and he leaned forward with a grin. "I hope a bit of both. I haven't had the pleasure of seeing you at any of the exhibitions before. I doubt I would forget such a face."

He stared a bit too long to be polite, but Sylvie forgave his curiosity. He had the cropped curls of the university student set, but his clothing betrayed his bourgeois background. She fluttered her fan so he could smell the sweetness of her perfume and sipped on the wine. *Too watered-down.*

"I've only just arrived to Paris. I made the journey with my brother."

His eyebrows rose. "Your brother? Is he here?" Sylvie nodded as he twisted to search the room. "I don't believe I saw another person of your . . . coloring in any of the rooms."

Sylvie's lips pinched together to hide her smile. "He's quite blond," she said conspiratorially, "I assure you."

He nodded, but his brow wrinkled in confusion. He took a drink during the awkward lull, still staring at her face. "And where did you two journey from?"

Sylvie's chest contracted, and she avoided his stare. His cravat, a vivid red, mesmerized her from its elaborate tangle beneath his chin. The richness of the color embodied the vibrancy of blood—as though he'd been slit across his throat and his blood gurgled from the wound in a tumble of silk. The artwork and din of conversations melted away, consumed by the prickling of a fire's heat and the sharp whines of yelping dogs. The bitter smoke from burnt sugar and coffee clung to the wallpaper. "Mademoiselle?"

She refocused again. Her breath steadied. Slowly, the fiery blazes became lit candles and the screams became polite laughter. Her lips curved into a tight smile. "Saint-Domingue."

He lit up in interest. "So you must know of the slave revolt! Was there terrible carnage? I must ask—"

She finished the wine in one large swallow, then gave the cup back to the gentleman. "I must beg your pardon, excuse me." Before he could intercede, Sylvie pushed her way to the front of the crowd to distance herself from his questions and the memories they evoked.

She studied *Le Déluge* at a distance again, specifically the inky backdrop of the night. Regnault filled the darkness with stars, and Sylvie counted them until the panic slinked away. The stars on Saint-Domingue sparkled like in no other sky she'd seen—each twinkle sewn perfectly into the black quilt of night blanketing a sleeping island. There were no stars the day they fled; the smoke concealed the heavens with an acrid cloud of ash.

"What do you think of it?" a young woman asked.

She had materialized by her side—either Sylvie had not noticed she was already there or the young woman had moved silently— with her head cocked as she waited for Sylvie's answer.

Sylvie considered her forward for asking an opinion of a complete stranger, but the blue-eyed woman's expectant expression hinted that she thought nothing of it. She wore a modern, high-cut gown and a bare face. Her hair swallowed all light, the inky blackness of her tresses matching the night in *Le Déluge*.

Sylvie leaned back on her heels to create some much-needed distance and said, "I have not been in Paris long enough to know the trends."

The woman's laugh was too deep to be ladylike but strangely pleasant all the same. "Come now, that does not mean you don't have an opinion. You frowned at the painting for five minutes like it offended your honor."

Sylvie balked at the woman's rudeness for having watched her and snapped open her fan to cool her warm cheeks. She did not wish to tell this woman anything and sincerely hoped that this impertinent manner of address was not becoming the standard in Paris.

"What do you care for a stranger's opinion?" she asked, a hair's breadth away from sounding cross. Her intrigue at the stranger, however, offset the dread building in her stomach.

Sylvie appraised her quickly; not a beauty, but her skin matched the creamy white of a naked canvas and thus was worthy of her envy. Her ensemble, an Indian-print dress with no adornments besides ribbon, was modern but unassuming. She sported a stylish mobcap atop her black hair; Sylvie had never met a white woman with hair as dark as hers.

Her slender frame was at least an inch or so taller than Sylvie's, but the slightness of her build did not match the steeliness of her steady gaze.

"You are new to Paris." Her smile broadened as though Sylvie's vexation amused her. She let her eyes run over Sylvie's attire and added, "At least, new to *this* Paris. I should like to know what you think of Regnault and his school."

This woman would not release her from this bizarre interlude without an answer, so Sylvie satisfied her.

She gestured vaguely toward the dreary tableau. "I do not care for this new trend—this *classicism*."

"Oh." The woman's lips—red like she wore cosmetics, but Sylvie doubted it—curled in amusement. "And why not?"

Sylvie snapped her fan shut, the dam restraining her frustration bursting. "It's miserable! No light or joy, no sparkle or shine. I miss the love gardens and the radiance." She had hoped France would be the wondrous marvel of her childhood dreams, but it was only the tight lacing of austerity. She crinkled her nose as she blew out an exasperated sigh. "Now it is only darkness and terror."

The young woman looked up into the eyes of the burdened youth portrayed in the painting above. "But there is virtue in terror."

Sylvie scoffed, thinking of Edmond and ashes dusting her clothes. "How can terror be virtuous? How can such pain be glorified?" She believed in the rebels' cause, but that did not mean she relished the thought of her island swimming in blood—no matter if the slaughter was deserved.

A gentleman appeared beside the woman as silently as she herself had minutes before. He was simply dressed with powdered hair, and his light build was offset by his severe expression. He could not have been older than thirty-five, but he wore both an air of agelessness and a well-starched white cravat.

"Terror is a natural consequence of democracy, and therefore life," he said in a mesmerizingly soft tenor. He gave Sylvie a cursory glance. "And nature, by its very essence, is virtue."

His tone may have been gentle, but his words were not—leadened by the sheer force of his conviction. He was not handsome: his jaw was too wide, his nose too sharp, his mouth too narrow. Yet, Sylvie shivered.

She was unused to such frank and complex discussions. Neither Father nor Edmond nor even Gaspard had ever truly cared what she felt or how she thought. Madame limited her education to domestic skills, music, and dancing rather than academics. Sylvie's natural wit and Gaspard's brief conversations with her on contemporary literature carried her through any soiree or dinner party.

Standing before these two strangers discussing the complexities of virtue was an exercise for which she was unprepared—especially when she had the distinct inclination she was being measured and coming up short.

The raven-haired woman smiled at the man with a warmth that hinted at a close friendship. "I'm all in agreement, Monsieur. A necessary evil."

This man interested Sylvie, and she would not have his attention wasted on his less-than-beautiful friend. "Well," said Sylvie with a sudden sweetness, "I would have no evils at all."

Her coquetry was wasted, as the gentleman sneered. "You speak of Paradise, Mademoiselle, not France."

His eyes, at first glance, appeared green. But as his stare settled heavily on her face, they could only be described as pale: flat, cool, and devoid of any outward emotion, like an endless void.

Her smile died on her pretty lips, his disapproval as obvious as her shame.

"But is it not the highest honor in the world"—she strangled the stem of her glass—"to be French? To love France above all else?"

"To love one's country is to call out her evils: to drag them out into a trial by terror until her stains are cleansed."

His words hissed like coals in a fire, but she laughed like he had made a charming joke. "Goodness—I hope you do not love your women as you love your country."

He shrugged, unfazed. "A true citizen may count their privileges and their grievances on the same hand."

"I know many men on Saint-Domingue who would disagree with you."

"They want the masses shackled watching shadows dance upon a wall in Plato's Cave. I care little for the small minds of slavers, as they are not before me now."

Saint-Domingue
1785

She scratched her chin; the ribbon keeping her hat steady chafed. But she was twelve and beginning to be pretty; she would take every opportunity to be in the public eye—even picking up Edmond from the fetid docks with Madame and Gaspard.

Holding a handkerchief to her nose, she whined, "It smells so foul." The seabirds squawked in a similar octave.

Madame shushed her.

While she often visited the old capital of Le Cap, this was only her first time coming to the harbor. She could have seen Papa and Edmond off months prior, but they had left so very early that she overslept.

Slaves carried the luggage down—she recognized the trunks as Papa's— and shortly after, both travelers descended the gangway.

Papa spent roughly half the year in France then, so Sylvie was used to his comings and goings. But this trip had been to Charleston, and Papa decided that eighteen-year-old Edmond should come along now that he had reached the age of majority.

"Look how sunburnt he is," Gaspard whispered. The eldest tried to disembark with grace, but the weeks at sea and youthful proportions had him wobbling like a newborn foal. She snickered into the lace covering her nose.

Papa had brought back more than he left with, and the children huddled together in conversation while everything was loaded.

"Take down that handkerchief. You look ridiculous."

"Oh, I missed you as well, dear Edmond." She fluttered the offending fabric in his face, and he slapped her hand away with enough force for the handkerchief to land in the dirt.

"Ow!" She cradled the smarting wrist. "That hurt!"

Gaspard smacked his shoulder. "Don't be such an ass. You've only been back a half hour."

"If this is how you treat your sister, then I can't imagine any American girls found you amiable."

Edmond laughed while she picked pebbles off her handkerchief. "The way they do things up in Charleston means I hardly have to worry about being amiable."

"What do you mean?"

Gaspard shook his head to discourage the gleeful Edmond from answering, but she wanted to know what he implied.

"They don't have to worry about stupid ghosts of dead vodou maroons or slaves poisoning their food."

"With your sour manners, I'm sure they considered it." She restrained herself from sticking out her tongue.

"You complain about not going to parties, but Americans do things right. They don't gift freedom to every squalling infant. You'd be our slave, same as them." He pointed over her shoulder, and Sylvie realized where the smell came from.

Shackled and mostly bare to the elements was a group of Black women. Their ashen skin was mottled from bruising, and one woman had vomit on her chest. The odor intensified, a blend of excrement and disease, as more slaves were led to holding cells. Some were crying and others shuffled along in a mindless shock. A woman's breasts were leaking milk, but Sylvie didn't see any babies.

Gaspard pulled her back in front of the carriage so as to obscure her view. "Mon Dieu, Edmond—"

She had never seen them like that before. Normally, they seemed well enough when she passed them in the coffee fields on their way into town or when they did her hair. Was this what it was like before they got to the plantation?

"Oh, don't look so bloody horrified." Edmond pinched her cheek. "A pretty, light-skinned negro like her would be a bona fide fancy."

"Ignore him."

"You're disgusting," she spat.

But Edmond went on, wistful and smiling. "A fancy would set me back four or five times what a field slave would. But you don't always have to buy the cow to milk it. Lovely, each and every one. A shame we do things so differently here. It was like Plato's Cave, going to Charleston. Freed from the shackles and able to see what the world could be."

Sylvie put the handkerchief back over her nose, the smell of soil and perfume wafting over Edmond's poison.

"Brother," Gaspard warned. "If you say another word—"

"She should know her privilege." He crossed his arms. "She should put the fleur-de-lis over her bed next to the crucifix and thank God every day that she is French."

She shuddered against the memory. "Are you all right?" his black-haired companion asked, her hand feather soft against Sylvie's arm.

"You're correct, sir. Forgive me, I have only recently escaped the Cave myself."

"And I can only imagine how blinding the sun must be."

"I prefer the harshness of the sun to the shadows of puppets."

He did not appear to be the smiling sort, but he did humor her with a small upturn of his lips. His sunlight was sweeter than all the days on Saint-Domingue.

He bowed and said, "We should discuss this further. I know you have more to say on the subject." He turned toward his female friend. "And you as well, I presume. You are very fond of the classics."

She touched his shoulder in an intimate gesture. "You just like hearing your own opinions echoed back, Monsieur. I am more a parrot than a lady."

"I prefer Mademoiselle Cornélie to Mademoiselle Parrot."

His words roused Sylvie from her conflicted sulking; perhaps the lady was not as unknown as she thought. This Cornélie displayed the complete lack of inhibition of most women.

"My mother, too, I imagine," said Cornélie after laughing.

He bowed over her hand while giving Sylvie a last once-over; her cheeks burned in a combination of embarrassment and interest. She was used to men like the fellow from earlier: stupid but smitten. But this gentleman—she had never met a man so completely without charm and admiration for her person.

She lowered into her deepest curtsy, showing off her décolletage, more of which she had to offer than the other lady, though he'd turned on his heel long before she lowered.

"Forgive him," said Cornélie with a rueful expression. "He does not do well with strangers—least of all ladies. He improves with time, I assure you."

"I hesitate to believe you, Mademoiselle Duplay." She grimaced and watched his retreat through the crowded rooms. His manners and opinions stood out starkly against her memories of the island. It unsettled her, but not in a wholly unpleasant way. "He seems the intractable sort."

"You both must share that quality." Then, upon realizing Sylvie had referred to her by her family name, Cornélie asked, "How, may I ask, do you know my name?"

For once in this entire encounter, Sylvie had the upper hand. "Éléonore Duplay, is it not? Though you prefer Cornélie. Your sister Élisabeth sang your praises over tea last week; she mentioned you are a student of Regnault's?"

Cornélie bowed in a smiling defeat. "All true, I'm afraid. I am at quite the disadvantage; you know of me, but I know not of you. I spend much time with Maître Regnault at his workshop, thus I am woefully ignorant of the neighborhood gossip."

"I'm Sylvie de Rosiers." She had forgotten the abolition of such titles—putting a *de* before the surname signified aristocracy, so she hurried to correct herself. "Forgive me. Sylvie Rosiers."

The *de* was a tiny thing, but she would erase anything that would draw attention to her carefully constructed veil of lies. The life she'd left burning on Saint-Domingue could ruin her even from its embers.

Cornélie gave a nod of approval. Lise and Gaspard appeared arm in arm, both pink-cheeked and beaming. "I'm so pleased you've found each other!" cried Lise, grabbing her sister's arm.

Cornélie frowned, the first one of the evening. Sylvie mused that she could see how someone as gentle as Lise would call her intimidating. The pleasant blue of her eyes became stormy. "You must inform me, dear sister, when you invite friends to the salon. I would have greeted our new neighbors properly."

Sylvie surmised Cornélie was rather embarrassed to be caught in this position; Madame de Rosiers would have been furious if Sylvie had snubbed a family acquaintance at such an event.

Lise's joyous expression faltered. "I am sorry, Cornélie. I only—"

Cornélie stopped her with a firm squeeze of the hand. "I discovered Mademoiselle Rosiers standing quite alone for some time. She is new to Paris, and yet you would abandon her so quickly"—she focused pointedly on Lise's and Gaspard's interlocked arms, at which point Lise hastened to remove herself—"to a sea of strangers?"

"I am to blame, Mademoiselle Duplay," said Gaspard with a gallant flourish. "I insisted your sister show me her favorite painting. I am a very poor brother, so chastise me if you wish."

Sylvie pitied the little sister; she was obviously unaccustomed to any sort of criticism. However, she found herself warming to Cornélie for her unapologetic support of etiquette, despite her strange introduction earlier in the evening.

Her hard blue eyes softened into something resembling understanding, and she waved the tension away. "I shall not chastise you, Monsieur Rosiers. I think Mademoiselle Sylvie will cut you to the quick the moment she is away from prying eyes. She was forced to suffer my company due to your negligence."

Sylvie enjoyed her first genuine laugh of the week; this new acquaintance knew her well. Either that, or Sylvie did not contain her displeasure as well as she ought.

The rest of the evening went on in a similarly merry way, though her mind wandered to the pale-eyed gentleman and his cold demeanor. Men usually left her presence in a dizzying fog of infatuation. This man almost reviled her flirtations—he was more interested in academics than beauty. Cornélie, who was pretty in her scholarly sort of way, held his attention with philosophy rather than smiles. Perhaps Sylvie's charms were also relics of an old world, like her dresses and powdered skin.

After Cornélie insisted they all share a carriage to return to Rue Saint-Honoré, Gaspard went out to fetch the coachman while Cornélie said her goodbyes to Regnault and fellow students. Lise remained with Sylvie, shifting from foot to foot with her normally smiling eyes downcast.

"I am deeply mortified for my behavior toward you," she began. "I left you alone and you knew no one. I hope you do not hate me, Mademoiselle."

Sylvie had no younger siblings, but she imagined it would feel something like the blend of annoyance and compassion she felt now. "Firstly, you may call me Sylvie. And secondly, my brother demands attention at all times—he is better suited to the stage than to the law—so I do not blame you for attending him as you did." The girl sagged in relief, her bright grin reaffirming its residence between her dimpled cheeks. "I do wonder if you could help me, however."

She wished to know more about that terse monsieur from earlier but was hesitant to ask Cornélie, who had an obvious attachment with him—romantic or otherwise. "A gentleman approached your sister and me. He had a slight build, powdered hair, light eyes, and a most serious mien. He knew your sister by 'Cornélie' rather than 'Éléonore.'"

Lise brightened. "Oh, you must mean our father's tenant; he left his previous lodgings after the Champ de Mars massacre to stay with us. Cornélie and he are"—her cheek dimpled in a half smile—"*close*. It's no secret, though: they take walks all the time."

Sylvie nodded: for obvious reasons, she was well acquainted with the concept of a mistress. But that answer alone did not satisfy her. "He said the oddest things." Her belly warmed at the recollection of his humorless countenance. His disinterest appealed to her. "He disliked me, I think."

"He is like that with everyone, at least at first." Lise looped her arm through Sylvie's. "But you will see him plenty; he's famous in Paris."

Sylvie was both anxious and glad; she would have an opportunity to improve his poor opinion of her. All evening, the other men at the exhibit stared at her, following her form with the restrained hunger she knew well. This monsieur would fall in line—she was sure of it.

Gaspard and Cornélie waved for the two to come toward the exit, and she and Lise wrapped their shawls around their shoulders and walked to the doorway.

"You never mentioned his name." She couldn't keep referring to him as "the monsieur." Though his air of mystery made up no mean portion of his appeal.

"Shame on me," Lise giggled, "and it's such an odd one, too. His name is Maximilien. Maximilien Robespierre."

Chapter Ten

Robespierre simply can't fuck, and money scares the hide off him.
—*Georges Danton*

For the remainder of November, the Duplays became regular fix-
tures in the Rohmer house. Aunt Fifi delighted in having so
many lovely young ladies to regularly speak to, even if Gaspard mo-
nopolized Cornélie's and Lise's attentions with philosophy.

The older woman seemed content to sit in her favorite velvet
chair, which was worn on the arms, watching her Parisian youths
debate the merits of Rousseau over Voltaire.

Cornélie often entreated Sylvie to join in the conversation—
posing questions about her opinions and life before Paris—but Sylvie
avoided her queries to keep both her sordid past and sordid concep-
tion secret. Despite the Duplays' liberalness, Sylvie didn't allow herself the luxury of trust.

Each time Sylvie changed the subject, Cornélie would purse her
lips in disappointment. She insisted on engaging everyone with the
same open honesty and interest, for which Sylvie both admired and
feared her.

The younger set all decided to go to the Tuileries Garden so they
might enjoy Paris fully before the city descended into the rainy dol-
drums of late fall. Lise and Gaspard attempted to fly a kite in the
autumn winds, chestnut and blond curls whipping around their en-

amored faces. The kite soared into the sky only to drop onto the grassy field as the pair laughed at their failure.

Cornélie and Sylvie became the second pair by default, sitting on an opposing bench in view of the couple's antics. Cornélie balanced her sketchbook on her knees and began a new drawing, her tiny nub of charcoal flittering across the page in a blur. Sylvie watched, noting that the other girl's fingers were always stained by smudges or paint. Black charcoal licked at the tips of her fingers, slowly encasing her pale skin in a gray veil.

She found it hypnotic; Sylvie never indulged in any skill for the sake of personal enjoyment. Cornélie sketched and painted for her own pleasure, whereas she herself always strove to please rather than be pleased.

Cornélie chewed on her bottom lip as she sketched a woman—faceless for now—nude and reaching for some yet-to-be-drawn object.

Sylvie held the second part of *Candide* on her own lap, but it remained unopened. As she'd left most of her gothic novels at the château on Saint-Domingue, she had few books of her own. So, when Cornélie noticed she had nothing to contribute during their morning discussion of Voltaire's novel, she insisted on loaning it to her friend.

But rather than read, Sylvie preferred to flit between glowering at Gaspard's indecent flirtation with Lise and watching Cornélie re-sketch hands five times.

Lise laughed loudly as Gaspard pretended to be hopelessly tangled in the kite. Her amusement unfolded, guileless and unrestrained.

Sylvie had never laughed like that—like no one watched nor cared. It was no wonder Gaspard gravitated toward Lise. Sylvie's very presence reminded him of his father's sins and by extension his own. He would free himself of her at the earliest opportunity, and Lise offered all the delights of a modern France and a modern French woman.

"What are Lise's prospects?" Sylvie asked, her nose in the air.

Cornélie smiled but kept her head bent over a fresh sketch. "Prospects?"

"For marriage," Sylvie clarified. "Gaspard is not a man of property any longer, and he has a tendency to fill girls' false hopes."

Even when he *was* a man of property, Gaspard preferred foppishness and flirtation to holy matrimony. He and Sylvie generally avoided anything with *holy* in the title.

"Ah. You are attempting to spare Lise heartbreak?" Cornélie asked with a sardonic twist of her lips, shading the shadowed side of a man's nose. "Or perhaps Lise is not worthy of your brother? She is, after all, only a carpenter's daughter."

Sylvie refused to meet Cornélie's eyes, for she knew they would be full of knowing humor. She flicked open her fan with a huff. "You are mocking me."

Finally, Cornélie put down her pencils. "No, dear Sylvie, I simply know you well. Gaspard is all you have, and you are loath to lose him to Lise."

Gaspard guffawed at Lise's attempt to keep her kite aloft, then they joined together—heads touching as they tried to untangle the unruly string. He looked fashionable and charming, blond wisps of hair dancing in the breeze. A perfect picture of French romance.

He thrived in Paris. He wore his tricolor pins with a gallant flare, his wardrobe of vibrant colors replaced with red and blue. The doctrines shaking the old tenets of the ancien régime came to him easily, and the Duplays welcomed him into their fold. Lise was the final jewel in his crown. Gaspard would fall madly in love and marry her—abandoning Sylvie until she was truly alone.

She had a sudden urge to cry, her fan fluttering as quickly as her heart.

"It was different before," she said. She didn't belong in Gaspard's new, happy tableau. Not that she ever really belonged on Saint-

Domingue, but at least then she knew her place—knew her prospects. "He's all I have."

Cornélie dipped her head lower to capture Sylvie's gaze hidden under the brim of her hat. "Before what?" Sylvie shook her head, squinting into the sunlight. "Before the slave revolt?"

Sylvie winced. "You know, then." She couldn't keep the shame out of her voice. The idea of Cornélie hating her filled her with an odd sort of grief. To her mortification, her tears escaped.

"I always did," Cornélie said as she touched Sylvie's arm. "Madame Fifi told us the truth, but she doesn't judge you or your brother for your father's decisions."

"And why should she? Why should anyone?" Sylvie snorted. "There are thousands of *indiscretions* on Saint-Domingue. But what does it matter now? I have no mother. And now I have no father." She hadn't meant to say so much, but like her tears, once the words escaped, she could not stop them. "*You* must despise us even if she does not. It is men like my father that fight against the reforms you dream of. I ignored my father's crimes until it was too late, and now his sins taint me."

Sylvie stared at her arms, half expecting to see those sins scribbled across her skin like charcoal on paper.

Cornélie's ungloved hand moved to rest atop hers. Her fingers weren't smooth like Sylvie's, or as bronzed. They had calluses along her thumb and pointer from holding pencils for hours every day, and the nails were short—cut straight and dull. An artist's hands. A sensible woman's hands. "Sylvie," she soothed.

But now Sylvie wept in earnest; the gulf that separated her from Saint-Domingue had filled with shame and doubt. "I feel trapped," she whispered. "Evil and trapped."

The material wealth and family that she believed defined her were either destroyed or in Charleston, leaving her nothing but lies, Gaspard, and her mother's blood that flowed in her veins. And now she wandered the streets of Paris, far away from smoldering fields and revenge killings, but still that terror lurked in the shadow of her mind.

Smoke from chimneys became smoke from a burning plantation; the crash of a fallen crate became the blast of a pistol. She'd crossed thousands of miles of open sea to find peace—and yet she felt no safer on a garden bench than in a carriage racing to the Saint-Domingue dock.

"Sylvie," Cornélie repeated. "You are not evil." She gripped Sylvie's chin, forcing her to look into those too-knowing eyes. "Robespierre told me the secret behind men like your father, men like the king, and it explained how the world could become the way it is now."

Sylvie's heart pounded at the mention of that strange man's name. "What's the secret?"

Cornélie smiled like the answer couldn't be plainer. "The secret of tyranny is ignorance. Ignorant tyrants, ignorant slaves, ignorant daughters and sons. You are not evil, Sylvie; it's only that no one taught you differently. Ignorance breeds evil, and education is the cure." She spoke with certainty—a certainty Sylvie longed to feel.

She gave a strangled laugh. "You have very strange conversations with this Robespierre." She wondered if her friendship with Cornélie would let her be privy to some of them.

Cornélie shrugged. "He speaks the truth."

Self-conscious, Sylvie pulled her hands out of Cornélie's grasp and dabbed her cheeks. "And how do I educate myself, then? Is Regnault taking on more students?" They both chuckled now, her tinkling laugh blending into Cornélie's deeper one.

"I'm afraid something less amusing than painting." She pointed to *Candide*. "Reading generally helps. You must come to my home tomorrow; Robespierre keeps quite the collection."

And perhaps he shall like me better, Sylvie couldn't help but muse, *if he thinks I am attempting to improve my mind.*

She read excerpts aloud while her companion finished her sketches, surprised she could enjoy the calmness of an afternoon without scenes of chaos flashing behind her eyes.

As Cornélie began packing her tools away, she said, "By the by, you needn't wear so much powder, you know." She motioned to the tan streaks of skin revealed under Sylvie's whitened cheeks. "You're not the first mulatto girl in Paris."

SYLVIE ASKED TO wash when they arrived at the Duplay house, and upon Cornélie's direction she found a bowl of water and a clean cloth. She sat at the well-worn vanity and began removing the powder on her cheeks and neck. She wiped off her beauty, her armor, her crutch—years of ingrained tradition that her skin was to be hidden.

She had avoided seeing her bare skin for most of her life. Even as a child, she scampered into Madame's rooms to slather her face in creams and powders. And as an adult, she only removed her cosmetics by the dim glow of candlelight right before bed.

Afternoon light offered no mercy.

Despite the shades of parasols and lightening creams, the honest mirror revealed the tan hidden under her powdery mask. Light freckles, the result of a reckless youth spent in the sun before the force of white superiority shattered any innocence, bedecked her slightly upturned nose. She fluffed the curls framing her face with a frown.

Cornélie told Sylvie she would be accepted here, though years of judgment distorted Sylvie's perception. Her skin was a burden to bear, a family secret that anyone could see, a symbol of sin. It may be the same girl in the mirror, but Cornélie saw one face—and she saw another.

Sylvie gripped the railing at the top of the stairs, barefaced and vulnerable. She took each step slowly with her eyes screwed shut.

Was she ugly now? Could anyone look upon her and think she was beautiful?

A male voice said, "Pardon me."

Sylvie opened her eyes, and Robespierre stood at the bottom of the steps with a stack of books in his arms. He wore no wig—the first time she'd ever seen his head bare—and ash-brown tufts of hair curled by his ears.

He remained at the foot of the stairs, white-knuckling his books. Sylvie shouldn't have been shocked to see him; he lived here, same as Cornélie. But still, she stuttered before saying, "Forgive me, I'm blocking your way." She skirted around him, hoping he couldn't catch her face in the low light.

She had never *not* wanted to be seen, but now all she wanted was to hide.

"Cornélie was asking for you," he said once he'd moved past like she carried plague. "Are you well?"

She had to look up now or risk offending him. "I'm fine. It's just difficult to adjust to a new city. Sometimes I can't tell if the world is changing or if I am."

He nodded but offered nothing else. Though instead of continuing upstairs, he shifted uneasily from one foot to the other. Sylvie liked to watch his hands grip the books and papers; he had beautiful hands. Little else about Robespierre could be considered beautiful, but she admired his broad palms and neatly trimmed nails. He read so much and knew so much—surely, his opinion was more informed than most.

"If it is not impertinent to ask, Monsieur"—she held on to the railing for support—"what do you think of me?" She hoped he thought of her at all.

Robespierre tilted his head, almost like a hound unsure of its master's command. "You are a good friend of Cornélie's," he said.

She cleared her throat. "I *mean*, what do you think of my—my background?"

"What do I think of your being mulatto?" he asked bluntly, and she struggled not to wince.

"Yes," she said. "What do you think of . . . *that*?"

He frowned in thought, keeping Sylvie in painful suspense. She shouldn't depend on one man's opinion. But in this raw moment, she needed someone—anyone—to offer some comfort.

"I've been clear in my writings that I support the Negro in his quest for freedom and the abolition of slavery—"

"No," she interrupted. She did not want to hear a pedantic essay on the "noble negro." She, and all the other Blacks still tied to the islands, were more than objects of pity. But his ardent support of the freedom of all men certainly secured her admiration. "*Personally.* Not as an academic. Please."

He came down several steps so he did not loom over her. He spoke deliberately, and Sylvie hung on his words. "The foundation of my philosophy is universal democracy. A man's faith or skin has no bearing on the rights bestowed upon us at birth. You are a citizen, same as me. The nature of your origins does not infringe upon your value as a woman, in my view—mulatta or no. You . . . you are crying, Mademoiselle."

She pressed a hand to her cheeks, and to her surprise she found them dampened from tears. "It appears that I am," she said, wiping them away with an embarrassed laugh. "Goodness, I'm quite sorry. It's only that no one has ever said anything like that to me before." No one had ever spoken of her *value*, only of her limitations.

He nodded, though he could not possibly understand the depth of her feeling. "Women are vital for the progress of this nation. All of them."

She smiled. "Thank you, Monsieur. I'll remember that."

"As you should. Now, if you'll excuse me." He bowed—more

like a jerk of the head—and went up to his rooms before she had the chance to rise from her own curtsy.

Sylvie leaned against the wall, half laughing into her hand. She was desperate to know his mind on everything. He was a man surrounded by walls, a one-man fortress of stone and ice. What secrets, what answers, did he hide behind that stoic facade?

His words may not have been poetry, or even romantic, but Sylvie found herself enraptured by something she had been little shown before: respect.

Chapter Eleven

There are no slaves in France.
—*French maxim*

décembre 1791

As Lise spent more and more time with Gaspard under the indulgent chaperonage of Aunt Fifi—their aunt often left the pair alone to do God knows what—Sylvie could be found at the Duplay household with Cornélie.

Originally, she hoped to see Monsieur Robespierre more often as well, yet business took him back to his hometown of Arras after the Assembly disbanded.

To her shock, he allowed Cornélie access to his private collection of essays and books to keep them sharp during his absence. With this ammunition, Cornélie taught her Montesquieu, Diderot, and translated works from Hobbes. Sylvie became her little pet project—her foundling student searching for a higher purpose.

Sylvie preferred tea cakes and gossip, but the new currency of Paris rested in knowledge rather than in champagne-soaked soirees. If she intended to stay in Paris—and the comforts and friendships it afforded meant she did—she needed to master this new world order. And so, she would rise to the occasion.

But that did not mean she did not blend her old proclivities into these new studies.

"Wine and philosophes—tell me there is no greater pairing."

She sat on the floor, essays and excerpts strewn about, and proclaimed that truth with a cup in her hand.

Cornélie sat on the ottoman facing her, smiling down at her pupil and pushing the stray curls from her forehead. "And tell me, how do Descartes and claret pair?"

Sylvie took a deep sip as though her third glass would suddenly have more nuanced flavors than the first. "A very fine match, I think. Perhaps a currant wine for Voltaire." After finishing the French red, she reached for the second bottle—which her tutor deftly slid away, spilling some onto her hand.

"You must prove you are learning something first!"

Sylvie pouted. "You are such a harsh mistress. However does Robespierre respond to such treatment?"

"With *merci*." Cornélie tapped Sylvie's wine-reddened mouth. The remnants of the claret stained Cornélie's finger, as Sylvie could taste when she bit the offending digit.

"*Merci*, then," she added with a wicked smile. "I know all of Descartes's Provisional Morals, the scientific perfection of ethics, and sum—" She wrinkled her nose and chewed over the increasingly slippery consonants of the Latin phrase: "Summum um . . . um bottom?"

Gaspard's laughter startled them both. "Summum bonum?"

"That's it!" She clasped her hands. "That's what I said. The ultimate good."

Robespierre slipped in behind him and sniffed the mouth of the almost-empty wine bottle. "I think you are more claret than reason."

She was too drunk to be shamefaced about his arrival. "I would prefer champagne, but my tutor says red wine is more egalitarian."

A smile flitted between him and Cornélie as she poured him a glass. "And she would be quite right. I see you're enjoying Descartes."

Sylvie frowned. "I prefer Voltaire. *Candide* was delightful, if a bit optimistic—or dare I say cavalier."

Gaspard snatched her cup for himself before she could drink. "Cavalier?"

"He discusses 'freedom' and 'slavery' like he hasn't actually encountered either." She let out a sigh, closing her eyes as she pieced together her meaning. "He and I share a country, but he uses 'slave' so liberally as to make it lose its meaning."

"Sister, to be fair, he could hardly have encountered any slaves in France."

She shook the drowsiness from her head. "Whyever not?"

"There are no slaves in France." Sylvie laughed at Gaspard's staid irony. She stopped when no one else joined her. He lowered his voice slightly. "Why do you laugh?"

She snatched back the claret and refilled the nearest empty cup. "Are you serious? I suppose next you'll say the Code Noir is a charming afternoon read."

He looked at the others for reinforcement, and no one did much beyond stare into their wine. "But there aren't! I haven't seen a single one, and France has never allowed bondage on its shores—since Louis X, at least."

Her wine sloshed, but she didn't care. "Really? Louis X said so? I hate that little maxim: 'There are no slaves in France.' Centuries old and still not true. I think I prefer 'There are only idiots in France,' or 'If a man does not see it, then it does not exist.'"

Gaspard's cheeks mottled in contained anger. "You embarrass yourself. How could you possibly feign such certainty?"

She set the cup down hard enough that she expected it to break. "I helped our father prepare the bloody paperwork."

Sylvie hurried to her father's office, eager to offer him help as he prepared for a lengthy voyage.

Most grand blancs *had others manage their businesses on the island while* they stayed in the more familiar comforts of France; their father was one of few who actually decided to remain on the island for a good part of the year.

But on the rare occasion he did return, a significant amount of preparation was required. Despite the competence of his secretary, her papa often asked her to transcribe a document or address correspondence. Since she was just seventeen, this seemed the most prominent position on the island—especially given that she had two brothers who often waned in favor.

After he called for her to enter, she curtsied neatly. "You called for me, Papa?"

"My pearl!" He waved her over to his desk—a bastion of authority—and kissed her hand. He smelled like coffee. "I hope your hands are ready and your mind is sharp." He pulled out papers, mostly prints of what looked like royal declarations, given the seals, and motioned for a servant to bring over a chair. "I'm bringing Jean-Luc with me to Paris, and that requires some tedious paperwork. Fortunately, I've been to France since '77, and I have copies we can transcribe."

The heading of the top sheet read Déclaration pour la police des noirs. Declaration for the Policing of Blacks.

She read through it quickly, noting its clear ban on interracial marriages or the entry of any African people. "It says no person of color is allowed to go to France?"

She had dreamed of seeing the glories of their supposed true home, but it seemed like their king did not want them—free or slave or mulatto. Her skin was her status.

"Bah." He fixed her a quill. "Any smart Frenchman knows how to smuggle a negro into France. But I won't be there long enough to require Jean-Luc, so he will be detained at the depot until I leave. Some work camp or other."

She put on her best smile despite the crushing end of the fantasies of her childhood. "I wouldn't want you to be without your valet, Papa."

"You know I helped him with minor tasks from time to time. I saw firsthand what a man was willing to go through in order to keep his slaves, even in France." She smoothed her dress and finished what was left of the spilled wine. "One thousand livres and days of bureaucracy. And yet you condescend to say, 'There are no slaves in France.'"

Gaspard said nothing, and only the hiss of his flask filled the silence until Cornélie supported her with, "Saying something aloud, no matter how many times, does not make it true."

Sylvie met her eyes and offered a weak smile. "But how I wish it did."

"And what would you say?" Cornélie asked, giving her pinkie a little squeeze.

"There's not enough air in all of Paris for that list." Sylvie poured another glass of wine, though smaller than her last few.

"Something silly, then?"

She could not remove her mind from that hypothetical list—the end of bondage, an hour with her mother, more liberty and less empty talk of it.

"I wish I were a poet like Molière," Robespierre's soft voice rang out, and it dispersed the ache in her chest like wind shaking snow from the trees.

She did not believe him at first, thinking instead that he was mocking her. "A poet?"

He swallowed his own wine before continuing. "I love poetry, always have. I'm mediocre at best and aspire to some artistic genius like Molière." Even Cornélie could not hide her surprise.

Gaspard spoke second. "I despise my calves. The day hose are no longer fashionable will be a grand day indeed."

Cornélie glanced downward. "Your calves?"

"I was advised this could be a silly request." He tucked his legs under the chaise as best he could. "Stop looking, the lot of you!"

Sylvie tipped her glass in salute toward Robespierre as the others laughed and teased, and he returned it in kind.

———

THE NEXT TIME Gaspard sat with them—teasing her when she struggled with the abstract origins of property—Cornélie was quick to insist that these lessons were reserved for her and Sylvie exclusively.

"It's only that I was never made to think before," Sylvie said once he left. "Not truly. I'm not bookish like Gaspard; he's become a regular bluestocking since Saint-Domingue."

Cornélie had just come down with an armful of essays from Robespierre's collection, with that serene little smile she wore whenever she was around his things or he was being discussed. "I wonder if your brother reads because he is impassioned by the words or because he thinks it fashionable."

Sylvie flipped through the pages of Diderot's *Encyclopedia*, tracing the branches of the Tree of Knowledge. "Very likely a bit of both."

Cornélie exhaled and said, "We have done enough educating today, I think. Robespierre would be proud of your progress." She closed the tome in her lap with a soft thud.

Sylvie's cheeks warmed. It was ridiculous, she knew, as she'd hardly had but a handful of conversations with the man—one of which had been hardly sober. But she read every essay, letter, and booklet Cornélie provided.

He even wrote her an encouraging postscript in one of his letters to Cornélie. She reread his note dozens of times, looking over his signature until she could see it even when she closed her eyes: the slope of the *R* and flourish of the *e*.

"Do you think so?" His quiet presence and resonating words stayed with her, a fleeting impression allowed to fester into something of an infatuation with the idea of the man rather than the man himself.

"Of course," said Cornélie, chucking her under the chin. "You must impress him with your mastery of *The Social Contract*."

"He'd laugh at me—if the man ever does laugh."

Cornélie covered her mouth to contain her giggles, and soon they both laughed like gossips. Once they caught their breath, Sylvie asked, "I have always wondered, why do they call you 'Cornélie' instead of 'Éléonore'? Even Robespierre calls you such."

Cornélie leaned back in her chair with her chin in her hand. "Have you heard of Cornelia Africana?"

Sylvie's expression signified that, no, of course she hadn't—at which her friend laughed again. "Cornelia Africana was revered as the very image of Roman virtue. She was a scholar, a devoted mother of twelve, an honorable wife—loyal and dutiful until the end."

She began stacking the essays in alphabetical order, showing the papers more reverence than Sylvie showed the Bible. "I was quite solemn as a child, and very focused on my studies. My father would say I had more virtue in my little finger than the entire Second Estate. Papa is a bit of an amateur classicist and started calling me Cornélie."

Sylvie raised her brows. "Twelve children? It sounds like fertility is synonymous with virtue, so you best marry soon." Cornélie hit her arm. "Very well, very well. I bow before you, most virtuous lady."

"Well, what about your name's origins?"

"My name?" Sylvie shrugged. "My father chose it arbitrarily, I think, beyond adding in 'Euphémie' for his sister. Bastards get the better names, at least. If I'd been his lawful child I would've had some god-awful familial name like 'Béatrice' or 'Agathe.' Why? Does it have some significance?"

Cornélie stood up on her toes to pull out a heavy text from an upper shelf. "You are familiar with the founders of Rome?"

Sylvie nodded, pleased she could answer. "*Oui*, Romulus and Remus."

Cornélie opened the book in front of Sylvie so they could both look at it together. They stood over the tome shoulder to shoulder, the floral notes of Cornélie's rose water adding to the warm atmosphere. "Rhea Silvia"—she pointed to the beautiful woman in the center of a print—"was their mother, and thus the mother of Rome. She claimed her sons' sire was the god Mars, begotten when she was a vestal virgin."

"Well, that must have made for an interesting courtship. All the best stories have virgins in them."

Cornélie dropped the book onto the desk, bending over to conceal her snorting laughter until tears pricked her eyes. "Honestly, *ma très chère*, no one amuses me like you can. In my weeks of knowing you, I declare I've laughed more than I have in my entire life."

Sylvie wrapped her arm around Cornélie's slender waist and rested her chin on her shoulder; she liked how neatly she fit by her side. "That's very fine, as I need someone to amuse."

"Odd, for you looked so dour upon first impression."

Sylvie pouted prettily. "Regnault's painting was dour. I do not know how anyone in the entire room managed a smile for all the bleakness. I hope your paintings are not so."

Cornélie narrowed her lids in concentration, staring at her in a hyper-focused way. Sylvie pulled away and tilted her head in confusion. "Why do you stare?"

Cornélie crinkled her brow and held Sylvie's chin between her thumb and forefinger—turning her jaw left and right at different angles. "Forgive me, but have you ever had your portrait done?"

Sylvie stood on a small stool in the center of the sitting room, wrapped in a makeshift white sheet meant to resemble a stola. Cornélie had woven a laurel of ivy leaves—meant to be olive leaves, but they could find none—into Sylvie's black hair.

What began as practice in portraiture became Cornélie's inspiration for a new painting. She styled Sylvie as Rhea Silvia, her arms reaching for her two sons playing in the Tiber. The rudimentary stola engulfed her frame, sliding down her shoulders every few minutes.

"My arms tire." She flexed her limbs to ward off the stiffness.

"Just a few minutes more," said the student artist, devoid of sympathy. She wet the tip of the brush before dipping into a dab of black paint.

"You said that an hour ago." Sylvie arched her back and heard a few satisfying pops.

"Most models stand for six hours at a time, you know—sometimes we suspend their arms with rope so they don't tire."

Sylvie rolled her shoulders to shake off the discomfort. "How undignified. I'm not a marionette." Cornélie shushed her, staring at her subject as late-afternoon light flooded the room. She stepped around her canvas to approach Sylvie, who gave up on her pose and whined, "It sounded so very fun to be painted, but . . ."

The older girl shushed her once more, readjusting Sylvie's curls around her cheeks.

"Your skin is the perfect olive; I am anxious to mix my paints to do it justice. With your coloring, you could pass as Italian—a true Rhea Silvia of Rome."

Sylvie took a corner of the sheet to flip it over her bare shoulder with panache. "Or Sylvie of Paris." Cornélie shook her head and moved the garment into a tidier arrangement. "And my sons shall be consuls of New Rome."

"Is that Paris's title? New Rome?" Cornélie tightened the rope serving as a belt. "And if I recall, you are childless."

"Well, I shall find two brothers, then, to lead us. Does Robespierre have a brother?"

"*Oui*, Augustin." Cornélie knelt to pin the sheet so it didn't drag. "He remains in Arras."

"There you have it: Maximilien and Augustin, masters of New Rome."

Robespierre himself appeared in the sitting room at that moment, still wearing his traveling cloak and dusty riding boots. "I daresay, Mademoiselle Rosiers, I only hope Augustin shares our ambition."

Sylvie froze. Her hair was mostly down, her bare calves and ankles exposed to the world. The only thing keeping the sheet over her chest was her hands—leaving her shoulders mostly exposed.

But Cornélie did not seem to consider the scene the slightest bit scandalous. She hurried to his side and pressed a kiss to his cheek like a wife greets her husband. "How does your brother fare? He likes his position at Pas-de-Calais?"

The spell broken, Sylvie curtsied in her heavy white costume, both embarrassed and exhilarated for the gentleman to have found her in such a state. But, to her chagrin, he perused her naked skin for only a moment before bowing to Cornélie.

"Well enough." He removed his tricorn and brushed off the dust on the shoulders of his coat. "He finds being the administrator rather dull. Though he would like Paris better."

Sylvie was determined to make him like her, and the education she received from Cornélie only improved her confidence. "Then you should force him to come," she said. "And he shall join our merry party of friends." She hesitated on her last words, staring at Cornélie's charcoal-marked fingers intertwined with Robespierre's.

With a wry twist of his mouth, he said, "My brother is as stubborn as they come, Mademoiselle. He cannot be *forced* to do anything he was not prepared to do himself."

Sylvie smiled, slowly pulling back her full lips to reveal her most charming and most practiced of grins. "You must convince him, then. You can convince anyone of anything."

His jaw ticked, the vein by his temple more prominent than usual.

"She's been reading your books," Cornélie said with pride.

Sylvie's sheet caught on the wooden crate she used as a stage. She felt stupid again, standing in a white sheet before such a man. "I hope you do not mind."

He leaned back, his face adopting the cool airs of someone accustomed to being the most intelligent man in the room. "Of course not. Education is—"

"Education is the secret to freedom," she said, echoing his own words back to him; they'd become a mantra, a guiding light, in her quest for purpose.

He nodded, his ghost of a smile her greatest reward. He released Cornélie's hand, stepping closer to Sylvie. She stiffened; he made her senses flutter until she could hardly see, smell, or hear anything but him. Sweat beaded under her stola.

With a complete lack of propriety—or self-awareness, she couldn't be sure—he touched the crumpled bedding wrapped about her form. "Dare I ask why you are wearing my sheet?"

Sylvie covered her mouth in mortification. "*Your* sheet?" She looked to Cornélie to dispute his statement, but she nodded with a gleeful twinkle in her eye.

"I knew he wouldn't mind," Cornélie assured her with a laugh. "The man would sleep on a wooden pallet without complaint."

Sylvie was horrified by such an intimate abuse of Robespierre's belongings, but he seemed unbothered by the scene—stroking the garment between his fingers in casual perusal. The heat from his hands burned through the sheet. "Don't worry, it looks finer on you than on my bed." A little smile lifted his lips again. He had to look up to meet her eyes, since the platform made her significantly taller.

If another man had said the same phrase, Sylvie would have recognized it as a compliment. Yet, Robespierre's manner did not lend itself to charm; he spoke to her in facts, not flirtation, though his words heated her all the same.

"I'm serving as her much-abused model today," she said, doing an awkward twirl on the too-small pedestal. She teetered unsteadily, but he gripped the bedding so she wouldn't fall. "For a portrait."

At any given moment, Robespierre's face only moved one element at a time: a quirk of the lip, a clenched jaw, a raised brow. This time, Sylvie was rewarded with the latter. "In costume?"

"Painted in the style of Rhea Silvia, actually. The mother of—"

"Romulus and Remus," he replied. "Seems only right, then, for the artist to be Rome's most virtuous woman."

It was the closest Sylvie had ever seen Cornélie to blushing, with her head lowered just a fraction as that serene smile reappeared.

"We are not in Rome, Robespierre," Cornélie said as she pushed him aside. She tied the sheet more tautly around Sylvie's shoulders before letting her palms rest on Sylvie's hips. Sylvie liked that Cornélie's movements focused his attention on her. "Unless the air in Arras has rattled your senses."

"New Rome, then," said Sylvie. Robespierre wanted the government to represent all rather than the few—forcing her to look outside of her own plight and see the struggles that many French people faced. She could see the new world he painted with his words, and she wanted to be a part of it. "A New Rome reborn from the ashes of the old republic."

Cornélie gestured for him to stand behind Sylvie to re-pin the stola. His fingers brushed against her skin, blessedly cool. She arched her back so he would touch more of her.

A breath above a whisper, he said, "A phoenix to break free of the chains of corruption."

With Cornélie pressed to her front and him to her back, every inch of her skin ached for something *more*. Knowing that her bare flesh brushed against his own sheet drove her wild. The tops of the stola finally pinned, he stepped around to face her. "You *have* been reading."

He divested himself of his coat, settling down next to Cornélie as she returned to her preliminary sketch of her subject.

Madame Duplay entered with a tray of refreshments for the recently returned traveler. She made a startled sound upon seeing Sylvie wrapped in a bedsheet on a footstool but recovered quickly; the Duplay household was used to such oddities.

Having overheard, the older woman said, "Let us hope Paris is not exactly like a phoenix; they die in flame."

"I have seen tyranny fall," said Sylvie, remembering the smoldering fields of Saint-Domingue. "Speeches and books cannot compare to the heat of real flames. A spark was not enough for Saint-Domingue; everything had to burn if the stain of injustice was to be purged."

She thought of Edmond and the cold mouth of the pistol pressed into her sternum. She would light Notre-Dame herself aflame if it meant she'd never know that fear again. "White masters die so Saint-Domingue may live, but things will not get so bad in Paris."

After the execution of Ogé, Sylvie remembered the invisible ash that hung in the air over Saint-Domingue's streets and warned of an eruption to come—the tension burned into every interaction, every glance between Black and white faces.

The taste of ash found her in Paris, but the conflict boiled under kettles of class rather than race. However, she remained sheltered among her brother and the Duplays; they were students of the revolution rather than active participants.

"I did not realize how close you were to the violence," said Madame Duplay. "Thank God you and Gaspard escaped."

Robespierre held a cup of tea but did not drink it. "Your father was one such master, was he not?"

Cornélie went to silence him, but Sylvie waved her off. "Yes," she said. "He was—is."

"And he escaped this justice?"

She nodded. "Edmond chose to stay. They are not good men."

She swallowed and lightened her tone. "That's why Gaspard reads as he does, to explain and cure the evils of our family."

Robespierre nodded. "I gathered as much from his letters." Her brother had not mentioned he'd been writing to Robespierre while the latter was in Arras. A seed of jealousy was planted in her heart. "Though you aim to absolve your father's sins through education as well."

She stepped down from the crate as gracefully as she could. "Despite my . . . *background*, I benefited from the profits of slavery all of my life. And I will spend the rest of that life paying penance for it."

Cornélie gathered her canvas and turned it toward Sylvie. "I think you already are."

The sketch, though in its infancy, captured her face and form with an intimacy that took her breath away. The outlines of Romulus and Remus grasped at her stola. Her left hand cupped her stomach like she guarded an unborn child while she pointed toward the yet-unbuilt city of Rome in the hills behind her with the other. Silvia's gaze beckoned the viewer, her eyes soft and sure.

"Cornélie . . ." she began. She had never seen herself so undone, so bare.

Robespierre moved to view the sketch beside her. "It's a vision," he said. Sylvie looked to Cornélie, who only smiled. His eyes did not stray from the picture, thumb following the flowing lines of his lover's pencil and brush. Sylvie shifted in her false costume, her vanity stoked and vulnerable as he stared.

"I'll continue to work on it," Cornélie said, waving off their praise. "But I believe I have the basic arrangement. You're quite the muse."

"And I will strive to rise to her example," Sylvie said, meaning every word. Her vulnerable heart warmed under this tutelage, and she decided she would never stray from the garden of their approval.

Chapter Twelve

It is the false shame of fools to try to conceal wounds that have not healed.

—*Horace*

janvier 1792

The icy rain and numbing cold kept Sylvie by the fire in the Rohmer house. Saint-Domingue lived in a perpetual summer compared to the coolness of France, so the concept of winter chilled Sylvie to the bone. On the island, sunlight drenched everything in heat. They had the occasional hurricane or summer storm, but the sweet warmth never left them. Here, the ice crept over each brick and flower until the entire city bathed in frost.

The bitter freeze burned her fingers if she strayed from the hearth, so she sat as close to the flames as she could without being singed. The only light seemed to come from fire: it was just in the past week that the sun lingered until five o'clock.

The days on the island did not vary, the sun and moon given equal time in the sky. Sunshine was fleeting in French winters, like the warmth of freshly baked bread.

Wrapped in a shawl and a blanket, she scribbled notes on a copied essay by Robespierre—at least, that was what she would *say* she was doing. In actuality, she tried to emulate the loops of his *L*'s and the way he crossed his *T*'s. His script took up as little space as possible, tight and uniform from one page to the next. Her writing looped and curved to excess, three words taking up as much space as Robespierre's ten.

Boredom and poor weather made unpleasant companions, so she sighed in relief when Louise came in with an unexpected letter in hand.

From Charleston.

She had not received a single letter from Julien. She knew her brother still received correspondence from their father; he'd answered the first letters, but at Robespierre's encouragement he ignored the rest. But at least he'd received any letters at all. Though Sylvie would never say so to Cornélie, part of her remained a loving daughter who hurt from her parents' complete rebuff, but she was too angry, too raw, too proud to reach out to Julien.

She was not disowned—one could not disown a bastard—but forgotten. Gaspard, who would never truly be cast out, as the only remaining heir, had given her the choice to leave Charleston, but her choice came with more consequences. She stood at a forked road and chose the path that offered her redemption as a woman of color but meant betrayal to her family.

And as the silence from Charleston continued, her loyalty to the Duplays and Robespierre grew.

So when their maid placed the missive in her hands, conflicting voices battled for dominance. She could toss the letter in the fire, disgusted by her father and everything he represented, or read it in the vain hope that he could redeem himself in the eyes of his disillusioned daughter.

However, the name of the sender, Madame—not Monsieur—de Rosiers, was scrawled on the back.

"Forgive me, Mademoiselle. Monsieur Rosiers told me to send all correspondence from Charleston to him only. But as this letter is marked 'urgent,' I thought to give it to you."

She tore her eyes from the weather-beaten paper. "Did Monsieur Rosiers give a reason for his request?"

"He said such communication would upset you."

So like her brother to think she couldn't handle something so asinine as a letter from his mother. "I see. Have I had many letters?" The maid looked askance, wringing her apron between chapped fingers. "You will not be punished, Louise."

"A few, Mademoiselle," she answered. "Two from Monsieur Rosiers and three from his wife."

Sylvie gripped the missive so tightly that the wax seal cracked. "And the fates of these letters?"

"Burnt, miss. Monsieur Gaspard tossed them in the fire."

"Thank you for your honesty, Louise; you may go." The girl curtsied and fled the chamber.

After she heard the maid scurry down the servants' stairs, she went to Gaspard's room, letter in hand.

"How *dare* you?"

He was buried in the paper, and a half-eaten plate of cold chicken sat next to his long-cooled cup of gunfire.

"How dare I what?" he asked as he turned the page. She slapped the paper onto his desk, and he jumped out of his chair.

"Louise told me about your outrageous order," she said. "How could you burn my own letters? Julien wrote to me—*twice*—yet you cut me off and write to him yourself."

He shook his head, his lips pressed into a tight line. "You wouldn't have wanted to read them."

"Perhaps, perhaps not!" she cried. "The choice was mine to make. You burned them without reading—"

He smacked his hands on the desk, his cheeks blooming red in anger. "I know what they *said*. The same things he wrote to me. Disappointment, coward, traitor, revolutionary, ungrateful. Yours could only be worse. I'm surprised he did not outright forbid Fifi from housing us. I wrote him once because I had a duty to do so. That man will receive no more than the minimum from us—I daresay ink on paper is more than he deserves."

She fell into her chair, balancing her head on the tips of her fingers. "You cannot protect me from the world, Gaspard. It reached us on Saint-Domingue, and it shall reach us here. Burning paper cannot stop it."

He chuckled, a wry smile breaking his stormy expression. "My sister, a picture of wisdom. Robespierre had mentioned as much, but I supposed I hadn't noticed."

Her chest churned both from Robespierre's praise and jealousy of her brother's growing intimacy with the gentleman. "He said you've been writing him," she said, a sour note in her tone.

"He was a deputy to the Convention"—his face softened into dreamy admiration—"a writer of the Declaration of the Rights of Man, a man of justice and of law. I wish to serve him, prove myself useful to his cause."

She seethed in envy. He decided he wanted to work with Robespierre, and in no time at all he became a protégé. While she drank tea with Robespierre's mistress in the hopes of becoming more than a useless reminder of a dead regime.

She wondered if Robespierre would condemn her for longing to read the letter from her aristocratic parents. He favored justice over compassion, virtue over pity, and he would think her weak. But she felt weaker still for knowing that if she so much as beheld Madame's writing she would burst into tears.

"Tell me what she writes. I must know."

He poured more rum into the cold tea. "It can do no good—"

"Read it." Sylvie paced in front of his desk, playing with the rings on her fingers.

He snatched the papers from their resting place and read, *"My dearest Sylvie, I write again to . . ."*

"Not *aloud*," she groaned. "Read it yourself and tell me what she writes, if anything is worth mentioning."

He read the letter silently to himself as she kept her back turned, running her fingers over the growing collection of books—bought and borrowed—in her brother's room.

Gaspard skimmed the lines. "She has written to me as well," he murmured. "But yours reached us first. She misses you, she's sorry she did not treat you better—"

His voice caught and she whirled. "What? What has she said?"

"It is of no importance. The rest is just her begging for you to leave France."

He went to toss the letter in the fire, but Sylvie clung to his arm like a drowning woman.

"Give me the letter," she demanded with a bravado he knew better than to believe. "I'm stronger than I look."

He took a deep sip of gunfire, the tepid amber liquid rippling when he rested his elbows on the desk, before reading it himself. "*The slaves—the Blacks now control a third of Saint-Domingue.*" Sylvie nodded as he spoke, having heard about the ex-slaves' success through discussions between Gaspard and Robespierre. "*While we knew better, it seems the Assembly just now realizes the gravity of the situation. We expect them to grant full citizenship to all free Blacks by spring.*"

Any joy she might feel at this news was tempered by Gaspard's distress.

His eyes averted, he focused on the drink to protect himself from whatever truth had been inked onto the paper. He turned back toward her, the whites of his eyes reddened from tears. Staring at her brother, she feared whatever came next.

She skimmed the next lines, and Madame revealed that their brother was dead.

"It is as we expected," he said softly. "Edmond is gone."

Unprepared for his sobs, she could only hold his blond head against her stomach as his tears dampened the blue cotton of her gown. She dropped the letter on the ground—she did not need to read more. "I hate what he is," he said. "What he's done. He is everything we rally against—the very image of corruption. Edmond put a *pistol* to your chest." His wracking sob threatened his words, but he powered on. "And still I weep for him. He is both my brother and my enemy."

He felt young in her arms—and she felt younger still—as she smoothed his curls like Madame did before. The motion felt awkward and unfamiliar, but she did her best to offer him comfort.

"How did he die?" she asked, unsure if she hoped it was torturous or quick.

He pulled away from her embrace, his mournful gaze worlds away from Robespierre's flat, observant one. "The rebels burned down the château and dragged him out. They killed him."

She pictured her brother's corpse bloated and rotting in the island heat. "But someone found the body?"

Perhaps it could be sent to Charleston for a burial. She did not consider that out of sentiment for Edmond, but out of some sympathy for her parents.

"No," he said. "They found *pieces.*" He dissolved into fresh tears, clutching her skirts, as she digested the loss.

Sylvie recalled the last memory of Edmond: spittle flying from his hate-spewing mouth, blood on the hand that struck her, pistol cocked and prepared to slaughter slaves and kin alike. She let Gaspard weep, but she refused to share his grief.

GASPARD'S EMOTIONAL DEMANDS wore Sylvie down over those next few days. She needed time away from her grief-stricken brother, so she asked to join the Duplay sisters on their errands in town.

They waited to head out until after luncheon; the morning chill cut through even the thickest wool redingote.

By noon the weather had warmed some, but here the overcast skies never cleared. Sylvie's soul longed for sun.

The girls locked arms—Cornélie held the large woven basket for purchases—and set off.

They shared the streets with quite a crowd today. Poorer folk had small baskets of bread or simple fabric. Rambunctious children wove throughout the carriages and pedestrians with squeals of laughter. Bourgeois ladies and gentlemen had maids scuttling behind them with large boxes filled with the day's purchases. Small troops of sans-culottes—the lower-class revolutionaries who wore long trousers rather than stylish silk stockings—roamed the streets in bright-blue short coats and red caps.

"We should take Sylvie to the clothier," Lise said. "She can get some tricolor cockades or a red-striped handkerchief."

Sylvie noted that most Parisians, even the wealthy, wore some element of the national colors commonly in the form of a blue, white, and red cockade sewn onto bicorn hats or lapels. The more dedicated citizens wore full ensembles devoted to their country's flag. Even the Duplays limited their wardrobe to some variation of this patriotic theme when they went out.

Wool or cotton replaced silks and jacquard once Sylvie's dress orders came in, but she didn't care about the color scheme beyond whether it flattered her complexion.

"She has a point," Cornélie said. "Not wearing a cockade—at the minimum—looks unpatriotic. You don't want to attract attention."

Sylvie smirked. "You mean more than I already do?"

Cornélie turned away to hide her laughter. "With all that vanity, I hardly know how you manage to leave your reflection in the morning."

Sylvie shrugged. "It's a daily struggle."

Lise rolled her eyes at their banter. "If you're both done being ridiculous, we're at the clothier's."

Sylvie eagerly poked through the displays of ribbons and patterned fabric. She found a beautiful white silk ribbon trimmed in a pink lace and held it up for Cornélie to admire.

"No, no," Cornélie chided as she put the ribbon back in the box. "No fineries or fripperies. You're lovely enough without it." Sylvie frowned but returned the length of silk to its spool with a longing glance.

Lise came between them with an armful of tricolor cockades, fichus, and neckerchiefs. "More like *these*."

Sylvie groaned. "Can't I be a good citizen and still wear a little lace?"

"It's different here, Sylvie. I don't expect to dress you like a nun—"

"Good, I look awful in black."

"—but you must understand why the old ways must go."

The old ways meant slaves, hypocrisy, and pain. Sylvie took one of the cockades and pinned it to her bodice. "I do."

Cornélie smiled and leaned in to whisper, "And I imagine you look very fetching in red."

Sylvie's grin grew wider.

"Cornélie!"

Two ladies Sylvie did not recognize hastened over. The Duplays seemed to recognize them, though Cornélie's stiff posture revealed she may not be as happy to see the pair as they were to see her. Lise bounced over, grabbing both women's hands and smiling profusely.

"*Bonjour*, Henriette, *bonjour*, Charlotte," Cornélie said. "Sylvie, these are Maximilien's sisters. Mesdames, this is Sylvie Rosiers."

The sisters Robespierre shared their brother's looks. Both appeared to be in their late twenties, with blue eyes and light brown hair. Charlotte looked rather plain, but Henriette still had a girlish youth about her.

"A pleasure," Sylvie said, her interest piqued. Any relation of

Robespierre's mattered greatly if she wanted to get—and remain—close to him.

Charlotte nodded with a slight frown. "Are you two acquaintances?"

"Neighbors, actually," Sylvie said. Cornélie squeezed her arm, though she didn't know why. "I'm friends with your brother."

"Friends?" Charlotte asked.

"Yes," Sylvie repeated. "My brother and I are honored to spend much time in the Duplay household. Monsieur Robespierre is a brilliant man—so I'm very pleased to meet you both. I didn't realize he had sisters! I should scold him for not telling me."

"Oh," Charlotte said with mild surprise. "You enjoy my brother's works?"

"The ones I have read, yes. I greatly admire his fight for freedom."

"Sylvie has become a bit of a student," Cornélie said in a clipped tone.

"Mmm," Charlotte hummed, eyeing Sylvie's basket of blue, white, and red splendor. "I can see she's become a regular revolutionary."

Cornélie kept pulling her arm, but Sylvie wanted to impress the sisters. "He's been quite the influence. I've read some Cicero, Voltaire, and Montesquieu." She leaned in conspiratorially with a playful smile. "Though I must confess I've enjoyed Rousseau most—he's the least tiresome of the lot."

Charlotte made a sidelong glance to her sister, Henriette. "You're not *from* France, are you?"

Sylvie's palms began to sweat within her gloves. "No—"

"Well, then let me inform you that in Paris we find a true interest in the classics and academic study, unlike whatever barbaric island you're from." She narrowed her eyes at Sylvie's elegant dress. "We may not put the same emphasis on fineries, but what we lack in expensive fashions we make up for in substance. We do not put on our cockades as you put on your string of pearls. I doubt my brother would call you a true friend, unless his standards for companionship have dropped further still." She made a pointed glare at Cornélie, though the latter did not falter.

Sylvie may allow others to comment on her own origins or ignorance, but she'd never countenance such remarks directed toward Cornélie, who had shown her compassion in ways unknown to her on Saint-Domingue.

"I *beg* your pardon," Sylvie said.

"Sylvie, don't—" Lise began, but Sylvie handed her the basket of goods, which Lise held without complaint.

"I am honored to be in the same circle as the Duplays. They offer true hospitality and humility without pretense. I am certain that Monsieur Robespierre shares that opinion threefold, especially re-garding Cornélie. She is a shining example of womanhood, and you do your own gender a discredit by failing to recognize the strength of her character." She made an exaggerated curtsy. "We bid you good day."

Henriette's mouth twisted in amusement while her sister's hung agape. "The same to you, Mademoiselle," she said, laughter dancing in her eyes.

Sylvie locked arms once more with a giggling Lise and a dumb-founded Cornélie to lead them out of the store and back to Rue Saint-Honoré.

No one spoke on the way home.

Sylvie chewed her lip, furious with herself for crossing swords with Charlotte. She imagined all sorts of awful consequences for her impertinence—worst of them Cornélie being so embarrassed that she severed their friendship and Sylvie's window to Robespierre.

But Cornélie stopped her at the threshold of the Duplay house after Lise went inside. "Thank you for saying those kind words ear-lier. In all my time knowing Charlotte, she's always despised my family. She actually lived with us for a time until her animosity practically dripped from the rafters."

Sylvie fiddled with her new cockade. "But what will Robespierre think? I berated his sister."

"He would never say so publicly, but he finds his elder sister . . . wearying."

Regardless of Cornélie's assurances, Sylvie didn't want to face Robespierre just yet. She'd rather focus on her grieving brother than her shameful outburst. She returned home, the basket of cockades heavier than before.

When she went to check on Gaspard, she found him slumped over his desk asleep. The empty bottle of rum lay on its side, though by the look of his tearstained cheeks, the rum had done little to soothe him.

Sylvie pinned a cockade on his lapel; they'd both find comfort in the balm of revolution.

Later that evening, she decided to send a note to the Duplay house to invite them to dine—knowing that Lise would improve her brother's spirits better than cold tea and rum.

Gaspard did not advertise their loss with any outward displays of mourning or grief, but he didn't wear his sorrow well. His skin looked sallow from too much drink and too little sleep. He offered little in conversation or good humor, mostly just sulking and picking at his dinner.

Only Lise and Madame Duplay visited, since Cornélie remained at home in raptures over her newest painting. Monsieur Duplay was down in his workshop, and Monsieur Robespierre stayed with friends.

Sylvie only nibbled at her chicken and lentils, pushing the little legumes around her plate in disinterest.

Madame Duplay chatted with Aunt Fifi at their end of the table while Lise and Gaspard drank in each other's presence over the silver candelabras. Sylvie sat between the two pairs in a sullen mood.

"Robespierre enjoyed discussing the slave rebellion with you the other day," she overhead Lise say to Gaspard. "He said your opinions provide context to a world with which he is unfamiliar." Lise squeezed his hand in pride, while Sylvie grimaced behind her wineglass.

But Lise's company improved his mood with her sweet smiles and sweeter laughter. She sat with him after supper ended, their knees touching as he relayed the truth behind his red-rimmed eyes—while Sylvie brooded over her own inadequacies. Cornélie did not judge or ignore, and she longed for her attention.

She envied both sisters; they had good parents, good humor, and good sense—all of which she lacked. Her brand of charm did not lend itself well to Parisian commoners, and only Cornélie seemed truly comfortable in her company thus far.

The group sat by the hearth sharing smiles and conversation. Sylvie kept to the fringes of the room to drink her brandy—first sips, then gulps. That dark melancholy pulled on her limbs and mood like an anchor, dragging her thoughts into the cloying bleakness that made her want to sleep and never wake up.

"I'm going to the Duplay house," she croaked from the burn in her throat. Not waiting for a response, she slipped on the nearest cloak and left without notice.

January in Paris meant blistering cold and endless rain, so even the short walk across the street demanded heavy outerwear and thick gloves—neither of which she wore. A light snow dusted the streets, disguising the ice beneath, but she liked the burn in her fingertips from the chill.

Saint-Domingue nights meant an orchestra of tropical birdcalls and buzzing insects; the neighborhood here, mostly well-to-do bourgeoisie, smothered her with its silence. The grimy stones glittered under a sheet of ice and a bright moon.

Sylvie had never seen her own breath until France, and she didn't like being aware of her own mortality every time it got cold.

Her silk and leather clogs offered no protection, and she walked without her usual grace thanks to the brandy burning in her belly. A loose cobblestone sent her reeling and, unable to regain her bearings on the black ice, she slipped backward onto the weather-hardened ground, her head striking the street with a *thump*.

Her eyes fluttered open but quickly closed again to protect against the falling snow. Frightened to move for fear of broken bones, she didn't immediately rise. The cobblestones dug into her aching spine.

She rolled onto her stomach, unable to lift herself off the ground just yet—cheek pressed into the icy sludge of the street. Her head felt like a bucket overflowing with water: sloshing, heavy, and difficult to manage.

The brandy held them off for as long as it could, but slowly pain seeped into her muscles and bones, as did the cold.

She raised her head with precarious slowness to orient herself in the darkness. The area was unoccupied save for her groaning form lying on the road. The dirty snow crept into her wool round gown and soaked her front with slush and filth.

With a huff, she managed to get to her knees and then onto her feet. She swayed with the wind as the houses spun around her. Her eyesight wavered, streetlamps multiplying at the edges of her vision. After taking a few tentative steps—and discovering nothing broken—she stumbled to the Duplays' doorstep. She tripped up the stairs and had to grip the banister to stay aloft.

Taking a few quaking breaths, she then pounded on the door, resting her cheek against the white stone doorframe. Their maid answered, her eyes round as saucers when she took in the muddied and disoriented Miss Rosiers. She ushered Sylvie in—as well as some of the growing storm behind her.

Sylvie found the nearest chair in the sitting room and flung herself into it, pressing her fingers to her temple in an attempt to ease the throbbing in her skull. Mud and water dripped onto the carpet.

"Mademoiselle, shall I call for a doctor?"

Despite the maid's nearness, she sounded miles away. "No," Sylvie croaked with a curled lip. Even the servant's timid voice hurt her head. "No need. Just a fall. Some tea would do just as well."

The girl went off to brew a kettle, and Sylvie divested herself of her cloak and hat. Melted snow dampened her hair and gown, but wet clothes did not stop her from lying on the inviting chaise. Everything ached now that her senses returned to her, and the allure of sleep tempted her heavy lids and pounding head.

Cornélie's voice roused her from her half slumber. "I'm sending for a physician."

"Don't you dare," Sylvie said, her hand covering her eyes. "I despise doctors. I've no need for third sons with wandering hands and beady little eyes."

The mild delirium that so often accompanied head injuries filtered any etiquette or gentleness out of her tone. She turned her face into the worn velvet pillows.

Cornélie picked gravel out of her hair with one hand and rubbed soothing circles on her back with the other. "What happened?"

The deafening roar of the tea tray clattering made the ache in Sylvie's head flare, but, thankfully, Cornélie's gentle voice was no more unpleasant than a feather brushing against her skin.

"Your poor roads will cause more deaths than your kings," she replied into the pillow. The older girl kept her laughter to a quiet chuckle.

Sylvie lifted her head off the cushion, and Cornélie placed a cool hand to her head. "A fall, then?" She brushed dirt from Sylvie's cheek with her thumb.

Sylvie went to nod, but the movement caused the room to move as well. "I hit my head. But it is not so terrible now."

Cornélie knelt to examine her dripping hem and frowned. "You're ruining my mother's upholstery."

"Hardly," Sylvie slurred. She slumped back into the seat while Cornélie removed one of her sodden shoes. "It was already hideous."

Cornélie laughed behind Sylvie's outstretched foot. She studied the injured joint and the pretty footwear that contained it. "I see the cause of your demise—these ridiculous heels of yours."

Sylvie frowned at the torn and wrinkled leather. "Ruined from the snow, I imagine."

Cornélie clicked her tongue as she perused the heel of the shoe. "You oughtn't wear them at all. The heel is *three* inches tall, Sylvie. I'm surprised the ice did not humble you sooner." With an almost maternal tenderness, she removed the other offending clog. "Your ankle looks injured as well."

Bolstering herself up on her elbows, Sylvie peered over her volume of skirts. "I must have twisted it when I fell. I didn't notice—*ow!*" Cornélie had squeezed the swelling flesh to test for a break.

"It's not broken, foolish girl." She glanced out the window. "But you must stay here for the night; the snow is piling up. Also, I do not trust you to brave the treacherous landscape of a city street."

Sylvie waved her hand in a show of defeat. "I shan't argue."

"I worry at you being so accommodating," Cornélie said with a smirk. "You must have hit your head quite hard. But first things first; let's put you in something less frigid."

With Cornélie's arm for support, they walked up to the shared room of the Mademoiselles Duplay. They were not a wealthy family—Sylvie's father would have called them common—but they enjoyed a certain degree of comfort from Maurice Duplay's success as a landlord and contractor. Thus, the rooms were spacious and well decorated, if a little simple for Sylvie's exorbitant tastes.

She fiddled with the laces on the back of her gown, and Cornélie shooed her hands away to undo the dress herself until the invalid stood in only her chemise. Sylvie allowed her weight to press against her temporary nurse while layer after layer fell to hurt, aching feet.

Her chemise remained unspoiled, so she kept it on. Cornélie slipped a dressing gown over her arms, and Sylvie enjoyed being coddled.

Cornélie pulled back to see her face. "Better?"

She nodded, touching her stomach where the stays no longer constricted. Most women did not lace as tightly as she demanded, but she enjoyed how the boning molded her form however she liked.

The robe was not as finely made as her own, but it was worn and loved and *Cornélie's*—so she preferred it to any silk creation she kept from Saint-Domingue. She ran her fingers along the old lace details, wondering if Robespierre had done the same.

Her addled mind was vulnerable to melancholy. So the loneliness—despite her well-meaning aunt and like-minded brother—crept into the cracks.

"You're lucky to have Robespierre," she murmured. She looked at the slope of Cornélie's white neck. "I'm jealous of you." She hadn't meant to say that aloud.

Tactlessness crept in as well, apparently.

Cornélie guided her to the vanity and began combing through her curls with her fingers. She had the good sense to avoid a comb. "No one *has* Robespierre. He belongs to the people, not me."

"He cares for you; everyone knows it." Sylvie swayed away from her helpful hands, but Cornélie removed the tiny pins meant to set Sylvie's hair in place with a determined focus. "He *smiles* at you. He lets you kiss him. You have the love of the Jacobins' great prophet. But that man hardly speaks two words to me each day, no matter what I say or what I study." Cornélie braided Sylvie's hair, frowning while she struggled with the unfamiliar texture. "And Gaspard has his precious Lise. Well, no matter. It's only right that I am alone."

Her self-deprecating laugh sounded more strangled than sincere.

She came from tainted stock, and she didn't deserve happiness. The slightly oversize gown slipped down her shoulder.

"I forget that even though you may know its language, Paris must seem a foreign place to you," Cornélie said while she knelt to tie the ribbons on Sylvie's dressing gown—clinical and sure in spite of her invalid's fidgeting. "But you are not alone, Sylvie."

"I should be." Tears blurred her already unstable vision.

"Why on earth should you be alone?" Cornélie shared the bench beside her. Sylvie's head ached, and all she wanted was to keep her head buried in the older girl's shoulder. "You are charming, amusing, and—"

Sylvie groaned, but the sound was muffled by Cornélie's sleeve. "I'm heartless."

Cornélie pulled away, holding the glassy-eyed girl up by the arms. "Why would you speak thus? What have you done?"

What *hadn't* she done? "Edmond is dead," she whispered.

"Your brother? He was in Saint-Domingue, was he not?" Sylvie nodded. "Then you are blameless for his death. Do not make yourself sick with grief, dearest."

Sylvie's shoulders shook, giving the illusion of sobs. But on closer inspection they shook from laughter.

"*Grief?* I feel none. And he would be insulted if I called him 'brother' in polite company. I am his father's seed sown on an unworthy field. Gaspard protected me from the worst of his contempt, but it stung all the same. And when the revolt reached us, Edmond aimed his pistol at the rebels—and then at me when I tried to protect them. He looked at them and saw property. When he looked at me, he saw a stain on the Rosiers name." She swallowed, but her mouth was bone-dry. "And I am glad he is dead."

Cornélie fetched the bowl of water warming by the hearth, dampening a cloth to brush across Sylvie's muddied forehead. "Robespierre only speaks of terror, but you have lived it, Sylvie. In

the grips of chaos, you put yourself between a bullet and the innocent." She placed her whiter hands over Sylvie's shivering-cold ones.
"That is the furthest thing from heartlessness. And your brother died
at the hands of Justice, a fitting end by all accounts."

Cornélie guided her to the edge of the bed. She moved slowly
and with a gentle purpose. First, she peeled Sylvie's wet stockings
down her thighs, now gray instead of white. Then she grabbed the
warm cloth to clean her feet and hands, removing mud from her
nails.

In the warm light of the fire, Cornélie's skin glowed orange. She
seemed angelic: a picture of virtue as she dabbed away Sylvie's doubts
with reason and tenderness.

Sylvie let herself be persuaded, if only for the night.

Chapter Thirteen

I prayed one word: I *want*.

Someone, I tell you, will remember us,
even in another time.

—*Sappho, "Six Fragments for Atthis"*

Cornélie continued to distract Sylvie with shallow conversation and affection throughout the evening. And Sylvie didn't mind in the slightest.

"Would you like to see your portrait?" Cornélie asked. "The preliminary sketch is nearly done; I've been working on it in class. Regnault says it is not horrible, which is high praise indeed." She went over to a chest—filled with canvas and paints rather than gowns—to retrieve it. "Despite your constant movement, I captured you rather well."

The tableau was now more painting than sketch. The likeness *was* good, if romanticized. Sylvie, or rather Silvia, stood on the rocky foot of one of the hills of Rome by a rushing river—presumably the Tiber. She extended well-proportioned arms toward two hearty babes, both naked and plump, with rosy cheeks.

Silvia herself wore only slightly more clothing than her famous sons; she sported a gossamer stola that revealed more than it concealed, with one sleeve having fallen off her golden shoulder to expose the curve of her breast. Her hair looked wild, as if a strong river breeze moved through the black curls. Her expression bespoke great pride as she gazed at her sons, hazel eyes framed by thick lashes that kissed tawny cheeks.

"How is your coloring?" Cornélie pressed. "And your hair? I

agonized over your eyes; it is so difficult to recall them once you are gone." Sylvie said nothing, running her fingers over the glossy oil paint that captured her so well as the artist went on. "Many modern depictions of Silvia feature her with Mars, but I prefer to explore her relationship with her sons and with the land we'd call Rome."

Sylvie chewed on her lip before saying, "I have no eye for art, but I like it very well." Her response felt stiff to her own ears. The placid seas of Cornélie's eyes froze over, and the artist went to re-cover the unfinished work. "Stop, do not—" Cornélie held the cloth sheath away from the portrait. "Do not cover it. Forgive me, I am unused to receiving gifts of this nature. I know how to show appreciation for finery or gowns, but not . . . Friendship like this is new to me."

The ice in Cornélie's gaze melted, and she said, "It is strange to see oneself in a portrait. But you make a beautiful subject."

Sylvie withered; opulence and physical pleasures had had their reign, and their grim successor disapproved of the old excesses. She only wished that she might wear fine things *and* support liberty. "No one cares for beauty here."

"I do," Cornélie said, examining a lock of Sylvie's hair. "I'm an artist; we find beauty in the barren. So I found you." She gave a husky laugh, the one like waves crashing against the shore. "And I suppose that's why I felt compelled to speak to you at the salon last November. No one in Paris looks like you, not really."

"There are many mulattoes in Paris—"

"That's not what I meant." She re-covered the portrait to protect it from the effects of sunlight and candle smoke. "You were this odd combination of haughtiness and fragility, like a wildflower growing on a cliff face: lovely, out of place, and determined, in spite of every-thing, to be exactly as you are."

"Such an eloquent way of saying I'm stubborn." Sylvie giggled, sinking into the pillows, which smelled like Cornélie's lavender and rosewater perfume. She preferred the bolder scents like citrus and jasmine, but Cornélie was her opposite in most ways. "Well, I thought *you* very odd."

"I could tell; you are very poor at concealing your inner thoughts." Cornélie glanced down at her dazed friend, her hand resting on the part of Sylvie's leg exposed by her chemise.

Sylvie's feet burned hot, so she rucked up the chemise to her knee as Cornélie continued. "Everything about your dress and presence spoke of wealth—the kind of company I would have avoided on any other evening. But you looked so lost in your pearls and fine clothes, surrounded by art you thought was dreary. My curiosity—and a bit of pity, too—insisted I discover the identity of that dark, scowling girl."

Sylvie always felt a bit lost in Paris, but perhaps not so much in Cornélie's company. She had a certainty in everything she said and did, which soothed Sylvie's disjointed existence.

But, like an omnipresent phantom, Robespierre haunted her thoughts. "What did Robespierre say of me?"

Cornélie smiled at the memory. "He said something along the lines of, 'The girl is either remarkably ignorant or remarkably bold to come here.' I found them both to be true." Sylvie pinched her thigh at this teasing. "Yet you suit us quite well. After that scene with Charlotte, Lise is terrified of you."

Sylvie recalled Lise's happiness with a rush of jealousy and scowled. "Lise is a ninny," she said.

Cornélie laughed like Sylvie had made a joke, ignoring her friend's pout. "So warm," she murmured, staring at the parts of their legs where they touched. "Your hands are burning. I hope you do not catch a chill." She rested the back of her hand on Sylvie's cheek.

Sylvie closed her eyes and pressed her cheek firmly into the other woman's palm, enjoying the brief intimacy. How long had it been since she'd been touched so tenderly? She wished she and Cornélie could share this intimacy without the pretext of injury.

Cornélie's beauty grew upon closer inspection, like a dormant tree in a Parisian winter; at first, its leafless branches could hardly be called enchanting, but with a second glance the icicles weeping from her boughs mesmerized. Her inky plait brushed her neck and ended by her heart, and her skin shone from rose water.

"Why hasn't Robespierre married you?" Sylvie asked. Despite her humble origins and manner, she would have married Cornélie if she weren't a woman. "Lise says you lie with him."

"Lise *is* a ninny," Cornélie echoed. "He's known women, though not many. He is a man of great passion and greater restraint. But we refrain from more for different reasons. He for ethical ones, I for moral—desire for marriage, specifically." Sylvie could not imagine denying anything Robespierre requested or even wanting to. But Cornélie did not walk this world in innocent wonder but in self-possessed strides. She was a woman who knew her own worth, and Sylvie was mesmerized by the lady who held Robespierre's iron heart.

"He is a complicated man," Cornélie said.

"And very much in love with you."

"Things are not always as they appear." She stared into the fire, still idly stroking Sylvie's calf.

Sylvie wanted to peel away the veneer piece by piece until the full truth was laid raw before her. They sat in silence for a moment before she blurted, "What is it like? Kissing him." Her head pounded still, and her normal inhibitions were loosened from drowsiness and the odd glow of pleasure.

Cornélie did not hesitate and was unfazed by her prodding. "Sometimes a brush, a whisper; other times it's hungry. He is a man who makes a study of self-denial." She sighed and lay down next to Sylvie, their shoulders pressed together as they looked at the ceiling. Cornélie touched her own mouth with a brush of her fingertips, her eyes unfocused, like she imagined his kisses as she spoke.

Sylvie made a snort of disbelief. "You pour his tea and read his books and hold his hand. You live as man and wife." She fiddled with a long strand of dark hair that had fallen out of Cornélie's braid. "I'm sure you grant him liberties—"

Cornélie looked away, something like embarrassment playing at the lines around her frown. Sylvie would feel no shame if Robespierre wanted her. "Robespierre is not the sort of man to be distracted by . . . carnality."

Sylvie turned on her side and rested her head on her hand so that she could see her bedmate's silhouette. "A man is a man. No one is incorruptible." Her lips curled into a teasing smile made a little more crooked from her injury.

Sylvie stared at Cornélie's lips, imagining Robespierre biting on her rosebud mouth. She envisioned his own face next to Cornélie's, stern and intractable even when presented with pleasure. The memory of Robespierre's steady gaze and wide jaw resting on his fingers fueled the simmering arousal creeping through her veins, with Cornélie's sensual figure bringing it to a boil. In vino veritas—though, in this case, it was a blow to the head.

Would Cornélie taste his wine on her lips? Did she leave charcoal smears on his coat when she gripped him during an embrace?

"I'm no beauty, not like you," said Cornélie. Her neckline was splotched with red, either from the heat of the hearth or from something else. "I do not make him wild with lust."

Sylvie curled her aching body closer, nestling her head in between Cornélie's neck and shoulder. *But you have* him, she thought. *You have him and Lise and wonderful parents and talent and the prettiest white skin I must touch.*

Sylvie pressed her dry lips to the throbbing pulse of Cornélie's neck. She tasted the roses on her skin, the scent spreading over her tongue and into her nose. Cornélie inhaled sharply and made a small noise in the back of her throat before biting her lip with small white teeth.

With two older brothers—now one—Sylvie was no stranger to tales of pleasurable female company. Cornélie felt good in her arms, under her mouth, beneath her fingertips. She wanted to possess her in the ways Robespierre had. And perhaps if she had not injured her head, her inhibitions would have protested louder—but she struggled to deny the demands of desire.

Cornélie said her name in a soft, plaintive cry. But the syllables were lost in labored breathing and the crackles of the fire.

Moisture collected in the shallow dip of the artist's collarbone. Sylvie chased the taste of roses with her tongue down the valleys and curves of Cornélie's chest.

When she extricated herself to look at her, Cornélie had her eyes screwed shut, dark brows pinched together so tightly that they almost kissed in the center of her forehead.

"You see much of my figure in the portrait," Sylvie murmured into the sharp line of her jaw. "How does an artist paint what she has not seen?"

Cornélie kissed the inside of her wrist, eyes still closed. "Imagination."

Sylvie fell back against the pillows, her dark hair spilling across the sheets. Slowly, she undid the ribbons of the robe. "So you imagined my breasts? Imagined my shape?"

"*Yes*," Cornélie whispered, leaning forward almost imperceptibly. She opened her eyes, their lids hooded with want.

Sylvie pulled down her chemise to reveal her breasts and traced her fingers over the supple skin. "And how does your imagination compare?"

Cornélie crawled over her, enraptured. "It does not." She gnawed on her lower lip—the veneer of control and modesty cracking under the power of Sylvie's wandering hands.

She kneaded Cornélie's breasts with increasing fervor, relishing their softness underneath her thin shift. Her breasts were smaller than Sylvie's, with bright pink nipples visible through the fine linen. Sylvie ached to consume Cornélie's mouth with her own, and so she kissed her lips and neck, savoring the bouquet of salt and flowers.

Cornélie's figure did not yield to her touch as easily as her own: she walked and worked daily, whereas Sylvie's body presented only softness from years of leisure.

Cornélie shoved her leg between hers. Sylvie wanted more, but she did not know what *more* entailed. Cornélie's body, at least its anatomy, was so much like her own—and yet the sensations she wrought were alien.

Sylvie wanted to see their naked bodies pressed together, to see her tanned curves against Cornélie's porcelain form, pale fingers working between her folds—the same parts fitting together in ways no man and woman ever could.

The older girl rubbed herself against Sylvie's thigh, moaning in pleasure and frustration. Limited by ignorance and head injuries, Sylvie just stared up at Cornélie's flushed face in a blissful daze, hips arching off the bed in search of her hands.

After they parted for air, Cornélie traced Sylvie's nose with her pointer finger. She skimmed over the dips and hills of her lips and cheeks, enraptured. "Your face is perfectly symmetrical," she murmured. "Bow-shaped lips, a rounded chin. I could sketch you for hours."

Sylvie turned away, laughing. "You could never subject me to such torture. I am not made to sit still."

"You most certainly are not, darling girl." Cornélie descended lower until she rested her head on Sylvie's thigh. Her irises had narrowed to tiny ribbons of blue. "But patience is an art of its own. And you are too greedy for control." She slid her hand up to Sylvie's knee, dragging her chemise up with every creeping inch. "A lady must learn to wait. To savor." She rested one hand on Sylvie's stomach as the other brushed between her legs. Sylvie arched toward her touch, seeking that sweet pressure. Yet, Cornélie withdrew her fingers. "And when you master self-restraint, you will be handsomely rewarded."

"*Please*," Sylvie said. The heat from the hearth and their bodies let a bead of sweat gather at the hollow of her throat. Cornélie's nightdress had fallen from her shoulder, exposing a creamy expanse of almost pearlescent skin. Sylvie's mind waded through a fog of want.

Cornélie wet her lips as she ghosted the skin of Sylvie's inner thighs. "Please what?"

Sylvie could hardly say the words—to concede to the power Cornélie held over her. The room spun and her head ached, but all she wanted was those beautiful hands to *touch* her.

"But for tonight"—she pressed an openmouthed kiss to the inside of Cornélie's wrist—"be greedy."

And Cornélie did not deny her muse.

As Cornélie drew absentminded shapes on her exposed skin, Sylvie watched the fire's shadows dance along her closed eyelids.

She had begun to fall into sleep's embrace when Cornélie spoke. "We must never do that again."

Sylvie fought to keep her mind sharp and her eyes open. "Why not?"

Month by month the tethers that bound her to the ground snapped free, threatening to let her float listlessly through the dark nothingness of sorrow. But Cornélie's touch, her kindness, brought her back down.

Cornélie rested her forehead against Sylvie's shoulder. "I will not be unfaithful," she said.

"You are not married," Sylvie reminded her—as well as herself. Even in the embrace of his lover, she rejoiced that Robespierre was technically free.

Cornélie served as an extension of the exalted Parisian leader, not by being *like* Robespierre, but by being *what* he liked. Sylvie could not kiss Robespierre, but she could kiss whom he had kissed. Touch whom he had touched.

Cornélie was a balm to her rampant infatuation, the answer to her prayers for closeness to the unsmiling revolutionary—all while being the subject of her envy and her affection.

"He will know—." Cornélie looked away and furrowed her brow.

Sylvie chuckled. "There is a reason they call it the 'silent sin.'" She never developed any closeness to God, at least no closer than reciting the Paternoster or the Ave Maria, but she rather liked the sordid name of her crime. "You have more knowledge of such liaisons than I do, but I see no reason why anyone should know but us."

"It must be because of that portrait." Cornélie threw off the sheets and paced in front of the fireplace. "Having to look at you for hours, memorizing the curve to your mouth and the shape of your hip. Regnault says you have to fall in love with a painting—that love gives it life. To paint you, I had to love you."

Sylvie fancied that Cornélie looked more beautiful now than she ever had, brooding and sullen while she teased through the explanation for her actions.

"And now you're in my bed, suffering from a head injury no less, and I don't understand what's happened. I don't understand what we are."

"Suffering?" Sylvie teased from her throne of pillows. "I am quite well—*very* well, actually—though a bit cold"—she patted the empty side—"now that you've left the bed."

Cornélie did not respond, sitting in abject loathing at the foot of the mattress. Sylvie placed a comforting hand on her arm. "Forgive me," she said without humor. "It seems my pleasure has given you nothing but pain."

Cornélie squeezed her fingers. "No, *you* give me nothing but happiness. You cannot help that you are so beautiful. A sort of beauty one wants to consume." She kissed Sylvie's palm. "Which is why I painted you, I gather. My feelings distressed me so, but when I painted your likeness, the ache lessened."

Sylvie sank into the sheets, her lids half-shut. "I've never been someone's muse before."

"And I've never had one," Cornélie said as she snuffed out the remaining candles and crawled into bed beside her. "Sleep now, my Silvia."

"Silvia, Cornelia, New Rome." Sylvie yawned and Cornélie pressed close, their legs intertwined. "The ancients would be proud."

"Sappho would be, at least," Cornélie said with a smile against her hair.

"Who is Sappho?"

She fell asleep to Cornélie's soft laughter.

Sᴙʟᴠɪᴇ ᴡᴏᴋᴇ ᴜᴘ cold.

Winter in Paris made this not a completely unreasonable occurrence—except she'd anticipated that sharing a bed meant she'd be spared the worst of the damp chill. She ran her fingers over the cotton, now devoid of warmth without Cornélie's lithe form.

Her head felt heavier and more burdensome after her clumsy injury from the evening prior. The sun had been up for hours, and her head throbbed from the late-morning light.

The only pleasant ache came from her pelvis. She swept a finger between her legs, testing the soreness, and smiled at the—albeit somewhat muddled—memory of Cornélie's unerring attentions the previous night.

The hearth boasted a small fire to keep out the worst of the winter, and Cornélie had laid out a spare dress—the green one of Lise's—as well as leather slippers for her over the chair by the window. That kindness warmed Sylvie's belly better than any fire could. Still, she would have preferred waking with her friend's arms securely around her.

I wake up without her, and suddenly I feel jilted. How missish I've become.

She wanted the reassurance of Cornélie's skin beneath her hands, her kisses in her hair. Sylvie needed the tethers to bring her back down again—to know that last night was no pain-induced fantasy.

The scrape of chairs and low voices rang out from belowstairs. She did not relish the imminent headache, but she missed Cornélie.

Snow had ruined the careful pressed curls from Louise's handiwork. Wigs had gone out of style years ago for women, and without a hot iron or castor oil, Sylvie's hair remained a tangled mess.

Sighing, she teased and pinned her curls as best she could. But her Black blood was most visible through her hair.

Thankfully, Paris had forced her to learn how to do her toilette without the cautious glances of a maid. The gown, though less fine than her preference, required no additional help.

With a light dab of perfume, she descended the stairs and went toward the commotion in the salon. The smell of Cornélie, from her rose water to her sheets to her sex, permeated Sylvie's every layer— like an intimate blanket only she knew she wore.

The moment she stepped into the doorway, Gaspard rushed to her to begin his condescending tirade.

"Cornélie told us about your fall," he said. "I hope you know that Aunt Fifi was near hysterics when she realized what happened."

He looked more peeved than worried, and she rolled her eyes. "I collapse in the street and you don't seem any worse for wear."

He gave her a once-over. "Well, *you* do. That's a handsome bruise, if I may say."

Her fingers flew to the side of her head. "Oh God, I've forgotten to powder it. I must look like I've been in a brawl."

"And lost," he snickered.

She ignored his jibe and found Cornélie's reassuring presence on the chaise by Robespierre. Madame Duplay served tea and refreshments between her two girls.

Sylvie possessed an awareness of Cornélie that she hadn't before. She looked lovely, if a little less serene than was her wont. Sylvie imagined her mouth to be a little pinker than usual, kiss-bruised, no doubt, which she happily attributed to herself. Her narrow, shapely lips curved slightly more upward when she caught eyes with Sylvie. A secret written in the lines of a smile shared between two women.

Until a stranger's voice pulled her away.

"Behold, our beloved Silvia!" a man exclaimed with a sardonic smile from behind Gaspard.

After acknowledging the stranger with a polite nod of her head, Cornélie returned to speaking in low tones to Robespierre.

Gaspard turned so Sylvie could see the large gentleman pushing past him. It required all of her social graces to avoid gasping at his face; he had a large, disfiguring scar down his cheek. The rest of his face had little to recommend him, though his presence—from the breadth of his shoulders to his fierce expression—commanded attention in a way not dissimilar to Robespierre.

"Danton," her brother said. "This is my sister, Mademoiselle Sylvie Rosiers. Sylvie, this is the formidable Georges Danton—Paris's deputy prosecutor." She knew the name well—he was an incredibly influential Jacobin: a member of the more radical party in French politics to which men like Robespierre and Marat belonged.

The origins of his disfigurement were no secret: when he was a child, a dog had bitten his face and caused a twisted scar to force his features into a permanent grimace.

"I know her name, Rosiers," Danton said as he lowered his chin in acknowledgment—not quite a bow. His wig only made his head that much larger.

Cornélie did not even glance her way, nor did Robespierre.

She grimaced; she had not anticipated being ignored by *both* objects of her affection. She forced a broad smile and indulged this unknown by saying, "Goodness, not yet in Paris half a year and already my reputation precedes me?"

"Paris is a whore for gossip." His voice, deep and brash, shook the porcelain tea set.

"I didn't realize renowned politicians engaged in gossip."

"Oh, but of course. Politicians are the finest whores of them all." He guffawed, and she couldn't help but admire his forthright manners. "Robespierre has called me here on matters of state, though I found myself incapacitated by your portrait. A very fine attempt, though the original is preferable."

She rewarded him with a teasing smile. Such an ugly countenance must surely avoid women and conversation, but he spoke and flirted with the confidence of a gentleman used to getting what he wanted. "One is obligated to say so. The subject would take great offense if viewers claimed the portrait to be the lovelier version—even if that may be the truth, as it so often is."

Gaspard laughed. "You do not know Danton, sister. He does nothing out of obligation and delights in offending anybody and everybody. When he's not offending he's—"

Danton kissed her hand. "Fucking or drinking. Ideally at the same time." Robespierre stiffened in his seat, no doubt bristling at the coarse language.

She laughed at Danton's twisted manners. "Then surely you've found a companion in my brother." The Duplays and Robespierre had mentioned the man a few times, speaking of his tendency toward private hedonism but public principles with admiration. He was Robespierre's age and of similar background, but their temperaments clearly opposed each other.

Where Robespierre was of slight build, Danton was tall and imposing. While many claimed Robespierre to be emotionless and cold, Danton radiated passion and charisma. Their alliance defied logic, but their opposing personalities blended together into a formidable political force when their goals aligned.

Danton looked over Gaspard doubtfully. "He seems a bit soft for any of my exploits, but we'll see if a night of good wine can bring him up to snuff. We'll leave the ladies to their art."

"I am but the humble model," Sylvie said with a curtsy. "I refuse to take the credit from the artist. Though I am surprised Cornélie would reveal the portrait unfinished."

"While the invalid slept, I decided to make a bit of progress," Cornélie said from her perch across the room. "By eleven I had an audience."

The thin skin beneath her eyes had darkened from too much thought and too little sleep. Sylvie wished to go to her, to reassure herself of their friendship, but the roguish character before her demanded attention.

"The process is fascinating, is it not?" He leaned in as though prepared to tell her a great secret. "But Robespierre prefers artists. I prefer the *subjects*."

Sylvie stood on more equal footing with this man—not because of situation or shared experience, but because he spoke in the language of innuendo she had mastered from dozens of soirees.

"Of course, sir," she purred. "Everyone knows of his fondness for Monsieur Jacques-Louis David."

His full lips opened to release a barking laugh. "We have not known each other ten minutes and you tease me already? Robespierre, your warnings ring true. He said you were quite the spitfire."

Both Robespierre and Cornélie, to Sylvie's pleasure, had already been watching the flirtation unfold. She decided she liked this Danton, but she liked the attention he garnered more so.

"More like Mars than Silvia. Speaking of which, where is our god of war?" He motioned to the portrait, devoid of the Roman god so often depicted ravishing the beautiful vestal virgin.

"We have no need of him," Sylvie said, and pointed to the still-unpainted toddlers. "He's already served his purpose." Danton conceded her point with a wink. "Just because Rome was begat by the god of war does not mean he must remain."

Robespierre scoffed and said, "I fear he is already among us. The Assembly itches to set our unprepared army against Austria."

The royal family's escape failed in June, leading to the imprisonment of the king. Ever since then, Austria had been skirting around the outright proclamation of war. The king of Austria was Marie Antoinette's brother; if Sylvie were the imprisoned queen, she knew Gaspard would do anything in his power to free her, politics be damned.

Danton's teasing mien transformed into fire, his blue eyes burning hottest. "The idiots of the Assembly would use anything to garner fame," he said. "They seek to glean glory from the carnage of war without ever taking part in the fighting themselves."

Good, thought Sylvie, *let them fight and die in Austria. Just keep it far from here.*

Cornélie looked unsurprised by the information discussed nor by Danton's outburst; she and Robespierre shared everything, including the goings-on of the Assembly—even if he was not a deputy. Sylvie hardly cared about military strategy, but she still envied Cornélie's position as Robespierre's ear.

"But surely Brissot will not be successful in his campaign for battle?" asked Gaspard. "No one can seriously consider the Declaration of Pillnitz a declaration of *war*. It's politicking on behalf of the noble émigrés and nothing more. Leopold knows, Holy Roman emperor or not, that any intervention will mean chaos."

Robespierre only shrugged. "A man who truly cared for the welfare of the French people would think thus, but Brissot is nothing if not persuasive. His extensive diplomatic experience—"

"From under the damned king!"

A muscle in Robespierre's cheek twitched. With his eyes on Sylvie, he said, "There is a young lady present, *mon ami*."

She bristled at the implication that she was delicate; while she appreciated Robespierre's defense, she would not demur to the language of revolution—even the coarser parts of it. She planned to occupy the same role as Cornélie: respected confidante and sometimes lover.

"Do not restrain your passion on my account, Messieurs," she said with more confidence than she felt. "Your anger is well-placed. With food riots flaring and untrustworthy generals, France cannot fall victim to war due to one man's hubris. But I do not doubt Monsieur Robespierre's powers of persuasion."

"You overestimate my influence."

For as long as Sylvie had known him, Robespierre served the people, first as a deputy to the Assembly and then as a public prosecutor—a representative of the people. He *spoke* for the people. He knew power in ways Sylvie would never know.

"I don't think I do, Monsieur. You will lead Paris—and then all of Mother France—away from those who would see her crippled. I am sure of it."

Her certainty was exaggerated, but his pale eyes finally possessed something other than cool indifference when she spoke of her loyalty. Like all men, his pride needed stroking. And she was a happy volunteer as she drank from the fountain of his gospel.

A brief smile lifted his thin lips. "Then I must be off to the Jacobin Club to see if this Girondist poison has tainted its waters. Gaspard, you must come as well."

Sylvie struggled not to snort as Gaspard's eyes glazed over in blatant worship.

And in a great whoosh of movement, the men stood and made their goodbyes. Gaspard placed a hasty kiss on Lise's palm, so anxious was he to accompany his mentor.

Robespierre would never do something so intimate in public, choosing instead to bow over Cornélie's outstretched hand. He brushed his thumb over her knuckles, and their eyes spoke while they did not.

Sylvie would have given anything to understand that silent language.

"Do you visit the Duplays often, Mademoiselle?" Danton asked as she walked him to the door. Robespierre, who walked ahead, turned his neck just noticeably.

"I live just across the street," she said a hair louder than necessary. "I spend more time here than Robespierre, I imagine. I should offer to pay rent."

Danton lowered his voice, somewhat impossible, and his words dripped with insinuation. "If you lived here, then I suspect Robespierre would never leave—I know I would not. Both Mademoiselles Duplay and Rosiers? A bachelor's paradise."

My paradise, she thought.

"Robespierre has better to do than take tea with silly girls," she said. "Besides, he is tormented daily with my portrait even when I am not here."

"Tormented?" Danton chuckled. "My dear Miss Sylvie, if your face is torture, then throw me in the Bastille so I may endure it forever."

In an irritated tone, Robespierre said, "That painting will become more than a pretty portrait, if Jacques-Louis David can be convinced to take my commission. I want a larger version made, and with the right . . . patriotic imagery, it could be a masterpiece."

Frankly, Sylvie preferred Fragonard to David—but she supposed that Greek philosophers were more suitable subjects than love gardens in today's France.

Her portrait belonged to her and Cornélie; it served as a tangible reminder of what they shared. But if that painting could be the link to bind her to Robespierre, then Sylvie would let him do with it what he wished.

Robespierre bowed over her hand while keeping his eyes on her face. They had never touched before now, though she imagined it plenty, and his fingers were soft and smooth like the hands of a man who had never lifted anything heavier than a book.

She recalled the lingering caress he gave to Cornélie's alabaster hand, and her jealousy stole some of the joy from his touch. But the knowledge that she'd savored more of Cornélie than even Robespierre at least whittled the flames of her envy down to a flickering candle.

"You shall be made immortal," he said. "The Mother of the Revolution."

Early mars 1792

Winter stoked not only the fires of war but the pangs of hunger.

People did not starve on Saint-Domingue like they starved in Paris. Branches always sagged from the weight of ripe fruit, and harvests flourished under generous sunlight and quenching rain. And if the land had no food to spare, the sea promised everything from fish to conch.

But the streets of France went barren when the days went short, and the brutal freezes left nothing in the fields to glean. The summers were deceptively fruitful and warm, but when winter came the starvation did as well. In Étampes, a little town outside Paris, the people lynched the mayor for not capping the price of food.

Bread fed the masses, but when reserves ran low, it fed their rage.

Tensions ran so high that Aunt Fifi made Gaspard buy flour once a week so their maid, Louise, did not have to face the violence surrounding the baker's shop.

Sylvie went downstairs with her hand on her stomach. She'd overslept—as per usual—and missed breakfast.

She caught Gaspard pulling on his coat. "Are you going out?" she asked.

He reflexively touched the knife on his hip. "We're out of bread, and we need more pork."

With forced levity, she said, "Do you remember the type of confections we ate at home? I'd give my weight in gold for a plate of sugar."

Gaspard grimaced. "The prices aren't that high—yet. At least we can afford food at all."

She handed him his hat. Despite their being weary of slush and snow, Paris insisted on clinging to the vestiges of winter; angry flurries painted the pale stone of their neighborhood even whiter.

"Be safe. It's too cold for me to come running after you." He tipped his hat and headed out, leaving her and her growling stomach to wait for his return.

She decided to pick through the pantry while Aunt Fifi and Gaspard were away on errands. They did not go hungry, but even the slightest suggestion of insecurity made her want to eat. And without Gaspard's judging eyes, she could filch dried fruit and buttered rolls.

"Mademoiselle?"

She jumped when Louise called her, stuffing a handful of apricots into her pocket. "Yes? What is it?"

"Monsieur Robespierre is here for Monsieur Rosiers. Shall I tell him he's out?"

Ever greedy for Robespierre's attention, Sylvie could not close the larder door fast enough. "No need, I'll let him know myself." She wiped the crumbs from her mouth and shoved the apricots into Louise's hands.

She hesitated outside the salon door, trying to rein in her giddiness at the prospect of time alone with the nonpareil. Once she schooled her features into something resembling pleasant surprise, she allowed herself inside.

Robespierre stood facing the window in a dark wool coat, free of snow despite the weather. The winter light cast an icy glow across his skin, and it made his severe features almost hauntingly beautiful.

"It seems my brother makes a terrible pupil," she said, referring to Gaspard's absence.

He turned and, upon seeing her, made a polite bow. "In all fairness, I do not always warn him of my arrival."

She laughed away the dark coil of desire in her belly. "Warn? Goodness, you're an intellectual—not a storm."

He glanced around the room. "So I gather your brother is not here?"

"I'm afraid not." She sat to pour tea for both of them. The ritual of serving tea had long become her standard reflex whenever she needed to calm her nerves. "He does shopping for our maid, since buying bread has become siege warfare."

His eyes went wide and fierce. "You mean he is out at the market *now*?"

"Well, yes. We need food, Monsieur."

"The people are worked into a frenzy because of the riot in Étampes." He pulled on his gloves and hat. "It's madness at the shops."

Sylvie remembered the glint of her brother's blade, concealed at his side and ready for blood. Now she doubted he could keep off more than one starving mother. Fear made monsters of men, and a cool sweat dampened her neck. "We hadn't heard about any—"

Robespierre's cheeks went from white to ashen. "It's only just started! I assumed your brother had the sense to avoid the markets."

Her brother had saved her more times than Sylvie could count, and not only in the obvious sense. He'd saved her from death, surely, but also saved her with humor and compassion, brazen confidence, and unwavering loyalty.

She could have been left to grow up in the shadow of her beloved white half-siblings, yet he insisted on loving her like she wasn't a shameful mistake. Sylvie would not leave him to the ravages of hungry townsfolk.

She bolted down Rue Saint-Honoré, Robespierre's shouts muffled by the crunch of soiled snow.

Chapter Fourteen

Oh Liberty! What crimes are committed in your name!
—Madame Roland

The late-winter snow was jaundiced with stale piss and dirty footsteps blanketing the square in a blur of gray.

But blue, white, and red were splashed across every door, every lapel. While it was meant to invoke community, Sylvie watched the flag whip in the breeze with sinister promise.

Men, women, and children pushed and shouted, their demands for a bread price they could afford lost in the roar of desperation. She pushed and shoved her way through, searching for Gaspard's forest-green coat. The slush seeped through the thin layers of her cotton petticoats as easily as tea on paper without her protective wool coat.

She screamed his name when she could get a gulp of air, but he did not answer her call—and most likely could not hear it at all—in the clamor of the mob.

Bread riots rarely ended without violence; hunger made men blind to fear and numb to pain.

Sylvie imagined his body broken and bleeding in the snow, the crumbs of bread stuck to his lapels. Her cheeks burned from the tears freezing on her cheeks.

"Gaspard!" she shouted in a half sob. She could not bear Paris without her sibling—another brother to blame her for his demise. Another casualty of her existence.

Pushing elbows and hands slowed her progress to the storefront of the bakery, until the rusting metal sign of a baker making bread came into view.

"*Gaspard!*" she yelled again, searching wildly for a gold head face-down in the snow.

She heard him call for her before she saw him. "Sylvie?" he answered, her name thin with panic. She found him facing the crowd, forcibly placing himself between their empty bellies and the baker. An angry red welt bloomed on his cheekbone, and his lips dripped blood onto the ground in a delicate stream. A few rocks littered the area, which explained the injuries. His wounds made the snow bloom with little pink flowers from the blood around his feet.

She sighed in relief that the mob hadn't come armed with deadlier weapons. "I'm taking you home."

Gaspard held up his hands to keep her distance. "I refuse to leave Monsieur Cambron to die in his own shop. But you must go home. *Now.*"

He must have tried and failed to calm the crowds—instead only riling them up as a well-dressed bourgeois commanding them to leave without food.

"So," the mob's large leader said, "you even brought your Creole whore to this little gathering." More people shouted around him in agreement, shuffling closer until Gaspard's back pressed against the brick. He wore multiple tricolors and the perpetually fearsome look of a sans-culotte.

She moved between him and the encroaching crowd. She did not know politicking like her brother, but the uprising on the island had sharpened her ability to sympathize.

"Your righteous anger is misplaced, *Citoyen*," she said in a strong but gentle voice. Despite her tears, she was resolute. "I am his sister, not his whore. And my brother *fights* for you. He left our plantation across the ocean to fight for you. He works with Robespierre to fight for you. He sends letters and proofreads petitions to fight for you. We abandoned a life of excess and barbarity to fight for you."

She put forth her hands, like a supplicant, in a silent appeal for the rock he held in his fist. "Killing your ally does not fill your belly or make the snow melt or make Austria withdraw her troops. It only adds another victim in the fight for freedom."

"I do not want any more blood on the snow today, *Citoyen,*" Robespierre said from a rapidly parting crowd. Their eyes went from rage to wonder and awe as they murmured *"Incorruptible"* among themselves. She had not seen his power over the people in its raw form—it was hypnotic. "Especially not the blood of a good French citizen and fellow Jacobin. Your pain is virtuous, but I do not want war in the streets while my brethren demand war on our borders."

He did not speak in loud, commanding tones like Danton or wave a gleaming sword high above his head like a war hero. He did not wear the face of arrogance or conceit. He only spoke in a soft tenor, with the most intense eye contact she'd ever witnessed, and everyone in his vicinity was compelled to listen.

In shock, the man dropped his rock into Sylvie's waiting hands. She hurriedly grabbed Gaspard, and the three left the scene while the crowd dispersed with slumped shoulders and empty hands.

Her brother walked with her support, blinking in the sun's glare. The blows and the tension had left him disoriented, so Sylvie shushed him and offered comforting words until his breathing became less labored.

Once they arrived at Chez Rohmer, Charles helped Gaspard to his bed.

Sylvie sagged onto the sofa in relief. "Thank you," she said to Robespierre. "You saved him."

He shrugged. "That man was going to drop the rock into your hands regardless of my words. You spoke well today and met him as an equal."

Fear is a powerful motivator, she thought. *For both sides.* "But you didn't have to chase after me—you didn't have to risk your life."

"Gaspard is a good man and a good secretary," he said.

A dot of happiness for Gaspard warmed her. "I didn't realize his role as secretary had been formalized."

Robespierre looked up the stairs toward Gaspard's room, then pointedly down at her. With a light smile, he said, "It was a *recent* decision."

She flushed. "Won't you stay for a cup?"

He declined and put on his hat. "Let me know if Gaspard requires any further care; though judging from today, you are the strongest woman this side of the Seine."

Sylvie heard of no more bread riots for the rest of the spring.

avril 1792

The chill was slow to leave, but at last tiny buds of green appeared on the frost-covered branches. Cornélie insisted on bringing Sylvie outside to help her tend to her garden once the earth thawed.

Using her hands like an *animal,* Cornélie dug a shallow pit in the center of the plot. Strands of her Stygian hair fell out of her plait and around her cheeks.

Sylvie sat on an opposing bench studying the basket of tulip bulbs nestled like figs in her lap. "Are these the *seeds*?" she asked, incredulous. She had never eaten a fruit with even a pit as big as those.

Cornélie's eyes crinkled with amusement, but she bit her lip when Sylvie pouted. "No, they are not tulip seeds. We use bulbs instead—the seeds take years to finally bloom. Bulbs flower within a single season."

Sylvie raised her eyebrows in mock astonishment. "So you mean to say that you use bulbs because you are rewarded more quickly?" She placed the basket on the ground and leaned forward, resting her elbows on her knees. "Such *impatience*, Mademoiselle. And after you so recently extolled the value of patience."

Cornélie's cheeks matched the rosy hue of the future tulips. Sylvie wanted to stroke the line of her flush from her jaw to her throat. "You can't help me from over there," Cornélie said, refusing to take the bait. She wore no hat, and the sun had already begun to change the skin of her nape from white to pink.

Sylvie grimaced under her straw bergère, itching her chin where the ribbon scratched. "We could play cards? Or I can model for you? Anything that doesn't involve"—she gestured toward the brush and weeds—"all of *that*."

Cornélie laughed from her little spot in the dirt, her smile wide enough to split her face in two. Wisps of hair clung to the parts of her skin lightly dampened from sweat. Sylvie lowered her voice and beckoned. "Can we not go inside where we have privacy? If you desire flowers so much, I shall send Louise to the market at Les Halles."

Cornélie dabbed her forehead with the back of her hand before patting the soil beside her. "I do not wish for you to buy me flowers; I want your company."

A line of hedges concealed them from the back door that led to the garden, but still Sylvie glanced over her shoulder before saying, "My company can be much more pleasing indoors." She arched her neck and bit her lip in her best attempt at seduction. "I appreciate your touch much more than a tulip can."

Cornélie's smile turned rueful, unable to deny her. She brushed her hands on her apron and stood. "What a man could accomplish with your powers of persuasion." She pushed back Sylvie's hat, exposing her face to the early-spring light.

Sylvie took Cornélie's thumb lightly between her lips and swept her tongue across the pad of her finger to sample the earthy taste of the garden. "Man has no power here." Cornélie's flush crept from her throat to the tops of her cheeks once more, and Sylvie tugged her silk ribbon to bring their faces close. She savored the lemon and black tea on Cornélie's breath, loving the control she had—and the control Cornélie was willing to surrender.

"*Cornélie*," Robespierre called out from the other side of the hedge. Sylvie pushed her lover away and straightened her hat. Cornélie stumbled backward, her arms still extended in a phantom embrace. Sylvie prayed Robespierre would not notice the redness around their mouths.

"I'm here," Cornélie answered in a daze, panting softly. Sylvie pointed to her lover's gown in exasperation, the top hooks of her bodice having been opened by Sylvie's deft touch. Cornélie tugged the bodice closed, covering the floral design of her stays inch by inch. "Do come round. I'm only doing my spring planting."

Sylvie fussed with the ribbon holding her hat in place, though when Cornélie moved to help, she swatted her hand away with an annoyed huff—insistent on doing it herself.

Robespierre emerged from the budding greenery, cravat askew, a thunderous shadow hanging over his brow. Gaspard trailed behind him with an armful of notes taken at City Hall, or the Hôtel de Ville.

As the Assembly didn't allow members of the previous government to serve as representatives, Robespierre and the most powerful voices pulled strings at their headquarters in the Hôtel de Ville—technically demoted to civilians, but in actuality influencing the Assembly with their power over the people.

Sylvie rarely saw her brother or Robespierre during the day, and she bolted upright so quickly she was shocked her spine didn't shatter.

"There's been a development," Robespierre said. After the bread riots quieted, the only stir that season had been the edict demanding mass collection of ex-aristocratic property. Sylvie knew that had caused a good deal of grumbling abroad, but beyond that edict no grand plans had reached her ears. She looked to Gaspard for a clue, but he frowned and kept his gaze on his mentor. "Cornélie, I must have words with you."

She went to him with a new determination written in her eyes and her back turned on the intimacy she and Sylvie had shared seconds ago. The remnants of dirt and tea and charcoal—the unique flavor of her kiss—soured on Sylvie's tongue. Despite her studies, despite her devotion to the couple, she was still an *other*.

The Incorruptible and his lover, framed by the untamed wilds of the Duplay garden, were the very image of modern French romance: Cornélie with her wholesome, windswept beauty and Robespierre with his modestly cut coat and tricolor cockade.

"I shall leave you," Sylvie said with false cheeriness. "And only add that whatever has befallen us may be solved with your cleverness."

As she passed them, Cornélie grabbed her forearm and said, "Do not go." She turned to Robespierre. "Has she not proven her loyalty to our cause? If I am worthy of your esteem, then so must she be."

For most of her life, Sylvie's very existence had been defined by doubt and mistrust. Her heritage created a cage that prohibited not only her ability to engage with her world but others from getting close. In fact, many went so far as to believe the devil himself lived in her very skin. But Cornélie, like a loving blacksmith, bent and shaped those iron bars into a Sylvie-shaped door that offered an escape.

Robespierre glanced between the three of them and solemnly nodded. "Tomorrow," he began, "the Assembly will announce war on Austria."

"*War?*" Sylvie repeated, aghast. She imagined columns of smoke rising from Paris, women dragged out of homes by their hair while children screamed. Taking short, shallow breaths, she tried to calm herself. Perhaps war was different from rebellion—the battles happened far away in distant fields, not outside one's door.

But Cornélie, stricken with shock, said what Sylvie could not. "Our country is in no position—financially or politically—to fight the Austrians."

"Exactly," Robespierre said with a tick in his jaw. "Marat and I vehemently opposed it at the Jacobin Club, but the Austrians represent the ancien régime that we ache to dismantle. It's the motherland of our disgraced queen, and the Jacobins want to take a stand." He ran his hand over his face. "Formally, they plan to declare war against the Habsburg monarchy." *The queen's family.*

Pale, Cornélie asked, "They vote tomorrow?" He nodded. "Is there any chance the motion will fail?"

She sounded hopeful—no, *desperate.* Gaspard only chuckled joylessly. "From what I've heard, the vote is naught but a formality."

Cornélie smoothed the invisible wrinkles in her apron, her bottom lip red and raw from anxious biting. "I believe I might take some tea," she said. "Sylvie, would you join me?"

"In a moment." Sylvie needed air and space before Cornélie started spouting off dark soliloquies about the looming war.

Gaspard offered to join Cornélie for refreshment, which Sylvie assumed meant rum, and they both returned to the house.

But Robespierre lingered behind, his back to Sylvie. Looking skyward, he said, "It may rain. You should be cautious." Several clouds hovered in the expanse of blue, though sun shone unfiltered over the garden. She could not tell if he spoke in riddles.

Pointing to the sky, she said, "But the sun shines, Monsieur."

"The heavens can be misleading. One can feel it; the air is heavy on the skin." She held out her palm, trying to feel the weight of the air. On Saint-Domingue, the rains came and went so suddenly, it was useless to predict them. Here, the seasons were defined and intractable. "I will take to my chambers. Good day."

All her life she'd been surrounded by fields of white coffee flowers, and Sylvie had never planted a thing. Though she must have played in the dirt as a child, she had no memory of earth under her fingernails or watching ladybugs scurry up her arm.

Slaves had dirt on their aprons and coffee cherries in their baskets. *You did not belong in the fields,* her father had told her as a girl when she asked why she did not have to work; she belonged in salons with a pretty fan in a crisp white linen dress. In her desperation to distinguish herself from her mother's people, Sylvie abandoned true childhood.

She knelt by the forgotten basket of tulip bulbs and dug a hole as she'd seen Cornélie make before, digging as deep as the length of her hand. Her ringlets kept brushing against her cheeks as she worked, and she wished she wore a tignon.

Time moved slowly as she planted those bulbs in neat rows. The tactile pleasure of moving earth to make way for potential life soothed her in the wake of a declaration of war.

When the rain began to patter on the upturned soil, Sylvie hardly noticed.

WITH MUD ON her petticoat and raindrops on her lashes, Sylvie entered Cornélie's bedroom triumphant.

"My darling, you are soaked to the bone!" Cornélie admonished. "Why is it that every time you open my door, you're in some state of calamity?"

Water dripped from the brim of Sylvie's hat, making it appear as though it had rained indoors. Cornélie rushed to find a towel as her damp companion laughed.

"No calamity at all." Sylvie revealed her mud-encrusted hands like a returned soldier brandishing a battle scar. "In fact, I planted all of your tulips."

Cornélie straightened in surprise and laughed in delight. "My little woodland nymph," she said, kissing Sylvie's smiling mouth as she wrapped her shoulders in a towel. "You will make spring arrive all the sooner with your efforts. But I think that we should leave the garden outside." She ran her finger down Sylvie's hand, drawing a line of clean skin beneath the dirt. "Perhaps a change of clothes and a wash?"

Sylvie agreed with a chuckle. She untied her hat and tossed it on the bed, which rustled the pile of papers she hadn't noticed sitting there. As Cornélie fetched a fresh gown from her wardrobe, Sylvie peeked at the scribblings.

Most of the sheets were letters from women, based on the flourishes of the writing, though the penmanship indicated several different correspondents. The wax seals, all unbroken, remained unstamped with insignia. And the letters themselves had been poorly treated—most crumpled and smudged.

Sylvie jumped when a metallic scrape echoed, but it was only Cornélie pushing the basin of water toward the hearth. "Come sit," she said, setting up a stool.

Sylvie obliged, letting Cornélie remove her fichu and unhook her bodice before she sat. Tenderly, Cornélie took the warm cloth—steam carrying the sweet scent of rose water—and wiped away the dirt from her neck and shoulders.

No matter how many times Cornélie undressed her, tended to her, Sylvie would always marvel at being serviced by a white woman and swallow a burst of shame. On Saint-Domingue, every need was attended by a blur of Black hands.

Cornélie wrung out the cloth in a separate bowl before soaking it again. After leaning into her touch, Sylvie asked, "Did you speak to Robespierre about this ugly business with the Austrians?"

Cornélie's mouth, already small, disappeared into a tight line. "Yes.

He and his faction obviously want any enemy of the Revolution destroyed, but they know the time is not right for war." Their faction, a triumvirate of Marat, Danton, and Robespierre, existed within the larger dominating party of the Jacobins.

Sylvie tilted her neck so Cornélie might reach her other shoulder. "Can he not persuade the Assembly?"

"He was forced out when they formed this new government—any previous elected representatives couldn't run again. He plans to work from the outside in with Marat and Danton."

Sylvie pulled away and turned to face her. "That sounds rather ominous."

Cornélie knelt so they were at eye level. "I meant what I said in the garden—I trust you. Am I right to?"

She may as well have asked if she could trust an anchor to hold a boat steady: in theory, yes, but chains break, currents are strong, and winds wail.

Instead, Sylvie skirted the question. "Is something wrong? Is Robespierre in trouble?"

Her deflection worked, and Cornélie paced in front of the fire. "He's going to organize a group of leaders to meet here to combat the Assembly's influence. In secret, of course. The mayor of Metz, journalists—"

Robespierre wanted to raise a mutiny in a carpenter's attic. "This could get him killed."

Cornélie disagreed. "In combination with the power of this group, he'll be impervious to scrutiny. We need action, not hiding behind closed doors and writing more pamphlets." She gripped the edge of the basin with both hands. "The Jacobin Club, of which we all are publicly supporters, grows more radical with every passing month. They shoot bullets at the government's feet and call it a dance."

Sylvie grabbed the cloth to clean under her nails. "Robespierre knows what he's doing."

"Does he?" Cornélie asked softly. "His notoriety may become his undoing. He's like a horse on the track—his blinders keep him from seeing his enemies in the same race—whose only goal is the finish line. Winning doesn't matter if everyone in the stands is dead."

Sylvie flinched at Cornélie's disloyalty. "How can you doubt him thus? He guides all of France through this turmoil, and rather than support him as you should, you disparage his efforts." She remembered the array of letters and asked, "What are all those letters on your bed?"

"They are what I wanted to speak of. We knew this war would come eventually, just not so soon."

"Who is 'we'?"

"A society," Cornélie began, "of women like us. Women who see everything yet have no ballot to voice their opinions. They think they've relegated us to the shadows, but they have only given us the cover of darkness." Cornélie fetched a letter and pointed to the addressee. "We use noms de plume when referring to one another, and code names for the Jacobins. This letter was meant for me, as it is addressed to La Muse. Your name would be La Mère."

Sylvie laughed, more out of shock than actual humor. "How you could possibly think that I'd want anything to do with this treasonous scheme is beyond me." Secretly meeting to sabotage the Jacobin party, the undisputed puppeteers of French politics—as a woman, no less—violated the fabric of society.

She could tell from Cornélie's flush that she very much wanted to shout, but the thin walls forced her into a harsh whisper. "Is it not more treasonous to see corruption and to do nothing?"

"You ask if you should trust me, but I think Robespierre should be the one asking you that question."

Cornélie traced the droplets of water falling down her chest. "I do not go against him; I only work against those who'd see his work destroyed. The people are fed on a diet of lies and fear, and with enough of that poison they will turn rabid."

Sylvie went to the bed and held up fistfuls of the soiled letters, throwing them in Cornélie's face. "You are a *spy*."

"And you are a coward." With that last burst of venom, Cornélie visibly deflated. "Forgive me. That was unfair."

Sylvie scoffed and plopped into the stool. "No, it's a fair assessment." She had run from revolution on Saint-Domingue, and she ran from it now.

Cornélie knelt before her again, her eyes less icy. "What do you want, Sylvie?"

"I want to feel *safe*," she choked.

"Safe?"

Sylvie crossed her arms against the chill in her heart. "All I ever wanted was security, safety. I came to this damned country looking for it—only to find Paris in a bloody shambles. I don't want to fear that my entire existence will be burned up in a night. I don't want my own family despising everything that I am. I will do anything I must to ensure my survival, despite everything working for my demise. Sneaking off to clandestine meetings for whisperings in the dead of night behind Robespierre's back will not make me safe."

"But what of the survival of France?"

Sylvie pushed two fingers against Cornélie's sternum, echoing the memory of Edmond threatening her with his gun. "I hope you never have a pistol pressed into your heart, my darling. It has a nasty way of rearranging your priorities."

juillet 1792

Once France officially declared war on Austria—the queen's home country—Sylvie saw less of Robespierre the man and more of Robespierre the leader.

As Cornélie foretold, the tension between the Jacobins and the more moderate Assembly catapulted Robespierre to the forefront of politics.

He and Danton fluttered in and out of the Duplay house like restless insects in the oppressive Parisian heat, cementing their influence over the increasingly anxious Jacobin Club. Marat, the always absent but never forgotten third member, often hid in sewers or attics to avoid persecution from the government—like a rat fleeing the cat.

And while Paris sweltered, Sylvie rarely left the house. Aunt Fifi assumed the heat was too much for her delicate constitution—a ridiculous notion, of course, as she had known nothing less than boiling temperatures since her infancy.

No, she stayed in to avoid not the heat but the menacing dread that prickled at her neck like sweat.

She had lived in Paris for close to a year now, and anyone could note that the physical natures of Paris and Saint-Domingue were vastly different. The streets were much busier, the architecture much older, and the faces much paler than those on the island.

And yet, the summer haze buzzed with the same friction that had sparked in Saint-Domingue—harbored in every hungry child's face or vengeful sans-culotte rather than slaves or *affranchis*. Though the bread riots had ended in late winter, she doubted the tension would lessen. The eerie sense of premonition kept her in her rooms or with Cornélie, who faced those uncertain months with the calm equanimity she had come to expect.

Her fears, despite Sylvie's vehement support of Robespierre, crept into the cracks left behind from the turmoil of Saint-Domingue.

With Robespierre so invested in preserving the fragile nation, Cornélie devoted more time to her. And the less time Sylvie spent with Robespierre, the more desperate she became for his lover. The passion for Cornélie trickled in, like a leaking dam, until her mind swam in thoughts of naught but her.

They retired to bed after a light supper of consommé and sullen stares over bread. Both women wore their thinnest chemises rucked up to their hips to try to keep cool.

"I'm sorry for what I said in April," Sylvie murmured, kissing Cornélie's white shoulder. Apologies did not come easily to her, nor did the vulnerability that often followed. But the tension was exhausting, and she preferred white flags to dueling gloves.

"As am I," Cornélie said, gracious as always. "I should respect your reticence to get involved."

They held each other in silence for about an hour, just enjoying the beating of their hearts and the familiar rhythm of each other's bodies. Cornélie rested her chin on Sylvie's shoulder—pressed so closely that her eyelashes tickled the line of Sylvie's jaw. The darker girl, her body soft and yielding in a way Cornélie's was not, draped her arms around her lover's middle.

"I do wonder, though," Sylvie said. "Why would my name be 'the Mother'?"

Cornélie smiled against her throat. "You emerged from a revolution that is the mother of ours." The language of the Enlightenment fed a people ready for freedom on Saint-Domingue, which in turn fed France. She'd escaped one revolution and fallen into another.

Mother of the Revolution, a title begat by circumstance, weighed on her head like a lead crown. She didn't want it, but duty rarely comes when bidden.

She ran her fingers through Cornélie's tresses, admiring the strands coiled around her hand. "And we are to just forget about the Americans?"

Sylvie practically felt her bedmate's eyes roll. "Pfft, we will not be grateful to them for bankrupting us for their freedom."

Cornélie moved through this world with a confidence she could not help but admire. But still, conviction alone could not spare even the most ardent of patriots from an untimely demise. "Promise me you'll be cautious," Sylvie said, tugging on those tresses just hard enough to add weight to her demands.

The artist picked at the charcoal under her nails. "I am neither alone nor unprotected."

"If I have learned anything, it's that politics are a most unwieldy mistress. One moment you think you're above reproach, and the next you're in prison, dying from the Italian disease."

"And would you still love me?" Cornélie bit the lobe of her ear, teasing it between her teeth. She stroked and caressed Sylvie like a brush on canvas. "Drunk on power and mad with syphilis?"

Sylvie pulled back with an arched brow and a cheeky smile. "And who says I love you at all?"

Cornélie rolled atop her muse, their noses brushing. "Your eyes do." Her own smile dared Sylvie to deny it, and not even she was so skilled an actress.

She had heard of love described as being pierced by Cupid's bow. But as charming as a plump cherub impaling innocents with arrows may be, her own experience reflected something more insidious. There was no moment of overwhelming realization, an arrow struck through her chest. Love began, for her at least, as an innocuous graze. But steadily it festered—the pestilence crawling up her limbs and into her heart—and she was doomed forever.

A slower process, to be sure, but as potent and as inescapable as an arrow drenched in asp venom. And so she succumbed to this condition, this love, pliant under Cornélie's generous tutelage and unwavering compassion.

Soft sighs, tender kisses, and muffled laughter made the music of that summer, deafening her ears to the battle drums just outside her door.

———

SYLVIE LOUNGED ON Aunt Fifi's most hideous chaise, again reading a book and grumbling about the rain. The torrent had not stopped since the day before.

The Paris Commune, the moderate council that governed municipal matters in the capital, had been falling out of favor as the Assembly had. Both governing bodies reflected a public opinion of moderation that no longer existed. Given this weakness, Robespierre and Danton's faction demanded space to operate out of City Hall—rather than a carpenter's salon.

This left Rue Saint-Honoré devoid of entertainment. To make matters worse, it was Wednesday; Cornélie studied with Regnault and his students across town—leaving Sylvie to entertain herself with a fair French translation of *A Sicilian Romance* until her brother burst in to disturb her peace.

Gaspard slammed open the double doors that led to the salon. He was fresh from some meeting, as always, waving a damp newspaper in her face.

"Perhaps if the newspaper sat still," she said, wiping the droplets off her cheek, "I could actually read it."

She preferred Robespierre's paper, *Le Défenseur de la Constitution*. Anything else she learned came by word of mouth in the Duplay house. Or from her excitable brother.

He didn't have the patience to let her read. Pink-cheeked with excitement, Gaspard declared, "Paris is in an uproar."

That was hardly news—Paris was in a permanent state of chaos. Discord clung to it like briars on wool. "When is it not?" she asked, turning the page of her newest romance novel.

He slammed the book shut, the pages snapping at her fingers like a recalcitrant dog. His eyes bored into hers, the still blue disturbed by his angst.

"I've just been to the Jacobin Club," he said with more calm. "This is different."

She waved him off. "Neither Robespierre nor Danton said anything about any disquiet," she snapped. "At least no more than the usual."

"Robespierre could not have foreseen *this*." He smacked a hand over the waterlogged newspaper, though the ink bled through the damp sheets. "Read the bottom of the first page."

She skimmed the small print, asking, "The Duke of Brunswick has issued demands upon France? Should I know this man?"

He gave a solemn nod. "He *wishes* you did. His Grace threatens to burn Paris to ashes if we harm the king or his family."

Gaspard quickly explained that Brunswick answered to the band of escaped nobility—rich aristocrats who had fled France and now wielded significant political power abroad—as well as serving as commander of an Austro-Prussian army. This Allied army marched to Paris as they spoke, ready to free the royal family and reestablish the old ways.

She crinkled her face in confusion. The more bloodthirsty revolutionaries called for executions, but that was just talk. "Robespierre says we do not need to kill the king; a constitutional monarchy is best," she said. "Why, then, does France fear this duke?"

He snorted. "We do not *fear* the duke. This little proclamation is a farce. We cannot be frightened into submission by ink on paper. But our enemies shall find that their manifesto has had the opposite effect."

She still did not understand and threw up her hands. "But nothing is amiss!"

"Come with me." He led her to the doorway of the house and onto the front steps. A familiar blanket of heat settled on her shoulders. "What do you see?"

She looked out into the Rue Saint-Honoré. The pale roads bespoke no riots or rage, only the listless air of early August. Putting her hands on her hips, she said, "I see nothing, Gaspard."

He ran his hands through his hair, already expanding in the humidity. "Exactly. It's a Wednesday—where are the shopkeepers? The wives? Truant schoolboys? The gardens at the Tuileries are abandoned; only the Swiss Guards remain."

On a second examination, the streets were not quiet: they were deserted. She strained her ears for any activity—horses' hooves, rolling barrels, the groan of a rusty water pump—but the only thing she heard was the thump of blood in her ears.

A flushed Lise hurried toward them, her chestnut curls poorly concealed by a hastily thrown-on cap. Gaspard ran down the steps to meet her, squeezing her hands and shoulders.

The short run had winded her, and she huffed a few times before asking, "*Mon chéri*, have you heard?"

"Of the manifesto? *Oui*, those insolent fools dare to—"

"No," she whimpered, gripping his arms. "No, not that. The Allied army has crossed the Rhine; they're on French soil. They brought the war to us." As the twilight of that blistering summer neared, it was clear that the battle drums had become cannon fire.

A WEEK HAD passed since Austria's army had arrived in France. As the distance between Paris and the invading army shrank, so did the people's loyalty to the king.

Effigies burned. Riots raged. The poor whispered about a rebellion similar to the one at the Bastille, about gutting their impotent sovereign and killing his wife in their virtual prison within the decaying Tuileries Palace. The masses blamed this war on the royal family; they assumed the absurd Duke of Brunswick came to the king's aid like a mindless hound.

Sylvie shared no hatred for the royal family as so many others did.

She often imagined the queen to be like Aunt Fifi: a sweet woman with a love of Rousseau and fripperies.

She put her energy into hating poverty, enslavement, injustice—rather than the last vestiges of a royal line hardly qualified to run a household, let alone a nation. Louis XVI had accepted a crown burdened with hundreds of years of atrocities and did not have the means, intellectual or financial, to rectify them. But he wore it anyway, bearing its weight to the detriment of millions.

And she had done the same: How could she hate an individual for a sin she herself had committed?

Nonetheless, Paris hungered for blood, and her denizens would find it at the Tuileries. Sylvie was no political savant, but she had seen a city before a revolt, tasted the iron in the air, smelled the ashes in the breeze. Paris planned to riot; half of the Tuileries' guard fled at some point during the day.

The sun began to set after their late supper, and the rumble of chaos shook the walls. Musket fire reverberated throughout the neighborhood, disturbing the relative silence of the meal. Aunt Fifi's nerves became so frayed she retired early.

After another shot echoed, Sylvie slammed down her fork. "This is unbearable. I'm going to the Duplays'."

"You will not," Gaspard said with a mouthful of bread, like he had the authority to stop her. "There are all sorts of sans-culottes looking for trouble. And a bourgeois lady like you is just the sort of trouble they're after."

She resented that she didn't have the street-savvy know-how that Cornélie or Gaspard did, but she liked to think her very image didn't attract hellions. Besides, dusk offered her some degree of protection.

She strode out with nary a second glance. "I refuse to sit and wait for a musket ball to burst through the door."

In truth, she was terrified, and only Cornélie and Robespierre could console her.

Ignoring her name on Gaspard's lips, she stumbled into the street. The sun nestled into the Parisian horizon, and a half-moon glowed in the violet sky.

Groups of men and women—all rather poor—stalked the streets. The Tuileries Palace was but a ten-minute journey on foot from Rue Saint-Honoré, thus attracting many would-be rioters to prowl the area and plan. Many carried axes, some muskets, others crude kitchen knives, the rusting weapons secured at their sides. Rust and blood looked identical in the dark.

She kept her head low and hands clasped over her bodice; the Duplay house was only a quick walk down the street.

An unkempt woman wearing a red liberty bonnet stepped in her path. She held a tiny carving knife in her left hand, looking Sylvie up and down with her lip curled in contempt. When Sylvie attempted to move around her, the woman blocked her steps.

"*Bonsoir,*" the stranger said. It was but one word, but Sylvie could hear the gutter in her accent. The odor from her clothes wafted nearer, and Sylvie struggled not to put her handkerchief to her nose.

She tried to rein in her disgust; it wasn't fair to judge a woman who could not afford jasmine oil and rosewater baths. Instead she offered a shaky, "Good evening, Madame."

"*Madame?*" the woman repeated before laughing. Her raucous chortle rattled her thin chest.

She looked at Sylvie as Alice had looked at Edmond: like a beaten dog who'd chewed off its chain. "Runnin' somewhere, queenie?" The knife twirled in her hand, itching to find purchase against skin.

"No." Sylvie lifted her chin. "I'm going just up the road." *I am a friend of Robespierre*, she wished to scream. *I'm not your enemy.*

"An awful nice dress yer wearin'." The woman proceeded to touch the fine sage cotton, her fingers leaving brown stains wherever they roamed as Sylvie failed to not flinch at her touch. "And 'n even prettier necklace."

She knew a threat when she heard one. "Yes." She lifted the string of pearls with trembling hands. Pearls were a cursed thing anyway: precious stones of salt and sand from the oceans where countless Africans met their end. "Would you like them?"

When the lady took the rusted weapon to her throat, Sylvie failed to stifle her cry. The woman gripped the necklace with her free hand and cut the strand with the knife, nicking Sylvie's skin in the process. The sans-culotte's smile widened as her victim whimpered.

She rested the cool edge of the blade at Sylvie's throat; a line of blood ran over the aging metal as well as the pearls, though Sylvie felt none of it. There was an intimacy in looking into the eyes of someone who wished her dead. Edmond's eyes had hidden nothing when he pressed the pistol between her breasts, a dark lust for her blood and for her body painting his face.

This sans-culotte's gaze spoke of hunger, of illness, of desperation, of revenge, of twisted satisfaction. The terror sewn into the fabric of her existence seeped into the hollows of Sylvie's chest.

The woman's bounty fell into her hands, and she shoved her hostage back with a sneer. "Thank you, Madame."

"Leave 'er be," an older sans-culotte woman said, a minute too late. Her expression didn't glisten like her partner's did. "We've got no quarrel with 'er." The thief shoved the necklace into her pocket with a grimace, the pearls in her fingers already smeared gray.

Between the fear, the smell, and the theft, Sylvie's eyes burned with tears. "*Vive la nation,*" she said, her volume just a hair above a whisper.

"*Vive la nation,*" the sans-culottes echoed before backing away. The elder woman pulled her companion along, and they both disappeared into the encroaching night.

Chapter Fifteen

Five or six hundred heads cut off would have assured your repose, freedom and happiness.

—Jean-Paul Marat

Air flooded her lungs once the danger passed. Ignoring the stares, Sylvie ran the rest of the way to the Duplays'. Banging on the door until a maid opened it, she stumbled through the entrance as her shock gave way to belated panic.

The Duplays were night owls, especially on an evening like tonight. She needed the quiet scratch of Cornélie's sketching and Lise's atonal hums while she embroidered—she craved the easy rhythm of normalcy.

She was never above false fainting spells for attention—or more often than not, for getting out of undesirable engagements—but she feared her fluttering heart may demand a real swoon. Her vision blurred at the edges like her head was submerged underwater, but a pair of firm hands kept her from slipping into the abyss of unconsciousness.

"Cornélie?" she asked softly.

"Send for a physician. Mademoiselle is not well," ordered a masculine voice. Her vision had yet to clear, and the ground seemed closer than it should be.

The man led her to a settee, guiding her down slowly by her shoulders. "No," she said. "Please, Monsieur, I'm fine." Now that she was off her feet, her senses trickled back to her. The blurry face of her companion focused into Robespierre. What little calm had returned left again; his hands still rested on her shoulders.

"You're bleeding." He spoke without any of the panic she felt. He covered the small wound on her throat with his palm, his hands scalding her clammy skin. He put pressure on the side of her neck; they appeared like two lovers about to kiss. "Fetch a poultice," he called out.

She shook her head, forcing a weak smile to her bloodless face in a way she knew wasn't half as beguiling as she hoped. "Monsieur, it is nothing. You needn't fuss; you have more important matters to attend to than the consequences of my clumsiness." It was easier to lie and claim she fell than to confess the truth.

Robespierre's palm never left her throat, his thumb grazing her jaw. She let the weight of her head rest in his hands.

"You have lost your senses, girl," he said almost to himself. "Are you mad? Why were you out at this time of night? Must you insist on jeopardizing your safety at every turn?" His gaze roved over her dirtied gown and tearstained cheeks; her idol's brow furrowed further with each smudge and errant curl.

His normally soft tenor had lowered an octave, and her paper-thin composure frayed under his criticism.

"I heard about the rumors, the plans—the musket fire wouldn't stop. Everyone knows what's coming," she said, and chewed on her lip. How could he understand the terror that leeched off her very soul? The leech grew fatter and fatter with every new threat to her safety, draining her of sense and calm. "And Gaspard *tries* to comfort me, but I feel safest here."

With you, she wanted to add. *Always with you.*

His frown made his severe face even fiercer. "Safe? *Look* at you." His grip on her shoulder tightened. How soft and supple her flesh appeared under the immovable grip of his fingers. "You have a wound on your neck. Your gown is filthy. I have two sisters, and I assure you I would not have let them out this late in Arras, let alone in Paris."

Cornélie would be furious. *Don't you care about your own life?* she'd say. *Are you truly so stupid as to think nothing would happen? Paris is not like Saint-Domingue!*

"I'm sorry," she sobbed as tears fell. "I'm sorry, Monsieur. It is my fault. *You* would have known what to do; *you* would have known what to say." She touched the space where the pearls should have been. "The sans-culotte—"

He pulled her closer. "Is that why you're distressed? Did a man . . . ?" His eyes ran so cold they could blacken flesh. Ice was a luxury she'd discovered in Paris, and while it made for a refreshing dessert or cooling ablutions, extended exposure could brand skin as a flame could.

His righteous fury at her supposed ravishment warmed her, despite the frigid tone. She enjoyed the sudden expression of emotion so much so, she was tempted to lie. Disgust with herself made her eyes burn.

"No," she said with emphasis. "A woman . . . she stopped me and wanted my necklace. She cut me. Laughed at me. The hatred danced in her eyes, Robespierre. But another sans-culotte woman stopped her, and she let me go."

He said nothing once Lise arrived with the poultice, only then releasing his grasp on her injury. Lise began exclaiming about her appearance as she tended the wound—clearly a bundle of nerves herself.

"Please make something for Mademoiselle from the kitchen," he interrupted. Sylvie's silent tears had yet to stop, and Lise's presence hardly discouraged them. "I think we could all appreciate the distraction."

Happy to be of use, Lise did as he bid.

"Something will happen tomorrow; the entire city knows it," Sylvie said as her trembles calmed. "Will they kill the king?"

Most Jacobins wanted Louis-Auguste dead, but this man could

not be the source of all their complaints. One man did not represent the entire Bourbon dynasty and all of its guilt.

Robespierre dabbed a salve across the circumference of her throat. "I do not pretend to know the future."

She shook her head, unwilling to let him pretend he was anything short of brilliant. "You knew about the war. You knew it would go terribly. You knew the *famille royale* was sending messages to Austria. You know *everything*."

He was silent as he finished cleaning the wound where Lise left off; like in all things, he tended with quiet precision and care. His knees brushed against hers while he cleared away the excess poultice from her neck. It stung, but no worse than the cut itself. She wished she had more injuries for him to mend.

Men die on the battlefield and you wish for more wounds? You deserved worse than what she dealt you.

He removed a strip of linen from a basin of warm water and pressed it into her palm. "Hold it against you like this."

His own hand now covered hers, their pulses bounding together in an erratic tempo. She hoped the wound would scar—a permanent reminder of this moment—and she sent a silent prayer of thanks to any and all deities for that sans-culotte.

"Will they kill the king?" she repeated. "Tell me."

He set his mouth into a firm line. "The Girondins claim to be moderates, and they control the government. But this storming of the Tuileries shows that their war-loving, passive politics are falling out of favor. The people will take the future of the country into their own hands, and they want the king's head." Her fingers twitched underneath his own. "I believe he should be tried for his crimes, though insurrection is the true trial of a tyrant."

The fire in his words, no matter how evenly he said them, added to the heat from his hands. His very being scorched her, and she adored every burn he left.

"*Should* they kill the king?"

He let a weighty pause linger in the charged air. "Men should use law, not swords."

A lofty axiom, but after her skirmish that evening and the memory of the hungry mob armed with rocks and bitter revenge, she acknowledged that law did not satisfy the people as violence did. When a wolf howls in hunger, you do not offer books and statutes: you feed it a bleeding carcass.

"But you"—her shaking hand went steady once placed on his chest—"are not like other men."

The ice left his eyes, replaced with an emotion she could not read. She arched her neck so his fingers touched more of her. His breath hitched before he said, "No." He dragged his hand from her neck, skimming her fichu and the line of flesh it concealed. "No, I am not."

I would let the sans-culottes steal every jewel, she thought, *if it meant he would touch me again.*

"Why did no one tell me you were hurt?" Cornélie stood behind the settee with Lise beside her. Robespierre clenched his fists in his lap, though his face remained impassive. "What happened?"

Guilt pricked at Sylvie's skin like tiny nicks from that rusty knife— not only because of her lust for Robespierre, but for her disregard for Cornélie's warnings. The people's rage had outgrown their means to contain it, and her impassioned pleas for her support now seemed less paranoid.

Sylvie moved away from him as she explained again what had happened. The cut stung as the poultice did its work.

Cornélie bent between them and turned her head to peruse the wound. "And he tried to play nurse, I see." She gave him an affectionate smile as Lise giggled behind her hand. "Well, I am glad he is a lawyer and not a physician."

Despite her earlier efforts to remain ensconced in her own envy, Sylvie had long ago accepted her love for the eldest Duplay; yet she schemed to ingratiate herself with her friend's virtual husband. He left an ache in her belly that only Cornélie could soothe.

And crueler still, even in that moment she desired Cornélie. Based on the green smudges between her fingers, she had been painting. She looked prettiest when she worked at her art; Sylvie loved watching her practice in the Duplays' private garden when the weather permitted. Sensuous and focused, her expression appeared almost vulnerable—only in her art could she be exposed.

Cornélie was strong, virtuous, and loyal, and every time Sylvie touched her, she hoped her lover's goodness would spread. Shame made her tears return.

"May I have a dress?" she asked now, motioning to the blood and grime from the sans-culotte's rough handling. "Brown is not my color."

They moved upstairs, where Sylvie could strip down to her chemise. She propped her head on Cornélie's shoulder while they lounged on the half-made bed. She stroked the exposed skin of her lover's ankle.

"You were very foolish today," said Cornélie. "It could have been much worse."

"Robespierre said the same. Sometimes I wonder if you share the same soul." She bit her lip, worried that Cornélie would hear the longing note in her voice.

But Cornélie only laughed, suspecting nothing of the infatuation. "I hope I am not too like Robespierre."

Offended, Sylvie asked, "Why not? He is the best of men." Cornélie insisted that he had faults aplenty, but Sylvie was unconvinced. "He may not be the handsomest of men—he has a pockmark or two—but his virtues more than make up for that failing."

Cornélie continued dragging her fingers along the slope of Sylvie's cheek and down over the muslin chemise that revealed more than it hid. "We cannot all be as beautiful as you."

Sylvie flushed, drunk off her desire. Mirroring Robespierre's earlier touch, she splayed her fingers over Cornélie's to guide them to her breasts. The fairer girl exhaled as she closed her eyes, allowing Sylvie to take what she wanted.

A knock at the door jolted them apart, and Cornélie called for the visitor to enter once her bedmate readjusted the chemise.

Lise came in and didn't pause for breath before saying, "The Paris Commune has been overthrown: Danton leads a new Insurrectionary Commune now."

Danton's words spoke loudly from Sylvie's memories, and his stormy eyes shone hungrier in hindsight. She saw him now—his imposing figure on the steps of City Hall, with shrewd Robespierre waiting in his broad shadow. "He called for all the newly appointed members to meet there, so Robespierre has left for the Hôtel de Ville."

If their faction controlled the governing body of Paris, then that meant they would hold a knife to the throat of the Assembly.

Sylvie's arousal flickered out, and she curled her limbs inward like a dying spider.

The girls crowded together in the bed for the rest of the night, waiting for news. And by three in the morning, a message from Gaspard revealed that the entire new Commune had convened at City Hall, and he had gone to join Robespierre as his secretary.

Cornélie slept in the middle of their trio, with Sylvie tracing the taut lines of her back.

Throughout the early morning, the dreadful tocsin bell clamored in the distance, making sleep an impossible feat. The tocsin rang specifically to announce the coming of war. But as she recalled the burning eyes of the sans-culottes, she was certain it was a war fought within France herself.

SYLVIE STAYED AT the Duplay house overnight, sharing the bed with both sisters as they waited for the imminent horrors the day would bring. The younger Duplay pressed her face into her sister's back for comfort, while the elder traced the shadows on Sylvie's cheeks.

Sylvie had heard so much talk of revolution—from the moment she landed on this unstable ground it was the thrumming hymn that never ended. But this overtaking of the Commune, the lifting of the anchor while a storm raged and waves crashed, signified a ship untethered to the past and free to sail into uncharted waters.

And while it wasn't immediately clear in those early-morning hours, the Insurrectionary Commune did more than order the old Commune into submission: it wanted the Tuileries as a trophy.

The storming of the Tuileries began at around eight in the morning, the sounds of musket fire and screams rousing the girls from their shallow slumber.

They were so close. Too close.

None of them wished to get out of bed, preferring the feathered comfort of the mattress and one another.

"Will Robespierre be all right?" Sylvie asked. While she gnawed on her lip and stared helplessly at the outline of the Tuileries through the window, Cornélie was the image of ease sitting at the end of the bed.

"He is more than a ten-minute ride from the palace. His faction controls Paris in all but name." Only when an especially loud gunshot fired did she flinch. "They will suspend the king's power and demand a new National Convention."

"No king. No queen," Sylvie said, more to herself than the others. "We shall be a *republic*."

The word weighed heavily on her tongue. All those books, those letters, those essays—they would amount to something tangible.

But revolutions demanded payment; while the people called for bread, she knew they meant blood.

SYLVIE SNUCK OUT the next morning at dawn, dressed in a plain blue gown of rough cotton with her head covered in a tignon, to face the remains of the insurrection.

The storming of the Tuileries lasted a single day, which she thought was hardly enough time to dismantle a regime.

The only thing she could say brought her to the edge of the Tuileries Garden was morbid curiosity. She had fled Saint-Domingue before any of the mass bloodshed reached her door; the only violence wrought was at the hands of Edmond, rather than those of the revolutionaries.

In her romantic mind, she wanted to prove her mettle—and prove she could stomach the justice that her Robespierre extolled so frequently—and see the consequences of liberty.

The Tuileries Palace used to serve as the royal residence whenever monarchs came to Paris. Designed in the Renaissance style, the perfectly symmetrical palace rose out of the garden's expansive hedge grove. It was old, ornate, and ostentatious in its grandeur.

She stood in the Place du Carrousel, staring at the main gate, which usually concealed the inner courtyard. But the gate hung, bent and twisted, by broken hinges—exposing the Cours du Carrousel.

The bloodstains crawled up the walls of the Tuileries like ivy.

Roughly a dozen red-uniformed guards, known as the Swiss Guards and the solitary defenders of the Tuileries, were strewn about the gate. The rioters had run them through with bayonets. The red of their coats camouflaged their wounds, but blood coated their gray faces. Scavenging birds scattered when she approached the bodies.

The flies did not scatter so easily. They freckled the bodies, lapping at the pungent sheen of fluid coating the exposed flesh.

Despite their training and superior weapons, the Guards had lost their battle with the French people. She gave the poor men credit:

they defended the Tuileries Palace even after their king fled in the night to stay at City Hall and under the Assembly's protection.

But the sans-culottes wanted to destroy the source of all their ills and breached the walls of the king's home to bring a definitive end to the monarchy. No guard nor army could match the fury of the mob—the people did not fight for duty but for their futures.

An era was over, and the new one had been ushered in with a bloody christening.

Sylvie stepped over the corpses to pass through the gate, walking the same path the sans-culottes had just a day before. Some said hundreds had died, others said thousands. All she knew was that the green grass now grew red.

She continued toward the maze of bodies, avoiding the eyes of other Parisians picking through the pockets of the dead. She overheard one man say to another, "Every gold louis goes to City Hall, you 'ear me?"

It comforted her some that the sans-culottes held to their code of honor.

The Garden had always been a source of pleasure to her in those early weeks of being in Paris, but now this veritable Eden seemed more like a circle of Hell. The carnage at the Tuileries was the Jacobin motto of "Live Free or Die" personified.

As she neared the deepest courtyard, the bodies became more and more butchered—the vast majority of them Swiss Guards. The red of their uniforms still hid the worst of the blood, but no amount of careful tailoring could hide their missing limbs and hacked faces. Cannon fire had done the worst of the damage; bits of singed flesh clung to the stairs.

Laborers had begun tossing the bodies and appendages into large carts, presumably to inter them in the catacombs for burial.

One particular young Swiss Guard lay at her feet, partially concealed by an equally youthful *fédéré* of the national militia. The fallen guard reminded her of Gaspard, with his yellow curls and angelic face, untouched by blood or anguish. His eyes were closed rather than open and blank, giving the illusion of peaceful slumber.

In a day or so the entire property would be cleared of bodies—the evidence of the Swiss Guard's sacrifice tossed into a mass grave and swallowed by the earth, while his fellow guards rotted in prison like the king. Perhaps compelled by his similarity to her brother, or by his beauty, or by his innocence, she removed one of his gleaming gold buttons. No blood or tissue besmirched its polished surface, and she slipped the token into her reticule.

The corpses began to smell after hours and hours in the August heat; the lack of a breeze allowed a blanket stench of rot to settle over the lush gardens. With her nose firmly planted in a perfumed handkerchief, Sylvie pressed on until she stopped at the interior of the pillaged palace. She had no desire to go farther, and the pile of bodies obstructed much of the entrance anyway.

To her disgust, some of the soldiers had been mutilated in more . . . personal ways. In a postmortem—at least, she prayed it was after death—means of humiliation, the rioters had severed their man parts and stuck the bloodied manhoods in their mouths.

Atrocities equal to and worse than those she witnessed at the Tuileries had occurred on Saint-Domingue. You could not judge a man for his actions done in pursuit of freedom—at least she had not been in the position to do so on the island. Those people endured true slavery, rather than the dramatic abstraction that Marat and other radicals used to justify their cries for blood.

But this violence, a raw rage manifested as slaughter, could not be the only way to win this war for liberty. She squeezed the golden button.

It would be rude to be sick near the dead, so she waited until she returned to the outer rim of the palace before vomiting into a bush. She wiped her mouth and walked slowly back to the Duplays'.

Chapter Sixteen

Let us be terrible in order to prevent the people from being so!
—*Georges Danton*

The household had just begun to rise when Sylvie returned. A maid exclaimed at the blood on her skirts, but she paid her no mind. She wearily headed toward the sisters' rooms, running into Robespierre as he descended the stairs. He looked almost as poorly as she knew she did; he had been up for a full day planning France's future. And yet, he was dressed to go out. He most likely had come home to change before returning to City Hall.

To her shame, her heart fluttered, and her cheeks burned at the sight of him, the destruction she'd witnessed somehow still not enough to douse her ardor.

"Mademoiselle," he greeted, though the inflection in his voice implied a question. She kept her eyes downcast, tugging the light cloak around herself. His gaze went first to the healing wound on her throat, then lower to the muck and deep-red stains on the hem of her gown. "You've been out."

She nodded, not trusting her voice between the earliness of the day and her tears.

He dropped down several more steps so that he was level with her. "Tuileries?"

She lowered her head farther, if that was possible, and nodded again. She refused to weep in front of Robespierre a second time. Progress demanded payment, and the price was steep. She'd witnessed that firsthand once before.

"You were very brave to go." She looked up then, her eyes shining from his praise. "Half the Assembly flees to the provinces," he muttered. "And yet a girl of twenty goes to pay her respects."

He bowed and prepared to leave, but her hoarse whisper held him back. The gold button weighed heavily in her reticule—a pretty token of an ugly sacrifice. Necessary evils are easier to bear when their victims don't decorate the nation's capital.

Touching the outline of the button, she said, "There were so many men. Hundreds."

The exquisite dead boy had died for a fleeing king and queen, died for a regime that could not protect him from the worst of their consequences. The Tuileries steps bled for a future she now feared, but Robespierre could prevent such a tragedy from happening again. He had to.

"Do not judge the people too harshly," he said, then set his mouth into a firmer line. But she did not judge the people; she judged *him*: Robespierre had power—he was a deputy to the Assembly. He couldn't pretend his colleagues did not orchestrate this insurrection to further the cause. Danton and Marat, the Jacobin sword and pen, led the charge with Robespierre as bannerman. "You have to break a few eggs to make an omelet."

She almost laughed at the absurdity of such a phrase. The slaughter at the Tuileries was not a few eggs or a few sorry, unlucky souls trampled under the weight of progress. She could be swayed to believe their sacrifice meant a brighter future for the rest of France, but she refused to accept that the nearly one thousand men doomed to an unmarked mass grave were only worth such trivial words.

He himself carried a shadow of shame about his shoulders: While his fellow men cried out for Prussian blood, he denounced the call to war. And when others wanted the king's head, he still insisted on a trial all men were due. But following the will of the others in his triad would mean doom for Robespierre and for herself.

Cornélie knew this tragedy would happen. Wild propaganda and self-interested leadership did nothing to curb the people's rage. This swift vengeance was like a doctor's remedy—the dose alone determined if it was a poison or a cure.

And Sylvie had preferred to hide behind Robespierre's promises rather than ensure his security, as well as her own. Cornélie offered her a role in the solution to this endless violence, and yet she chose cowardice.

She wanted to survive, and she could not depend on Robespierre alone. She took a shuddering breath. "I couldn't have put it better myself."

AFTER SHE SCRUBBED the smell of day-old death from her hands and face, Sylvie rushed to Cornélie's room. Huddled over a basin of murky gray water, Cornélie washed her paintbrushes as she hummed.

Sylvie knelt beside her and pressed a kiss to her rose-scented cheek. "I will help you end this massacre in any way necessary."

Cornélie looked at Sylvie's hem and reeled. "Why are you covered in blood?" She grabbed Sylvie's skirt to examine the browning stains. "You're positively ashen."

"I had to see it," she murmured. She gathered some brushes and lathered the coarse bristles with soap. "I had to see the Tuileries."

Cornélie did not scold her like Sylvie expected; she only resumed washing, but her gaze was focused on the hem. "And the Tuileries changed your mind?"

"I want to feel safe—that remains the same." The red from the paint stained the fingers she'd just cleaned. "But I realized leaving my survival to a mob"—she cracked a wry smile—"decreases my chances of making it out of this Revolution alive. No one is protected while innocent men are butchered with less dignity than a pig."

She had first put her faith in family and then put her faith in men. Both had failed her, so she needed to put faith in herself.

Cornélie, dirty hands and all, gripped Sylvie's face and pulled her into a kiss. It lingered until she rested her forehead against Sylvie's. "You magnificent woman."

Sylvie grimaced. "What do I need to do?"

Late août 1792

Sylvie's new resolution was easier said than done. Since the insurrection at the Tuileries, roughly half of the Assembly had fled the city—fearing the very populace they swore to serve. Given the fresh graves dug for those who rose against the people's will, Sylvie did not judge them too harshly.

But with an impotent Assembly and an all-powerful Commune, there was little they could do except keep the pathways of communication clear. So she accepted the role of carrier pigeon—dressing in plain clothes befitting a shopkeeper's daughter rather than a bourgeois princess.

Sylvie kept the letters in her bodice, the paper cool but warming from her skin. Her brief rendezvous with that sans-culotte had made her more cautious: if anyone were to demand she empty her pockets, they would only walk away with a few assignats and some lint.

September was only a few days away, and already the temperature crept lower. Without a summer sun keeping watch over her errands, she could navigate the sections with a modicum of pleasure. Delivering missives throughout the city gave her the opportunity to better understand the organization of Paris.

The capital was recently reorganized into a hierarchy of forty-eight sections rather than sixty districts. The Duplays and Rohmers lived in the first section, known as the Tuileries section, and shared that distinction with the Tuileries Gardens and the Place de la Révolution.

She walked parallel to the Seine to meet her last contact near the Place des Victoires. The place boasted a near-constant flux of crowds or passersby. Its most iconic feature was an ostentatious statue of Louis XIV atop a horse at the center of the circle.

As she approached the place, the cries of a crowd overwhelmed the normal sounds of activity. A herald stood on the statue of the Sun King, holding the rearing steed's hoof for balance, as he shouted into the raging crowd.

France contained a patchwork of languages from Flemish to Basque, and the general public was semiliterate at best. Heralds, usually just men with newspapers, shoveled the news directly from print to greedy ears.

"The People's Friend," the herald declared, referring to Marat's nickname, "beseeches his brothers and sisters of liberty to begin a new bloodletting to purge our nation of mutinous enemies." His audience cheered, and he held up a hand to silence them once more. "*The Prussians draw nearer, the prisons overflow with conspirers—we must unleash a fury of our justice greater than the Tuileries or the Bastille, so that all of the monarchs of Europe tremble upon their thrones.*"

The Tuileries had *just* hosted a public memorial to those who lost their lives breaching its gates. The king rotted in a cell.

And still Marat ordered a massacre from his sickbed?

They sang out his name and pledged their muskets, their kitchen knives, and even their broomsticks to his rallying cry.

Sylvie backed away in horror and shielded her face with her cloak. To witness his words work their blood magic over the vulnerable— it was not love or fear, but witchcraft. And Robespierre could not afford to go against a man who wielded the influence of a prophet.

The flickering thoughts of La Mère and secret societies were snuffed out. The letter burned in her bodice, but she only had the wherewithal to return home.

29 août 1792

Sunset wouldn't begin for hours, but Sylvie hardly cared. She sank into her bed and prayed for the numbing promise of sleep.

And yet, deep sleep is a luxury that revolution does not afford. Ever since the fateful night when Gaspard had roused Sylvie from her bed, glass breaking in the distance and smoke clouding the air, she never allowed her mind to fully succumb to the beckoning call of restful sleep. She lay in bed, muscles tightly coiled and ready for use, chasing the dark promise behind her lids.

A faint whisper could jolt her awake—so the screams breaching Chez Rohmer's walls from outside sent Sylvie running from her bed before her eyes had even opened.

Gaspard and Aunt Fifi sat in the salon, both rod straight despite the exhaustion weighing down their features. The shouts and cries rang out continuously, but no one moved to find the source.

Sylvie ran a hand over her face, trying to wipe the tunnel vision from her eyes. "I hear a woman screaming, but neither of you seem inclined to do anything about it?" Aunt Fifi let out a shrill sob.

Sylvie strode toward the door, but Gaspard held her back. "Don't—there's nothing to be done."

Sylvie tore her arm away, recoiling from any touch at all. "Done about *what*?" She didn't wait for an answer but instead went to the largest window facing the street. Dusk danced across rooftops and painted the street with blush and gold.

With both hands pressed to the glass, she searched Rue Saint-Honoré.

Across the street, a National Guard member pulled a bourgeois woman down the steps of her home by her hair.

The woman, dressed in her nightclothes with a robe thrown over, wailed and kicked her bare feet as her children looked on in tearful distress. The children sobbed and reached out to their mother, but another guard restrained the father—suffering from a beating of his own—from going to her.

She spat at her captor, earning a backhanded slap across her face. A rivulet of blood ran from her nose and down her mouth, leaving her bared teeth a shade of pink.

Something cold and sharp bloomed in Sylvie's chest, wrapping its tendrils around her heart and lungs. The air warmed and seabirds shrieked overhead. Wind carried salt and ashes from frothing waves and burning fields.

"The arrests are happening everywhere. If you try to intervene"—Gaspard placed a steadying hand on her wrist—"they will consider that treason and imprison you as well."

She shoved him away and flew out of the house while Aunt Fifi yelled after her. The tidy row of gray houses shimmered under the lamplight, making them glow orange. Rage made her limbs lighter, her feet faster, and her mind loud and quiet at once.

The guard dragged the woman toward the carriage, more of a jail cell welded to a cart, and did not notice Sylvie's silent approach.

She tackled them both, the officer and his charge, to the ground. The other guard hesitated: he alone kept the husband, a burly fellow, from barreling toward his wife.

But Sylvie did not pay him any mind; an army of men could have surrounded her and she would only see the guard snarling beneath her. She applied nails and teeth and elbows to pry the mother free. She wished she carried a knife. His white waistcoat and breeches, unlike the Swiss Guards' uniform, did not hide blood. A stab wound could paint his uniform red.

After a fierce bite to his wrist, the prisoner twisted out of his hold. But Sylvie did not stop her assault. Edmond, Marat, Gaspard's stupid friends—they needed to taste blood and fear in their mouths, feel the warmth of urine spilling down their thighs, tears burning their eyes. Then she would be safe, then she would be free—

The *click* of a pistol stole her breath.

Unbeknownst to her, several guards had emerged from the victim's house with boxes of goods and two muskets. One drew his weapon in her sight line, and the view restrained her better than all the chains in every prison in Paris.

She crawled backward from the encroaching guard. They all shouted at her, from the family's pleading to the officers' demands, but the mouth of the pistol spoke the loudest.

Her bare feet couldn't find purchase on the cobblestones, slick with rain and filth. Edmond was going to kill her. Rage melded into terror, two sides of a toxic coin.

"Edmond," she moaned in a soft plea. "Please, please, *mon Dieu*, please."

Arms wrapped around her—more yelling, more orders.

"I will put lead in her *fucking* skull." The pistol trembled, untested and unsure. Edmond's pistol never trembled: his hands had been so steady.

"She was overcome. She did not understand the scene in the poor light." That was not Gaspard's voice; it was too soft.

"She tried to claw my damned eyes out!" Edmond's eyes were not so round or blue. They had been black and red rimmed.

The interior of the de Rosiers château faded into a residential street. She wore no more than a chemise: the island air of her imagination vanished, replaced with the brisk chill of a Parisian night.

The arm holding her steady belonged to Robespierre. "Which is inexcusable. I will personally see it addressed, *Citoyen*."

The guard she'd attacked did not wear her violence well. Scratch marks bled on his jaw, and his lip matched the wound he had given to the mother. She undoubtedly left imprints of her teeth all over his torso.

"And the delegate is a man of his word," Gaspard added. The shaken guard immediately lowered his weapon, and Sylvie shuddered against Robespierre's chest. He wore no wig, revealing cropped brown curls. Sans powdered white hair, he did not seem so old and sage but more like a man a few years older than her brother. "Surely, there is something I can offer you, sir, for this affront?"

A bribe offered to the wrong man meant political suicide, but the guards nodded in agreement. Again, her family's wealth and privilege spared her from the consequences due.

Assignats exchanged hands, and the mother—once again in custody—left in her mobile prison. The official snapped his whip to urge the horses forward. A dog yipped and whined around the wheels.

"I'm so sorry," Sylvie whispered to no one in particular: to the family she couldn't save, to the enslaved men and women she didn't try to save. Robespierre placed his coat around her shoulders.

"You wanted to spare her."

"I wanted to see him suffer. And all men like him suffer." She needed to clear the guard's skin from under her fingernails.

"It is not unreasonable to want vengeance for centuries of wrongs. But it would take years to satisfy that bloodlust." She nodded, still holding on to his arm like it kept her above water. Gaspard remained with the weeping family, most likely offering his ample connections and soothing words. "Your passion does you credit."

She turned in his arms to face him. "I'm frightened of myself."

"I'm not scared of you," he said.

She draped the coat around them both and leaned into his shoulder.

He wore only his shirt haphazardly tucked into breeches. The sole thing separating them was the scratch of wool and cotton. "Then I hope you never incur my wrath."

"I admit a weakness for dangerous things," he said with a gentle smile. He had once said he didn't so easily reveal his vices, and here he was—bare to her as she was to him—confessing to her. "Cornélie will be home shortly." Her name doused the burn in Sylvie's skin.

They walked down to Chez Rohmer with Gaspard at their heels.

Robespierre returned home, leaving his coat on her shoulders. She watched him until he disappeared down the street.

The family's cries echoed like birdcalls.

A thin pane of glass separated her from the brutality outside, but it may as well have been an ocean.

"*Who did this?*" she asked through clenched teeth. Her nails scratched at the window.

"Our precious justice minister," Gaspard spat from behind her. "Danton, the fucking weasel."

She had made a villain of Marat and did not see Danton for who he was. Evil did not always lurk in shadows and pens but wore fine clothes and roguish grins in broad daylight.

Gaspard continued, "After the Assembly issued a curfew, he ordered the section commissioners to go to each of their sections and arrest any suspected militants. They're just ransacking and arresting on rumor alone."

Working as Marat's conduit, Danton would provide his pound of flesh. Scenes like this were happening all over Paris, and the dam would burst—resulting in a mass panic as the Prussians pressed closer and Paris destroyed itself from the inside out, like a dog gnawing on its own tail.

A few houses down, Sylvie spotted Cornélie, a vision in pale blue, standing on the landing of Chez Duplay. She held herself, looking pale and slight like a single unlit candlestick lingering in the dark.

Sylvie let her forehead fall against the window as the silence of defeat crept over the street.

Chapter Seventeen

In a few days, I will have them all guillotined in Paris.
—Jean-Paul Marat

30 août 1792

The salon held at the Duplay house was more of an extended political meeting than a social party. But Sylvie dressed with the same care she would have if it had been a ball held in her honor.

The hopelessness of the past few days left her bitter—she anticipated that tonight the endless cross talk of brilliant minds would ground her like Robespierre's arms did.

Cornélie had sent a short note advising her to keep to patriotic dress. Her handwriting leaned heavily to the right and took up as little space as possible. She pressed too firmly with the quill and left a series of small blots—the heaviness of her angst made the slip of paper weighty in Sylvie's hands. The absence of an affectionate closing stung.

Sylvie wore a newer gown, a higher waist than she was used to. Fashions changed so quickly, she could never keep up. But the damned thing was at least covered in blue, white, and red. Louise helped her pin a tricolor to her fichu.

Gaspard, frustrated with his limited role as secretary, seethed to her as she set her curls. "Marat will be there," he said around sips of gunfire. "He pretends to be a sans-culotte, uncouth and abstaining, but it is a curated act."

Marat had a troubled start in academics due to a modest upbringing and unfortunate appearance. The nobility only sought his care as a physician once his enlightened mind made him patently famous. "Marat was a court physician and a favorite of many a noblewoman," Sylvie soothed. "Do not let him belittle your own background you had no choice in."

His most recent public appearance, a rarity due to his few periods of relatively good health, was during the insurrection at the Tuileries— putting even more weight on tonight's salon.

As a final touch, Sylvie tied a red ribbon around her throat. The macabre detail sent a tiny thrill down her spine.

She headed to the Duplays' alone, as Gaspard had left prior. The front door was unlocked, and when she opened it, a wave of male voices blasted out into the street.

Danton's voice drowned out the rest. He banged his fists on the table as he berated another deputy: "Did you not learn your lesson the first time, you idiot?" Sylvie hung just behind the wall, pulling back her skirts to keep her presence hidden. "Arrests flow like the Seine. Haven't you had enough?"

She suspected the object of Danton's ire, and a darting glance confirmed it. She had walked in during a heated debate between the scar-faced Danton and pockmarked Marat.

Each man lacked the subtle manners of Robespierre, and their notorious disfigurements made them both iconic and fascinating. Danton cut the most imposing figure in any room he entered. But Marat, while lacking Danton's bulk or baritone, captured the room's attention with skill.

"We must sound the alarm bells," Marat said. His voice contained a slight rasp—like he was being choked. "The people have the right to know that the Prussian army is practically outside our gates!" His skin never shook its clammy pallor, except for the red spots of healed scars. The odor of medicinal vinegar for his rashes reached Sylvie's nose from across the room.

Danton's natural sneer deepened. "That will incite mass panic, which I believe is exactly your intention."

Marat persisted. "They *should* panic. If the royalist scum filling our prisons catch wind of possible rescue, there will be a mutiny."

Danton threw his fists on the table. "Prisoners are more easily eliminated than Prussian mercenaries. So forgive me for not caring for your unfounded fearmongering."

"I care about having a city to protect," Marat replied, spittle flying from his mouth. "The monarchists have spies and allies to spread their poisonous ethos of greed and corruption. Paris cannot be safe until the people devour those traitors' palpitating hearts!" He readjusted his head wrappings, presumably soaked in vinegar, since they had shifted during his tirade. "And I still argue that you, Robespierre, should serve on the Tribunal to see that justice is handed out."

Robespierre sat in front of the shuttered east-facing window, the evening glow obscured by heavy curtains meant to ensure privacy. Cornélie, clear-eyed and calculating, stood behind him with a steadying hand on his shoulder. He had been more of a listener than a participant, taking in Marat's paranoia with a neutral expression. They had the presence of co-regents staring down their squabbling advisers.

Swirling a cup of watered-down *vin rouge*—the Jacobin drink of choice—Robespierre said, "The same man ought not to be a denouncer, an accuser, and a judge."

Marat glowered at Cornélie and took a bitter swallow of brandy.

After a few minutes of anxious debate, the deputies agreed to ring the alarm bells if the Prussians took Verdun.

They digressed into mumblings among themselves, and Sylvie took the opportunity to go to Gaspard's side. "I don't understand Marat's anger," she whispered in their corner of the room. About a dozen people occupied the salon—a combination of deputies, allies, and Duplays—as they discussed the repercussions of the insurrection just weeks before and the weight of the encroaching army. "The vigilance committees are already arresting everyone. The Church is dissolved, the monasteries closed, émigrés' property confiscated . . . what more do the people want?"

Gaspard leaned back against the wall, his arms folded across his broadened chest. The year or so under Robespierre had brought about many changes in him. The Revolution had stolen his boyish grin, and his light hair had darkened from spun gold to an ash blond without the constant sunlight, while his increased activity strengthened the soft body left underworked in Saint-Domingue.

"It's the Prussians," he said. "The Duke of Brunswick approaches Verdun—"

Sylvie flapped open her fan and spoke behind the painted silk, an opulence she refused to abandon. "I know, I know. But we have an *army* to deal with such things. We are enlisting thousands at the Champ de Mars as we speak."

Gaspard snorted. "An army of cobblers and bakers."

"Truly, things are not so dire? Verdun is still so far away."

He traced the filigree on his flask. "He is cutting his path to Paris, and I assure you that the duke will make good on his promise of retribution."

Sylvie made an irritated huff. "So why are we arresting priests instead of training soldiers?"

Gaspard let his head rest against the wall molding. His Adam's apple bobbed when he swallowed. "Marat believes the detainees must be cleansed. A time for daring, he says. Danton agrees."

"The prisoners are in jail cells. How are they a threat?" She looked over to Robespierre. He never advocated violence directly, but he sympathized with the people's hunger for revenge—just as he had sympathized with her rage the day before. "They are half-starved rat feed."

She could tell her brother shared her confusion, but he, too, had a talent for echoing the opinions of others like they were his own. He sipped from his gunfire flask. She sighed: he drank too much these days. "We fear a counterrevolution if the Prussians breach our walls."

"What does Robespierre think? He didn't say much when Danton and Marat went on their rant."

Gaspard shook his head. "Danton may speak the loudest, but Marat has the people's hearts. Robespierre will never risk going against popular opinion, and Marat controls it absolutely. It's uncanny." He took another swig from his flask and went to Robespierre's side.

Sylvie moved to pour herself a glass of wine. She missed the champagne of old, but the decadent drink was considered too unrepublican. She finished her glass and poured herself another.

Marat's claws dug into every person here. Even in her hatred for him, his talons scraped along her spine.

"Pour me some, would you?" Cornélie asked a touch louder than necessary. Sylvie offered her a cup, watching the red wine slosh along the rim of the glass.

"Breathe," Cornélie said, for her ears only. "He is just a man. Beneath the fury and costumes—he is just a man." Sylvie let her fingers graze Cornélie's, but she did not reach for her hand. The ribbon on her throat tightened with every sip.

The smell of vinegar grew more pungent, and Sylvie went rigid. Marat approached them with a limping but purposeful gait. "Duplay," he said. She felt the warmth emanating off him from an arm's length away—fever, most likely.

"Marat," Cornélie greeted him with a polite dip of her head. Though he stood shorter than them both, he insisted on meeting her gaze.

His eyes flicked briefly on Sylvie, disinterested, then focused on the artist. "What is your view of all of this? Robespierre keeps you close; you must have an informed opinion?" He did not move his lined, dark eyes away for a moment.

"I have opinions, surely, but they cannot be as informed as a deputy's, Marat." Cornélie could not speak without fear that any disparaging remark would get back to Robespierre, and she only smiled tightly. "I must speak with our cook. Do excuse me," she said. "Sylvie, care to accompany me?"

"Go ahead without me, my friend," she declined. She wanted to put flesh on the shadow she feared—to learn what she could from the man who threatened the security of herself and others. Cornélie hesitated briefly before removing herself with a diplomatic air.

Based on gossip about his betrothed, Marat was not impervious to a woman's charm. But Sylvie did not know him as a man, which would be necessary to encourage loose lips. She needed to gild her interrogation in a sensual, patriotic package. "The People's Friend," Sylvie said with delighted pleasure. "I haven't had the honor of meeting you formally."

"You're the mulatta who hangs about with the Duplays," he deadpanned. He spoke in plain, ragged French. She doubted the accent was genuine and pretended his manners didn't unnerve her.

"I am, though I prefer answering to Sylvie Rosiers. I must wish you congratulations on your role as head of the Committee of Surveillance." She prayed his position would not have him ruling over graves.

He swirled what little remained of his brandy and ignored her comment on his promotion. "Your brother has become Robespierre's little shadow. Surprising for a nobleman from a coffee plantation."

Now was the time to sharpen her blade. She leaned forward as if to whisper a secret. "My brother and I left that world, renounced it in its entirety. The crossing to France was the end of an old life and the beginning of a new—a baptism, if you will. It certainly rained enough on that blasted voyage."

Marat's jaw twitched with what Sylvie hoped was humor.

"I'm sure you can understand regretting past luxuries," she continued. "Why, you were a court physician, were you not? I cannot imagine anything so grand!"

She *could* imagine it, but she played the simpering and awed newcomer with glistening eyes. Marat fed off sycophants and dread, and she would keep him satiated if it meant he revealed himself to her.

"It is how you said: we cannot be bound by our past transgressions."

"And nor should France," she said, hoping to guide the conversation into specifics. "We move toward democracy, but I worry that sympathies for the old ways may turn treasonous. Even Danton seems to have gone soft."

"Danton is a toothless hunting hound. Do not let his barking frighten you." A cruel joke, given the origins of his scar.

"But if *you* cannot rein in those moderates, then who can? The prisoners may mutiny."

Marat's face twisted like a child's when tasting a lemon for the first time. "Danton knows how to heel like the dog he is. When the time is right, he'll submit to the will of the people." He emptied his glass, bringing a flush to the apples of his prominent cheeks.

"And who knows the will of the people better than their Friend?" She withdrew her fan, letting its silk ground her in the moment. In a man's effort to show strength, he often reveals his weakness: Marat had all but confessed to private dealings with Danton—the invalid wielded influence over more than the masses. This explained Danton's aggressive ordinance increasing arrests.

A hopeful lilt in her voice, she asked, "And he will take the suspected villains to trial?"

Marat shook his head like she was a simpleton. "A trial is not needed when I have the honest accusations of loyal citizens. And our fair justice minister will happily exercise the people's will."

"Imprisonment does not prove guilt, Monsieur," she said, trying to keep her tone gentle and questioning. "Surely, a man of the world such as yourself knows that a person could have much to gain by falsely denouncing a neighbor? Some of those detained must be innocent by sheer numbers alone." Bloody teeth and children's screams gave weight to her words.

He narrowed his eyes. "Well, you have a poor opinion of the French citizenry."

Her gentleness left her like the air in her lungs. "My good sir, I *am* a French citizen."

"You are a colonist," he spat out. "And a woman, for that matter. You were not raised here. You did not plow this land—"

"Only because my father gave me my freedom and denied my mother hers."

He stepped closer, one part indignant and one part intrigued. The vinegar made her eyes water; she hoped he did not think his bullying could make her weep. His skin may cause him pain, but so did hers, a pain that no number of vinegar baths could soothe. "I will not know happiness until every enemy to liberty has been washed from this earth."

Sylvie shuddered. Marat contained a ferocity that could destroy a thousand men. His eyes glinted with that same darkness Edmond's had had. It bespoke obsession, intractability, and reckless youth. Instead of using his gifts to heal, he only sought to fracture.

She snapped her fan closed and tucked it into her reticule. He needed to trust her, or at least be attracted. She doubted he experienced any physical closeness given his painful condition, making him susceptible to the heady powers of touch. With steady fingers—due to the calming power of two glasses of wine in an empty stomach—she buttoned the top part of his undone waistcoat while saying, "Then we have a common goal." Sylvie let his black eyes capture her own, and she pressed her fingers against his chest. "I am glad you are the People's Friend, but I hope I may be yours as well."

He grazed her fingers, which still lingered on his waistcoat, with his own. He had calluses from hours of writing, a badge of honor among all these men of letters. "I would not dare deny your friendship, Miss Rosiers."

After giving her one last hard stare, he returned to his place by Desmoulins and Danton.

Gaspard replaced him in seconds, but Sylvie spoke before he could ask why she held Marat in such rapt attention.

"He's like Edmond," Sylvie muttered. "He doesn't *see* me, not really."

"You're a woman," Gaspard said with a shrug.

She snorted into her third glass of wine. "Half of this country is women. Women stormed the Bastille. You'd think he would listen to what we have to say if he's trying to control it."

He smiled sadly. "He doesn't see it that way. Most men don't."

"Then they should open their eyes. I remember all the dead men at the Tuileries; women killed scores of those soldiers. And I promise you, they didn't die thinking, 'Oh, if only a man had killed me instead.'"

The creaking and shuffling of chairs interrupted them. Deputies rose from their seats en masse and collected their coats from the sisters Duplay.

"We're off to City Hall, Rosiers," said Robespierre, but he looked to Sylvie while he said it—a worry line between his eyes. Gaspard donned his frock coat like battle armor.

"I didn't know it would be like this," she said to no one in particular. She thought back to the beautiful Swiss Guard dead at her feet, and the notion of a peaceful republic seemed no more than a fantasy.

Later, she sat at Gaspard's unused desk to write her account of the evening with Marat. Cornélie encouraged writing her accounts of the things that terrified her most: a library of horrors. Her hand cramped from the hours spent detailing the suspected duplicity of Danton.

Unaware of the ink stains, she massaged her hands with rose oil, smearing the ink all over her fingers.

She rested her hands flat on the desk, marveling at their strangeness. Normally, her hands were unmarred and kept soft. Yet, the top of her palm had red welts where calluses would form, and her fingertips had black blots from pressing too close to the end of the pen.

Sylvie decided she liked them better this way.

Chapter Eighteen

Finally, I saw a woman appear, pale as her underclothing, held up by a counter clerk. . . . They made her climb onto a heap of corpses. . . . Then a killer seized her, tore off her dress and opened her belly. She fell, and was finished off by the others. Never had such horror offered itself to my imagination.

—Nicolas-Edme Rétif, on the September Massacres

3 septembre 1792

September in France meant the oppressive humidity of August drifted away, but the chill of autumn had yet to descend.

The uprising in Saint-Domingue had unfolded before Sylvie's eyes with perfect clarity. Slavery in and of itself was an absolute evil, and under Robespierre and Cornélie's tutelage she decided all free men should share the same rights—regardless of skin color. The war in Saint-Domingue was brutal, but she had no trouble sympathizing with the ex-slaves' plight even if she wasn't in perfect agreement with their methods.

In Paris, however, her world was not so neatly divided.

When surrounded only by the Duplays and Robespierres, the tenets of their utopia so clearly outlined on paper, she understood. But monarchs were imprisoned, guards mutilated, and children left orphans. The very appearance of wealth condemned people as traitors.

Sylvie wrote to Cornélie in short notes back and forth—she didn't dare leave her house as the tocsin rang. She did as Gaspard asked and kept the windows covered and the door locked, oblivious to the justice—or revenge, depending on the newspaper—occurring in the streets.

Until she received Gaspard's message insisting she take the carriage to meet him at the Hôtel de Ville. He wouldn't send for her unless something truly dire propelled him to.

"Shall you come with me, Aunt?" she asked, mostly out of politeness. The arrests, many of which were of people Fifi knew, kept her aunt abed and rattled.

Fifi clucked nervously, like a hen smelling a fox near the roost. "I've never in all my years seen Paris so fraught. I would rather walk on hot coals than on those streets."

Sylvie shrugged and sent for a more modest coach to be fitted for her journey to City Hall. She did not have the luxury of doing nothing. Gaspard needed her; she couldn't afford to be afraid.

She had never been inside the Hôtel de Ville, despite its easy distance from the Rohmer house. It was a stately, grand, and imposing building—filled with notables and leaders like her Robespierre.

After confirming that Rue Saint-Honoré was quiet with a quick peek out the window, she said her goodbyes. She smoothed the front of her *chemise à la reine*, anxious as she locked the door to the carriage. Thomas, their coachman, slipped a pistol within his coat before climbing to his seat.

The carriage bounced roughly over the cobblestones. She lightly touched her liberty cockade, gleaming in the traditional tricolor, and focused on some Rousseau quotes she'd memorized to keep the tightness in her chest from strangling her.

Once the carriage merged into the main but narrow thoroughfare flanking the Tuileries, Sylvie immediately regretted her decision to join Gaspard.

The insurrection was nothing compared to this chaos.

Under the shadow of the Church of Saint-Jacques-de-la-Boucherie, an ornate Gothic cathedral, a raging horde of dozens stood in the streets. Red liberty caps and buttons glared among the gray stone and gray skies of Paris, but the red on their weapons glowed brighter.

"*Mon Dieu*," she whimpered. She melted into the worn brown leather behind her, praying that whatever fed the sans-culottes' ire would distract them from the finery of the coach.

To avoid the advancing mob, the carriage lurched back to the road that hugged the Seine. They sped toward the spires of the Grand Châtelet and away from the blood-tipped weapons, only to be confronted with a furious crowd three times larger. The coach jerked to a stop.

Eager to press on, she banged her fist on the roof of the carriage. Hearing no response, she stuck her head out the window to hiss over the din of the mob, "*Move*, Thomas! Why have you—"

A mountain of bodies cast a shadow over the street in front of the Grand Châtelet, Marat's vision of revenge realized.

Men and women—some with heads, some without—had been piled high in the street while their slayers shouted "*Vive la nation!*" in a grisly chorus. Intestines spilled out of gored bellies, and some bodies twitched with a desperate attempt at life.

Their sentencing was public execution: not done in front of the mob, but *by* the mob.

A municipal building, the Châtelet contained prisons and courts. But it held little justice today.

At the insurrection, the sans-culottes had declared no women to be harmed: a code of honor to separate themselves from true heartlessness. Yet today no poor creature was spared from their savagery, from priest to petty thief to suspected counterrevolutionary.

But the mob was still in the throes of its vengeance, waving pikes with disembodied heads. Blood was smeared liberally over dozens of sans-culottes, and the air was heavier from the metallic stench of iron. Sylvie's eyes burned from not blinking.

Marat's words rang in her head. *Traitors. Treason. Purge.*

The prisons were filled by his orders, and on his orders were emptied.

She snapped the coach windows closed, covering her mouth to keep the smells and sobs at bay. The horses whinnied in distress, pulling at the reins and causing the carriage to creak.

"*Bonjour, Citoyen!*" she heard a man say, presumably to the coachman. Despite the wooden panels of the coach and ample cushioning, the voices reverberated throughout the dark box.

"*Vive la nation,*" Thomas answered. That phrase was a greeting, a promise, and a threat.

"*Vive la nation.* Who do you have inside?"

"No one." She wasn't sure what she'd done—if anything—to deserve his loyalty, but she heaved a grateful breath. "I am simply returning home. My master is one of the deputies."

"Which deputy?" Dark coats moved in front of the cracks in the carriage curtains. She was surrounded. "We know them all."

"Where is your liberty cap, *Citoyen?*" asked another. "What house do you work for?" Thomas gave no answer. She twisted her silk gloves until they crinkled like paper. "Open the coach."

"No."

Her heartbeats were so quick that one beat was no longer determinable from another, thrumming like a plucked harp string.

The tiny latch began to turn, and Sylvie couldn't find enough air in her lungs to scream.

The door flew open, revealing three bloodied men who had broken away from the larger group beating a prisoner behind them. Their eyes glinted when they found the crouching bourgeois pressed into the corner.

She only found her voice when one of the men grabbed her ankle, eliciting a piercing scream as she kicked with all her strength.

This is how I die, she thought. *Ripped apart by the people I tried to save.*

They pulled Thomas down from his perch on the carriage as she continued to thrash—half in and half out of the coach. Thomas was a burly if older man, and the sans-culottes struggled to contain him. But the click of a cocking gun rose above the skirmish, stilling the scene in an instant.

Thomas commanded, "Release the mademoiselle. *Immédiatement.*"

The men did as he bid and relinquished their grip on her legs. Her nails had left scratches in the seats like a lion had sharpened its nails on the leather.

The carriage door still open, Thomas leaped onto the roof and cracked the reins.

City Hall crept into view only minutes later.

No one came in or out of the enormous facade; every available deputy was either politicking inside or hiding in his home like the rest of Paris.

Sylvie flinched when Thomas opened the door, covered in scrapes. He had blood on his cravat.

He slowly extended his hand to her, saying, "Let's get ye to your brother, miss." Not wanting to leave the safe darkness of the coach, she shook her head.

He braced his arms on the side of the door and lowered his voice. "You're safe here. None of those folk would come to City Hall. There are no enemies for them to kill here."

As a mulatta, she was an enemy of royalists. As a bourgeois, she was an enemy of the sans-culottes. Vinegar dripped from the walls of her mind until Sylvie could smell it emanating off the walls of the coach.

She shuddered and shrank away farther. She wasn't safe, not while there were bodies to butcher and fury to feed.

Thomas gave up and closed the door once more, returning minutes later with Gaspard. He had less care than the coachman and flung open the doors to check his sister for injuries despite her reluctance to leave.

"I want to go home," she whimpered, so overburdened with dread that it could not be expressed.

"Sylvie," he said more gently, "come inside. I summoned you here to keep you safe."

"No." She struggled against his grip. "I'm fine. I don't want to be here." Who else had Marat put on his list? What number of his personal enemies would rot in the sun?

"You're not well. You've had a terrible shock. We have several deputies who are physicians inside."

"Like Marat?" She said his name like a curse. "I said no."

"Sylvie . . ."

"Let's leave." She stroked his stubbled cheek. "Let's leave like we did before."

He wrapped his arms around her, and she sagged in exhaustion. "The gates are all closed. No one leaves; no one enters. I'm so sorry, little sister."

Trapped in the walls of the carriage and trapped in the walls of Paris, she gasped for air. The cage of his arms did not give, so much like the sans-culottes just moments before. Her awareness of her surroundings slipped, replaced with a serpentine grip of anxiety. The man entrapping her was no longer her brother but a faceless threat from which she needed to flee. Sylvie twisted and tugged against his hold and struck her brother across his face when he did not release her.

He let go instantly and clutched his smarting cheek.

Trembling, she stuttered, "I'm sorry. I—I don't know what came over me."

"You're frightened. It's all right." He approached her more cautiously this time, speaking to her like she was a spooked horse. "I had hoped you could get here before the worst began, but it seems I was a fool to think . . . Just come inside where it's safe. Robespierre has offices here where you can be treated."

No, Robespierre could not see her like this—so vulnerable, so weak, so unlike him. Not again.

She pinched the tears in her chemise together. "I am uninjured.

They did not hurt me—I swear to you. Please, just let me return home."

Gaspard looked toward the hall and the conflicted assembly bickering inside. "Let's go home together, then—or perhaps to the Duplays'. I refuse to leave you alone."

"You already did," she snapped.

He winced. "I know. I'm sorry."

They stared at each other for a few moments before she conceded, allowing him into the coach. He sat across from her, careful not to accidentally brush his knees against hers. Every touch was magnified to an unbearable degree.

"I have neglected you," he said after the horses began their trek home.

"You're important." She spoke with a mixture of envy and resentment. "Assistant to the Incorruptible himself. You're a different man."

He put up his hand. "I'm a *better* man now."

Gaspard did good things for France. The well-being of a nation superseded her own needs. But he was her brother before he was anything else. "Which takes you further and further away from me! You cannot understand my position."

He fidgeted. "You have Cornélie—" How little he understood. It enraged her.

"A friend is not the same as a brother, Gaspard. You and I have shared everything except mothers . . . but I cannot share this new life with you. You cannot share Lise. You cannot share Robespierre's respect."

The coach hit a loose cobblestone and jostled. Her heart thrummed again, and she closed her eyes against the fear that threatened to overcome her every moment of the day.

"I may share your ambition," she said in a choked voice. "But you cannot share your success."

His hand covered hers. "Paris may tear us in separate directions, but I am first and foremost your brother. I said that on Saint-Domingue, and I say it again now." She took in his words, hoping rather than knowing that he meant them.

"Something's happening at La Force just ahead, sir," Thomas shouted from above. The only thing she knew of La Force prison was its famous current captive: the Princesse de Lamballe. There were so many prisons now, and so many prisoners. The people filled them with supposed enemies and went mad trying to empty them again.

"Christ," hissed Gaspard. "What now?"

The shouting grew louder from scores of sans-culottes and guards congregated at the front. Gaspard stuck his head out of the coach and cursed.

Sylvie could now make out the people's cries.

"Death to Lamballe! *Vive la nation!* Kill the queen's whore!"

She trembled as if the carriage were filled with ice.

"Sister," Gaspard said, his voice sounding far away. "Look at me. Nothing will happen to you."

He did not remember the dead Swiss Guards, the blood on the walls, the hate in their eyes. Marat's gleeful promise to pull the strings of the poor into a murderous riot. Wherever his words went, so would bloodshed.

"They will come for us," she whispered. "They will come for us, too."

"No, they won't." He grabbed her shoulders, shaking her slightly. "Sylvie, you *must* keep calm."

But the terror had already taken hold. The urge to escape—this coach, this street, this city—blinded her to reason. She needed to run. It didn't matter where.

She opened the coach door and darted down the street, the princess's screams driving her every step.

Out of breath and out of energy, Sylvie finally stopped running. Street names, buildings, and faces blurred uselessly together.

Sweat pooled under her arms and stays, and she lost sensation in her exhausted legs. The outline of a café called to her with its promise of wine and a place to rest.

Every smell rushed her at once; she noticed every face. Every scrape of chair legs and peal of laughter hurt her ears. Every fiber in her gown itched and rubbed her sensitive skin.

Once she could speak without panting, she requested a small table in the corner. Few women dared to eat alone, but if anyone tried to proposition her, she'd give them a string of curses so foul, they'd have to be rebaptized.

She knew she couldn't eat much, but she ordered a pastry anyway.

The wine, though cheap, slowed her pounding heart and frenzied breathing. She rested her head in her hands—probably garnering herself more than a few worried looks. Her *chemise à la reine* lay in tatters, the white cotton soiled into a somber gray.

She ignored the concerned looks and chose to enjoy the relative peace of the café, though she couldn't fathom how anyone escaped the gruesome theater a few miles away to quietly sip wine.

How did Robespierre reconcile the atrocities occurring under Jacobin leadership? He'd said time and time again that answering cruelty with more cruelty served no one. Then why did men like Danton and Marat encourage this lawlessness? One can't make an omelet without breaking a few eggs, but how could one make an omelet when burning down the henhouse?

She nibbled on the pastry without tasting anything. A young group of students argued over the classics beside her, and a bourgeois couple chattered about moving to Marseille. The thrumming banality of the everyday world first brought her back to a semblance of calm, then exhaustion.

Compared to her breathless flight just an hour before, Sylvie felt ready to collapse in her chair in sleep.

Her lids weighed heavily as she rested her chin in her hand, wishing she could fall into a sweet dream of an island beach without slave blood spoiling white sand. Without angry, political brothers. Without Cornélie, Maximilien, Marat—without any more pain and confusion and violence.

"More wine, Mademoiselle?" The serving girl smiled tightly, holding the heavy vessel with both arms as she waited for a response.

Sylvie lifted her head slightly to view her before letting it fall once more. "*Oui*," she mumbled into her hands. "And fill it to the *top* this time."

She waited for the welcome sound of wine tumbling into her glass but was greeted with silence.

"Did you not hear me?" she asked. "I said yes."

The serving girl continued to ignore her, staring over Sylvie's head and through the window.

In fact, conversation in the entire café had ceased. Everyone was engrossed in the scene approaching from up the street—the room silent save for the quiet gasps of nearby patrons.

Sylvie turned to view whatever justified ignoring her drink order.

At first, she thought it was a remarkably large man with an absurdly narrow neck. She gaped with the rest of the restaurant; a monsieur as tall as a horse was surely worthy of such awe.

But everything looks better at a distance—few people can recognize true horror unless it stares them in the face. When the cries of "*Vive la nation*" reached the café, Sylvie knew death was close behind.

The serving girl screamed and dropped the metal tankard on the floor, murky beer and watered wine splattering the ground.

The monsieur's skinny neck turned out to be a pike, and his delightfully bobbing blond head was the severed remains of the Princesse de Lamballe, the ex-queen's dearest friend and renowned beauty. She had not escaped the violent plague that came for the denizens of Versailles.

The sans-culottes had killed her and led her decapitated head on a morbid parade of Paris. Sylvie hesitated to think of what they did with the rest of her body.

The earlier escape had stolen what energy she had. She could only tremble in her chair, gripping the edge of the table so tightly that splinters found a home in her fingertips.

She turned her back to the window, praying to the soulless deity above that they'd be content to walk by. But God or Fate or Fortune left her two years ago, and she was unsure of what hell remained.

She refused to look at the door, ignoring the sans-culottes' jeers and patriotic fervor. The mob crammed into the café and went from table to table with their prize.

"Say *bonjour* to Lamballe before she goes to visit Marie Antoinette," said the man holding the remains of the princess when he reached Sylvie's table. Blood ran down the pike and dripped onto her shoes.

She shook her head, her eyes screwed shut. The man continued, "Don't you want to see the death of a tyrant? The face of your oppressor?"

He lowered the pike so that the eyes of the royal were level with hers; she could smell the fetid remains. Sylvie kept her own eyes closed.

If she weren't inches from the dead stare of royalty, she would have laughed from the irony of it all. She and Lamballe were the same: wealthy women with a taste for Enlightenment literature, ensnared in a web of politics out of their depth. It easily could have been her own head bouncing on that pike.

She refused to open her eyes. Opening her eyes made this real.

"Mademoiselle," said the tiny voice of the serving girl beside her. "Please."

She heard the pleading note, the unspoken request. *Please don't do anything foolish. Please give them what they want so this will end.*

So she lifted her lids and faced Lamballe. Her gray-skinned face held no anguish or hint of her brutal end—just the blank gaze of death. A few inches lower, the ragged line of her severed neck met the bloodied column of the pike.

This did not feel like freedom; this did not feel like justice.

"Why don't you give the lady a kiss?" the pike bearer asked.

The image of Cornélie's face flashed unbidden as Sylvie pressed a shuddering kiss to the princess's cool lips. Sylvie had kissed two women now, and she wondered if she would ever be able to look at Cornélie again without recalling Lamballe's unmoving mouth.

"Do you see that?" the same sans-culotte shouted. "She weeps tears of joy. *Vive la nation!*" Sylvie touched her lips, tasting the flecks of blood left from Lamballe's kiss of death. The boisterous and triumphant mob left soon after.

No one spoke because there were no words.

She carefully removed her liberty cockade and placed it on the table beside her payment.

The moment she was outside the café doors, Sylvie spewed her meal into the street, staining the cobblestones red from her vomit.

Chapter Nineteen

I've already told you: the only way to a woman's heart is along the path of torment. I know none other as sure.

—*Marquis de Sade*

Sylvie's throat protested, now raw from purging the wine, but she was thankful that her gown escaped the ordeal free of stains.

She walked home as slowly as her muscles would allow. Images of screaming mobs lurked in her periphery, haunting her until she whirled back to make sure they weren't real. Fringe groups of sans-culottes ran past—presumably to empty a new prison. She kept her head low and her arms crossed.

She went toward Rue Saint-Honoré, but the comfort of Robespierre and the Duplays did not beckon. She did not have the stomach to sit at the center of their republican utopia.

When Louise spotted her from the window of the Rohmer house—presumably perched there to alert Gaspard should she arrive—the front door flew open.

"Do you take delight in making us all worry?" Gaspard asked. His hair was overgrown, hanging loosely on his forehead. Golden stubble lined his jaw, and his fair skin did not hide his dark circles well.

She swallowed the remnants of bile still in her throat. "You sound like your mother. I'm sorry you worried, but clearly I survived the walk home unscathed."

"I disagree." He took in her ragged appearance. "You look awful."

"Can you continue insulting me *inside* the house?" she said. "I'm exhausted and filthy, and it looks like rain."

Gaspard opened his mouth to say something more but thought better of it and led her inside. She went to remove her gloves before remembering that she'd left them in the carriage.

Fifi's cloak hung on its hook, indicating that the lady of the house was at home. "Keep Aunt distracted so I may have some time to bathe," said Sylvie. "I have no patience for her chatter. At least not before I've had some tea."

He pulled out his rum flask. "Here—you look like you need it more than I."

"Thank you." She sipped the bitter rum and tea mixture greedily. "You know, Gaspard, I think you'd be the pride of the British navy. You certainly already drink like a sailor."

As a point, he took a swig before guiding her upstairs.

Once in the tub, she washed her arms and neck in the basin of warm water. She hoped the bath would calm her gooseflesh, but every hair on her arm stood straight.

Louise's voice called out from behind her modesty screen. "Are you hurt, Mademoiselle?"

Sylvie checked her wrists and ankles. No more than bruising and scrapes. "Not that I see. Why do you ask?"

The maid came over with the *chemise à la reine* crumpled in her hands. "There's a stain—many stains—on your chemise. It's blood by the looks of it."

"It's not blood," Sylvie corrected. "I went to a café on my way home from City Hall." Louise did not respond immediately, so Sylvie went on. "The clumsy girl spilled some wine as she refilled my glass. Must be from that."

Louise folded the garment on a nearby chair. "It wouldn't matter, though; blood and wine are removed the same way. Just a bit of salt and boiling water and—"

"Very well," Sylvie cut in. "Go fetch some, then." Louise flinched at her brusqueness and left to concoct her solution for cleaning the linen.

Sylvie sank deeper into the tub. Her hair fanned out around her, like ink dispersing through water.

When the demand to breathe became too great, she came up gasping. Her desperate gulps of air reminded her that she was alive despite the numbness settling on her like a yoke.

Louise had folded the gown as best she could, but no careful handling could disguise its ruin. Sylvie touched the red blots on the bodice, hating the rough texture of drying blood under her finger. But she wasn't injured, and that wasn't her blood. The corpse-gray face of Lamballe brandished on a pike danced across the room like a shadow puppet.

Lamballe.

As a little girl on Saint-Domingue, Sylvie would pretend that Château de Rosiers was her own personal Versailles. She kept court with dolls and forced Gaspard to play the role of courtier. Devoted to her dream, Sylvie stuffed pillows under her petticoats as makeshift panniers and had imaginary conversations with the queen and her ladies over equally imaginary cake. And at the same time, over a thousand leagues away, Lamballe sipped tea with the real queen. But perhaps Lamballe's world was just as much an illusion as Sylvie's.

She wept for them both.

GASPARD INSISTED ON a family dinner the next evening, drawing Sylvie out of her room. The killings hadn't stopped, just escalated. Sylvie focused on keeping her countenance pleasant and pushing the savory ragout around her bowl. She couldn't bring herself to drink the wine, no matter how fine the vintage. Her throat still burned from heaving up the beverage the day before.

". . . But in light of it all, I think London should make a good home," Fifi said after a long-winded speech to which Sylvie had paid no attention. "And I trust both of you to maintain Chez Rohmer."

Gaspard jerked his head up so violently that Sylvie felt its force from across the table, startling her out of her reverie. "You can't *leave*, Aunt Fifi," he said. "Not now."

"Leave?" asked Sylvie. But Gaspard was too shocked and indignant to pause his tirade.

"France is finally a republic! How can you abandon her when she needs us most? Running into the arms of our enemy? I understand that the Tribunal is getting out of hand—"

"They killed a princess, Gaspard," Sylvie bit out. "In an alleyway."

He looked askance. "She was tried, and a verdict was rendered."

He could put on all the disaffected airs he pleased; this brutality went against his noncombatant nature, and she could not sit quietly while her brother feigned callousness. They were both scared—but only she could admit it.

"A show trial! A bearbaiting!" Sylvie stood up and slapped her palms on the glossy wood of the table. "In the end, it's a row of cowards setting mad dogs on a chained beast and calling it justice."

The clatter of his silverware falling made their aunt jump.

"And you're so quick to give up on our goals because revolution is messy?" he asked Fifi, ignoring Sylvie's indignant claims. "You know I disagree with the violence, but fleeing to England? *That* is cowardice!"

"Cowardice?" repeated Fifi. Despite her rouged cheeks, a choleric pallor went over her face. "Cowardice? I grew under the shades of the great *philosophes*, and I've been attending the salons for thirty years. I shared a room with Rousseau while he read from his memoirs. My husband witnessed the Tennis Court Oath. This was not the France we dreamed of. This was not the price we were willing to pay. You punish a man for his *crimes*, not for what he represents."

Her voice—the one that so annoyingly carried throughout the entire house—was softer than Sylvie had ever heard it.

"Forgive me, Aunt." Gaspard's face crumpled contritely. "I spoke out of turn."

Fifi lightly tapped her spoon. "This was a surprise for you, I know. But I'm sure you and your sister will come to appreciate the peace and quiet."

Sylvie valued stability more than anything else. She was accustomed to Fifi's laughter, her chatter, the clink of her jewelry. Fifi embodied the Old World, and when she left them she'd be taking the remains of a dying regime with her. Once again, someone was deserting Sylvie, and once again, she'd be alone.

Dinner finished shortly after that, with Gaspard leaving the table with a thrice-emptied wineglass and ignoring a bowl of ragout—though Sylvie had done no better.

Her aunt had new lines around her eyes and a deeper slope to her shoulders. With her brother gone, her aunt's eyes went soft as she looked upon Sylvie. "You mustn't think I'm abandoning you, Sylvie dear. This decision was not made lightly."

Aunt Fifi had always been a source of friendship—no matter how disregarded, Sylvie could count on her banal conversation, on her unflappable warmth. When all she heard was talk of war and factions and fear, brief chatter about lace was a welcome respite. But now, even if her aunt denied it, she planned to abandon them.

Sylvie studied her reflection in her knife, the red upholstered walls bearing down on her overburdened shoulders. Paris had stolen all her softness. "I'm not angry that you're leaving," Sylvie said. "More people would flee if they had the means."

The idea had merit. Though she spoke no English, almost anyone worth knowing spoke French. The fashion was dreary and the weather drearier, but Britons didn't murder their neighbors and call it liberty.

"There is room aboard the ship for another, my girl."

Sylvie shook her head to knock the idea loose. She had run before, and it almost destroyed her. She had seen what happened when men gave life to their nightmares.

"I fled once—I won't flee again. I won't abandon Robespierre." And she wouldn't abandon Cornélie.

Fifi stood and went to cup her cheek. "*Ma bichette*, self-preservation is not a weakness. I remember what it was like, being young and beautiful and obsessed with great men. Indeed, I even married one, so enamored was I with their ideas and their passions. But the horrors of the past days—"

Sylvie clenched her hand. "Robespierre won't let this happen again. He *can't*."

Fifi raised her hand to silence her. "I esteem our Robespierre, but I do not trust the men he keeps close. To take a country is one thing. To govern a country is another. Marat and Danton have a good deal of blood on their hands; no number of elections will wash them clean. They are incorruptible, not infallible."

As always, Sylvie was torn in two; the wealthy aristocrat feared the men she adored, while the Black escapee who knew the horrors of unchecked privilege prayed the sacrifices would pay off. Robespierre was not at fault. It was the madmen who loved him.

But she could not say as much to her aunt. So she hid behind the hypocrisy she knew so well.

"I hope you do not share these misgivings with your friends," she said. "Many would consider it counterrevolutionary."

"Yes," said Fifi with a wan smile. "Disagreement is treason nowadays."

Sylvie flinched at the truth. Her aunt could also be relied upon to not mince words.

"I know how lost you feel in Paris," she went on. "The climate, the food, the fashion—it's all such a departure from the world you knew. But I'm offering you a chance to find it again. In London, with me. The city is no stranger to French émigrés, to women like us."

The demons that plagued Sylvie were not hindered by mountains or seas; they would follow her to Paris, to London, to Heaven or Hell. "The world I knew is dead," she whispered. "And I must learn to live in this one." Paris held all the things she feared most, as well as all the people she loved best. So in Paris she'd remain. "But I am sorry."

Fifi squeezed Sylvie's fingers. "For what, dearest?"

"I was never kind to you. You opened your home to me—to us—and I never treated you as well as I should have. I wasn't kind to Madame de Rosiers, either. You were both generous, yet I repaid you with coldness and conceit." She fiddled with her thumbs. "I suppose I always thought I didn't deserve affection."

"You deserve love, Sylvie. Everyone does. Even a little mulatto girl with a bad temper." Sylvie's heart fluttered with warmth from her aunt's comfort—and acceptance. Fifi knew more than Sylvie had ever given her credit for. "The world would be a gentler place if people loved one another as they ought."

Sylvie sniffled and laughed. "You're such a sentimentalist."

Fifi cupped her cheek with a soft, plump hand. "That doesn't make my words any less true. But I hope whoever keeps you here loves *you* as much as you love *them*."

HISTORY WOULD CALL those days the September Massacres, but for Sylvie it was just September. She never told Gaspard about Lamballe and assumed he interpreted her new skittishness as a result of the attempted assault at La Force.

She remained in bed, surrounded by pages and pages of memories— a collage of terror and regret. She wanted to improve the world once, wanted to see men who hid behind grandiose caricatures pay for the pain their words wrought. She wanted to stand by Robespierre as a woman who could protect him and be protected in turn.

Several servants left their service when news of Fifi's decision was made known, and only three of them remained: Louise the maid, the cook, and Thomas the coachman. Sylvie struggled with the sudden onslaught of domestic chores laid at her feet, even if most Parisians wouldn't consider hanging laundry to dry as particularly humiliating.

And while Gaspard's presence at home was minimal before, it was wholly absent now. Her brother had been her one true comfort these past years, but now he was a stranger.

The few times they crossed paths in the hallway were when he came home for a fresh set of clothes. She complained, but he assured her that his absence was due to the demands on his time given the impending elections.

"But you're not running," she said one afternoon. "Let Robespierre write his own letters; I demand you take tea with me."

"If you're so lonely," he countered with a wry grin, "why don't you spend more time with Cornélie? I know she comes over, but Louise says that half the time you tell her you're indisposed."

What used to drive Sylvie—Gaspard, Robespierre, Cornélie—flittered away into abstractions. And when her mind swam with the disembodied head of Lamballe, she struggled to even get out of bed.

CORNÉLIE FOUND HER thus—sheets up to her chin and tearstains on her pillow. Louise called up the stairs, protesting that Mademoiselle Sylvie was indisposed and not to be disturbed, but Cornélie's determined steps warned of her intent to see Sylvie regardless.

Sylvie's entire body hurt, though she could not pinpoint any single injury to cause her pain. She faced the window. Days blurred together well with the curtains drawn.

The door opened and closed, punctuated with the light pad of Cornélie's careful steps. The bed sank under her weight, but Sylvie did not turn from her vigil.

"The society of women," the painter began, "will meet this week. The streets are clear, and we need to regroup since . . . everything." She squeezed Sylvie's calf through the duvet. "I won't ask you how you are: it's an offending question. But I'm selfish enough to confess that I've missed you terribly."

Sylvie pressed her foot against Cornélie's thigh in a quiet show of affection. "How can you meet," she croaked, "when you cannot win? When you fight against the most base of human misery?"

"If our influence, no matter how slight, can spare just one person, then it is not for nothing. Maybe one day we'll even be a proper public society—"

"Piles of bodies," Sylvie said. "Piles of them. They emptied the prisons like culling cows from a herd. Robespierre is too good to serve those monsters."

Cornélie came around the other side of the bed so as to see her face and knelt. "I want there to be something *left*." Tears slipped down her pale cheeks. "I refuse to kneel to men like Danton and Marat."

Sylvie turned into the pillow and mumbled, "Robespierre will—"

"He is terrified of losing public opinion, and once elections are held for an entirely new Assembly there will be no one left to temper him. He needs us."

Sylvie pushed away from the pillows. "Surely, there is something we can do."

"There is," Cornélie said with a small smile, resolution straightening her shoulders. "And it cannot wait until your first meeting as La Mère."

She went to Sylvie's desk and scratched out a missive, wiping

tears away before they could fall on the wet ink. "And once the elections are held, our chance to have someone within the Assembly will
be lost." Cornélie's hunched form hid the contents of the note.

Tentative, Sylvie set her feet on the floor for the first time in two
days. "And who do you have in mind?"

Cornélie turned around and blew on the paper—not taking the
time with wax and a seal. She shoved the note into Sylvie's hands.
"Do I still have your support?"

Sylvie refused to let all of that blood stain Robespierre like it
stained her. She pressed her forehead against Cornélie's and skimmed
her hot mouth with her own. Sylvie wanted to be a succubus and
drain her lover of all her inexhaustible strength. "Undoubtedly."

"Then take this"—Cornélie squeezed her hands—"to Olympe
de Gouges."

Chapter Twenty

Women, wake up! The tocsin of reason sounds throughout the universe: recognize your rights. The powerful empire of nature is no longer surrounded by prejudices, fanaticism, superstition, and lies.

—*Olympe de Gouges*

S ylvie followed Cornélie's instructions to Olympe's house, though she would have to enter through the servants' door. Olympe, arguably the beginning of her personal enlightenment, had achieved some degree of sainthood in her mind. She wiped her palms on her plain skirt.

It seemed that Cornélie had some powers of manipulation herself—she knew such a task could not fail to restore at least some of Sylvie's shaken spirit.

After pulling down her hood to obscure her face as much as possible, she rapped on the door and waited.

A servant girl opened and seemed unsurprised by a cloaked woman on the doorstep.

"You've a message for de Gouges?" Sylvie didn't speak; she only extended the letter. The servant sniffed and took it, but Sylvie did not leave. "What? You hungry? We can offer some soup, but—"

"No, no. I was told to wait until she's read it."

The servant stiffened at the elegant vowels and unfamiliar accent. "*Oui*, a moment, then."

Only two minutes later the servant returned and ushered her inside. Sylvie had no idea what the letter contained, but she was unprepared for anyone as fine as Olympe to *see* her. Sylvie was dressed for anonymity, not a social call.

The girl deposited her in a small but elegant sitting room, and Sylvie took the opportunity to pinch her cheeks in the gilded mirror.

"Forgive the poor reception," said a woman's reflection.

Sylvie turned swiftly. The lady had powdered hair and a round, elfin face. She offered her hand, and Sylvie took it without hesitation.

With a deep curtsy, she said, "Madame Olympe de Gouges, it is an honor."

"Tch, no curtsying here," Olympe chided with a smile. Her beauty, by no means little, was enhanced by the intelligence evident in her brown eyes. "We shake hands, Sylvie."

Sylvie did as she asked, shaking Olympe's ink-stained hand. It appeared that, regardless of the hour, the woman was bound to her desk.

"Thank you so very much for bringing this note to me. A bitter shame that we must meet in secret to be agents of progress. But it's an honor to meet you as well." Sylvie's surprise must have been poorly hidden. "Surprised I know of you? Don't be. I admire your tenacity. Cornélie sings of your devotion to the liberation of all peoples in spite of an upbringing determined to keep you bound."

"Cornélie is overly generous."

Olympe crinkled her nose in disagreement. "Heavens, no. That girl is as prone to exaggeration as Marat is to moderation. You're a living ideal of a most dearly held belief: regardless of the barriers confronting women, it's within our power to free ourselves. We must only *want* to."

Olympe's admiration and praise were bursting in Sylvie's chest. "Your plays, Madame—"

"Tch," she said again. "We haven't the time to talk, though when this Revolution ends I should very much like to." She winked. "But I will not let you leave empty-handed."

She exited the salon and returned with a man. "I do not think a man is a fair parting gift, Madame," Sylvie said with a smirk.

The stranger looked no older than thirty and wore well-cut if provincial clothing. He stood out from the other men of the Parisian political circle—he wasn't infamously hideous like Danton nor markedly ill like Marat. He was handsome but unassuming; his air of banality intrigued her in this city of extremes.

Instead of a gallant introduction, he squinted his eyes, staring at her like she was a cloud in a much-too-sunny sky.

"I assure you, Sylvie," Olympe teased, "he is a man worth his weight in gold."

SYLVIE ESCORTED THE man back to the Duplay house as advised by Olympe—her heart fluttering still from her meeting with such a formidable woman. She was unsure what to make of Augustin— who declined to give his last name—however, and kept her racing thoughts to herself.

Yet, he clearly thought midnight missions were ideal for chatter. "Are you Mademoiselle Rosiers?" Suspicious and cool, she nodded. "Forgive me, your reputation precedes you: Gaspard's mulatto sister from Saint-Domingue."

Sylvie had grown spoiled among the liberal company—the word *mulatto* almost forgotten during her tenure as a Parisian. He said the phrase with interest rather than malice, and she feigned serene confidence at his blunt greeting.

"I did not realize I had a reputation at all," she said. "But clearly word of my reputation has journeyed far."

He grinned at her cheek. "At least as far north as Arras. But by the look of things"—he kissed her hand—"it was well worth the effort to meet the lady herself. An honor, Mademoiselle."

"I would return the sentiment if I knew who you were." They

approached the Chez Duplay steps, and the door swung open before he answered.

"*Mon frère!*" Robespierre greeted the gentleman with more animation than was his wont. The brothers grasped forearms in a Roman handshake, and Sylvie curtsied with an embarrassed flush creeping up her neck.

"Forgive me, Robespierre. I had not realized he was your brother. I was not expecting . . ."

He said Arras, you stupid girl, she thought. *How many gray-eyed republicans named Augustin hail from Arras?*

"Nor was I," said the elder brother. "I've been beseeching Augustin to serve France in Paris, but if you recall me saying—"

"He cannot be *forced* to do anything he was not prepared to do himself," she said.

Augustin chuckled, his open amusement so unlike his more restrained sibling. "I daresay, Max, she remembers your words better than you do."

Chewing on her lip to keep from laughing in surprise, Sylvie said, "'Max'?"

The elder winced. "A horrid nickname I expect you never to repeat." His face transformed into rueful amusement. "Gus likes to bait me, as little brothers often do."

She laughed outright, disbelieving that either nonpareil could have a boyish name such as Gus or Max. And why did Augustin hide in Olympe de Gouges's house as a weapon against the radicals of Robespierre's faction? "I shan't repeat a word."

The rest of the Duplay household came in one after another to greet the new tenant, but, unlike Sylvie, they had met the younger Robespierre several times before. Augustin embraced Cornélie and Lise like one would a sister and bowed handsomely to Monsieur Duplay and his wife.

As always, Madame Duplay insisted Sylvie stay for supper—as

well as sending Lise to collect Gaspard so he could meet the newest addition to the Robespierre campaign.

Sylvie sidled beside Cornélie and whispered, "Shall we refresh ourselves before dinner? Everyone seems rather preoccupied with our two Robespierres."

The only indication Cornélie had heard was the twist of her lips, her tiny mouth made as small as a rosebud. She walked to Maximilien, who was engaged in conversation with Gaspard and his brother, and placed a white hand on his shoulder as she murmured that she was going upstairs for a spell. "Come," murmured Cornélie to Sylvie. "They shan't notice."

Tangled in Cornélie's bed and suitably disheveled by kisses, they rested in each other's arms as they caught their breath. The familiar wave of guilt blossomed on Cornélie's face, and Sylvie swiftly pressed closer to bring her lover back into her arms and out of her gloom.

"He is not wondering about where you are," she said. "He's too preoccupied with his brother. His quite handsome brother."

"He's more than just a handsome man," she chided.

"An ally to our cause, surely." Sylvie nibbled on her jaw. "But I can appreciate him all the more, knowing he answers to reason."

IN THE FOLLOWING days, the revolutionary fervor did not die down; it simply changed into an omnipresent force that became as much a part of Paris as Notre-Dame. While the moderates decried the Jacobins' insurrections as bloodthirsty—singling out Danton for instigating them in the first place—the Jacobins worried they had not been fierce enough.

But amid the chaos, Robespierre conquered with his quiet words and blaring message. The ballots revealed the people's devotion and trust in him following his support for the insurrection; he became the first deputy to the newly minted National Convention, a true republic. His brother, miraculously, also earned a seat despite having only recently arrived in Paris.

Sylvie watched Maximilien become master of the Duplay domain—now serving as the de facto patriarch of all of those who crossed its threshold. And surrounded by his supporters, on his territory, Robespierre shone.

Whenever he strayed from City Hall or the Jacobin Club to remain at home, his republican court stayed with him. The Duplay house became a sea of dark coats and powdered wigs, keeping her and Cornélie on the periphery pouring tea while nodding in agreement whatever their conversations.

Today was a Sunday, and even revolutionaries needed a day of rest. But *revolutions* did not sleep.

Thus, the afternoon saw her and Cornélie walking into Regnault's studio. Cornélie assured her that it'd be abandoned given its state of disarray. "He's sleeping at home, a wine bottle in his arms," she said as she unlocked the door.

The studio more closely resembled a warehouse than an artist's den. Scratched-out canvases were piled high, and frames leaned against walls—a strong draft away from toppling over one by one. Plates of partially eaten meals, all in varying degrees of staleness, sat on miscellaneous surfaces. The air smelled like old paper and watery paint.

Sylvie wiped her nose with a handkerchief. "Well, at least we know he isn't a starving artist." The dust made her eyes water. "And no one would find all of us meeting here suspicious?"

"Regnault is a prominent tutor in Paris." Cornélie pulled out a mismatched assortment of stools and chairs. "Many of his tutees are daughters from bourgeoisie families. No one would bat an eye at students coming here to practice after church." Sylvie crossed her arms and sniffed into her handkerchief.

She narrowed her eyes at a familiar pair of legs partially covered by a white sheet—or, rather, a once-white sheet. She pulled it back, releasing a plume of thick dust. Once her coughing fit subsided, she recognized the painting as a larger-scale version of the one she had posed for months prior. The majority of the painting was no more than a sketch, but the hills of Rome—Paris, in this case—had been filled in with verdant greens. Her eyes, too, had begun their journey from lifeless sketch to lively warmth.

"At last, Rhea Silvia has joined us," a pretty woman said from the doorway. She resembled Lise with her girlish smile and upturned nose. Her brown hair looked a bit wild, but her gown, while reflecting a degree of wealth, was rather plain. Her style may have been dull, but her blue eyes were sharp.

Cornélie exhaled through her nose. "Sylvie, this is Charlotte Corday, a friend from Caen."

Charlotte smiled, though it was more mocking than polite. "I've heard much of you, Mademoiselle."

Sylvie shrugged. "And I've heard not of you."

"I daresay that's the point," Charlotte returned with a curled lip.

"Stop bickering," another woman said. Sylvie nearly fell off her chair in surprise—her skin was as black as night itself. "Forgive Charlotte. You'd think growing up with nuns would've taught her some humility. I am Simone." She wore an ornate canary-yellow tignon, with dark puffs of hair peeking around her ears.

Her accent brought Sylvie back to the streets of Le Cap. "You're from Saint-Domingue?"

Simone nodded and said with cheek, "Though you and I most likely went in different circles. But a few friends and a blessedly dead master led me to freedom."

Sylvie flushed and kept her eyes on the ground.

Several other women trickled in, their clothing ranging from the bourgeois to the truly humble. Augustin was the last to arrive, and she noted that everyone seemed to have expected his arrival. They studied him with suspicion but no surprise.

"I've kept this meeting small," started Cornélie, eyeing Sylvie's stiffness. "The fewer people who know about this discussion the better."

Augustin withdrew a letter from his breast pocket. "This society, aware of my desire for political restraint, requested I come to Paris under the guise of serving my brother. I will not impose on your meeting again, and only come to you to show I have no ulterior motives beyond serving France."

The society formed a circle around them, Charlotte the most fearsome with her arms crossed tightly over her chest.

Sylvie ignored their affronted glares as she pushed her way to the newest arrival and Cornélie. "What is he doing here, Cornélie?" she asked, her voice low. Cornélie could not answer before Simone spoke.

"Men are volatile, easily misled," she said, dark eyes flashing fire. "This is a society of women for a reason."

"And I have the utmost respect for that," he countered, taking a seat on a paint-splattered stool. "I do not seek to breach your sanctum, only to help at the request of Olympe."

Their hackles lowered, but Sylvie still could not fathom it. "She sent for you? That's why you left Arras?" she asked.

"Cornélie sent a letter marked as her own so as to avoid suspicion," he explained while displaying the letter from his breast pocket. "Olympe heard rumblings of something bloody—even more so than the insurrection at the Tuileries—and sent for me. Though I arrived too late to do much good."

Sylvie felt played for a fool, running around Paris for no real benefit. "Then if you were already with Olympe, what was my purpose as a courier?"

"They don't let just *anyone* in here, you know," he teased. "Cornélie keeps these meetings very hush-hush—even Olympe is kept blind as to their specific times and places in case of her arrest. Your letter was my invitation."

Sylvie glanced in surprise at Cornélie, who smiled gently. She should know by now that Cornélie trusted her.

But Charlotte studied the letter with her natural skepticism. "And you are so eager to betray your kin?" she asked.

"I do not consider putting my countrymen first as deceit. I *will* be serving my brother." He stood up from his chair. "The first matter of business will be the king: the monarchy will be abolished; that much was certain when my brother kept the royalists from running. So, whether the king is exiled, imprisoned, or executed, he will not stay king for much longer."

This was not a surprise to anyone, and they all hummed in understanding.

"Our goal is restraint," Simone advised them. "The war with the Prussians has turned in our favor, and that means that the delegates can focus wholeheartedly on conflicts at home. Augustin"—he nodded—"keep your brother from capitulating to political deadlock. Division in the Assembly led to its downfall; we would not see those party lines redrawn."

"Let us watch the debate over the king with a close eye," Cornélie added. "The future of France hinges on how they punish a man for the transgressions of his ancestors."

Simone spoke up. "Though we must remember to look beyond the king: the Revolution is not threatened by a powerless ex-sovereign."

Cornélie slapped a stack of newspapers down before her. "Which brings us to our next point. Who *is* the Revolution's greatest enemy?"

"The Jacobins," Charlotte said.

"Be more specific," Cornélie replied with a weary moue.

"Marat is the Revolution's greatest enemy," Sylvie said, the print from his *L'Ami du peuple* glaring at her from its resting place, though he had since renamed it *Le Journal de la République française*. Cornélie and Charlotte nodded. "He's a proper delegate like Robespierre now, which makes him doubly dangerous."

Before the massacres, he published from darkness, driving the forces of change into whatever destructive direction he desired. The collapse of the old Assembly provided him with a concrete pathway to more power.

"But the people love him; I fear losing him would only increase their unhappiness," Simone countered. "Danton and Robespierre know to keep him in the fold." They witnessed his power when he summoned violence like a hunter calls a hound.

Charlotte sneered. "Poisoned fruit is the sweetest."

Simone looked askance. She was a wiry woman with a sharp chin and a clever sparkle in her eyes. "And he may have already poisoned the well."

"We must still *try*."

"But what can we do?" Sylvie asked. "He can mobilize the people with a flick of his quill. I do not know all of you well, but I cannot imagine you have better political connections than Cornélie. And even she could not get an audience with such a man without suspicion."

Machiavelli insisted it was better to be feared than loved, but under Marat's thrall she acknowledged that even a beloved tyrant was just as potent. Sylvie used love as protection the same as he did, only the objects of her affections did not suffer violence at her whim.

Cornélie flipped through a packet of copied letters. "For now, we wait. We watch the tide of the Revolution. We have Augustin now"—she gave a nod of acknowledgment—"a delegate free of royalist ties and suspicion."

Charlotte rolled her eyes. "I'm less willing to plant all my faith in the Incorruptible's brother. And waiting means more death."

"And rushing into an ill-developed plan will mean our own,"

Cornélie said. "We cannot help France from a grave, nor can we help without allies."

Simone squeezed Cornélie's hand. "It took my people centuries to end the yoke of the *grand blancs*. We can wait a few months." It was hard for their worries to not seem insignificant in the midst of Saint-Domingue's battle for true freedom, and the group appeared chastised by the reminder.

The women smoothed their skirts and said their goodbyes. Augustin made it a point to bow over Sylvie's hand, and she trusted him enough to offer a smile.

She hung by Cornélie's side until the last member left the studio. "I wonder who leads you: surely, you alone cannot organize all these people?"

"Olympe—"

Sylvie didn't need her to finish. "*Olympe de Gouges?*" Olympe guided the strings of their group? Sylvie assumed some connection with their society, given Olympe's harboring of Augustin, but it was another thing entirely to be its grand master.

Cornélie smirked. "*Oui*, Olympe de Gouges. But she's too well-known to come to our meetings; she hosts her own salon and publishes a newspaper. Ever since she published the Declaration of the Rights of Woman she's had a target on her back."

Sylvie enjoyed memories of Edmond referring to Olympe as "that radical bitch" when she published her abolitionist play years ago. It had endeared her to Olympe from the start.

"She marvelous. But no more so than you," Sylvie said. Cornélie chuckled, tidying up the notebooks and papers. "I admire you, you know. For having the strength to do what's right despite your closeness to the Jacobins."

Cornélie's eyes softened, and she took Sylvie's chin in her hand to kiss her mouth.

"When does Regnault come back to his charming château?" Sylvie asked, motioning to the tea-stained cups piling up on a plate.

"Not until tomorrow afternoon when we have lessons."

She tugged on the ribbon trailing from the artist's waist. "Perhaps I need a lesson myself. I'm a very shoddy painter."

Cornélie smiled over her white shoulder. "And how would you like to begin?"

Sylvie checked the shadowed corners and doorways for visitors before she unhooked the front of Cornélie's bodice. "A canvas is the first step, no?" Cornélie nodded, moving her arms to give Sylvie room to work. "An artist is only as good as her materials."

Her eyes, half-lidded but focused, did not waver. Sylvie had never seen blue so remarkably dark.

"We must work on your brushstroke," Cornélie said. The student removed all of her canvas's clothing until Cornélie was left in only a chemise. Sylvie grabbed a rounded brush that looked respectably clean and offered it to her for approval.

"A filbert brush," the painter murmured. "It has wide-ranging uses—from detail work to blending."

Sylvie's heart ached with affection. Cornélie always wanted to share what she knew—her insights, her knowledge, her feelings, her burdens—with the world around her. Sylvie thoughtfully stroked the still-moist bristles, firm but soft to touch.

"I chose well, then." She pulled down Cornélie's chemise so that it gathered about her narrower hips. So clean and fair, she glowed amid the dark chaos of the studio. The novice ran the damp brush down the planes of her stomach, mesmerized by the subtle tremble of her muscles and the control she had over her canvas. "I've never been much of a painter, but you certainly make a fine tableau."

She dragged the brush up to swirl around Cornélie's breasts and ribs—then farther still to her jaw and lips. She traced the line of

Cornélie's mouth like she applied imaginary rouge, not that she needed it. "Your lips are the finest shade of pink; I wish I could take the color with me when I leave you."

The chemise pooled around Cornélie's ankles, and the naked artist stepped closer—so close that Sylvie couldn't fit the width of the filbert between them. "Then do not leave me."

She learned the name of every brush, and not an inch of her canvas was left unmarked.

THE FLOOR OF Regnault's studio wreaked havoc on their hair, so Cornélie re-pinned a lock of Sylvie's hair as she knelt behind her.

"You two would make a comely pair," she said, twisting a curl. Her willingness to learn how to manage Sylvie's hair, worlds away from her own tresses, never failed to please her lover.

Drowsy from their activities, Sylvie wiped at her eyes and yawned. "Who would?"

"You and Augustin," Cornélie mumbled with a pin in her mouth.

Sylvie always enjoyed the attentions of handsome men, though in her experience beauty of form meant emptiness of mind. Not because handsome people could not be intelligent, but because rarely did a handsome man have to use his mind to get what he wanted. She understood better than anyone how much people would excuse for a pretty face.

Nonetheless, Augustin appeared neither vapid nor unintelligent.

"If he is like his sibling, I doubt Augustin is ready to settle." Besides, she hardly knew him beyond his political allegiance and family name.

But Cornélie only shrugged and removed the pin she held between her lips. "He shares Robespierre's ambitions for France, not his temperament. I think the idea of a wife is not an unwelcome one."

Sylvie bristled at her suggestion. "So ready to be rid of me?" Cornélie was not Robespierre, but Sylvie had grown accustomed to her touch and her skin and her affection. To be so summarily discarded after months of . . . *friendship*, well, that was an affront she refused to stomach.

Cornélie's china-blue eyes widened in surprise. "No, my lovely girl, of course not," she stuttered. "But people talk. Marriage could cement your place here. Robespierre and I have been speaking—"

"The only marriage you should be needling for is your own," Sylvie said, shrugging off the artist's hands. She pulled out of her embrace and reset her curls herself. "I'm hardly a spinster at twenty."

She enjoyed Cornélie's flabbergasted expression and the flash of hurt in her eyes. It lightened her own burden, if only for a moment, to see that Cornélie was not above plots and machinations.

Her anger moved between Cornélie and herself. Her efforts to bring herself closer within Robespierre's inner circle appeared to have been working—but apparently they'd worked too well.

Did Robespierre see her as a younger sister? He had two of them, and his paternalistic nature primed him for adopting a brotherly if not fatherly role toward her in his own mind. But those lingering looks as he tended to her wounds, the contractions of his arms around her—surely, those did not stem from familial affection.

She prided herself on her ability to read men well, but Robespierre eluded her.

"I suppose I should be grateful for the Incorruptible's blessing," she said. She did not want his blessing; she wanted the security his love would provide. But the true object of his respect and affection sat on the bed behind her, flushed from her kisses and confused by her sudden unkindness. "Seems unfair for me to become Madame Robespierre before you. But I see why he's reluctant to make you his wife; I wouldn't want you needling in my affairs, either."

Cornélie pushed herself up onto her feet. "I thought you said you wanted to feel safe. Marriage is just another tool. I'm trying to help you."

"I never asked you to procure me a marriage, for Christ's sake." Sylvie pulled some curls out of her coif to frame her face. "I can hook a husband on my own."

"Is that what you did to me? Was I simply a worm on your line?"

She refused to meet Cornélie's accusatory stare. "You know you're well-connected. Befriending Robespierre's mistress was a wise decision."

"How could you be so cruel?"

One of Sylvie's hairpins now bent in her fist. "Acting on a will to survive makes me cruel?"

"No, ignoring your own heart does." Cornélie's hair fell in unbrushed waves down her back, and her crinkled chemise drooped off her shoulder, highlighting the marks dusting her collarbone. Her undress and hurt made her look vulnerable, giving Sylvie a thrill of control once again.

Fully dressed and properly refreshed, she turned on her heel and left without a second glance.

Chapter Twenty-One

We swallow greedily any lie that flatters us, but we sip only little by
little at a truth we find bitter.

—*Denis Diderot*

For four days Sylvie refused to visit the Duplay house.

She pretended not to see Gaspard when he returned home.
He warily eyed his sister, who lounged on the yellow chaise with
forced nonchalance, as he divested himself of his coat.

"Cornélie asked after you," he said. She sniffed. "She seems out
of sorts. Have you had a falling-out? Robespierre mentioned something about a quarrel."

"What did he say?" she asked, refusing to reveal her interest in his
answer.

"He does not know the details, but Cornélie has been rather sullen;
she is not the kind of lady to give in to melancholy." Her heart twinged;
Cornélie had not deserved Sylvie's meanness. But she sighed in relief
knowing Robespierre did not know the truth.

"So Robespierre does not know why?"

"No," he said, suspicion creeping into his tone. "Is he the source
of the discord?"

She turned away. "No." *Yes.*

"Well, you'll be pleased to know that everyone is asking after
you." She was indeed pleased by this information and did nothing to

hide that fact. "Lise is not enough to keep the house cheerful, and the deputies have no one to moon over."

"You are good to safeguard my honor."

He rolled his eyes. "It's less about your honor and more about my sanity. *Mon Dieu*, even Augustin pines for you, and he only spoke to you for an hour at most."

She smiled; what he meant as a criticism she enjoyed as flattery. "It is difficult to imagine a Robespierre pining over anything. What excuse did you give regarding my absence?"

"Said you had an abominable cold." He shrugged. "Whatever it is that keeps you hidden here—you cannot hide from it forever."

She could try. Sylvie wanted to avoid the Duplays and their enticing tenants for the rest of her days, knowing that she would always belong to Maximilien, but he would never belong to her.

"Stave off their curiosity for as long as you are able," she said as Gaspard frowned. "Let me hide for a little while longer."

ANOTHER TWO DAYS of quarantine in the Rohmer house, and Sylvie was no closer to returning. Her longing for the company of Cornélie and Robespierre was inflamed, but she satisfied herself with rereading his Jacobin speeches from months ago that Gaspard had transcribed.

Her brother only returned home to sleep. This left Sylvie to her own devices for much of the day.

This evening, however, the maid, Louise, interrupted Sylvie's daily monotony. "A Monsieur Robespierre for you, miss."

The girl's sparkling eyes betrayed her excitement at seeing the famous lawyer, and Sylvie hoped her own expression was better contained.

"*Which* Robespierre, Louise?"

"Maximilien."

Every sort of fancy and hope flitted through her mind, but she channeled her angst into organizing throw cushions. "Fetch us tea," she said. "And comfits. The ones with the fennel seeds; he likes those best."

Louise wrung her apron. "Of course, miss."

Sylvie heard his familiar steps approach the salon, and she hastily concealed her well-loved Radcliffe novel under the opposing chair's pillow. As the door opened, she tossed herself into a casual repose with a copy of Marat's *Journal*.

He walked inside, and she mused that time away from him had made his effect on her more potent. He wore his favorite emerald coat—the one that brought out the flecks of green in his mostly color-less eyes.

"You are in good health," he declared. She could say nothing in response; the accusation was true. "You have not been at the house in some time."

She nodded, but once again there was no question or invitation in his tone. He looked ridiculous surrounded by her aunt's brightly colored finery. He became aware of that as well, observing the gilded knickknacks and porcelain figurines in pseudo-erotic poses with a frown.

Louise fluttered in with the tea tray and spared them from con-versation for a few minutes.

"Won't you sit?" Sylvie asked. He stared at the proffered fuchsia chair like it was going to bite him before finally sitting down. "Cream? Sugar?" She knew he did not take either, but she asked out of politeness. He shook his head and accepted the tiny cup.

"Surely, you know I did not come for idle chatter." Frankly, she had no real idea why he had come, but she nodded anyway. "Your brother said it was only a cold, but I needed to appraise your condi-tion for myself. Gaspard serves me well, yet he is neglectful of his duties as your brother."

She tried to speak with the same dignified softness he so often had. "The health of France supersedes mine. Gaspard keeps quite busy."

"That very well may be, but that does not mean that your welfare and situation are to be thus ignored."

She motioned to her person. "As you see, I am perfectly well."

"Then your absence is due to me and Cornélie?"

She desperately wanted to sink into the velvet chaise. "So she has told you."

"Only that the subject of a husband clearly upset you. And I understand a certain reluctance to settle down, but I believe you are the sort of woman to benefit from marriage."

If she weren't so uncomfortable, she would have laughed at his complete misinterpretation of her motivations. But there he was, looking every inch a stern father rather than an ardent admirer.

She focused on Marat's newspaper crinkling in her hands. As always, the articles were more alarmist propaganda than news. It was a prop for Robespierre's sake.

He let her fester under his gaze until he shifted in his seat—odd, as he was never one to fidget—before he reached underneath the cushion to reveal her battered copy of *A Sicilian Romance*.

"I take it this is not Gaspard's?"

Had she been paler, she'd bet her cheeks would match the violent pink of the seating. "It is mine, Monsieur. I know you must think me ridiculous for reading such nonsense, but I do not read it often, and I . . ."

He would call her stupid or silly, ridiculing her shallow taste in literature. Half of the time her own mind frightened her, and familiar romance novels allowed her a few hours of respite. Sylvie prepared herself for any manner of embarrassment.

He ignored her frantic explanation, thumbing through the book with a ghost of a smile. "My littlest sister, Henriette, reads these

English romances. I was tempted to ban her from them, but Augustin insisted they were harmless."

"I promise there are no coded messages from Britain hidden in the pages."

His eyes flashed at the very notion of espionage, then cooled when he caught her jest. "We all have our private proclivities, Mademoiselle."

Over years of practice, Sylvie had mastered all manner of subtlety—to rebuff, to ignore, to beguile. She chose to beguile, lowering her voice. "And what is yours?"

"Not one that can be hidden with a chair cushion," he said, handing her the novel. She gave a self-deprecating laugh and put the book back on the end table. When she returned to her seat, she found his expression to be quite changed. "If I may be so bold—"

Her heart fluttered in hope. "Your life is a study in boldness, Monsieur," she told him.

"Then your life should be a study in good sense. My brother would be a good match for you."

He very likely would; however, *she* rarely wanted things because they were good for her. Perhaps if she had not met Maximilien she'd be happier to consider Augustin's suit. But Gus could not match his brother in fame or authority.

"Perhaps I should marry Cornélie," she challenged, feeling reckless. If he would be willfully obtuse, then so would she. "You love her, and I know her better."

He did not take her bait, and instead pondered the suggestion with a wry smile like it was a legitimate possibility. "You are too-similar creatures—you would know no happiness."

She scoffed. "*We* are too similar? You and Cornélie are married yet identical in all ways: serious, devoted, republican to the core . . . I would say you are the same person twice over."

"She is a very dear friend whom I will cherish for all my days, but she is not my wife." She had more or less made the very same accusation the previous week, but hearing it from Robespierre's lips caused a welling of passionate defense for her friend to rise in her breast. Despite the polite language of friendship used to conceal it, they were lovers: to drive a wedge between them now would be cowardly and cruel.

"My brother does not lack social charms as I do. He is a good man, ambitious but principled. He is comfortable—you will want for nothing."

She leaned back with a raised brow. "And what does your brother think of me?"

"He holds my opinion in the highest of esteem, despite his stubbornness. And after having met you, he is eager to continue the acquaintance."

Sylvie did not have enough fingers and toes to count all the men who wanted to get better *acquainted* with her. But Augustin was not like other men; his closeness to Maximilien came from blood, not just shared philosophy or political party. And for reasons she could not articulate, he did not seem the type susceptible to her charms.

"If your brother is half the man you are, then I would be the happiest woman in all the world." That was a lie, of course. But she would wound his pride if she said anything less than complimentary about his beloved Gus. When faced with his resolute expression and the possibility of his happiness, she was powerless. "He is your only and dearest brother. If you deem me worthy, then I must at least consider your proposal."

Satisfied with his success, Robespierre finished his tea and allowed her to explain the finer details of *A Sicilian Romance*.

She did her best to be sweet and pleasing, but unintentional hurts cut the deepest—and Robespierre seemed entirely unaware of the pain he had caused her.

———

"Bloody high-handed of him, if you ask me."

Sylvie rubbed her temple. "I don't recall asking you, Gaspard," she said as they walked to the Duplays' for a late supper at Monsieur Duplay's invitation. After Robespierre's visit the day before, she could not decline. She was privately honored by his condescension, even if her brother was not.

"I am your brother." He unscrewed his flask so fast, she was sure it would spark. "I alone decide when and who you marry."

She burst into laughter. "Honestly. The last time we discussed marriage you couldn't be bothered."

"It's different now," he whined. "Augustin is an upstanding fellow, but you—"

She placed a firm hand on his chest as they approached the Duplay entrance. "Are you going to forbid me if I choose to pursue the match? I don't think Robespierre would appreciate his secretary denying his brother the wife of his choosing." She only knew Gus in passing and doubted that this matchmaking scheme would survive longer than a few weeks if she had her way.

Gaspard exhaled slowly and removed her palm. "No, of course not. But promise me you'll think this through. Sometimes you rush into decisions without considering the consequences."

"I think," she chuckled, "that you are confusing my character for yours, Gaspard. And if my crime is rushing, then yours is delaying. When will you give poor Lise a proposal?"

With time and some romance of her own, Sylvie had accepted Gaspard's choice. But the idea of sharing her brother's home with a woman from outside their world—or, rather, their past—made her heart pound.

He crossed his arms and leaned against the stone wall like an intractable youth. "It is *she* who hesitates, not me."

Sylvie laughed. "Then she has more sense than I thought."

THE MOMENT SYLVIE seated herself in the Duplay salon, she wished she hadn't come.

Devoid of its usual guests, she had only the Robespierre brothers and Cornélie to converse with—as Lise and Gaspard took their usual spot in the corner of the room.

Cornélie greeted her with restrained civility, but Sylvie recognized the worry simmering beneath her milky-white exterior. She ached to embrace her friend, to soothe her concern and apologize for her earlier unfairness, but Sylvie's loyalty to Robespierre overpowered any independent will.

Augustin was overly accommodating—offering tea, refreshments, blankets, and a pillow should she need it—in an effort to ease the tension.

Robespierre simply looked on in muted pleasure; she had long ago learned that there was little he liked better than being obeyed. As Augustin flattered her, Cornélie sat in dignified silence. Paris was days away from forming the French Republic, and Sylvie knew Robespierre enjoyed his orchestrated plan coming to fruition.

"Sylvie."

Cornélie's alto snapped her out of her reverie. "Pardon?"

A gentle smile. "I asked if you wanted to view the new flowers? Mother just finished putting in the rest of the tulips."

Sylvie understood her intention, but Robespierre did not and said, "It's dark out; she may see them tomorrow."

Cornélie's smile turned rather thin, but her grace remained. "There is still some light out yet, dearest."

"I would love to see them," Sylvie interjected before Robespierre could argue. She curtsied to both brothers before following Cornélie out into the family garden.

"Such a brilliant man," said the elder girl once the door closed. "But sometimes I both curse and praise his obliviousness."

Sylvie fidgeted under her kind gaze. "I apologize for my outburst. You were only trying to help."

Cornélie waved her off, stroking the still-closed bulbs of the tulips. "'Tis I who should apologize. I cannot imagine how insufferable I must have sounded; a dear friend making machinations about your marriage. I had no right. I begged Maximilien to speak to you, to apologize on my behalf."

A rueful smile played on her lips. "He failed you spectacularly. Robespierre all but commanded me to come to dinner."

Cornélie exhaled slowly, glowering at the flower beds. "Well, then I must apologize twofold."

Sylvie ran her fingers through the loam. "As always, he made fair points. But I was mostly confused: Why would Robespierre want me married?"

"I confess it was I who planted the idea in his head. Between the turbulent nature of revolution and your romantic tendencies, I feared the day I'd lose you. I thought a union to Augustin meant you'd be close to me forever, or at worst you'd be married to a decent man who shares your beliefs and accepts your background. Robespierre liked the idea—"

Sylvie struggled to feel worthy of Cornélie's affection when she had Robespierre's. "You have *him*. Why do you need me? Love me, even?"

"We still take our walks, read together . . . but things are different now. I know him better. I love him still—and I always shall—but working under Olympe broadened my horizons. I know how easy it is to fall into his gravity. How easy it is to lose yourself in his orbit: never straying and never getting closer." They sat side by side, and Cornélie rested her head on Sylvie's shoulder. "He's always been a man of the people, yet now he drifts further from me than ever. But you and I, Sylvie"—she wiped a tear away with the back of her hand—"we can be lonesome together—friends for the rest of our lives, married or not." She ghosted her lips across Sylvie's, sighing sweetly at the brief touch.

Sylvie fed from her until she was as swollen as a tick, full of her praise and tenderness until she fooled herself into not needing any more. A wave of guilty longing washed over her, unbidden and traitorous, until it manifested as anger.

She pushed her back, saying, "Married or not, I don't like to share. I never have. And I understand that our new world order may allow for such . . . indiscretions. But how can you content yourself with clinging to a man who refuses to wed you while keeping me as a bit on the side? Haven't you any ambition?"

As she burned hotter, Cornélie went frigid. "Unlike you, my ambitions are for France and not for myself."

"So you are content to cling to Robespierre until he tires of you? To play house?" Sylvie's duty to Robespierre and her love for Cornélie dueled for dominance; she wanted him to herself, but not at the expense of her lover's integrity. "How can your parents allow your reputation to be dragged through the muck? You are his mistress, Cornélie. When I challenged him on the subject of marriage between you, he would only call you his 'friend'!"

Instead of matching her vitriol, Cornélie remained calm. "We have an understanding—why does it enrage you so? I don't mind being what I am. I don't mind that he does not wish to marry. And my pride is not so great that his choice wounds me."

Cornélie's attachment to Robespierre was unshakable, as was hers: therein lay the conflict Sylvie had ignored for the better part of a year. Though a handsome portion of her anger lay in the truth that Cornélie would be so at ease at the idea of her marriage, let alone the one who would suggest it. "We both have a duty to him. And we dishonor Maximilien by continuing this temporary charade."

Only then did Cornélie allow some resentment to crack her

smooth glass exterior. "It was not a charade. And certainly not temporary—not to me."

Sylvie laughed: humorless and cutting. "You're smarter than I am; you should have known this—"

"Yes," Cornélie snapped. "I *am* smarter than you." She collected the woven basket and tiny shears at her feet to gather clippings from the garden. "I've been patient with you, Sylvie. When you hid away in that pink monstrosity of a house, I waited for you to collect what little sense you had and return to me." She cut the stems of several flowers, the tulips snapping like the necks of baby birds. "But to hear you belittle the life I lead, to belittle my plans for you when my only wish is to keep you safe against your own arrogance . . ."

Her words trailed off as she sheared several more red bulbs, an angry splotch of color bursting on either cheek. "I do not know what you aim for, nor what you seek to gain by feigning heartlessness. But I can assure you that it will not be worth losing me." Another tulip was severed under her merciless blade. "And without me, this Revolution will consume you, like a fire consumes kindling."

Cornélie gathered the tiny flower corpses resting in her basket and brushed past.

Trembling, Sylvie kept her chin high as Cornélie's rose perfume fell over her in waves—unable to sweeten the bitterness settling in her bones.

Chapter Twenty-Two

One wonders why there are so many women who follow Robespierre to his home, to the Jacobins. . . . It is because the French Revolution is a religion and Robespierre is one of its sects. He is a priest with his flock.

—*Marquis de Condorcet*

21 septembre 1792

The first session of the National Convention had arrived, and while half of Paris fled to City Hall, Sylvie hid in her rooms with the coverlet pulled up to her chin.

Nightmares rendered sleep an exercise in torture rather than rest. She dreamed that she took tea with Lamballe, and the princess's head was only attached by rotting tethers of flesh. She woke up screaming, hands clutching her own throat. Louise rushed in at the sounds of her cries—though, as a servant, she could only offer to stoke the fire.

Thus, Sylvie kept to her bed, wallowing in memories old and new. She'd gotten up only to change into a fresh chemise.

A soft knock—only Louise knocked so timidly—disturbed the silence of the afternoon.

"I'm not hungry, Louise," she called. The girl was always sending up food trays, but Sylvie had no appetite. When the maid knocked again, she lost her patience.

"I told you, girl: *I'm not hungry.* Stop trying to fatten me up like a Christmas goose."

Louise cleared her throat on the other side of the door loudly enough for Sylvie to hear. "A Mademoiselle Duplay to see you, miss."

Her heart constricted. If she'd known Cornélie was coming, Sylvie would not have chosen to wear a wrinkled, unwashed nightgown. But the chemise let the afternoon light reveal the shape of her legs and hips, so she left it on. She bolted upright, her braid whipping out behind her like a dark tail.

Living in practical isolation had made her more agreeable to Cornélie's company. In fact, she longed for it. Cornélie was distilled rum: addictive, strong, and burned all the way down.

And Sylvie was parched.

"Send her up!" she called as she pinched her cheeks in the vanity mirror. Purple bruises mottled the skin under her cloudy eyes.

Her room hadn't been tended any better than her hygiene. Half cups of cold gunfire tea sat on the windowsill, ribbons and half-eaten pastries covered her end table, and newspaper articles littered the floor.

I should be an artist, she thought. *Regnault's studio is nothing compared to my room.*

She pushed what she could under the bed, but there would be no hiding her sorry state from Cornélie's blue gaze.

"Hello, Sylvie," she said, her voice flat and distant. Cornélie wore a dark wool coat with wide-cut lapels in the masculine style so popular in Paris. The fine tailoring complemented her narrow waist and creamy complexion.

Sylvie's loosely-thrown-on dressing robe did nothing to obscure her sheer nightdress, which was at its most translucent in front of her window—as planned.

"You look well," Sylvie said.

"I wish I could say the same," Cornélie replied. "It's noon, Sylvie. Why are you not dressed?"

Sylvie crossed her arms, now self-conscious of her cheap tricks. "Did you come here to mother me?"

Cornélie poked at an uneaten bread-and-cheese plate. "No, I came to bring you to the National Convention. Though it seems you need some mothering, from what Gaspard has said."

"Gaspard knows nothing of what I need." Sylvie pushed back her hair and took a cleansing breath. "Forgive me; I'm certain you did not come to argue."

"No." The other woman's lip curled. "I did not want to come at all." Sylvie let her face fall as Cornélie's discomfort crashed into her like waves.

"Then how can I help you, Mademoiselle Duplay?"

Cornélie sat on a small stool in front of the vanity. Sylvie traced the dark wisps of hair at the nape of her neck with her eyes. "You can help yourself. I tire of watching you make a show of being miserable and yet rejecting all offers of friendship."

Sylvie took a step forward. "So, you're extending an olive branch?"

Cornélie held up her hand. "Nothing between us resembles peace, and it never will. You made certain of that when you cast me out."

Sylvie looked down at her bare feet. "I'm sorry. You know I'm sorry."

Cornélie removed one of the dying tulips from the dressing table, peeling off the orange petals one by one. "You're not sorry; you're lonely. You've buried yourself in this genteel hovel to nurse your self-pity while the rest of us watch the birth of a nation." She put the bald flower back into the vase. "And I, for one, have lost my patience," she added. "But my family has not, nor Augustin nor Maximilien. So here I stand, most unwillingly, to lure you out of this little cave of despair."

Sylvie knew Cornélie would not have come if she did not care for her.

Sylvie pressed her lips to Cornélie's—to silence the ugly words with lips and tongue. If she dug deeply enough, she could unearth the affection masquerading as cruelty. After all, Cornélie only needed reminding of how good Sylvie could be to love her again. Sylvie missed the tethers that bound her to Robespierre, as well as Cornélie herself.

Cornélie's mouth did not move under hers, but her hands be trayed her. They instinctually touched the swell of Sylvie's hips, either to push away or pull closer. In the end, Sylvie remained fixed in place.

"Do you not feel how well we fit against each other?" Sylvie asked against her neck. "How long it has been since you've held me? Love me like you used to, Cornélie."

Cornélie pushed her face into Sylvie's hair. "You hurt me that day. Hurt me in a way Robespierre never has."

"And I've been hurting every day since then," Sylvie said as she undid one of the buttons of Cornélie's coat.

"You used me."

Sylvie pulled back, asking, "What of Robespierre? When I want you I am disloyal. When you want me it is love."

"They cannot be compared," Cornélie snapped. "Robespierre's heart is not easily touched, nor easily broken. When a man is so surrounded by enemies, I cannot afford to be expendable."

Whether it was Sylvie's or Cornélie's love for him, Robespierre would consistently bring them apart. Cornélie belonged to him, even if he could not belong to her.

Sylvie tied her dressing robe tighter, already regretting exposing both her body and her feelings.

Cornélie re-buttoned the front of her coat and raised her chin. Sylvie knew that she would never fall prey to such manipulation again.

"As you have always preferred his word to mine," Cornélie said coolly, "Robespierre wishes for you to come. And staying in this room will not make you any happier. I'll be waiting downstairs."

ONCE SHE COULD take in the enormity of the National Convention herself, Sylvie understood the alluring thrall of politics.

The deputies decided these early sessions were to be held within the Tuileries Palace—long cleansed white and cleared of its bloodstains and corpses. No Swiss Guards lining the gate or bejeweled nobles strolling its gardens; only a sea of sans-culottes and white-wigged deputies culminating in a roar of republican fervor.

The women—Lise, Cornélie, Sylvie, and Madame Duplay—stood among the crush of onlookers.

Robespierre and his party sat across the hall, perched upon their mountain of righteous enlightenment high above their fellow deputies and followers. Robespierre's gaze was fierce enough to be felt in the stands; Sylvie pretended his approving look was for her and not Cornélie.

When a representative approached the stage, the Convention silenced their cheers. The entire hall thrummed from the thousand heartbeats hammering in the seats and in the stands.

"*Citoyens!*" said the deputy. "Deputies! Beloved France! I stand before you, eager to begin a new century of *liberté et égalité*."

Cornélie leaned close to whisper, "That is Deputy Jean-Marie Collot."

"But to usher in this republic," Collot continued as he white-knuckled his podium, "we must purge the dying tree of the ancien régime and its poisonous roots, so they may not defile the soils of France. The monarchy shall be abolished—once and for all."

The thunderous roar of celebration could make one's very bones shake. Robespierre and his brother showed their approval with more subdued applause.

"We are all in agreement that the monarchy must be held accountable for the evils it's wrought," said another deputy.

"Basire," Cornélie named him for Sylvie. "One of Danton's favorites." Sylvie shuddered at Danton's name, but she still listened with the rest of the enraptured crowd.

"But we mustn't let our passions detract from the issues at hand," Basire went on. "While the persons in this room have demonstrated their deep hatred of the king, do they speak for all of France? Would it not be reckless to make such a decision without thorough deliberation? We should discuss—"

"Discuss? *Discuss*?" an abbé cried out. "What need do we have of discussion when everyone is in agreement? Kings are as much monsters in the moral order as in the physical order. The courts are a workshop for crime, the foyer for corruption and the den of tyrants. The history of kings is the martyrology of nations!"

If there was any dissent, Sylvie didn't hear it. The bloodcurdling cries of "Down with the king" and "End of the monarchy" were a chorus too powerful to silence. The trauma of the past month left Sylvie with a deep aversion to crowds, and she fought against the urge to bolt.

"*Mon ami* Collot is correct," said a moderate whom Cornélie identified as Jean-François Ducos. "After the events at the Tuileries, there can be no denying that discussion is fruitless. France will be a monarchy no longer. Let us vote."

The audience and the deputies hummed in agreement, and the men began to cast their ballots while the rest of them waited in suspended silence.

"Will the proposition pass?" Sylvie asked. She knew it was at least very likely, but she was wary to ever assume in regard to the will of the people given their constant fluctuation.

"Undoubtedly," Cornélie answered without turning. "And our children will know this as the moment we truly became free." Lise bobbed her head excitedly, leaning over the banister to watch the proceedings.

Even with the great gulf of the hall separating them, Sylvie spotted Gaspard darting from the lower seating to the highest sections where the Robespierres and other leading Jacobins sat.

Her brother wore no wig, so she could follow his excited movements from his yellow crop of hair. He whispered into Maximilien's ear as the chamber settled and the votes were tallied.

Like Cornélie and the society predicted, the proposition passed unanimously. Pride for Robespierre's triumph buoyed her, and for once, Sylvie could join the echoes of "*Vive la nation*" that shook the rafters without a surge of panic.

And when Robespierre moved to speak, her broad smile threatened to split her cheeks in two.

"The National Convention has decreed that the monarchy is abolished in France. Let it henceforth be known that today, *le vingt et un septembre*, shall forevermore be the first day of the republic!"

As he spoke, their fellow women screamed in ecstasy. They fluttered ribbons and shouted, "Our Robespierre!" in a great clamor of idolatry. Their eyes shone with the same adoration Sylvie had carried since the first moment she truly knew him.

Some women shouted marriage proposals; others, "*Vive le Robespierre.*" But all Sylvie heard was the disconcerting sound of her own obsession blaring in her ears. Her love for Robespierre no longer felt so rare, so treasured, so special. She stood helpless among masses of wailing women fluttering over the banister, screaming for their savior, their beloved. And while once Sylvie would have considered Cornélie the only true obstacle, now hundreds stood in her way.

Robespierre must notice his devoted followers madly falling over themselves before him, Sylvie thought. *Surely, he is repulsed by them.*

He was far, but she made out his telltale quirk of the lips despite the distance. Though it was a slight gesture, Sylvie knew Robespierre well enough to understand its nature. He not only acknowledged his fans; he reveled in them.

She looked toward his mistress for some comfort or at least to share in mutual disgust, but she remained unperturbed by the borderline manic display of fervor. This was not passion for republican ideals; this was a passion much more vulgar and base.

And yet, she lusted for his body and mind in the same way, only without the theatrics.

She could not—would not—be like those women.

During celebrations with the Duplays the next day, as France had finally won a battle against the Austrians at Valmy, Sylvie could not stomach the festivities.

At last France had found its voice, if the renditions of "La Marseillaise" outside the window were any indication, but Sylvie had never felt more lost.

Chapter Twenty-Three

When one meddles with the direction of a revolution, the problem is
not how to make it go but how to keep it under control.

—*Mirabeau*

décembre 1792

Sylvie's bond with Cornélie remained unnamed and unknown to
the world. This made their separation all the worse; no one could
have shared in her joy, and now no one could comfort her when the
relationship ended. Their courtship was an invisible dance between
masked partners; when the music stopped, their hands parted and
tears were shed without an audience to gossip or mourn.

After the fierce bloodletting quarrel, she fought against the up-
welling of regret at rebuffing Cornélie. She despised her for being
able to reduce her to this state.

Both women were talented actresses; no one in the Duplay house
nor in Robespierre's clique noticed their estrangement. Lise, perhaps, did not miss the tight-lipped smiles and the distance dividing
them when they sat together. But to everyone else, the ex-lovers
shared a filmy veil to hide behind. Their relationship dissolved like
sugar in water, leaving a sweet varnish over her memories, detect-
able only to those who had tasted it.

She was at least thankful that Cornélie wasn't the vindictive sort.
Cornélie did not inform either Robespierre brother about the truth
of their tender but oh-so-sinful winter dalliance.

Had he not Lise, Gaspard would've noticed the subtle changes in his sister's mood. But she did her best to not begrudge him his happiness. She focused on attending Duplay salons, always careful to remember significant comments that Olympe's society could use.

And the fearsome debate over the fate of the king—now known only as Citizen Louis Capet—meant another meeting with Olympe's network of women.

Sylvie made the trip to Regnault's studio alone for the first time. She grimaced at the dust coating the hem of her gown; they hadn't seen rain in weeks. Flowers wilted in window boxes, and stray dogs whined on doorsteps.

She licked her lips again. The air on the island was never this dry and cold, always laden with humidity from some recent downpour. Paris relished extremes, in both politics and weather.

The studio, with its roaring hearth, brought instant relief. She immediately recognized Simone, who smiled warmly. Charlotte sulked nearby, her pale face pink from the chill outside. But the vast majority of women were unknown to Sylvie, and Cornélie had yet to arrive.

While everyone chatted, free to share pamphlets and opinions without censure, she scanned the canvases for Rhea Silvia. The tether between Sylvie and her mythical counterpart grew tauter every day as she continued her cautious foray into rebellion.

The canvas had been moved nearer to the windows for better lighting, though now the shutters were closed. The sheet covering the painting lacked its previous layer of dust, signifying that Regnault—or perhaps Cornélie—had been working on it regularly.

Not wanting to draw attention, Sylvie only peeked under the sheet. Romulus and Remus, no longer faint outlines of charcoal, clearly reached for their mother's outstretched hand. Silvia's other hand extended toward the viewer—beckoning them into the republic.

She placed her fingers on Silvia's, their coloring so similar that it appeared that her own flesh melted onto the canvas. The old adage that art imitates life did not ring true; she knew she wanted to be Silvia, the faultless legend, and not a coward desperate for validation.

The din of conversation fell into whispers, and she pulled away from her double—worried that her likeness had caused the hush over the studio.

But it was Cornélie and Augustin who provoked the unease. Gus stood in the center of the studio with a placid smile on his face while the women stormed and raged in a low hiss. He looked like a pigeon who had stumbled into a murder of crows.

"We were told"—Charlotte pointed an accusatory finger at his chest—"that your presence was for that one instance only. And how little you have accomplished! The trial of Louis Capet is days away, and his death is all but set in stone!"

He winced. "The Convention's grudges grow deeper with each day."

Charlotte rolled her eyes. "No one argues over his *guilt*."

"A single man's death will not heal this country," Simone said with crossed arms, the melody of her island accent soothing and terrifying Sylvie all at once. "And I worry that the resentment this trial will cause might send us down a dark path."

Gus nodded. "The Convention knows this. But a wounded dog will not seek out aid. It is only once you remove the thorn from his paw that he knows it was for the best."

"And who is this thorn?" Sylvie asked, though she suspected the answer.

"Marat," he spat, "grows hungry. He whispers of spies and mutiny in the ears of every hungry sans-culotte, of every Jacobin eager to make his mark on the Revolution. He despises the moderates for their supposed softness toward Capet, and as his ire grows, so does the people's."

The tense silence erupted into a clamor of disagreement. A woman said, "The blood is not yet dry in the Tuileries—"

Another: "He cannot be allowed to continue this reign of terror!" They all agreed Marat's unchecked influence continued to push Paris further off the proverbial cliff, but they disagreed as to when and how that influence ought to be redressed.

Simone's voice overwhelmed the rest. "And what does Olympe suggest?"

It was Cornélie's turn to answer. "A successful arrest: he's skirted the law for three years. Augustin can convince the Convention to sign a warrant, but Marat will simply go into hiding as he always does. We need to draw him out."

Sylvie averted her eyes—afraid her love and admiration for Cornélie could be discerned by others. She was beautiful like this, commanding a room with her nerve and resolve.

Charlotte grimaced. "Like at your house? But we cannot all storm a Duplay salon without arousing suspicion."

"Marat is suspicious of everyone," Simone said, exasperated. "He knows Cornélie is Robespierre's eyes and ears."

How many mass graves had Marat's words dug? Sylvie sharpened her rage into something useful and said, "Then I will lure him to me." The warble in her voice betrayed the fear in her veins.

"He is a radical, not a trout!" Charlotte protested.

Cornélie's eyes softened. "Sylvie, if anyone has experience with radical egoists, it's you."

Edmond's firebrand lectures and extreme conservatism came to mind—Marat simply lived on the opposite end of the same spectrum. Nothing scared her quite like the madness of a man convinced by his own lies.

She did not want to look into that darkness again, but she longed to prove her commitment to Cornélie—as well as make that monster bend to the power of her will. He had caught her unprepared before; next time he would not have the element of surprise.

"Cornélie may correct me if my impression is wrong, but I believe I intrigued him. He professed an interest in *friendship*, as it were."

Charlotte vehemently refused such a plan. "We cannot use you in such a way. The man is a demon in human skin."

"I wish I could disagree with her assessment"—Cornélie winced—"but I cannot. And we know how difficult Marat's good opinion is to procure."

"Then it is settled," Sylvie said, with only a little bile rising in her throat. "Cornélie will write to Olympe, and the details shall be arranged in ink."

The society mumbled among itself over the various possible outcomes of the king's trial and Marat's subsequent arrest—if her ruse proved successful.

Among the din of discussion, Augustin asked, "Might I request a stroll?" like they debated over tea cakes rather than lives. She knew little of him outside of his relationship to Maximilien—though now he was more of a mystery with his involvement with de Gouges.

While the group argued over solutions with Cornélie, Sylvie took his proffered arm.

They walked arm in arm in the Faubourg Saint-Germain, though this ancient suburb had become less fashionable over the past few years. "I should like to know more about your home," he said. His attention on her was absolute, and she was grateful he did not want to immediately demand she discuss a plan to ensnare Marat.

"I'm not really the best source of information on Chez Rohmer." The bright late-summer sun pricked at Sylvie's exposed skin. She readjusted her parasol. "Aunt Fifi *lives* to talk about its golden age, however. Though she left for Londres some time ago."

He chuckled. "No, I meant your actual home—the island. You must have had such an exciting childhood on an exotic island."

She recoiled at the word *exotic*. "It wasn't exotic to us. I daresay a pine tree is stranger to me than a palm."

He laughed outright. "A fair point. Forgive me."

"But I will confess I miss it"—she stared at the Parisian skyline—"despite the ugliness of its origins."

He nodded in understanding. "One cannot choose to love in pieces; you must love the whole."

She dipped her head. "Well spoken, Monsieur. Though most men fell in love with the island for its money rather than its beauty."

"Then tell me why *you* love it."

She let the parasol slip, allowing a ray of sun to fall on her face. She closed her eyes. "Fewer people than Paris, obviously. I loved the silence. I loved the sand and the orchids. Sugar made the air sweet. And for all its burdens, it looked like Heaven. But for the vast majority of its inhabitants, it was Hell on Earth."

"I cannot take you across the sea, but I can perhaps give you a taste of home without the sin of those who call themselves master." She opened her eyes, and Gus pointed to a grand building to their left. "We are close to the Hôtel Biron."

"I've seen enough rich family châteaus." And she didn't need reminding of the wealth and grandeur her family sacrificed lives for.

"It's not the house—though it's quite a sight—but the gardens."

They approached an enormous freestanding home covered in rococo-style boiserie and passed through the entrance on the Rue de Varenne. Parterre gardens surrounded the estate, the cone-shaped shrubberies and square hedges a marvel of symmetry.

The grottoes and Chinese pavilions surrounded her in foreign wonder but not the authentic beauty of home. "While I appreciate the gesture," she began, "I'm afraid Saint-Domingue is not known for Oriental architecture."

He laughed again. "Ye of little faith. Come into the hothouse." She squinted at the gleaming glass building with reluctance.

She had never been inside a hothouse before; tropical islands had all the heat and sun a flower could need to grow. The glass walls separated the fragile foreign flowers from the harsh seasons of France—letting plants from faraway places call Paris home to the delight of nature lovers.

They stepped within the structure, and immediately she shivered with familiarity.

The heat and humidity prickled at her skin, beckoning the memories from her birthplace to come to the fore of her mind. Cuckoos did not chirp above, and the wind didn't carry the sweet singe of burning sugarcane, but the air was warm and heavy like home.

The room overflowed with greenery she recognized, from palms to hibiscus. Pink and red petals bloomed, eager to show their faces to French tourists. Sylvie touched a violet orchid, the stem bending from its weight. A whole bunch grew along the branch of a mango tree, the flowers reaching out for light streaming through the glass.

She turned to try to thank him. No words came, but the tears did.

His eyes told her he understood. She smiled at him—not to entice or to charm or to distract, but because this room held a piece of her soul. Like the seeds the sailors brought to France from Saint-Domingue, Sylvie had put down roots in strange soil and survived. That island, for all of those who sought to spoil it with sin and pain, would always be a part of her.

Augustin stood beside her to admire the orchids. "I've heard orchids are notoriously fickle plants," he said softly, like they were in a church. Surely, a man who spoke thus could not be real? She kept her suspicions close, but his words crept closer. "But look how beautiful they are, how determined. Is the labor not worth such a reward?" She focused her gaze on the magnificent flowers while she weighed the double meaning of his words.

"That is for you to decide, Monsieur Robespierre. Orchids will grow regardless of admiration. They only know to survive."

"And no one would know an orchid was capable of such wonders by appearances alone."

She clicked her parasol on the ground in exasperation, and her worries tumbled out. "But I would not be growing up a tree. I am working against the aims of Robespierre and every Jacobin in the city."

"Marat signs the death warrant of any man or woman he wants. His pen cuts cleaner than any blade. He will come for everyone you love until only you remain. And then you will mount the scaffold, wondering if there's something you could have done."

Sylvie stroked the petals of a particularly vibrant purple orchid. "This man cannot be swayed by beauty. He bears his soul in his writings, and there is nothing but darkness in them." Augustin opened his mouth to speak, but she held up a finger. "But I have faced that darkness before and failed. I don't want to fail again."

He reached for her hand, his fingers cool despite the feverish air of the hothouse. She took that as a good omen. "This time you won't be alone."

mars 1793

Despite the purge last September, and the beheading of an ex-king in January, France found no satisfaction. The country lived in a state of perpetual war.

Those months following the opening of the Convention and the subsequent trial of the king had been the darkest months of Sylvie's life, so surrounded was she by the virulent rhetoric of justice and bloodthirst.

She accepted the king's treason—his damning letters to foreign supporters had been found in a locked iron chest—and her mind often wandered to Ogé. Both men had committed high treason and were considered traitors of the state, but one was killed to end a war while the other's death started one. It was almost an insult to the suffering of Ogé to compare him to a simpleton and an incompetent king. Equal or not, she wished both men had been spared their humiliating ends.

Gaspard had the sense not to invite her to see the king's death sentence carried out, but Augustin did not. She politely declined him; Sylvie had seen enough headless bodies in her lifetime.

France threw itself into war with Great Britain and the Netherlands, but many battles at home may as well have been fought against phantoms. Marat's paper sang songs of counterrevolutionary uprisings and the evils of the moderate faction in every edition. A man can be silenced; words on paper cannot be.

But with their plan to trap him set in motion, she prayed that iron bars could contain him.

Dear Citoyen Marat,

I fear among the past months' successes you have forgotten our acquaintance. But my desire for friendship, as well as your guidance in a most sensitive matter concerning the safety of our young republic, has not ebbed.

This letter is one of hundreds, I am sure, but I long to see you in the next weeks to discuss a matter of a most intimate nature. I fear a traitor lurks among my circle, and I depend upon you, Citoyen, to advise me.

Your words set me alight with passion and fury for those who would tear us asunder, and I hope, with your generous aid, to bring this suspected turncoat to justice. I pray my next words to you shall be shared in your company.

Je t'embrasse,
Citoyenne Sylvie

If only saliva made a good seal. But spitting on the letter would not inspire the passions she sought.

She had Augustin read it for tone and appeal. They stood in the hallway of Chez Duplay.

He smiled, a touch grimly, and said, "You have quite the skill for this, Sylvie. I suspect he will be at your door in a day."

She exhaled, twisting the ribbon from her bodice around her finger. "You will be able to ensure its delivery?"

He tucked it into his breast pocket and patted it twice. "I am not *wholly* useless. Write another note in anticipation of his acceptance, recommending a time at Chez Rohmer when Gaspard will be absent. Make sure you emphasize that you will be alone."

"Honestly," she chided while putting on her hat, "you act like this is not my first time assisting in an arrest."

Chapter Twenty-Four

History is not a web woven with innocent hands.
—*Abigail Adams*

Early avril 1793

As Augustin and Cornélie suspected, Marat accepted her invitation without hesitation. The Convention, still technically controlled by moderates, eagerly signed yet another arrest warrant.

Sylvie missed Robespierre, but the knowledge that Marat would be far and away from the Convention's rostrum gave her comfort and a not insignificant thrill: she would bring Marat to his knees where others could not.

The rain stopped around the time Louise cleared the dishes of her dinner. Gaspard worked until midnight at City Hall—leaving the house silent and dark.

Sylvie set out brandy glasses—she took a hefty gulp or two to settle her nerves—and comfits to avoid any suspicion. Traitors do not set out a light supper before the National Guard is summoned.

She dressed humbly to appeal to his disdain for finery, but she still took care with her toilette. The heaviness of her perfume would call to him, even if the plainness of her dress did not. He needed to believe she desired him as she desired Robespierre. Two glasses of rich wine gave her the appearance of flushed desire rather than the disgust seeping from her pores.

She told Louise and the cook to retire early and waited by the servants' entrance at the rear of the house.

The wine did not slow her pounding heart, but it did make her vaguely nauseated.

His knock came at around nine o'clock.

He had been in good health those months—she did not feel the heat from the ever-present fever that clung to him. Besides a general pallor, his skin betrayed no malady beyond scarring, and the only telltale sign of his condition was the damned vinegar-soaked turban.

The scent, though most likely mild, never failed to overwhelm her.

She adopted a breathlessness to convince him of her pleasure. "*Citoyen!* You have come—I dared not dream that you would." She ushered him into the kitchen with the intent of keeping him there: the richness of the rest of the house would set him on edge.

The liquor and food sat on the wooden slab, along with stacks of various essays and letters.

"I'm disappointed that you thought I would not," he said as he sat on the proffered chair. She only needed to keep him engaged for a few minutes until the guards arrived.

She poured him some brandy with a steady hand and a steadier smile. "You are a busy man—"

"I am called the People's Friend"—he sipped the brandy, and some tension left his shoulders—"not the Friend of a Few."

"I have some *vin rouge* if the brandy is too fine," she said. "We drink little more than that and watered beer, but I recalled your preference."

He waved away her offer. "You have a keen eye."

She found speaking as truthfully as possible kept her heart and hands from betraying her true intent. "You are not a man to ignore,

Marat." He said nothing and smirked around the rim of his glass. "The moderates should see that before it is too late."

He let the pause draw out before saying, "You mentioned something of an intimate nature."

She shouldn't have been surprised that he was a man who preferred directness. She made a show of biting her lip and twisting in her seat like her very soul raged in a conflict of conscience. He leaned forward—a trout about to bite the line.

"Can I trust you?" she asked, shifting the burden. *Where are the guards?*

He ran his thumb along the artery bounding in her throat. "One can always trust a Friend."

How easily she could end him then, taking more than his freedom—his life. Marat's lust and greed fed the flames of her hatred, and how she wished she could snuff him out.

The door flew from its hinges, and her panic did not need to be forced. The glass of brandy crashed to the ground in a shatter of light. Four National Guardsmen rushed in with muskets drawn.

"How dare you?" she screeched as they dragged Marat to the ground. "Release the deputy at once!"

"He is wanted by the Convention, *Citoyenne*," said one guard, holding her back. She made a show of resistance and outrage.

With no doubts of her loyalty, Marat beseeched her, "Don't fight them. I would not see you stained by their *incompetence*." She was almost offended that he so firmly believed her incapable of duplicity. "They will all fall in the end. But speak to no one; you are an innocent." *Ha.*

They pulled him down the servants' steps and to the jail cart. The guardsman holding her released his grip the moment Marat was out of earshot and eyeshot. "The Convention can promise anonymity: no one shall know where he was found."

She smoothed her skirts and curtsied. The door closed, and the house was quiet once more.

juin 1793

Sylvie enjoyed the warmth in the Rohmers' small garden despite the shade from her parasol.

"Why come outside at all," said Cornélie from the doorway with Gus beside her, "if you're going to hide under a parasol?"

Sylvie put down the letter she was writing to glance over at her visitor. Augustin looked handsome in his navy frock coat and dark curls; unlike his brother, he frequently went without a wig. Cornélie wore a *robe à l'anglaise* with her head uncovered. The green of her gown made her eyes dance and glitter.

Seeing her leaning against the doorframe in repose made Sylvie's heart ache—from longing for the closeness they had once had, and for the future they had fought for and lost.

"I'm only writing letters," she added as she unfolded a tray on which to set her quill and ink. "So I will be rather dull company."

"Writing to whom?"

"Aunt Fifi."

"Is she well?"

"She is. She loves London but despises the English—calls them 'mousy, boorish, colorless dullards.'"

"And let us hope poor soldiers," Augustin murmured. France had enemies at every corner and could not afford to lose its gains at this stage; they had all sacrificed too much. He picked up the newspaper beside her to occupy himself and noticed the author. "Been reading Marat's paper?"

"Unfortunately, yes. Though I prefer papers that do not inflame the fears of the stupid."

Cornélie took it from his hands and folded the paper up. "He is like strong wine: too much renders even the most reasonable man a reckless idiot."

"Or a murderer," Sylvie said, dry and biting. Marat, due to his sheer charisma and legal acumen, had been acquitted several weeks prior.

Cornélie knelt by her feet, sighing before saying, "It was not your fault. You did your duty, and at least now we know that he's impervious to traditional methods."

Sylvie rested her cheek in her palm. "You all worked so hard, and it amounted to nothing."

"That's not true—"

Sylvie kicked the small table, the ink and papers scattering on the ground. "Paris runs out of graves. Men like Marat exist outside of the world we live in. They cannot be bound by reason, by compassion, by justice. And it is men like Robespierre"—her throat constricted—"who are tainted by the poison they sow."

"My brother serves the people," Augustin acknowledged. "And the people like Marat." Even a Marat turned sickly from his jaunt in prison—bound in his medicinal baths for hours and hours a day.

Cornélie stood and went over to a plot of fleurs-de-lis, studying their stems and leaves. "Our national flower," she said, her voice soft like the petals she touched. "The English call them French irises, but it's all the same. You can't find a French garden without a plot of them somewhere."

Sylvie, surrounded by splatters of ink, stared at the purple flowers with a despondent indifference. "I'm shocked they don't turn red from all the blood in the soil."

Cornélie picked up the knife meant to sharpen the quill, lying by Sylvie's feet. "As lovely as they are, they're quite susceptible to disease." She pointed to the tiny splotches of brown and yellow dotting some of the leaves. "And sometimes they must be culled to save the rest." She began cutting the infected parts of the plant—the knife hissed as it sliced through the papery leaves with ease.

"Olympe understands this," Augustin said. "If we sever the infected limb, we may be able to save the body."

Cornélie knelt before Sylvie again and placed the sharpening knife on her lap but said nothing. Sylvie touched the silver filigree along its side. Her reflection in the blade was blurred but unmistakable.

A pistol hard against her chest.

The crack of Ogé's bones.

Lamballe's cold lips pressed against her own.

Marat wanted to turn the Seine red with his enemies' blood, but she would turn his bath red with his own.

THE KNOWLEDGE OF what she planned to do gave Sylvie an alien kind of peace.

The Montagnards, Robespierre and Marat's radical faction, had seen a divisive increase in power within the Convention.

Despite the purge of the prisons, paranoia of counter-rebellion led to the establishment of the Committee of Public Safety. Danton, his scarred face made uglier by his duplicity, oversaw its formation and the execution of policy—which had been focused almost solely on the expulsion of moderates from the Convention.

But Sylvie could only hope that the people might come to prefer political restraint over runaway vengeance, and she felt confident that the catacombs would be fed no corpses this year with Marat gone.

With her mood so improved, Sylvie decided to visit Gus at the Duplay house. He spent more time there than at his own lodgings and had assured her that she was always welcome. And with so many months separating her from the sad business with Cornélie, the warming of Sylvie and Gus's blossoming friendship meant she could navigate the Duplays with less crippling regret.

As she approached the door, a dark-haired gentleman opened it before she could knock.

"Monsieur Le Bas," she said in surprise.

She had met Philippe Le Bas a few times during Duplay soirees, but he had never made a lasting impression. He was a severe, quiet deputy to the Convention—even more so than Robespierre—and a longtime companion of the Montagnards. And, most unfortunately, he hadn't the good looks to counteract the coldness of his demeanor— though she'd heard he was intelligent and fiercely loyal, which she supposed was more important to Robespierre.

"Mademoiselle Rosiers," he said with a stiff bow.

"Good day to you, sir. I was under the impression there were no meetings today; I hope I am not interrupting."

"You've heard correctly; I was only here on a social visit of a more personal nature. Please excuse me."

He moved too quickly to acknowledge her bow, and Sylvie bristled at his brusqueness.

"What an odd man," she mumbled.

The maid ushered her into the salon, where Madame Duplay and Lise stood in animated conversation.

"We will need to write a quick announcement for the paper about your engagement," the lady said to her daughter. "I think an August wedding is appropriate. You'll be wed before he goes to the Armée du Nord."

It was only then that she realized they were not discussing Gaspard.

"You're engaged?" she asked without preamble.

Lise exchanged a dark look with her mother. "Yes—"

Sylvie gripped the back of the settee to keep from falling down in shock. "To whom?"

"Philippe Le Bas."

For reasons she did not understand, Gaspard adored Lise. And now Lise was engaged to another.

"Mother, would you mind giving us a moment?" Lise asked as Sylvie trembled in her rage.

When they were finally alone, Lise gave her explanation. "We met at the Convention a few times. Robespierre suggested the match; in fact, it was he who introduced us. We're very well suited, you see. And with Philippe being such a dear friend to—"

"You're well suited?" Sylvie spat. "You are about to break my brother's heart because you and Le Bas are *well suited*? What does Cornélie have to say of all this?"

Lise looked askance. "She will always support Robespierre."

Sylvie would not accept that pitiful half answer. "She is your sister," she pressed. "She'd want you happy. And you are happy with my brother."

"My happiness is nothing compared to Robespierre's will. And he wills that I marry Le Bas; that's not something my family can afford to ignore."

Lise did not have the same independence of mind her sister possessed, though Sylvie hoped that her love for Gaspard could overtake loyalty to Robespierre. Such a desire ran afoul of all Sylvie's devotion to him, but her loyalty to Gaspard surpassed all things.

"And when were you planning on telling my brother of your plans?"

She gnawed on her lip. "We were going to announce it at a dinner."

Sylvie envisioned the evening unfolding: Le Bas standing at the head of the table surrounded by comrades and intellectuals, wine and cheer flowing. He'd announce the engagement with pride, and Lise's eyes might glisten with tears her onlookers would wrongfully assume sprung from happiness. Gaspard would fly into a tearful rage as Sylvie attempted to restrain him. He'd declare a duel, which he would not survive—emotions made any man a poor shot—and Sylvie refused to see another brother buried.

Her voice rose. "You would not even have the decency to tell him yourself?"

Lise wrung her dress between her trembling hands as her distress rose with every word. "How could I stand before the man I love and tell him I am to marry another? It's unfathomable."

Sylvie walked around the settee and gripped the girl by her shoulders. "No, what's unfathomable is how you could willfully mislead Gaspard into thinking you truly loved him."

Fat tears rolled down Lise's face, but Sylvie had no patience for them. "What would *you* do? Would you tell Robespierre no? Would you deny the most powerful politician in France because of romantic sentiment? It would bring shame to my name and dishonor on my house. Reputation is all a woman has."

Sylvie did not deny the iron truth in Lise's plea, but love for family overcame logic. "And what of my *brother's* honor? His reputation?" If something were to go awry with Marat and Sylvie succumbed to the guillotine's kiss, no one would be there to keep him from a drunken, broken stupor.

"Do not judge me, Sylvie. You have no right to." Lise began putting away the stationery for wedding correspondence.

"Of course I have the right."

"Then you are the pot and I am the kettle."

"I beg your pardon—"

Lise paused for a moment, studying the bunch of quills in her hand that resembled a swan's wing. "When the time comes, you will make the same decision I did."

Sylvie's fury did not allow her to parse Lise's cryptic warning. "But Gaspard has done nothing but serve him dutifully for years!" She never imagined that Robespierre would betray Gaspard's loyalty with heartbreak.

Lise shrugged, the bitterness carved into her face like gouges in a riverbed. "He is young and expendable, while Philippe Le Bas is deputy to Pas-de-Calais. Who do you think Robespierre needs to keep closer?"

She clutched Lise's hand. "But, *Lise*—"

Everything tidied and placed in her box, Lise gathered her things in her arms when she stood. "They would never say so, but we are rewards for loyal service. Robespierre is no feudal lord—he has no lands or titles to bestow. So instead he plays matchmaker, and my father is delighted to comply." She turned to leave but paused in the doorway. "Tell him I'm sorry. Tell him I love him, truly. But France needs this sacrifice: a marriage above reproach."

"France does not care who you marry."

"But Robespierre does. Robespierre speaks for us and for France." Lise closed the door, leaving Sylvie alone in the Duplay salon.

Perhaps she hated Lise because she saw her own weakness reflected back at her. She mirrored Sylvie's own choices—the betrayal of one's lover out of duty to another. There were critical differences, of course, but the tragedy had the same consequences. But Lise and Gaspard had not fallen in love in the shadows. They laughed and kissed and flourished out in the sun—which made Sylvie all the more bitter.

And though she wished it with every fiber of her being, Sylvie knew no amount of treason could spare her brother from this hurt.

Chapter Twenty-Five

There is no disguise which can hide love for long where it exists, or simulate it where it does not.

—*François de La Rochefoucauld*

Sylvie hurried home; she would have to tell Gaspard sooner rather than later or else she'd lose her nerve. She practically tossed her gloves and hat into the maid's waiting arms, ignoring Louise's attempts to speak.

"Gaspard," she called, moving from room to room like an angry storm. "Gaspard, are you home?"

"You just missed him." Robespierre stood at the unlit fireplace, a collection of letters folded under his arm. For the first time, he was the last man she wanted to see. "He will be home within the hour."

He looked nearly handsome with his tousled hair—such a rarity as to make him almost beautiful—and his arm casually draped across the mantel. It infuriated her.

She steadied her breath and lowered her voice. "Lise and Le Bas are engaged; did you know?" She already had the answer, but she wanted him to confirm it.

Besides a slight narrowing of the eyes, he remained unmoved. "Shockingly, I am not privy to the romantic entanglements of every deputy in the Convention."

She had a constant tempest of emotion trapped in the walls of her ribs at all times, and it thrilled her to see Robespierre reveal a little of his own. Raising her voice, she asked, "My brother risks his life for your cause, and yet you mock his loss?"

He chuckled, heavy with the memories and experience of an older man. "Your brother is young; he will find another."

She jabbed a finger in his chest. "That is not the point. Gaspard has so little in the world that brings him happiness. You would simply take it away?"

"Le Bas cares a good deal for her, and you must see why any union between your brother and Lise would have been ill-conceived."

She did not want his reason, his rationale. She wanted him to fix his mistake. "Gaspard is a fine catch," she said, her voice increasingly shrill and desperate as she switched tactics. "Lise is fortunate he gave her any attention at all."

He raised a brow. "You are biased."

"So are you."

He opened his arms like the answer to her frustration sat before her. "Monsieur Duplay cannot have a slave-owning son-in-law."

Gaspard worked too hard and sacrificed too much for their father's weaknesses to destroy him. She stepped closer, fury making the space between them evaporate like water on hot steel. "He does not own— A father's crimes should not taint the son."

Robespierre shook his head. "Past or present, it was a flaw impossible to overlook." He snatched the hat and cloak he had thrown over the hideous fuchsia chair.

"In another time," she shouted after him, struggling to keep up with his fierce strides, "the Duplays would be begging my brother to make an offer."

He whirled on her so quickly she ran into his chest. "Men like Le Bas are the new elite, Sylvie."

She did not step away but raised her chin and sneered, "He is common—so is Lise."

"And you are mulatto. We may accept you as you are, but I think you can see where you stand in the eyes of the people."

Maybe Marat's imminent demise falsely enhanced her confidence; perhaps knowing that Robespierre was not infallible made her reckless. But her hand connecting with his face surprised her almost as much as it surprised him. His eyes burned hotter than the handprint on his cheek. He paused in his shock before bringing her face to his for a fearsome kiss. The slur hung in the air, and the kiss branded it on her lips. He tasted like want and frustration, a bitter combination that left her mouth sour.

She shoved him away—uncomfortably aware of her choler and his closeness. In another time she would have preened at such a display by the man she'd so long admired. Yet, she had hardly seen him these many months, and his inability to stamp out those who would ruin his legacy drove her rage higher.

His forehead wrinkled in confusion like he didn't know what to do next. He opened his mouth to speak but closed it again.

"I think you will be missed at home," she offered through her teeth. To throw her station back at her like it wasn't a truth she'd sought to escape her entire life was a wound he knowingly carved.

He nodded and left in a hurry, leaving her wondering why he'd come in the first place—and her lips aching from his bruising kiss.

SYLVIE'S CONCERN FOR Gaspard served as a welcome distraction from Robespierre's uncharacteristic show of passion. The complication it presented for her tenuous bond with Cornélie, and the trouble it posed to their mission as they dealt with Marat, could not be afforded.

So Sylvie spent the next day hoping her brother never came home, if only to prolong his happy ignorance for a couple hours more. But even Robespierre slept, and eventually Gaspard came home an hour after Sylvie had eaten her supper.

She watched him from the doorway. Gaspard stood by the table, picking at the plate of meat on his desk while flicking through a newspaper. She despised being ignored.

"Why are you lurking?" he asked without looking up.

"I'm not."

"Yes, you are. Whenever you feel guilty, you hover until you can't help but confess what you've done. It's been that way ever since you were small."

Sylvie grabbed the newspaper away from his face. "I don't feel guilty." He quirked his brow and popped a piece of chicken into his mouth. "But, yes, I do have something I must tell you, though I am loath to do so. You ought to sit down."

"Well, goodness," he said, wiping his fingers on the abandoned newspaper. "This *is* serious."

She swallowed any biting remark and took a deep breath. "Lise is engaged."

"What?"

Now I have your attention.

"Lise is engaged," she repeated. "To Philippe Le Bas. It is done."

Gaspard gripped the arms of his chair. "That's impossible."

"I can assure you, it is quite possible."

"How can you be certain?" he asked, walking around the desk. "You hardly speak to Lise."

She bristled. "I ran into Le Bas when I went to visit Gus. He claimed to have been visiting the Duplays for a personal matter, and then I overheard Madame Duplay discussing the engagement. Lise confirmed the details."

He shook his head frantically, refusing to believe her. "Lise *loves* me."

"I do not doubt that, brother mine," she murmured. She put a hand on his shoulder, watching his face crumple. "She does. But that changes nothing."

Love is only powerful, she thought, *when we are* willing *to fight in her name.*

He pushed her away and paced. "Le Bas is no good for her," he cried. "He's cold and reserved, and . . . he will not read to her. He will not pick her flowers or sing her songs. How could she agree to such a scheme?"

She struggled to balance comfort and sympathy with her own annoyance. "Lise likes him well enough, and Monsieur Duplay would not dare go against Robespierre."

"What do you mean? Robespierre orchestrated this charade? He is the one who arranged the match?"

She nodded with a sorry sigh. "It was a surprise to no one except us. Le Bas has become a strong supporter, and I suppose Robespierre needed him closer still."

He threw the porcelain plate against the wall. She controlled her urge to wince when it shattered—Gaspard had maintained his own composure during many of her tirades. And his pain now was more deserved than her tantrums ever were.

"And what am I if not a loyal supporter?" he asked, enraged and tearful. "I have worshipped his every word, memorized every line! I may disagree with a few others of his party, but in *him* my faith is absolute. I've made myself sick rationalizing the things I've done. Why"—he dissolved in sobs, struggling to get his words out—"why would he take her from me?"

Robespierre gave Gaspard everything—and took it all away. Gaspard always got what he wanted; the world always obliged. She watched him navigate society with ease and access, while she moved with lead weights tied on each foot. He hadn't known true loss, which made this pain all the worse.

She kissed the top of her brother's golden head. "Though we may try, we will never be one of them, Gaspard."

————

As expected, Gaspard did not join Sylvie for dinner—consuming the weight of his meal in gunfire instead. So Sylvie blocked out the clamor and ruckus coming from his study, sympathetic to his heartbreak but unable to soothe him.

As she blew on a spoonful of soup, Louise fluttered in, wringing her graying apron. "Miss Sylvie!"

"Just ignore him, Louise," she said. "We have both borne far worse."

"But, Mademoiselle, he is *leaving*."

She dropped her spoon with a splash and a clatter. "Leaving? In this state? To go where?"

"To the Duplays': he's brandishing his sword about, declaring that he shall call out Monsieur Robespierre! He's half in his cups."

Sylvie ran out after her brother into the street. She heard him before she saw him.

"Come out, Robespierre!" called Gaspard, his rapier glinting under lanterns. The night air made his drunken cries carry farther. "I will have my satisfaction."

"Brother," Sylvie hissed as she clung to his arm. "Come home. Before someone hears you." It was just after dinner, and she feared what danger her brother may invite from men on their way to the taverns. "What do you hope to gain?" she asked. "No one would dare let you near Robespierre. Do not shame yourself, or Lise."

His red-rimmed eyes narrowed into a sneer, and he shoved her off, howling Lise's name.

"Robespierre steals my sister." Sylvie flushed, both embarrassed and confused at how he could possibly know about Robespierre's *inclinations*. "He steals my wife—"

She hissed, "Lise is not your wife!"

He sobbed. "She was *supposed* to be. We were happy. So happy. And she knew—she knew for weeks, and she led me on."

He stood beneath Lise's window and called for her once more.

"For heaven's sake, Gaspard. *Shush.*"

"He's a tyrant, he is. A despot. He'd replace the monarchy with a dictatorship. I want 'im ruined."

If anyone were to repeat her brother's slurs against the Incorruptible, the Tribunal would imprison Gaspard without hesitation. "Someone will hear you!"

He waved his rapier toward the Duplay house. "Let 'em hear. You adore him too much to see what he's doing. You all love him too much. He stole Lise from me, and I'll cut 'im down."

Lise's curls sprung out from the second-story window. "Gaspard, what are you doing?" she asked, and Sylvie could see her stricken expression from down in the street.

"How could you?" asked Gaspard, the anger gone and only anguish remaining.

"Please, my love, don't do this."

"I'm not yer love. Not anymore." He smeared his tears on the back of his sleeve, and the anger returned. "Bring out Robespierre! I would have him answer for his cruelty. You were not his to give." Several other windows propped open, and Gaspard did not have the awareness to sense the tension brewing in the street. "*Robespierre!*"

Augustin stood on the steps, looking down on her half-drunk, half-choleric brother. "I hear there is a buffoon screeching my name out in the road."

"Do not hide him from me, Augustin."

Augustin kept his hands raised and approached Gaspard slowly. "Luckily for you, *mon ami*, he is not here."

"Then where is he?" He whirled on the steps and stumbled back into the street. "I wish to string the blackguard up by his heels—"

Augustin muscled his way between Sylvie and Gaspard, holding the latter by his shoulder. Gus's mouth was so close to Gaspard's ear, one might mistake his threatening whisper to be a lover's kiss. Sylvie could not hear what was said, but Gaspard visibly stilled.

"It seems our friend is ill," Augustin said to the crowd of Duplays after speaking in a low tone to her brother. Cornélie clutched the railing, warily watching Gaspard. "Let me escort him back to his rooms."

Lise was sniffling above them, clearly distraught by the whole debacle. Gaspard kept his head low.

"We will put this unpleasant evening behind us, won't we?" Augustin asked the ladies Duplay as he pulled Gaspard's arm over this shoulders. "The lad is only miffed at the loss of his lover. No need to bring Maximilien or Monsieur Duplay into this ugliness, yes?" Augustin's suggestion was clear, and Sylvie breathed a sigh of relief when everyone nodded in agreement. "Then let us go home."

THE CHURCH BELLS rang out when midnight struck, and Sylvie was still dressed.

Gus and Gaspard had been speaking in the study for the past hour while she twiddled her thumbs. Gaspard had put them all at risk with his drunken confessions, and she was unsure how forgiving Robespierre would be.

Heart pounding and unable to sleep, she slipped downstairs and into the dining room, finding comfort in recent memories of meals and wine shared. She slumped into a chair. Her reflection, lit by a single candlestick, danced and warped in the silver candelabra.

Night made voices clearer and propriety less pressing, and she heard every word coming from the adjoining salon through the slightly opened door.

"I can hardly breathe without pain," her brother said, hoarse from yelling in the street. She crept closer to the *porte-fenêtre* separating the rooms and looked in through the pane. Gaspard sat doubled over, his forehead red and sweat dampened in the firelight. Gus knelt before him in only shirtsleeves with a hand on his shoulder, though his back was to the door.

"It hurts now, by Jove, I know it does. But it will not last." Gaspard shook his golden head, and Gus's hand slipped into the curls on the nape of his neck. She started to suspect why Gus did not yield to her in the ways she had learned to expect of men.

"No, no one will ever love me like she did."

"My sweet boy." Gus's other hand migrated to his cheek and wiped away lingering tears. "Now, I *know* that to be false." Their voices turned to whispers, dissolving in the space between her and the sofa. She pressed against the glass, and the hinges groaned in protest.

She whirled back against the wall and out of sight.

Gaspard spoke first. "I'm going to bed before I do anything else foolhardy."

"More tea, less rum, *mon ami*," Augustin called after him.

Only one set of footsteps left the room, and Sylvie waited for the sound of the front door. None came.

"Come out, *mon chou*. I know you lurk in the shadows."

"I would hardly call it *lurking*." She stepped into the salon and nearly gasped at Augustin's tearful face. "Pray, do not tell me you pine for him?"

He gave a watery laugh and sank onto an ottoman. "You're an astute girl. You would have seen it sooner had you not been so otherwise engaged."

She echoed his laugh, resting her hands on his hanging head. "You weep over my blockheaded brother? He's pretty to look at, certainly, but why not woo some other hapless dandy?"

He looked up, much like a fox would when the hunter approaches to make his final shot. "He's so good, so gentle. He gives himself so wholly to anyone and anything and—"

"You're better off tossing your heart in the Seine."

"Better than tossing it to wolves." The coldness in his accusation stung harder than any European winter.

She flinched and stepped away to keep from striking him. His shoulders sagged lower like they were anchored to the ground.

"Look at the two of us: you who love the wrong woman and I who love the wrong man." He swirled a half-empty cup of port before downing it. "I don't think any irreparable damage has been done. We all know that sacrifices must be made. Le Bas is a necessary ally, but Max is not so unfeeling as to scorn Gaspard for his very natural reaction."

Despite the added complication of his feelings, she valued Augustin immensely in these moments. She could trust him, and trust held incalculable value in times like this—but, like bread, was in short supply.

"In fact, I think it has strengthened Gaspard's loyalty to our cause. We shall redirect his frustration to those more deserving of his ire— Marat, specifically."

"My brother is a poor actor," Sylvie countered. She was willing to challenge the most powerful men in France, but she doubted if she was willing to bring her brother into that fold. "Will he be able to continue working for Maximilien?"

He finished the port with a flourish. "He'll have to. None of us can afford to fall out of Max's good graces. And, unfortunately, I don't think my brother will wear power well."

FOR ALL THEIR talk of resistance and strength, Sylvie decided Parisians were weaklings in the face of a little sun.

She and Gaspard found comfort during the peaks of French sum-

mers; it was only then that Paris felt anything like her childhood on Saint-Domingue. The French capital replaced palms with
linden trees and flamingos with sooty pigeons. But her body
would never forget how to adapt to the thick layers of humidity-
laden air.

Unattractive beads of sweat trickled along the brows of Parisian
citoyens while Sylvie's skin eagerly tanned in the afternoon light—
despite the thick parasols and wide woven hats—without soiling her
petticoats in perspiration.

And once Gaspard's melancholy weakened its grip after a week of
heartbreak-induced isolation, he emerged from Chez Rohmer with
her from time to time to walk the Tuileries—and his skin, too,
adopted a golden hue.

The girls on Saint-Domingue called him Apollo; his cheeks and
curls looked like he'd stolen a piece of the sun. He basked in the
gardens, while his already golden sister hid under layers of lace and
shady trees.

Maximilien and the other higher-ups preferred the indoors.
They were creatures of winter and shadow, not the picnics and teas
on which Sylvie was raised.

When she dreamed of France as a child, she envisioned dashing
hunters on horseback gallivanting through the woods and fields surrounding Versailles while powdered ladies cooed from manicured
gardens above them.

She did not expect those gallant nobles to be pale, bookish creatures who built upon a stone city with blood instead of mortar.

And besides, June had kept them busy.

Robespierre's coauthored Jacobin constitution was accepted without hesitation, and Sylvie mused that his influence was so profound
that tea stains on paper would've been lauded as genius. With the
moderates out, the Jacobin Club and its subgroup of Montagnards
held Paris—and therefore France. If they did not amputate the pu-

trid limb of their party, the infection would spread too far and too deep to stop.

"The moderates are out," Cornélie said after skimming a letter from Olympe de Gouges. She stood before a select group of their compatriots from the society. In May, they had formally named themselves the Society of Revolutionary Republican Women, but for their more counterrevolutionary enterprises they limited attendance to a few. "With no one to check their power, the responsibility falls to us." Olympe reconfirmed what they already knew.

Through Danton, the Montagnards expelled every moderate from office while cementing their own power, which left any hope of a strong moderating party as dead as the king. Men like Marat reveled in the promise of unopposed radical rule, while Olympe's society privately lamented the loss of their secret allies.

"Death is the only check these men understand," Sylvie said. How many times had she been at the receiving end of a deadly threat, tears streaming down her cheeks while she pleaded for mercy? For once, she wanted to be the one to see the terror in a man's eyes.

Simone put a gentle hand on her shoulder and said, "I know we are eager to restore balance, but we must not make such a decision lightly. They have tried to take our humanity for centuries; do not let them succeed."

Charlotte, the most vengeful of their lot, did not understand the nuance of Simone's advice. "We must kill one man to save a hundred thousand. And I will be the one to do it."

The room roared to life with disagreement and discord, but Cornélie raised her hands to signal quiet. "I cannot send you alone into that mad dog's den. And I doubt he'd allow such a stranger into his home unannounced."

Despite Charlotte's education and pedigree, she often looked unkempt or even wild. She wore her bitterness poorly, and Sylvie agreed that she alone would not gain access to Marat's home.

Marat had recently married, so Sylvie offered, "It must be when his wife is out. Even Marat would not be so reckless as to invite a woman upstairs while his bride is below."

Cornélie studied her with a pensive look. "Sylvie will accompany her."

Charlotte scoffed. "The girl couldn't stab a man with a sewing needle, let alone a knife."

Sylvie stepped close. "Unless you want all of Paris, including our target, to take one look at you and know you're a murderer, I recommend you accept my help. I agree, you have more experience than I, but Marat knows me. He never suspected I had anything to do with his arrest. Without me, he will cast you out like a common vagabond."

Charlotte pinched her mouth and turned away, which Sylvie took as understanding. Perhaps this was futile; perhaps this was reckless. But she thrilled at the promise of a future without Marat.

The Revolution had taken many lives, but it had finally given hers back.

Chapter Twenty-Six

That blood which thou hast spilled, should join you closely in an eternal bond.

—*Vittorio Alfieri*

Sylvie prepared for bed later that evening, snuffing out candle after candle until the soft patter of feet stopped her.

"We've settled on July," Cornélie said. Her hair was down, her curls blurring into the darkness of the hallway behind her. Sylvie let one candle remain. "So about two weeks from now."

"Good," Sylvie said. She sat at her vanity tying her hair into a tignon for bed.

Cornélie stepped across the threshold of the room, wringing her hands. "You agreed to our scheme rather quickly."

With the tignon partly tied, Sylvie spun on her stool to look at Cornélie. "Of course I did."

Sylvie dreamed about killing Edmond instead of leaving him to the mutilation of liberated slaves; it wasn't that he didn't deserve such a death, but more about the justice of having his "filthy-blooded" sister doing it by her own hand.

She dreamed about killing every sans-culotte parading Lamballe's head around Paris—to let them taste the screams and tears of a murdered princess.

And she dreamed about the death of Marat.

When murder is the order of the day, the thought of taking a life for the betterment of France becomes an increasingly palatable option.

"How can you possibly know the risk?" Cornélie asked as she sat on the bed. The intimacy they shared was harder to dissolve than their romance.

"How can I not? We invite that risk into our lives every moment we pray for the mercy of men who hardly think of us at all."

Cornélie reached toward her but thought better of it, wiping her palms on her knees. "This feels less like a risk and more like throwing your life away."

"Has it ever been said that a man who throws himself out the window to escape from a fire is guilty of suicide?"

Cornélie threw up her hands in exasperation. "Do not quote Rousseau at me, Sylvie. I doubt he thought his words would be used to rationalize an assassination."

"But Marat does! He knows his words are power." Sylvie could not keep still and began pacing. "Do you suddenly think he can be silenced in any other way?"

The muscles in Cornélie's jaw clicked and twitched. "I have no doubts that Marat deserves death."

"Then why do you fight me?"

"Because you frighten me!"

"Wanting to end Marat frightens you?"

"Your complete willingness, the lack of hesitation? Yes, yes, it *does* frighten me."

"Has anyone ever hated you? Not a nursery squabble or an argument between siblings. *Hatred.* Someone looking at you like you are vermin, like a sick sheep in their perfect flock?" Cornélie shook her head. "I have endured that hatred on Saint-Domingue. That kind of hatred takes time, education, and tradition over years to flourish. Here"—Sylvie pointed out the window—"I've seen a similar hatred sown by Marat, and it led to a similar fate: more dead, innocent people."

Cornélie did not hesitate to take her hands this time. "I hear you, Sylvie, every word. I do not pretend to know that pain, but I know *you*. Why are you so resolved to do this yourself?"

Sylvie sat back down to apply lemon cold cream as she spoke. "I despise men who do what they want and take what they want—who wield their power and their words like ribbons on a maypole."

Saint-Domingue
juillet 1791

The piles of loam looked like dark mountains in the grass. She reached out to touch one—warm from sitting under the sun but still damp and velvet soft. Perfect for growing coffee. Better for burying the bodies that grew it.

Little bugs burrowed within the soil, making tiny catacombs. How long did the bodies last in these graves, unprotected by mahogany caskets and lovingly bestowed last rites, before the bodies became soil themselves?

She wove in between those dark mountains, each denoting a recent burial. The darker the soil, the fresher the death.

How deep did the bodies go? How many mass graves fed the palms growing strong overhead?

Julien was fond of her mother. She knew he would not have put her in a mass grave. Her suffering earned her some dignity in death; Sylvie was sure of it.

She moved deeper into the forest, where the grass was interspersed with shoots and shrubs and larger trees. It had not been cleared for a decade at least, but she felt the graves in the spots where the saplings grew.

Finally, she spotted the shadow of a cross under the evergreen branches of a mature sabina tree.

The boughs protected the grave from the worst of the rain and wear, as well as discouraging much growth beyond grasses. Sylvie knelt in front of the stone cross and read, "Beloved Nicole, aged about twenty-three."

A small shell necklace was draped across the tombstone. Sylvie recognized them as cowrie shells, precious little things the slaves would hide and hoard all the way from West Africa. She had heard Edmond describe them as a combination of money and jewelry, but the tenderness of the image—tiny white shells tied around the unforgiving Catholic grave—seemed more than that.

Her mother was loved. Loved so much that someone gave away a precious symbol of home to let her mother have it in death. Her father sacrificed nothing but a pittance on rock; some enslaved person gave up a piece of their lost world.

Gingerly, she removed the necklace—only temporarily—and lay down on the earth with her eyes facing skyward. She pushed back her fichu and rested the necklace on her chest, secretly praying to any gods that her mother wore it in life.

She imagined her mother's hand, cool and smooth like the shells—not blistered and rough from the work before Julien snatched her for himself—resting on her skin as she sobbed in the silence of the forest.

Her tears slid down her cheeks and into the soil. She wished she could crawl inside her tears and down to the darkness below, drowning all of the enslavers in her wake.

A slow rumble of distant thunder woke her from her half-conscious state. She clambered to her feet, bits of dirt and grass falling from her muslin dress.

Hurricanes and storms and winds had not moved the necklace, and Sylvie wouldn't, either. She pressed the gift to her lips before wrapping it around the cross once more. She would steal nothing more from her mother than her father already had.

Sylvie whispered her mother's name over and over as she trudged back through the dampening grass. Julien could not take her mother from her, nor could death, if Sylvie knew her name.

Nicole.

Nicole.

Nicole.

She said the name like a prayer, like a curse, and mostly like a threat.

"I know that the consequence is death, regardless of what I choose," Sylvie added after pulling her mind out of the past Killing Marat would not bring her mother back or make her free, but if Alice's face had been any indication, it certainly brought deserved satisfaction. "I'd rather die knowing I took a stand rather than as a coward. But I do not plan to get caught."

"Charlotte will remain while you flee." Cornélie smelled the various jars and essences spread about. "Her intention has always been martyrdom."

Sylvie chuckled. "How vain."

"She has a dramatic flair."

Sylvie swiveled on her stool, looking up at Cornélie's moonlit face. "Do you believe I can do this?" Sometimes she wished she had taken her mother's necklace, to rub the shells in hope that a little bit of her courage would pass through her skin.

"The selfish part of me doesn't want to put you in danger." Cornélie traced the line of Sylvie's brow and down the slope of her cheek. "But I *know* that you can, and you must."

Cornélie was her salvation and damnation—the fantasy in her nightmares, the rot in a ripe apple.

The secrecy, the confessions, the closeness, the blood bounding through her veins—it all banded together into one intoxicating potion that threatened to dismantle her very soul. The moment before, Sylvie had been in her power, and now Cornélie was in hers.

Her pupils expanded, leaving only narrow circles of blue iris. "Sylvie."

Dire repercussions loomed if they failed in their quest to control the radical fringes of politics, but they moaned and sucked and tasted, throwing themselves into each other as they threw themselves into the hungry maw of revolution. They danced on hot coals; a wrong step and you'd catch aflame. Sylvie kissed like she was trying to taste Cornélie's heart.

At this moment, she'd almost take a severed neck over a broken heart. *Fool.*

They fell back against the softness of the bed. Sylvie let Cornélie bear the brunt of her weight as she swallowed every whimper and moan. The heat from Cornélie's skin burned through Sylvie's nightgown to her fingers, uninhibited by stays or boning.

She wanted more—more pleasure, more distraction, more intimacy—but the need for air stopped them both.

They separated to catch their breath, lips swollen and hair in disarray. Sylvie liked Cornélie like this. They had never loved each other in Sylvie's bed, and there was a special thrill in wrapping Cornélie in her scent.

"How I missed you," Cornélie said, cupping her cheek. "I should never have let you leave. I don't care what led you to me; all I know is that I cannot live without you."

Sylvie debated on whether or not she should tell her about Robespierre's kiss—if Cornélie still felt tied to him as she did. People often excused words born out of anger; perhaps Cornélie should excuse a kiss born of anger, too. Sylvie's passion and obsession with him blurred at its edges, where her love for Cornélie had never seemed so clear.

The scents of Cornélie's rose water and Sylvie's lemon cold cream mingled together as their bodies did. "I have never known a happiness purer than this," Sylvie whispered between kisses. "And I don't think I ever will."

Maybe the promise of murder heated their blood, and the threat of Sylvie's arrest made past hurts seem inconsequential. But in

Cornélie's embrace, she knew a peace that no treaty or war or marriage could ever promise.

juillet 1793

By tomorrow night, Marat would be no more.

Olympe had written with her final approval, and Charlotte stayed in a hotel near Chez Marat to watch for any sudden developments.

Cornélie worried over Sylvie at every other hour of the day, asking if she had changed her mind or needed consoling. When she wasn't worrying, they made love and whispered impossible promises into each other's skin.

But by late afternoon Sylvie knew they both needed a distraction—so she convinced the Duplays, Robespierres, and Rosiers to play *jeu de mail* in the now completely public Tuileries Garden. She also longed for green fields and lush flowers after such a cold and brutal winter.

Due to Robespierre's celebrity, little patches of onlookers strolled around the playing grounds, gawking at the Incorruptible. Maximilien would never do something so undignified as play pall-mall, so the gossipers would have to be entertained by Le Bas and Max making conversation beneath a tree. However, that did not keep him from casting stolen glances at Sylvie while she studiously ignored him.

"At least Gaspard spends more time at home," Sylvie said as she lined up her shot. She and Cornélie stood a distance away from the others. Augustin used his mallet like a walking stick, leaning against it as he watched them give a few practice swings. "*And* he's been civil to Robespierre." She avoided the gaze of the man in question by placing an unnatural focus on her shot. She struck the ball with her mallet, and the ball went widely off target. Gus snickered.

"Perhaps he could show you how to play properly," he said. "Try hitting the ball under the arches instead of at my shins."

"Lise has just been ignoring him, that heartless woman. And now Le Bas is always about, glowering at everything."

Cornélie tried to correct Sylvie's posture. "Space out your hands and loosen your grip."

"Robespierre sees none of the tension, of course. He is sympathetic to Gaspard, but what is sympathy in the face of heartbreak? We all want to further Robespierre's success, but at the expense of my brother's happiness?"

"No, no, not that loose. And square your hips."

"Lise seems happy enough with him. Though I don't know how she can stand his atrocious northern accent."

"Don't swing so hard. It's not a test of strength."

"That wretched artist Robespierre likes so much—Jean or Jacques David or something—has been lurking about here as well. Robespierre's commissioned some secret project, though I can't see how any poor creature could endure getting their portrait done by that man. Why must all the Montagnards be so horrendously ugly?"

"Hit the ball, Sylvie."

Sylvie let the mallet fall and crossed her arms. "If you're in high dudgeon, then I have no desire to play with you."

Cornélie pinched the bridge of her nose. "I'm not cross. Forgive me. Marat is fueling fires that have long needed to be extinguished. And I'm scared for you." She squinted into the July sun.

Sylvie struck the ball, missing its target. "There," she said with more gentleness. "I've made my shot."

"And I've no broken bones," Cornélie said with cheek, but the tears in her eyes betrayed her distress. Sylvie went to her and wrapped her arms around her quaking shoulders. In full view of the public, her means of comfort were limited.

Gus turned around to give them privacy.

"I love you," Sylvie said. "And you are too skilled a leader for us to fail."

"If it weren't for me, you wouldn't be in danger at all. I should never have brought you into this."

Sylvie held Cornélie's chin between her fingers. "Every morning I thank you for giving me a purpose—for giving a silly, spoiled girl from the colonies a means to rectify her past mistakes."

"And if his death amounts to nothing? If it does not give you the satisfaction you crave?"

Unsure of an answer, Sylvie pulled away. If Marat's end did not bring the peace she craved, the security she longed for, then what hope was there for France?

Without any target in mind, she swung her mallet with all the force she possessed, sending the ball flying off into the shrubbery.

13 juillet 1793

Sylvie slept ill that night, to little surprise. After taking a light breakfast in bed, she changed into a walking dress and set out for Chez Marat.

"What are you doing up at this hour?" asked Gaspard. The door to his study was open, and he caught the ivory of Sylvie's gown in front of his doorway.

Schooling her features into something resembling calm, she said, "It's nine in the morning."

"Exactly," he said. She smoothed his flyaway curls, wondering if it would be the last time she'd touch them. But she shook off those paranoid worries; she was going to keep them both safe—Gaspard worked safely at his desk, nowhere near the dangers she planned to witness.

"You look horrendous. Spending all your time with Monta-gnards is making you ugly."

He swatted her hand away and straightened his cravat. "Don't distract me with insults. Where are you going?"

Arms crossed, she answered, "What business is it of yours?"

"I'm your brother. I'm entitled to know where you're going."

"Oh, don't start wheedling me about brotherly responsibility now—where was it when you tried to teach me to count cards in vingt-et-un?"

"That *was* brotherly responsibility; I taught you vital financial skills."

"Those *skills* almost got you killed in a gambling den on Saint-Domingue."

"Almost." He grinned.

Laughing, Sylvie tied the ribbons of her cotton lappet beneath her chin. "I'm going to take tea with Cornélie and Gus in one of the *jardins*. Nothing scandalous, I assure you."

"Father would disagree," he muttered as he sipped his tea, most likely too cold to be appetizing.

"We disagree with Julien on most things," she countered, putting on her gloves one finger at a time.

"Just have a care while you're out, won't you? Stay with Gus."

"Gus? *Mon ange*, you can't depend on anyone," she chided. "Don't try to fool yourself into thinking you can." She kissed his cheek as he frowned. "Go outside today. I'm sure you could charm any lovely Parisian lady—they all have such charming black teeth."

He gave her his first genuine laugh in weeks, and she replayed it in her mind all the way to Chez Marat.

EVERYONE IN FRANCE knew where Jean-Paul Marat lived.

Charlotte, before the Society had reined her in, had desired to kill him publicly at the Fête de la Fédération. But his skin condition worsened in the summer, so the only witness to his death would be the four walls of his room.

Marat occupied a nondescript set of apartments on the Left Bank with his wife, and a small gathering of sans-culottes permanently cluttered the street hoping to catch a glimpse of him.

But they'd be disappointed; he'd been forced to influence his followers all from the confines of his medicinal baths.

Sylvie waited outside, obscured by an abandoned stall, but she did not have to wait long before Charlotte emerged. Only, she emerged from inside his house rather than from her neighboring hotel. Sylvie couldn't know how long she'd been at the house.

"Charlotte," she called in a half whisper, raising both of her hands to show she posed no threat.

Charlotte slipped into the stall to join her. She had done nothing to tidy her appearance.

Sylvie raised her chin. "I assume you came early to try and kill him alone. Why is he not dead yet?"

"How do you know he isn't?"

Motioning to the bustling street, Sylvie said, "It's too quiet—there's no hysteria. Marat has a constant audience. That will not stop when he's dead."

Charlotte let her shoulders fall, her face heavy with failure. "His servant would not let me in. I didn't know what to do. He always takes an audience with his supporters. I wasn't expecting—"

"Things not to go exactly as planned?"

Charlotte narrowed her eyes. "I've never done this before."

"It shows."

The two daughters of privilege stared each other down. Sylvie imagined those pretty chestnut curls making a fine wig without that impudent neck in the way. But arguing with this amateur assassin helped no one. Charlotte had at least some of her wits about her. Sylvie needed to swallow her pride if the deed was to be successful.

"Go to a hairdresser," said Sylvie.

"Wha—why? How will that gain me an audience?"

"You didn't sleep last night, and it's obvious. Go to the hairdresser and then to your hotel. Write a letter bewailing the conditions in Caen—make up royalist names if you must. Marat says he is a friend of the people; be a person in need of help, and he will come to your aid. And to ensure an audience, *follow the plan* and let me join you."

Charlotte nodded. Sylvie knew she was a willing martyr, but she was an obedient one at that.

"I'll come back before his dinner and shall try again."

Sylvie watched her leave in a mixture of awe and pity. Charlotte had committed herself to assured execution, and Sylvie couldn't decide if that was remarkable courage or remarkable stupidity.

CHARLOTTE RETURNED TO their previous meeting place well-groomed and handsome.

Sylvie took a deep breath. "Good, you look less deranged. Did you write the letter?" Charlotte sneered but nodded.

Due to the early Fête de la Fédération activities, the streets didn't boast quite as many people at this time of day, providing the women with some added degree of protection.

Still, Sylvie hid herself within the same abandoned stall—keeping her shoes clear from the rotting fruit that remained from the failed business. But when the afternoon sun dipped closer to the Parisian skyline, she knew they couldn't wait any longer.

She had dressed for obscurity, not to call on the Enlightenment elite. But she gave the servant her best smile when she received Sylvie in the Marat sitting room with a jittery Charlotte in tow.

"Do tell Citoyen Marat that Sylvie Rosiers calls on him. I have a message of some importance: I did not trust a courier."

"It is nothing," said the maid. "I understand his reluctance; our people are under siege by royalist madmen. No one is safe."

"Indeed. Their watching eyes are never far."

"France is well on her way to liberty. And Marat is bathing in his study, if you care to wait?"

Sylvie waved her hand. "I'll just give him the letter and leave him to his business," she said as she rose. He normally just slept in the bath; she could not delay until he finished. He even took meetings in that damned vinegar soak.

The maid scurried upstairs to relay their arrival. Sylvie smirked at how quickly the maid returned. "He is happy to receive you now."

"No need to wait for me. I'll see myself out."

Grateful, the maid motioned up the stairs. "His room is the last door on your left."

SYLVIE AND CHARLOTTE stood outside of Marat's bedroom door.

"Do you have the knife?" Sylvie asked, though she already knew the answer. She hardly recognized her own voice. Charlotte partially withdrew the butcher's blade from her pocket. Sylvie had never stabbed someone, but the brutal serrations lining the knife seemed deadly enough. The sunlight bounced off the virgin metal.

Charlotte opened the door slowly. Soft murmurings came from behind the linen curtain concealing Marat.

A single window let in little light, keeping the room in a state of constant night except for a few candles. The smell of vinegar that haunted Sylvie had never been stronger. But instead of triggering an insurmountable wave of panic, the fumes fueled the rage that led her here.

She turned to Charlotte, but her coconspirator had frozen in place. The woman palmed the knife, trembling too fiercely to strike true.

His mumblings stopped, and Marat called, "Citoyenne Sylvie? Is that you?"

Panicked, Charlotte shook her head, tears running down her cheeks. "Stay here," Sylvie mouthed. Defeated, Charlotte handed over the blade.

It was heavier than expected.

I wouldn't have come here if I wasn't willing to do what must be done.

"*Oui*, 'tis me," Sylvie said as she stepped into his line of vision. "Forgive the intrusion." He pulled the linen curtain back to the desk fitted to the tub. He spotted Charlotte's silhouette behind Sylvie. "She is overwhelmed by you," she explained.

Marat nodded like this was a regular occurrence. "Come closer," he said. "I can hardly see you in the poor light."

She did as he bid, keeping the knife tucked in the pocket tied at her waist. For some reason she was surprised to see him naked. And despite his poor health, the sinew of his arms and shoulders did not reflect a sickly constitution.

The rash, however, did. Angry red dots covered his sides and part of his arms. He kept his head covered in the same wraps of cloth.

She could not reveal any clues of her intent until the knife silenced any potential cries for help.

"I am sorry you've been unwell," she said. She sat on a stool near the tub, careful not to stick herself with the blade in her pocket.

He shrugged. "It is my lot in life, it seems. But my skin, though painful, has made me what I am."

I could not agree more.

"I confess I am glad to see you."

His lips quirked into a smile. He shifted closer. "And why is that?"

"I'm in desperate need of your insight. You once said that a few deaths would assure our happiness. When an enemy is killed, do you find some peace?"

He steepled his fingers in thought. "Violence is the language of revolution, the right of an oppressed people. So, yes, when I know the guillotine falls on a guilty neck, I know peace."

Sylvie nodded. "It may not be a guillotine, but it will bring me peace nonetheless."

Marat did not have time to understand her meaning, as she withdrew the blade and shoved it as deeply as she could into his flesh. She used the metal tub as leverage to ensure it cut through as much as the knife could reach. Vinegar splashed out of the tub and onto her dress as he twisted.

She met less resistance than she expected, almost like his body welcomed the blade rather than resisted it. She covered his mouth to silence a scream, but he was too weak to make a sound louder than speaking level. As the water went red, he slowly stopped writhing. He could not speak, just grasped at the wound while he gurgled on blood. When the tension left Marat's body, Sylvie knew he was dead. His right arm hung over the tub as his dead eyes stared into nothingness.

It did not feel good to kill; taking Marat's life only fulfilled Sylvie's duty to her country and Robespierre—a necessity to taper the violent binge that held so much of Paris. She found no joy or relief, only the prickling itch of dissatisfaction.

There was no peace in the eyes of the dead, just the reflection of her own face. "You lied," she said to Marat, panting for air.

"I'm so sorry," said Charlotte. Sylvie had forgotten she was in the room at all. "I'm so sorry I failed you. I failed Olympe. I promised you all I could kill Marat, to kill this evil."

Charlotte had come to Paris ready and willing to die for her crimes, but Sylvie had no patience for martyrs. Why sacrifice for a better future if she could not live to see it?

She pulled away and wiped the blood off her chin. "You did kill Marat."

"Wh-what?" Charlotte stuttered. "You did. I saw you."

"*You* brought the knife. *You* killed him. *You* are the martyr," Sylvie said. "You took one life to save a hundred thousand."

The unabashed gratitude in Charlotte's face sparked pity in Sylvie's breast—but only until she remembered that *she* had something to live for, and Charlotte did not. No one died for a cause if they had a reason to live—at least, not by choice.

"Every child will know the name Charlotte Corday and how she saved France."

"And you will not tell the Society of my cowardice?"

Sylvie looked at Marat's corpse; the cotton sheet around his shoulders almost matched the pallor of his skin except for the edges where the fabric met the pink-tinged water. His metal tub was three times the man's size and in the shape of a wooden clog, so large that it appeared to be eating him whole.

The wound in his chest looked clean and deep—Sylvie was tempted to leave the knife buried between his ribs for theatrical flair.

Marat believed violence was a necessary step to achieve true liberty. With his bathwater red like the Nile, Sylvie realized how right he'd been. In death, Marat got to live his truth.

"No," Sylvie said. "Only the three of us will know the truth. Now muss up the room. It must look like there was a struggle." They quietly tipped over writing desks and spilled ink to set the scene. "Do you know what you'll say when investigated?"

Charlotte nodded, smearing some blood on her hands. "I've rehearsed it with Cornélie."

Sylvie nodded. "Good. I'm going to leave down the servants' staircase." She fixed her hot-pressed curls in a mirror. Sylvie doubted Marat used it much. But her gown had streaks of his blood, and Charlotte's had none. "Help me get out of this." Charlotte got to work unlacing her until the gown pooled at their feet. "Take off yours and put mine on."

"Why?"

"I look like I committed a murder. You look like you're going to tea." Charlotte turned and let Sylvie remove her dress as well, and they both put on their respective costumes. The rush of the kill kept Sylvie's fingers steady. "Thank you, Charlotte."

Unflinching, Charlotte replied, "It's an honor to help our cause and our people."

Sylvie inspected her reflection. She thought she saw a fleck of blood on her cheek, but it was only a freckle. "Of course it is. Be sure to make a ruckus once I've left the house so that everyone knows what's happened." Charlotte nodded, staring at the knife embedded in the corpse. "Here"—Sylvie braced her hand against Marat's cool chest to force out the knife, fighting against the cartilage and bone—"keep the knife." Without the blade in place, more blood was free to seep from the wound.

Charlotte opened her hands like she was taking Communion. With the weapon and the stained skirts, Charlotte had transformed into an alluring vision of vengeance.

They will never look at us the same way again, Sylvie thought as she scrubbed her arms free of the darkening blood. *That a woman could see something wrong with the world and do something about it. Without hesitation. Without permission.*

Sylvie hoped that with Marat dead along with his conspiracies, the guillotine would stop being fed. France needed to fight real foes instead of faces in the shadows.

She dried her hands, only now shaking as enough time had passed, and hurried down the stairs.

CHARLOTTE'S TRIAL AND sentencing happened within three days, with her execution planned for the fourth. Cornélie tried to stay close, but Sylvie was too raw to allow her comfort. Charlotte had confessed without hesitation, feeding the investigators her well-prepared lines until their bellies would burst—but the relief Sylvie craved hadn't yet settled.

She'd told herself she'd never watch another execution after Ogé's death, but she felt duty bound to see Charlotte's end. She asked to join Robespierre and his posse to watch the beheading; he agreed with a raised brow.

Marat's followers would avenge their fallen prince with the bloody spectacle his memory demanded, so all of Paris came out to watch justice fall.

It poured overhead, but Sylvie and a few Montagnards watched the proceedings in a building overlooking the Place de la Révolution platform and crushing crowds.

Cornélie did not join them, and she disapproved of Sylvie going. She said she had no desire to see their comrade die. Sylvie never had the privilege of such a choice, but she bit her tongue and let Cornélie hide.

It took hours for the tumbrel with its lone prisoner to make it to the platform for the execution; the executioner gave the townsfolk plenty of time to harass and shame the assassin before her final stop at the guillotine.

Sylvie watched the overworked horse weave the cart through the crowds, Charlotte no more than a red speck in the drizzling gray of the streets.

To the people, she was a murderer—which was exactly what Sylvie and Charlotte wanted.

Charlotte stepped onto the platform, her long chestnut curls cropped to her chin. Sylvie knew her locks would make a fine wig for some balding Parisian. The thought made her laugh and gag at once.

Robespierre kept his back turned on the window, while Sylvie couldn't keep her eyes from the scene playing out below.

"Do you not like executions?" she asked without moving, the two of them alone at the windowpane.

Danton spoke animatedly in the background at the center of the room, making a loud joke and earning several chuckles. But Sylvie found the charisma and audacity that normally charmed only disgusted her.

Robespierre looked askance. "Justice is necessary, and therefore so are the consequences of justice."

"That wasn't my question."

"No, I do not. I dislike blood." His hypocrisy infuriated her. She had *killed* for him. She had killed for France. And he could not acknowledge the death on *his* hands.

He's like a butcher who doesn't eat meat.

"Do you think the people will calm after they're done mourning Marat?" Sylvie asked, trying to keep the emotion out of her voice.

Robespierre shrugged. "Hard to say. At the moment, I would say no." She hoped that, at least this time, he proved incorrect. "But regardless, we will lead them on the correct path. Marat was too volatile to lead the people alone."

"From the sounds of it, Charlotte Corday thought *he* was the murderer."

"There are bound to be more like Corday coming out of the cracks like roaches. We had all best watch our backs now." He sounded afraid. Sylvie warmed at his vulnerability. She liked seeing his humanity. Gods were above reproach, but man was not.

They led Charlotte to the front of the platform to face the crowds before her death. "Marat was paranoid and practically a hermit. The scariest monsters are the ones we can't see." Sylvie kept her focus, but Robespierre's intent gaze made her falter. "On Saint-Domingue, the white masters almost never went out into the fields. And if they did, it was the cruelest ones who liked to play with their things."

The executioner went to bind Charlotte's arms and legs once she removed her bonnet. "My father didn't play with his slaves, but he knew masters who did," Sylvie went on. "It's easier to destroy people if they don't have a face—if they hide from their evils. *You* don't hide. The people know you. They see that you're flesh and blood."

The guillotine fell, cutting Charlotte's pretty neck in two. When the head fell into the basket, a man picked it up and slapped it twice upon the cheek. They were too far away to see the gruesome details, but that obscene display was impossible to miss.

"Oh God, how vulgar. He can't do that, can he?" Sylvie asked. Charlotte did not deserve such treatment in death, and Sylvie could not help but look to Robespierre to rectify the injustice. His thin mouth went thinner still, and he motioned for a colleague to come near.

He spoke lowly, but she heard Robespierre's demand. "Have that man arrested and tried by the Tribunal for that offense."

The attendant left to do Robespierre's bidding, leaving Sylvie pleased to have given Charlotte some iota of justice. The rest of the world may have gone mad, but Robespierre still had his incorruptible integrity.

SYLVIE AND GASPARD went home together in the carriage, Sylvie pinching her dress as the metallic whoosh of the guillotine replayed in her mind.

Charlotte wore a red dress, which designated her crime as murder.

No one commented on Sylvie's gown—she'd had it dyed red for the occasion. She wore it not out of penance—Marat had objectively incited copious amounts of violence and had been at death's door regardless—nor out of patriotism. Nor did she wear it in solidarity with Charlotte, who died a scapegoat, a courageous fool, on a platform so burdened by victims the wood practically bled.

No, Sylvie wore red because it was the uniform of a murderess. But, she thought, there were no murderers in war, only soldiers.

Chapter Twenty-Seven

The lust for power, for dominating others, inflames the heart more than any other passion.

—*Tacitus*

Sylvie feigned illness to avoid Marat's funeral; neither Cornélie nor Gaspard fought her when she determined that she wouldn't attend. But, per usual, Cornélie knew insincerity when she heard it.

So, Sylvie sat at her vanity plucking her brows when Cornélie entered without knocking.

The darker girl flinched, the tweezers flying across the table. "*Mon Dieu!* I could have ripped off half my eyebrow."

Cornélie pursed her lips. "Are my suspicions correct and you're perfectly well? You missed a very important event."

Sylvie picked up the tweezers and attacked the other brow. "My senses are delicate—I can almost smell the vinegar from here."

"I know we had no love for him, but to skip his funeral would be unpatriotic."

Killing him was unpatriotic. "It's vulgar to attend our victim's funeral, is it not?"

"Sylvie—"

She'd expended most of her emotional energy yesterday, so Sylvie had no patience for Cornélie's patronizing. "Did you come here to condescend? Because I'm trying to force my eyebrows into submission."

"And failing, clearly." Cornélie pulled a stool in front of Sylvie and snatched the tweezers. "Let me help you."

She cupped Sylvie's chin with her thumb and forefinger, her own brows pinching together as she plucked. When her eyes drifted to Sylvie's mouth, Sylvie's lips curled into a smile.

Cornélie huffed. "I did not come here to help with your toilette."

"Of course not." Sylvie traced her lover's fingers. "But you do miss me."

Cornélie pulled away warily. "What's wrong? You only play the coquette with me when something's the matter."

Caught in her own web, Sylvie retreated. "You're right. You did not come here to be my lady's maid. What do you need?"

Cornélie leaned back. "Robespierre would like you to join us at Jacques-Louis David's studio tomorrow."

"Why?" Sylvie asked. A year ago she would have rejoiced, but now her hackles rose like a stray cat's.

Cornélie winced. "I don't know," she said, staring at her own reflection. Sylvie noticed the strands of silver blooming at her roots. She would give her the recipes from Saint-Domingue for hair dye— Cornélie was only a few years older than her, after all; she knew her maid could find the right seeds with enough time. "He doesn't talk to me like he used to."

Inside, Sylvie moved between shame and sympathy. The section of her heart that loved Cornélie hated to see her so disheartened. The other piece, starved for Maximilien and safety, felt the tiniest flicker of interest.

She agreed to attend, watching Cornélie's critical eye examine her face.

Despite years of flirtation, being with Cornélie was a dance unlike the hundreds she had danced before. She'd charmed dozens of powdered beauties—male and female—on Saint-Domingue, perhaps enjoying a sherry-induced kiss with one or two. The carnal nature of the pair's connection did not concern her; it was base and selfish and *theirs*. Lust, sexual power, the desire to satisfy and be satisfied . . . these concepts gave Sylvie no pause, regardless of the partner.

However, her feelings that veered into the realm of love made less sense. She knew she loved Cornélie as well as her shallow heart could love anyone, but what they shared did not exist in her gothic romances. She did not see a happy ending for them, only a tragic one.

So they sat together, knees touching, with thoughts and ambitions thousands of miles apart.

THE NEXT DAY, Sylvie dressed as finely as French society allowed—though she couldn't powder as much as she used to without someone making a comment about her "buying more flour for her face than I can to feed my family."

But fortunately her skin did not occupy her mind as much in Paris as it had on Saint-Domingue. Abolishing slavery remained on the Committee's agenda, and more than once she passed other Creole escapees in the streets.

Sylvie mentally prepared for interacting with Jacques-Louis David. They'd met before at salons and outside the Convention due to his friendship with Robespierre. But she and Gus regarded him as a Marat-like figure, though doubly as volatile but with less political influence outside of his art.

Fortunately, most held the same opinion, so Sylvie's sentiments on the artist could be less censored in Robespierre's presence. Unfortunately, she disliked his painting as much as the painter.

"Why is everything so grotesque?" Sylvie asked Cornélie. They stood together in David's expansive, well-supported studio. Dozens of canvases in various stages of completion leaned against the walls.

The artist spoke to his students and Robespierre on the far side of the room. "I miss when all the paintings had flowers."

"Three years in Paris and you still haven't learned to appreciate neoclassicism?" Cornélie asked before kissing her cheek.

"Why name it neoclassicism? Nothing about it is new. 'Tis old men in togas. Frankly, I think they've just run out of ideas."

Cornélie snorted behind her hand, her gray eyes twinkling. "Don't let David hear you," she said, gesturing to the wild-haired Jacobin. "He thinks he's doing a great service for the nation—and he is."

"If I remember, he couldn't even finish that Tennis Court Oath painting. It's an enormous sketch, hardly a masterpiece."

"Maximilien has faith in him."

"Well, if you need more women clutching their naked bosoms, then he is the right sort of fellow." Cornélie laughed again. Sylvie loved her laugh.

"If I recall," Cornélie said once she regained her solemnity, "you liked classicism when you were the subject. You made a fine Silvia."

"You're a better artist. You use lighter colors."

Cornélie scoffed. "I most certainly am not the better artist. I'm a student. He's a genius."

"Says who?"

"Says all of Paris."

"I don't let sans-culottes dictate good taste."

Sylvie's sourness evaporated at Robespierre's arrival with David. "*Citoyennes*, forgive us for making you wait. I wanted to work out the particulars before presenting this to you both."

David nodded and motioned to a small arrangement of chairs facing a covered canvas. Sylvie frowned at the lack of tea.

"We are in great suspense," said Cornélie. "Neither of us has the faintest idea why we're here." Sylvie envied how relaxed she appeared, freely looking at Robespierre without a hint of restraint.

"Permission," Robespierre answered. "I felt it unfair for David to model his work after your own without your approval." David huffed, clearly disagreeing with his patron.

"My own work?" asked Cornélie. Robespierre removed the cloth over the canvas, revealing Sylvie's old portrait. "Silvia?" she asked.

"*Mother of Rome*," David corrected. "*Silvia: Mother of Rome*. I intend to make it larger, with Paris in the background rather than Rome."

"With your permission," said Robespierre.

Cornélie put her hand to her breast. "It's an honor, sirs. I can think of no finer artist to improve upon my work."

Sylvie considered it a private, intimate image for Robespierre and Cornélie—she felt exposed with David and all of his works looming over it. The light and style differed, making her own face appear alien.

"If I may," she began. "Why did you need me to attend this meeting?" She only had eyes for Robespierre, but David answered.

"We will still use you as my subject. A Creole Silvia to represent the freed slaves of the French colonies. Paris rising out of the hills—Romulus and Remus still at your feet—with its citizens bathing and washing in the river. Black and white, and all of us French."

"Women are the foundation of the home," Robespierre added. "And so they are the foundation of the nation. It is only right that Silvia should be the focus. I wanted your approval as well."

Robespierre had kept his word; Sylvie would be the mother of a new France, a France where a mulatto girl could be the very image of liberty. Or, most importantly, Robespierre saw her that way. Tears pricked her eyes, and the emotion embarrassed her.

"You have it," she said after clearing her throat. Cornélie's hand moved beside hers.

"It will not be done until the next year," said David, appearing vaguely annoyed with her emotion. "But I will need you to model several times. I want the original Silvia, not a copy." Sylvie agreed. "Good. I do not have much time to spare, then."

"We shall leave you to your work," said Cornélie, eyes sparkling with pride. David had spun on his heel and gone off to his corner to continue mixing paints before she'd finished speaking. "We'll take our leave. Sylvie?"

Robespierre shook his head. "I would like to speak to her privately. Cornélie, have one of the students escort you if you like."

Her confused face offered Sylvie no idea as to why Robespierre needed an audience.

"As you wish," Cornélie said, hurt creeping into her tone. "I'll be at home."

Both thrilled and terrified, Sylvie stayed seated with her hands clasped in front of her. But Robespierre made no move to sit.

"Shall we walk?" he asked stiffly. She joined him, and they moved slowly along the walls of faces. David remained oblivious, mumbling to himself while he stirred paints next to a large unfinished piece. The face of the subject resonated with her in an unpleasant way, but she could not place where she'd seen his face before.

"What is he so anxious to work on?" she asked, trying to shake her discomfort at standing so close to him. Robespierre paused in front of an older sketch.

"Marat's death—I'm having Jacques-Louis David do a painting of it."

She swallowed. "The assassination?"

"Yes, to immortalize him. Modern martyrdom."

She turned toward David: the clear lines of Marat's turban were now more obvious. She could smell the vinegar. "But to be remembered in such a way? Sickly and bleeding in a bathtub?"

"You have a tender heart," he said, and resumed walking. "Though you hide it well. You're like Cornélie in that way." She disagreed but just nodded. "We'll keep it bare—no gore or illness. He made a sacrifice, and the people worship him. They need a memorial, a revolutionary Pietà, if you will."

"He's no Christ," she said, judgment coloring her tone.

"Perhaps not, but he is loved in a similar way." Sylvie kept her gaze on the painting, watching David write the names on the letter of condemnation Marat gripped in his hand. "Your painting will not be like that. Yours will be a celebration of a French spirit, rather than to avenge its loss. Glorifying an idea—not a person."

He read her mind. His intuitiveness stripped her barer than when her portrait sat uncovered. She wanted to change the subject.

"Certainly, you did not need to speak to me about art? You have Cornélie."

Robespierre frowned. Watching his facial expression change was akin to seeing a water droplet moving down a windowpane. "No. I wish to inform you about a meeting I had with Augustin."

She reined in her paranoia; if their treason had been discovered, she would not learn of it in David's studio.

"Is he all right?"

"Physically, yes. He is . . . displeased with my decision to send him to the Alpes-Maritimes for the remainder of the year."

Sylvie stopped walking, unable to stroll and process his words simultaneously. "Is he not of more use to you in Paris? How can he help France in the Alps?"

"Southern France rebels against us, and I need him to contain the Federalist revolts. They feel we have betrayed the principles of the National Assembly; Augustin must convince them otherwise."

"And you think they will be calmed by speeches?" she asked, more out of hope than reason. Augustin still loved Gaspard, as fruitless as it was. She feared how such a separation would impact their goals as well as Gaspard's heart.

"If anyone can, it is my brother. But if military action is necessary, then he is more than capable."

David's pencil scratched against the canvas, but Sylvie still kept her voice low.

"But the Committee could send *anyone*. They'd listen to you if you said you wanted him based in Paris." Augustin offered the intuition and insight the Society needed—and the friendship she craved.

"Gaspard will replace him at my side." Her brows shot up in surprise. Sylvie was no fool. Their money supported Jacobin propaganda. But she trusted Gaspard's financial decisions, and she knew Augustin had helped him put it to good use. So, Robespierre had welcomed her and Gaspard into his circle. But to give him such a promotion did not seem proportional. "Augustin understands my wishes and respects them. He knows that plans are susceptible to change."

"Plans?"

"I am to be made head of the Committee of Public Safety." Her heart dropped like lead in water. "I want to keep Gaspard close. And as you witnessed earlier this afternoon"—he motioned to the partially concealed portrait in the middle of the studio—"my wishes for your future have broadened."

His slate eyes, his only truly attractive feature, settled on her face in a way she now understood.

It was restrained, repressed even, but it was lust. He had looked at her that way a thousand times, and only now she translated its meaning. He wanted her. He also wanted the idolatry her image would come to represent, but he wanted her.

"And what are your wishes, Maximilien?" she asked. She let her fingers trace his, moving slowly so as not to startle or alarm. He needed the release of capturing her, but Sylvie had set her own trap—or perhaps she was entangled in it herself.

"More like a need," he murmured. He shuddered at her touch, and the consequences of his admission began to pull at her limbs like weights. But it was not the muslin of Cornélie's morning gowns or the smell of a garden after rain that surrounded her, just Robespierre.

She'd ached for this moment for years. Yet the answer to her prayers came attached to so many questions and broken hearts.

And so she ran.

SYLVIE DID NOT expect him to follow her. Maximilien Robespierre was not a man who chased after a fleeing damsel.

The urge to cry battled with the urge to laugh. She struggled to assimilate the past half hour with her previous understanding of the Incorruptible.

She made it to a scraggly patch of garden behind the studio before falling to her knees. She sat among the buzzing insects, as immobile as the statues in the Tuileries. The birds returned to their fence perches when they realized she posed no threat.

She and Cornélie had only just reconfirmed their bond, and already Robespierre threatened to dismantle it.

His appointment to the Committee of Public Safety following Marat's death was no accident. A fear, sharp and insistent, prickled at her neck. To remove a leader in such a violent manner: Was it ripping out an arrow from the chest of France—tearing the flesh further and leaving a gaping, bleeding wound? Marat's death had only assured his legacy and not the peace she'd wanted.

She had taken that man's life, and still she was at the mercy of his radicalism.

"I wanted to give you some time to consider my words." Robespierre stood in the doorway to the garden.

Would-be courtiers had called her an island queen on Saint-Domingue, as she fit in so beautifully with the fabric of the tropics—tanned and bathed in lilies. Robespierre's colorless visage was out of

place in the lush green of late summer even in the decidedly un-
tropical Paris. She always thought their disparity erotic.

She stayed seated in the overgrown grasses, adding tiny yellow
buds to a flower chain. "Time would have been a few days, not
minutes."

"I do not have the liberty of days. Augustin must prepare for his
leave in August; he wants this settled quickly."

"Why do his orders require my answer?"

"Gaspard's role depends on yours."

She wove a flower through the last stem, completing the bracelet.
She did not look at him for fear of forgetting all the things she
wanted to say. "Cornélie is your wife in all but name." *And I love her.*

"I care for Éléonore very much." She winced at the cold use of
Cornélie's given name. Sylvie hadn't thought of her as such since the
earliest days of their acquaintance. "She is, and will always be, one
of my most trusted friends. But the fondness I hold is not enough to
make her my wife." She spun the bracelet around her wrist, the petals tickling her skin.

"Then why me?" She despaired at the choice he threw at her feet.
"Why *now*?"

His voice sounded closer as he said, "You saw the slaves of tyranny overthrow the shackles of corruption and sin. You know that
terror is the vessel in which justice is carried. Saint-Domingue was
baptized in blood, reborn again. I want you as a wife for the same
reasons I want you to pose for David." He sighed and knelt beside
her. "Also, Éléonore is dear to me, but she has not endured what you
have. And I admire that."

She did not expect poetry, but she did not want such imagery
pervading her thoughts, either. "So I make a fine painting, and you
admire me."

"I do not indulge in lovemaking as others do. Many take pleasures of the flesh with a laxity of which I cannot boast." As he stood,

his coat hem brushed her shoulder. She looked up at him, her eyes challenging him to give her more. "Though I must confess an . . . attraction I have not felt since I was younger. I aim to restrain myself from weakness of both mind and body. Try as I may, I could not ignore you."

She knew her answer would be yes—his position leading the Committee meant survival for Sylvie and her brother—despite the tears she would shed for Cornélie.

"Have you asked Gaspard?" She did not require his blessing regarding anything she did, but she wondered if Maximilien had shown her brother the respect to at least ask for her hand.

"I have. He recognized the significance of our union but deferred the final decision to you."

He accepted your offer through clenched teeth, you mean. She would get an earful from Gaspard that night, though she deserved that and worse.

However, Cornélie occupied the most space in her heart and mind. She had a duty to tell her of her decision herself.

"Your Cornélie loves you, Robespierre."

"I've had my share of pain: my own father did not survive his heartbreak, but she will survive this with grace and dignity." His reply hinted at a great deal of history, but she knew not to ask now.

"You could have any woman in Paris," she said, her molten irises matching his own cold-burning stare. "You chose me. But I am not Cornélie." She meant that as both a warning and an apology.

He touched a spiral of her hair that had bounced free. The gesture seemed almost clinical rather than romantic, until his fingers brushed the curve of her ear.

"I do not want 'any,'" he murmured. "I want you."

Chapter Twenty-Eight

Surely the Women were created . . . for some better end, than to la-
bour in vain their whole life long.

—*Lady Sophia Fermor*

Sylvie went home in Robespierre's carriage, the skin where their
sides met driving them both to distraction. Evening settled on
the streets, and Robespierre insisted they travel together as far as
City Hall. He gave a shallow bow and did not go inside until he was
only just visible in the lamplight.

She did not want to go home, at least not yet—Sylvie wanted the
blur of color and hum of conversation to distract her from the decision she had just made. Surely, a soiree or exhibition could keep her
from the gates of Rue Saint-Honoré for an hour longer.

"Could we stop here, please?" she called to the driver. She recognized the house as one of a prominent salon. Servants and coaches
lined the streets, a promising sign.

He reined in the horses. "Robespierre said home, miss."

"And that is precisely where you shall tell him you took me if he
asks." She closed the door of the carriage. "You may wait if you like,
but we are near enough that I can walk home." She didn't linger to
hear any further complaints and let the warm embrace of chatter and
wine usher her in.

The salon—she could not remember the hostess's name—was
more of an art showing like that of her early days in Paris.

The exhibition had plenty of viewers, though it was certainly more intimate. But she acknowledged that she was hardly there to study art: the tableaux offered a brief purgatory while she mulled over Robespierre's grand plans.

She grabbed a cup of punch before the servant could offer it and kept to the fringes of the crowd. She hoped her casual dress could somewhat conceal her more notable characteristics.

The punch was ideally strong, and she let her eyes look without seeing as she passed portrait after portrait.

Sitting for Cornélie had been an almost sacred affair: no one would know of the painting's existence except those in their chosen circle. What Maximilien wanted was a loss of control—her control over her image and her legacy—in exchange for all the protection his offer implied.

She stopped in the corner of the larger of the open rooms that featured only one portrait, hoping to brood with her punch without running into deputies or their well-informed wives. She stared at the blank space between the painting and the wall, clinging to the tangible. The wood under her slippers, the smell of people and long-burning candles. The light tug on her gown.

A young Black girl smiled up at her.

"*Maman* had our friend Madame Sophie de Tott do my portrait."

Sylvie glanced around, briefly concerned that her years of haunted daydreams and nightmares of Saint-Domingue had finally manifested into madness. But the girl seemed real enough, from the youthful smoothness of her skin to the black puffs of hair tied in ribbons.

Sylvie was certain she gaped at her, but the child seemed unperturbed and kept referencing the painting Sylvie had yet to actually notice.

"*Maman* always says I am an angel, but I said I never see angels that look like me, so she had Madame de Tott paint me." Sylvie had calmed enough to get a good look at the portrait in question: a cherub, unmistakably the talkative girl to her left, flew with golden wings beside a marble bust of a man of some importance. The subject pointed to the wreath of flowers in her double's hands and giggled. "There I am putting a flower crown on the Maréchal de Beauvau. *Maman* says I am just like him, and she wanted her two loves in the painting."

Sylvie hardly knew her age, having rarely encountered children, but the girl could not have been older than ten or so. She spoke in a true Parisian accent, unlike Sylvie, and dressed in equal finery. At last she found her tongue. "And thank goodness she did, so you may admire yourself always."

"Well, yes, but *Maman* says that portraits are for other people. Now everyone shall be able to look and remember me forever!"

This small, undoubtedly personal portrait may not be the idol that sparked the hearts of all of France, but it still spoke louder than any other piece at the exhibition due to its subject alone. "You do not mind being painted for all to see?" The child engaged with unbidden glee about her likeness, just as any other French youth would.

A shadow of confusion crinkled her small face. "Why should I mind?"

The blissful ignorance of a girl who had never been taught to doubt or hide or wither. A free child—free not only from the bondage of shackles but from a bondage of the mind. At every moment of her life, her family and Saint-Domingue reminded Sylvie, with and without malice, of her skin and the limitations they placed upon it.

This little girl would not be shackled by the poison that followed Sylvie, the burning in the air that left her nose stinging and her chest tight—at least not on this day. "You shouldn't, not at all. You are the loveliest cherub I have ever seen."

The girl curtsied with a flourish, more of a bounce than a bow. "Thank you, Mademoiselle." If she was so enraptured by seeing herself thus immortalized, how would others like her feel when Silvia welcomed them to a world reimagined?

"Ourika!" a slightly frustrated woman called out. "*Ourika.*"

"Forgive me, I must return to my mother. Enjoy your evening." The girl bounced again and whipped off into the shifting crowd like a ghost Sylvie wasn't sure she'd seen.

WHEN SYLVIE ARRIVED at Chez Rohmer, Gaspard had already fled to one of Paris's many taverns—assumedly to avoid the certain confrontation that would erupt between the siblings.

Sylvie returned to her room, sober after her brush with the past—or future—and the short walk home.

Cornélie was sitting on her bed in expectation. Her pink lips spread out into a worried smile. "My darling, what did Robespierre want to speak about? Is Gaspard in any trouble?"

"The opposite," Sylvie said. "He is rising. Augustin is going to a post in the south, and Gaspard shall replace him."

Cornélie embraced her, and Sylvie relished the pressure of her lithe body against hers. Would this be the last time she would feel it? "That's marvelous! He shall be protected, then, and so will you."

"Actually," Sylvie said, trying to contain tears as she pulled away, "I will be protecting *him.* Robespierre will only keep him on the Committee if I accept his hand."

Cornélie took a step back. "What?"

"I killed Marat to save lives." Sylvie paced within the shrinking confines of the room and her own breaking heart. "But it would be a lie to deny that I wanted revenge. I wanted a taste of the power he had and then wanted to take it away. But all I made was a martyr. He is immortal, and I am nothing."

Still confused, Cornélie tried to soothe her. "You are not nothing. You just need to realize your strength—"

"Strength? *Strength*? I do not have the luxury of strength, the luxury of sacrifice. If Marat had had his way and my neck had met the guillotine's kiss, no one would mourn me. No marble plaque chiseled with my name; my death would mean no more than my mother's. Tossed into a mass grave, while unworthy men live on forever, if not in body, then in spirit."

Cornélie gripped her shoulders and forced her to meet her eyes. "*I* would mourn you."

"That's not enough. Your grief will not protect Gaspard; your grief will not protect *me*."

"So you are going to agree? If you accept him, he will own you like your fear owns you."

"And what? Is your relationship not for your benefit? Do you not use your closeness to further your family's security?"

"I knew what Robespierre was becoming. I kept him at arm's length because I could not stain myself with his misdeeds."

"His list of those he trusts grows smaller and smaller," Sylvie said, pleading for her to understand. This decision did not arise from an infatuation but from duty.

"And you needed to protect yourself."

She nodded, and nodded, and nodded, until her face erupted into tears. "I'm sorry," she cried as she buried her face in Cornélie's neck. "I'm sorry I did not fight for you. I'm sorry I'm not better," she sobbed. Cornélie held her, shushing softly and swaying back and forth. Sylvie pulled away to rest her forehead against Cornélie's, their tears blurring together. "He still cares for you. You must know he'd never let any harm—"

"I don't care about that," Cornélie said. "I do not care about losing *him*."

Sylvie guided her hands over her décolletage, over buttons and ruffles, and under the various skirts. "My brother is at the taverns. He won't be home until morning," she said. Cornélie's mouth hung open in slack–jawed admiration. "We'll be alone. Perhaps for the last time." Sylvie pressed her body against Cornélie's so that not even a hair's breadth could separate them.

"I'm scared for you, Sylvie," she whispered, like acknowledging the fear gave it life. Sylvie moved her fingers between Cornélie's legs, her gaze holding Cornélie captive.

"We are safe in this moment." Sylvie unlaced Cornélie from her clothes and bindings. She traced every plane, every freckle, to her memory: the flush on her chest, the curve of her hip, the dark waves of hair concealing her breasts. "I will keep us safe."

The sheets lay damp by morning, stained by shared sweat and tears provided by both in equal measure.

23 août 1793

"I'm surprised they even found a priest willing to do the ceremony," Sylvie murmured to Gaspard. She fanned herself lightly, her emerald earrings swaying with her movement. They had been invited to Lise and Philippe Le Bas's wedding. The couple chose to marry at Notre-Dame-de-l'Assomption, a convenient walk along Rue Saint-Honoré.

The church was over one hundred years old and, despite the inten-sifying anticlerical sentiment and vandalism, it still stood as a beacon of classical architecture. But since the people's rampant distrust of the Catholic Church ended with two hundred drowned clerics in the river, Sylvie was surprised the priest wasn't shaking as he blessed the couple.

"I've always hated being inside a church," Gaspard mumbled in the pew.

"That's because we're sinners, dear brother." She winked over her fan. "Us in church is like a fat sow in a butcher's shop." He made a snorting laugh, earning a glare from a nearby guest. Gaspard mouthed an apology but kept laughing behind his hand.

Sylvie was happy to distract him. He'd been in an anxious state all morning, retying his cravat six times before Sylvie threatened to hang him with it.

Regardless of the groom, Lise shone in a soft yellow gown and a lace veil that brushed her shoulders. Gaspard avoided looking at her.

"She looks happy, I suppose," Sylvie whispered. "It's a good match."

Gaspard scoffed. "Lise had a choice, and she made the wrong one."

Sylvie snapped her fan closed, staring at him in incredulous shock. "A choice? A choice? Lise had no choice. She wanted to survive this godforsaken hellscape of false justice, and she knew what Le Bas could offer her. I will not judge her when I share her crimes."

Gaspard remained silent, his head bowed in angry confusion. Sylvie softened her tone and said, "We speak of liberty, of freedom, but the fine print excludes *us*." She held up the fabric of her gown. "We storm the Bastille, we wave the colors, we bleed the blood, and yet . . ."

Sylvie let her sentence hang as she watched Lise say her vows. "Just remember, dear brother, when you serve on the Committee as Robespierre's second—a position you earned from skill and merit alone—that you are not betrothed to a man you do not love; you did not have to charm and flirt your way into that seat."

Gaspard followed Sylvie's gaze toward the now-married couple. Cornélie clapped and cheered as Lise and Philippe returned down the aisle, flinching when she met Sylvie's eye. "Freedom looks different in a dress."

septembre 1793

Despite their engagement, which Sylvie insisted Robespierre keep private until a later date, not much in her life changed once she reconciled losing Cornélie.

She did not see Robespierre any more or less often than before, except now she suffered endless boredom without Cornélie's love.

As forewarned, Maximilien had been elected to the still-young Committee of Public Safety shortly after Augustin went south in August. He told her he never wanted such a position, that every step he took was for the people. And yet, when a seat on the Committee was offered, he had no qualms about accepting it—the power, the celebrity, the crown he never asked for but wore so well.

The stays of the Revolution tightened, and Sylvie found it harder and harder to catch her breath.

Gaspard stormed into the sitting room with a pamphlet crumpled in his hand. His work as Robespierre's secretary wearied him, and he did not wear his haggard appearance and weight loss well. "Have you read it yet? The conscription was mad, but this is beyond *reason!*"

"Read what, brother? Sit down and catch your breath," Sylvie said over her tea.

"The Law of Suspects." He slapped the pamphlet over the tea tray. "Tell me, do you care a whit what he votes on? Or are you just happy with your secretly increased status?"

The irony was that she read less now that she was the Incorruptible's bride-to-be. She found rationalizing the Committee's decisions—and her fiancé's role in them—increasingly difficult. But after killing Marat proved meaningless, she accepted that only Robespierre could save her.

"Let me see it—drink some tea in between your insults," she said.

Robespierre did not discuss much of his work during the few instances they were alone. Most often, he worked in David's studio while she posed, his eyes lingering on her classically styled form no matter how determinedly he focused on his essays.

It was power if not intimacy, which suited Sylvie fine.

"Well, it's alarmingly vague," she murmured.

"*Immediately after publication of this decree, all suspect people who are to be found on the territory of the republic, and who are still in freedom, will be put under arrest.* Now read the fifth group of suspect people," he said.

"*Those former nobles, with their husbands, wives, fathers, mothers, sons or daughters, brothers or sisters, and agents of émigrés, who have not consistently demonstrated their commitment to the Revolution,*" she finished softly.

"We are dead, Sylvie. The moment we are no longer useful."

"But it says right here—*demonstrated their commitment to the Revolution.* Have we not done just that? You're paranoid."

"Marat was paranoid," Gaspard snapped.

"Then we must make ourselves invaluable." She added another lump of sugar. She liked her tea so sweet that her teeth ached.

"You don't understand!" he shouted, making her hands tremble as she stirred her spoon. "Robespierre can find a hundred Creole whores! We are not protected—"

She stood and struck her brother across his cheek hard enough to bruise her own hand. "You are afraid. *I am afraid.* But we have both sacrificed for this Revolution. Robespierre knows that. This chaos is temporary—"

"I'm sorry," Gaspard whispered, clutching his cheek. His eyes filled with tears. "There will be terror in the streets, Sylvie. Just like on Saint-Domingue. Do you remember the screams? The righteous hate in their eyes? You burned the newspapers detailing the mutilation; I *read* them."

"You forget to whom you speak," she snapped. "My own brother held a gun to my chest."

"And tomorrow it could be your brother under a guillotine!" he sobbed. "I am not warming the Incorruptible's bed. I have no such protection."

She held his face in her hands, his cheek hot where she'd slapped him. "*I* will protect you. You saved me that night; I can save *you* now."

He embraced her, his head curled on her shoulder despite being several inches taller. "I don't know what game you're playing, but Robespierre isn't the god you think he is; he's ruled by the same fears as us."

I know, she thought. In the beginning, Sylvie considered Robespierre untouchable. He held the key to the future in his hand, and she grew intoxicated on his power as he transcended this temporal world. But time makes all men mortal. And she would cling to this false prophet if it meant sparing her and Gaspard's lives.

She wiped her tears before he could see them. "He's going to free the slaves, Gaspard. Next year he shall abolish slavery in the colonies. We're making things *right*." She ran her hands through his blond tufts. "If we can bear this terror, it will all be worth it."

novembre 1793

The days moved so quickly then, but the fall of the guillotine kept better time than even the most accurate timepiece.

In another life, Sylvie might have been shocked by the execution of a queen. But once Marie Antoinette's end finally came in October, her death was swallowed by the deaths of so many others.

The public face of the Society was disbanded by decree and with violence—Olympe, their brilliant and invisible hand that formed the Society, met her end by way of the guillotine two weeks after the ex-queen.

Sylvie found peace in those hours with David and Robespierre. There she represented all of the ambitions she had for both herself and her country, while the Incorruptible of France lusted after her.

But today a series of condemned prisoners had been guillotined, for reasons unknown to Sylvie, and the revelers made their joy known loudly.

She'd murdered Marat, but this senseless horror continued anyway. Even still, the odors of blood and vinegar clung to Paris—Sylvie haunted less by the violence of his death than that of his life.

"I feel unwell, David. Could I return tomorrow?" she asked. The air thickened by the moment, and the walls of the studio pressed closer.

"I'm creating a masterpiece, and you're feeling 'unwell'?" he sneered. She had no time for his mercurial temper.

"David, give us a moment, would you?" asked Robespierre. Her periphery grew darker, and she sank down onto the wooden stand. David grunted and gave them privacy.

"Forgive me," she said. "I get these . . . episodes. The walls close in around me and there isn't enough air . . ." He shushed her, gripping her arms to keep her aloft. "And I know you're doing good work for France, but every day Paris looks more and more like Saint-Domingue. My brother is frightened; *I* am frightened. And I. Can't. Breathe." She clawed at her toga, the cool air of the room soothing her heated shoulders.

"You are safe here," he said, rubbing slow circles on her bare back. "*We* are safe from them in here." She wanted to believe him. But it was easy to agree with the words and not the consequences that followed them. She'd learned that lesson a thousand times already.

Her cheek sat flush against the buttons of his coat. She liked how he kept himself fastidiously clean; he always smelled of lye. The scent of his soap slowly pushed away the haunting scent of vinegar. Her heart settled, and she breathed in deeply for the first time in an hour.

Without Robespierre, she and her brother had nothing between them and the guillotine. Neither desire nor love kept her bound to Robespierre; it was necessity.

She hadn't been this close to him before, and he remained tense beneath her palms. As panic left, the urge to regain control replaced it.

"Thank you, I am much improved," she murmured. He hummed in response. She moved closer still, and his fingers dug into the flesh of her back.

"Maximilien," she whispered, and moved onto his lap. "I see how you stare at me—like a dog starved. I am to be your bride; you may do more than look." She felt his desire rise with her confidence. He reached out to touch her cheek, and she captured a finger with her lips, sucking lightly. Robespierre made a strangled moan.

She kissed the corner of his jaw, so fraught with tension it quivered. Yet that simple touch shattered his self-control, and Sylvie found herself flat on the floor of the studio. He bit her throat, shuddering at the expanse of uncovered skin. Sylvie gripped his shoulders and moaned.

"You will be the death of me," he groaned. He pulled down the toga to reveal her breast, suckling greedily. His roughness excited her, and she bit and nibbled with as much ferocity as she could muster in her limited position.

He took her hands and held them above her head. He bit at her chest, and she could not stifle her pleasure. Those broad palms squeezed the thighs exposed from the shifting stola. She arched toward him, but he pinned her with his pelvis.

She felt him sliding between her thighs, brushing against her cleft over and over but never entering her. She twisted in his hold, desperate for more control, though he seemed keen on holding her satisfaction prisoner.

He kept moving against her, not inside her, until she cried out into his shoulder. The friction was pleasurable, though not enough to bring her to her peak. Cornélie wielded Sylvie's desire with the knowing fingers of a prodigy; Maximilien had the clumsy skills of a new student. But the spontaneity and passion of the tryst were still enjoyable. And with a moan of her name and a shudder, he finished.

Robespierre did not move immediately, lying atop her, panting for breath. He then put himself back into his breeches and tucked in his shirtsleeves. He used her stola to clean her legs. The entire encounter lasted no more than a few minutes.

He looked down at her, still panting and flushed. "I have defiled you on a floor," he said.

"Which you may do anytime you please," she said between breaths. "You enjoyed it."

He winced. "I am above such base pleasure."

"And yet here we are," she said. He ran his thumb along the bites he'd made on her breasts, tracing their pattern over skin darker than his own. "You've seduced the vestal virgin Silvia."

"David's studio is hardly Vesta's temple," he said. "And I'm no Mars."

"The man's name matters not," she countered, choosing her words carefully. "The woman begets a legacy of liberty."

His eyes went hungry again—for both her body and the future she promised.

He helped her dress and escorted her home silently, leaving Sylvie to contemplate her progress with contentment.

Her satisfaction did not come from his sexual prowess—his inexperience showed—but in the knowledge that she'd corrupted the Incorruptible. And within his corruption lay her survival.

Chapter Twenty-Nine

How can you come to know yourself? . . . Try to do your duty, and
you'll know right away what you amount to.

—*Johann Wolfgang von Goethe*

décembre 1793

As winter cooled Paris, Sylvie held a secure and private position
as Robespierre's betrothed. He did not show his affection in
the more common ways, like flowers or doting words, but in sharing
his mind. He gave her short essays he wrote in his spare time regarding topics ranging from law to political theory—coupled with short
romantic poems he hid within the essay pages. His displays of fondness were endearing, bordering on absurd.

The Law of Suspects kept Sylvie out of the public eye and out of
the streets, Gaspard kept mostly to himself, and the female political
clubs had been disbanded—so analyzing Robespierre's gifts was her
sole form of entertainment.

Those papers focused mainly on his devotion to preserving the
Revolution from any who would dismantle it. In his defense of terror, he became a man terrified of his own mortality.

She clung to his rationalizations like the haunting scent of vinegar that never left her person.

Today, December's freezing fog kept the fires burning early at
Chez Rohmer, and Sylvie sat among her gothic romances in front of
the house's largest fireplace.

She planned to read more of Robespierre's essays on female

virtue—but she missed the comforting promise of melodrama and romance her old novels supplied.

Sylvie hardly expected visitors anymore now that Cornélie never came over, so Lise's arrival that late morning was met with surprise. She had not seen Lise since her marriage to Le Bas in the late summer.

"I'm still in my morning robe," Sylvie muttered from her perch on the carpet when Louise announced Lise's presence. "Tell her my brother is not here."

"She's asking for you, miss," her maid said. "And was relieved when I told her he was away, if you don't mind my saying so. I don't think this is a formal visit."

Sylvie leaned back against her pillows with a huff, snapping her novel closed. "Let her in, then. And some tea if you could."

The maid led the younger Duplay sister into the sitting room, and Sylvie gasped. "You're soaked to the bone! How long did you wait outside, Lise? And without a proper coat?"

Lise only then noticed her damp clothing, a dazed look on her face. "Oh, I suppose I've forgotten it, haven't I?"

"Sit by the fire, at least," Sylvie insisted, moving her novels off the chair. Lise was dripping everywhere. "Cornélie will despise me all the more if I send her sister home with a fever."

Lise removed her wet things and warmed her hands by the flames. "My sister doesn't despise you. She's only heartbroken."

The tea came in, and Sylvie served them with more focus than required. "All of Paris is mourning someone," she said instead. "In fact, you're in some terrible shock yourself."

Lise finished her drink in an impolite amount of time, holding the cup with both hands. "Oh no," she said. "Nothing terrible. I'm visiting my family and realized I never thanked you for attending the wedding—and to give you the news."

"News?" Sylvie repeated.

"Yes. I'm with child."

Sylvie's immediate reaction was to offer her condolences for Lise's doomed figure. But courtesy won out. "Congratulations, Lise. Your family must be pleased for you."

"Th-they don't know, nor does Philippe. You're the only one."

This entire interaction grew stranger by the minute. "I'm . . . *honored* to be your confidante," Sylvie said, though it came out more like a question. "Don't you think the father of the child should like to know you're expecting?"

Lise, whose affect up until then had been almost disoriented, crumpled into hysterics—wailing and weeping in Sylvie's startled embrace.

"I can't tell Gaspard the truth—he'd want to raise the babe as his own. And he knows I'd want nothing more than to run away as a family—"

"What does my brother have to do with your baby?" Sylvie asked, but then felt stupid for even voicing the question aloud. She pushed Lise back, holding her arms and forcing her to calm herself. "How can you even be certain the babe is not Philippe's?"

Lise sniffed. "I gave myself to Gaspard right before the marriage, and when I was due for my monthly blood days after my wedding, it never came."

Well, no one can say Gaspard doesn't make the most of a single opportunity, Sylvie thought. "I still do not understand," she said aloud. "You are married without a hint of suspicion surrounding your pregnancy."

"These are uncertain times; if something were to happen to my husband or to me—I want you to know. Someone who shares the same blood as my child—"

"A very, *very* little amount—"

"—and who would do anything to keep her family safe. Like me."

Sylvie knew Lise spoke truly, and she stared at her belly while her heart ached.

"But still, why did you come to me? Your sister would be more than willing."

"You're engaged to Robespierre; you understand marriage to a man like Le Bas," Lise said. Sylvie nodded, feeling a new sense of kinship. "Our protection one day could mean our demise the next."

She promised her protection while cursing the old adage that trouble came in threes.

février 1794

Sylvie had no trouble keeping Lise's secret—secrets were her dearest companions—yet Gaspard's melancholy pulled on her weathered heartstrings. Time bolstered his spirits some, but his disposition never fully recovered to the roguish charm of his youth.

She knew he'd be overjoyed if he discovered Lise's child belonged to him. However, through guilt or obligation or sympathy, Sylvie determined to honor her promise—by avoiding any contact with Gaspard at all.

But like brothers tend to do, he insisted on finding her anyway.

She sat in the kitchen, the warmest room in the house, picking at the leftover dried fruit that hadn't made its way into the cook's bread. Cook had gone earlier but kindly left the fire in the oven going for warmth.

With only two people to feed, the kitchen sat quiet and empty most hours of the day. Even the mice gave up on trying to find a meal.

"I'm astounded," Gaspard said from the doorway with a hand tossed dramatically across his brow. "My patrician sister sitting in a kitchen. I may swoon."

Sylvie rolled her eyes and put another piece of Comté cheese and bread in her mouth. But in her heart, she gladdened to hear her brother sounding more like himself.

"Your patrician sister is cold, and the kitchen is warm," she said, sliding the platter of cheese toward Gaspard as an invitation to join her. He sat down at the humble table—which looked more like a block of raw, ancient wood—and picked at the cheese while avoiding the rind. She groaned at his waste and grabbed his abandoned rind for herself.

"Ugh, that's disgusting," he said with a scrunched-up face. "How you eat the rind is beyond me. You've always liked sour things." She popped another piece into her mouth with glee. "I don't like to punish myself with such foulness after a good meal."

In a half jest, she said, "Gluttony should have consequences—even small ones. So I endure it." She wiped her mouth with a cloth. Gaspard stared wordlessly at the table, and Sylvie guessed he'd come to see her for more than good company. "Unless you're turning into a gourmand, I assume you aren't here to debate about cheese."

He chuckled. "No, at least not tonight. I'm going to come out with it: Gus thinks now is the right time to bring up abolition, and Robespierre agrees." Gus had returned from Nice, and apparently, Parisian politics were eager to have him back.

She swallowed thickly and got up to find the good wine that Cook hid for herself. "A noble endeavor, certainly. But what has that got to do with me?" She reached behind the oven, but no luck. She turned to the lower cabinets.

Gaspard spoke over the clanging pots as she searched. "Everything. Since half of the Society of the Friends of Blacks are on the run or executed, Robespierre needs new voices to speak on the horrors of slavery. He hoped to arrange for a few delegates from Saint-Domingue to speak, as they might sway the Convention. He planned on one white, one Black, and one mulatto."

Hunched over, looking through a crate of potatoes, Sylvie snorted sardonically. "Goodness, such variety."

Ignoring her, he said, "But the mulatto delegate got sick on his journey to Paris. So Robespierre is short by one. He believes you'd be an excellent replacement."

She stopped and turned around. "What? *Me?*" she asked, incredulous. "Is he an idiot?"

"Not in this case, no." He stood and grabbed her shoulders, trying to shake the confidence into her bones. "You recall how brilliant you were talking that mob down? I could've been killed along with the baker, but *you* persuaded them otherwise."

"This is not a horde of starving townspeople! The National Convention could destroy us *both* if they so choose. I'm no delegate. They deserve better than me."

Gaspard lowered his voice, now uncharacteristically gentle. "Why are you crying?"

She smeared her cheeks, but the crying worsened. She staggered into his chest, sobbing, "I'm not worthy. Those people deserve a hero. They deserve someone better than me." The slavery, the death—by her own hands and by the masters of Saint-Domingue— hobbled her with the weight of their lives in guilt. "I'm so ashamed, Gaspard. I'm so ashamed."

He peeled her away and said softly, "Then *help* them. You're worthy not because you've made no mistakes—but because you try to overcome them." She nodded and wiped her face. Gaspard, Robespierre, the *world*—they were asking too much of her.

Gaspard reached to the top of the cabinet and retrieved a rusty old pot. He opened the lid and pulled out a small bottle of cognac.

"Here," he offered. "I don't know where she keeps the wine, but she's been going through at least one of these a week for the past year."

She took a swig, relishing the burn. "I promise I'll think about it."

"Decide quickly. We're planning for the fourth."

Sylvie choked on the brandy. "That's in two days!"

He shrugged. "Revolution waits for no man. Or woman."

She didn't hear him leave. Sylvie glared into the mouth of the cognac bottle, the amber drink lulling her into a false calm.

Her island bled for freedom, burned for freedom; Sylvie owed her home and her people a speech—even if it did nothing, she could rest easier knowing she did not hide from her past.

Gus knew she'd agree, the bastard. He knew her strength where she did not.

Sylvie took a few more gulps but resolved to keep the rest for before the Convention. She didn't know how to speak to a room of murderous white men without it.

She was no one's champion, but she'd have to do.

SYLVIE REMAINED WITH Gus and Cornélie while the first two men from Saint-Domingue spoke to the Convention.

"I cannot watch them," she said. "It will only make me more nervous."

Cornélie understood and promised to stay with her until she needed to face the Convention. Robespierre and Gaspard had to remain within the hall to record the speeches and make notes. But Cornélie held her hand discreetly, providing small squeezes whenever she thought Sylvie would faint. Knowing Cornélie still loved her, despite her engagement, bolstered her strength.

Several Black and mulatto onlookers had come to hear the speeches, Gaspard had told her, which made her angst intensify. The cognac barely helped.

She groaned into her hand. "I'm going to look like a fool."

Cornélie squeezed her fingers again. "You're going to look brave."

Sylvie couldn't stomach the possibility of failure now. Money spoke louder than words, and she feared that France had too much money invested in the sin of slavery to liberate herself from greed.

Gaspard opened the doors. "It's time, sister." He reached out his hand, and Sylvie took it with a grateful smile.

While outside was quiet, chaos reigned within the chambers.

The deputies talked loudly among themselves while the audience shouted opinions from the benches above. Robespierre stood near the stage with the other head Montagnards. Gus went to join them and serve as a secretary to the Convention. Robespierre stiffened when she came in, but he gave his best attempt at comfort with a nod of support.

She wiped her sweating palms on her dress—a modest blue one—and squared her shoulders, adjusting the cockade pinned on her white lace fichu.

The din quieted as she arrived before erupting into surprised whispers. She could imagine them already. *Women belong in the stands, not on the stage.*

Whispers turned to murmurs, which turned to grumbling, which turned to loud complaints to Gus from several head deputies.

"A woman, Augustin?" one red-faced deputy asked. "God knows France doesn't need another Olympe de Gouges."

The Convention, it seemed, preferred to murder a woman than make her its equal.

Maximilien spoke instead. "Unlike Olympe, Sylvie Rosiers comes to speak as a sufferer under the yoke of tyranny—not as a monarchist. We shall hear her as we heard the other delegates."

Sylvie breathed a sigh of relief. The support of her secret fiancé bolstered her confidence. He nodded at her, and she took her place onstage.

The mumbling continued, but she took a calming breath and

closed her eyes. Sylvie allowed the pain and contempt of her life before France to escape the fortress she'd built to repress them. Dark faces, coffee beans, and the iron scent of blood filling a city square crept out of the recesses of her mind. Time made the blood less vibrant and the faces less clear, but time could not lessen the twisting vines of shame that wove themselves throughout her memories.

"*Bons citoyens*, thank you for allowing me to speak here today," she said. Sylvie had only a vague idea of what she wished to say. She had tried to write the speech the night before, but only a sentence or two survived before she'd returned to the cognac. "I am unsure of what the excellent men who preceded me have told you, so forgive me if I repeat their points."

She tried to clear her throat, but her nerves made it feel like she had swallowed rocks. "My name is Sylvie Rosiers. To be clear, I am not a slave—I never was a slave. I was born as free as any of the fine men and women here today. So I cannot tell you the horrors of being whipped or the exhaustion of picking coffee beans. I can only tell you what it is like to be me."

A few people shouted for her to leave—mostly men—but the majority seemed willing to hear her.

"I grew up on a prosperous estate on Saint-Domingue. My father, Julien de Rosiers, owned the surrounding plantation, which specialized in coffee—something I still cannot bring myself to drink." Her chest constricted, her ribs ensnaring her heart and making the air thin. "My father owned the mother of his child. He could sell her like he sells a horse. And, like a horse, my mother did not choose when she worked, when she was ridden, and when she would bear children. Even in her last moments, as the puerperal fever took the light from her eyes, she had no more rights than the bed she died in. And for that I face paralyzing shame—that I live free, and she gave the life she did not own for a child she'd never know."

Several people, mostly women, gasped at this. Their shock threatened her equilibrium; they had no right to be surprised. But she needed their sympathy, and she soldiered on in her speech.

"Most mulattoes' stories mirror mine; mulattoes follow wherever Black bondage goes. Mulatto babies are the cruelest symptom of the disease of slavery. We remind white wives that their husbands are unfaithful and remind Black men that their masters can defile their wives on a whim. I may have half brothers and sisters already dead—taken by suffering or by their war for freedom. I will never know their names." The words came without difficulty now. She spoke from an aching, scarred place. But the promise of abolition compelled her to tell her whole truth.

"Whether Black or white, our skin determines the certain types of clothes, entertainments, positions, and marriage partners we may have. Free but not equal. More than a slave but less than a citizen. White men think that because I came from the union of a white man and a slave, I am this vessel of carnality and pleasure—one they can own and exploit. I feel a constant isolation and fear, afraid men will hurt me because of their assumptions regarding my character. Yet, simultaneously, I feel beholden to that caricature.

"White, Black, or mulatto, we all should be born free. Slavery is an evil in and of itself, but its cruelty is far-reaching. I implore you, fellow citizens, to right a wrong so heinous that it will stain us for generations to come. Let my brothers and sisters in Saint-Domingue know the meaning of *liberté*, *égalité*, and *fraternité*. Let them taste the glory of our revolution."

Many men and women in the stands wept with Sylvie. She did not expect their compassion or support, but she found both in their applause. She was vulnerable and overwhelmed; Gaspard reached out to guide her down the steps. His own eyes glistened, too.

He took her outside while the Convention deliberated. They waited in a heavy silence, but her heart felt lighter than it had before.

An hour or so passed, and Gus came out to usher them in—his

face beaming with happiness. They entered as a secretary said, "The National Convention declares the abolition of Negro slavery in all the colonies; in consequence it decrees that all men, without distinction of color, residing in the colonies are French citizens and will enjoy all the rights assured by the constitution. It asks the Committee of Public Safety to make a report as soon as possible on the measures that should be taken to assure the execution of the present decree."

The foundation of their revolution—*égalité*—survived the violent perversions of the Law of Suspects; the Convention had voted to abolish slavery in the French colonies. Sylvie struggled to stay on her feet, and Gus reached out to hold her steady.

When she left Charleston for Paris, Sylvie had promised herself she would not sit on a throne gilded by hypocrisy and built on bones. And perhaps she broke that promise, but at least no woman would bear a child to a man she called "Master."

She looked to Robespierre and found pride in his eyes. Her original infatuation replaced the chaos of the previous months—the doubt and vinegar that spoiled her waking hours loosening their hold, and the cruelty of the Convention unable to besmirch the purity of their triumph.

Chapter Thirty

You [Robespierre] will follow us soon. Your house will be beaten down and salt sown in the place where it stood.

—*Georges Danton*

The night the vote passed, Sylvie brought Robespierre to her rooms.

He could not deny her; they both were high on the glory of their success and the brightness of the future. Sylvie could breathe a little easier, her list of burdens shortened by one.

She kissed his mouth until the tension left his jaw. He ran his hands over her curves without the reticence she'd come to expect. He did not lower his gaze when she let down her hair; he did not hesitate as he removed her gown and then her petticoats. Now he could be Robespierre the man rather than Robespierre the Incorruptible.

He took her with precision, with focus. She prepared for great pain, but there was only discomfort: her time with Cornélie made her a master of her own pleasure.

His intensity never left—nor did his gaze. He marveled at the texture of her hair and the darkness of her nipples, something she'd never considered particularly unique before. His interest reminded her of scientific study; he stroked and touched, observing her reactions for the optimal response. Robespierre's body did not yield to excess; though he was not athletic in any way, his muscles flexed and coiled under her touch. But he never surrendered control, and she let him think he had it.

She indulged in the fantasy of his perfection.

He remained in her bed for the rest of the evening, and Sylvie slept in the security of his arms and his power. Sleep made the Incorruptible a mortal man, vulnerable and calm. She watched him slumber, pleased with her success.

This night bound him to her, protecting her from both the threat his crusade posed and the potential wavering of his interest.

Based on his sated snores, Sylvie doubted he'd leave her bed or her side. But like the month of February, her confidence did not last long.

mars 1794

The end began as winter thawed.

Sylvie never would have described Robespierre's health as robust. He suffered from frequent bouts of lethargy and headaches, but never had Sylvie doubted his ability to quickly recover.

So once Robespierre became ill almost immediately following the liberation of the slaves, she embraced the panic Gaspard had expressed previously.

"We must prepare for the worst," her brother said. The worst, of course, meaning Robespierre's death.

Robespierre's skin went jaundiced, his eyes yellow and glazed. He hardly had the strength to leave his rooms, and he refused to let Sylvie see him. Desperate to see his condition for herself, she even visited the Duplays out of hope he'd greet her. Cornélie left the sitting room the moment she arrived, leaving Lise to entertain Sylvie with stilted conversation about her pregnancy until she gave up on seeing the invalid.

"The Convention could turn on his supporters," Gaspard said as he scribbled out lists and letters on the first rainy night in March. "I'm still serving as his secretary, as well as his second, and those closest to him will reveal your relationship under duress."

Robespierre's many enemies would eagerly take power if he were to succumb to his sickness. But their legitimacy depended upon delegitimizing their predecessor and his followers. The best way to discredit Robespierre would be to establish a show trial for his allies and feed them to the guillotine.

Even still, she could not help feeling a surge of reassurance at Gaspard's capabilities: he'd grown up from a sobbing boy racing toward the docks to a competent strategist. Perhaps she worried about him overmuch.

"So we'd run?" she asked. "Again?"

Once more she'd be an enemy in her own home—considered unsafe and unworthy.

She wondered if Gaspard would be so quick to escape if he knew Lise carried his child. Her brother lived as an established romantic, regardless of whether his absurd devotion to either people or ideas meant an assured demise. She did not intend to risk her only sibling's life by telling him the truth.

"We're the wards of an émigré and ex-noble; we'd be in line at the guillotine before sundown." He grimaced. "Aunt Fifi could house us in London, assuming we could find passage across the Channel without being arrested." Sylvie considered the gray English skies and shuddered.

Blessedly, the Rosiers avoided the dreaded British weather when Robespierre overcame his illness by the middle of March—but without his mind intact.

Gus had already been sent as a *représentant en mission* to the Army of Italy stationed in eastern France. Sylvie could not lean on him for political insight like before.

Robespierre rested in his bed, still recuperating from his illness, but he feverishly scribbled in a notepad on his lap. He had finally allowed Sylvie to visit.

"It shall be seen as a revelation," he said. "It's deistic in foundation—the people need organized religion in their lives. The Supreme Being supplies that social utility." She pressed her lips together, wary of criticizing his ramblings in this manic state. "A new religion for *all*."

"A new religion? But I thought the Cult of Reason replaced the Church—"

"It's different," he snapped. "The people need structure, moral guidance. Something laws and government cannot always provide. I shall present them with a new form of rational worship. I'll host a great celebration on the Champ de Mars to unify us all, a Festival of the Supreme Being. And in the center of it all, we will set fire to the great statue of Wisdom in effigy."

He spoke at such a speed, Sylvie barely understood him. He did not seem to notice her presence as he mumbled and designed plans for this festival. He kept repeating "the Supreme Being" as he wrote.

She envisioned Robespierre, arms raised, circling a burning statue while he praised his new God. How long could she stand by his side in the name of self-preservation? The fear of his instability began to outweigh her fears of retaliation.

Sylvie slinked out of the room—not that Robespierre noticed—enveloped by the acrid memory of vinegar.

mai 1794

Sylvie,

I greatly enjoy my role here at Haute-Saône, but news from Paris urges me to write to you.

My brother says that he is unwell and has withdrawn from the Convention for now. He says he keeps you away and the Duplays nurse him. He has a habit of keeping those closest to him at a distance when he is at his weakest, so do not judge him too harshly.

Nice was Hell. I condemned so many and saved so few. Toulon was a greater success, mostly due to a Corsican general named Bonaparte. I'm rather proud of myself for having discovered him, and I wish I could introduce the two of you. I consider him my closest friend, and he reminds me of you greatly through his wit and ambition—though he'd out-cheat you at cards. I wish I could have spirited you away from the pestilence of this terror. I worry for you and Cornélie. Max seems more paranoid in his writings, his passion inflamed. We have bolstered him out of the hope he could be moderated, and I worry the Committee seeks to fan his wildness rather than hinder it.

I beg you, Sylvie, that if a time comes when closeness to my brother means your destruction rather than triumph, you will do whatever you must to survive. I would offer you my protection, but my name brands me a prince of the republic now—it could later brand me a traitor.

And as the nights in Paris grow darker and the promise of dawn less certain, do not forget that it will come.

Your Friend,
Augustin Robespierre

The turmoil throughout France slowed the messengers, and by the time Sylvie received Gus's letter, his fears had long been realized.

Her portrait—or, rather, the painting of Silvia—neared completion. She kept the letter on her person as an anchor amid the waves, the paper crinkling softly whenever she shifted her weight on the platform. She did not need to wear the toga now that most of her body had been painted, sparing her the added vulnerability.

Robespierre sat in his usual spot a few feet away, scratching out speeches on a small writing desk. He had not accompanied her to David's studio in weeks due to his increasingly demanding schedule and the fact that her sessions became rarer with the preliminary sketch completed.

However, when she informed him David demanded his model, Robespierre had offered to accompany her in the carriage. He refrained from walking anywhere now out of fear of assassination.

The madness that had touched Marat had also touched her betrothed. Outside of convening with the Convention or committees, he stayed a recluse, seeing plots and traitors in every face. Sylvie rarely spoke with him for any extended period of time; his fastidiously clean scent now reminded her of vinegar. His "releases" were the only activity that remained consistent during those months.

She gleaned what pleasure she could from their unions, but he used her to exorcise whatever demons and self-loathing haunted him. He remained as clothed as possible and disliked mess of any kind, limiting their interactions to rutting against her or frustrated groping.

Every release secured Sylvie's safety while soiling her dignity, yet dignity was the one luxury she could not afford. So she missed Cornélie's love more with each passing day, but endured Robespierre's touches as penance for her weakness.

As David copied her image to a painting of a shattered dream, Sylvie questioned the veracity of her safety. The government of puppet masters turned on Danton and his ilk despite his closeness to Robespierre, and the Incorruptible condemned Danton with silence.

Even if the Revolution ended, she was still its victim. How long could his lust for her sustain his loyalty? Would marriage promise safety, or would it merely ensure a lifetime in a habitual state of uncertainty?

She now fully understood what he meant by terror. It was a beast unchained that fed on screams and blood and fear. And still the Committee chose terror as their weapon, with Robespierre one of their many blacksmiths to sharpen and shape it on the whetstone of the Revolution.

"David." Robespierre's voice pulled her from her morbid discovery. "Leave us for a moment?"

David closed his paints louder than necessary, tossing Sylvie a glower before going downstairs.

A tingle of dread sparked in her chest. She did not want to be alone with Robespierre.

"I wish to unveil the painting at the Festival of the Supreme Being," he said, circling the portrait. The festival, a hollow celebration of his invented religion, occupied his every moment. "I can think of no better setting to reveal what we've created."

The painting represented all of David's genius—from its drama to the play of light. Sylvie as Silvia embodied the glories of democracy in the form of woman, sensual and romantic but also warm and empowered. She welcomed the viewer to join her in the burgeoning paradise, but Sylvie saw the lie in her gentle smile.

She wanted to see the canvas burn.

"And we will announce our engagement then," he added, fingertips brushing the jaw of Silvia. "I see no point in postponing it any longer. The festival will show the people their new religion, and the true believers in our vision shall rejoice—your image shining before them. And those unbelievers, so surrounded by true virtue, will be exposed as the traitors they are."

His gray eyes glittered at the prospect. Robespierre and those who supported him believed they controlled terror, but experience had taught Sylvie that terror cuts the hand that wields it.

And she knew terror as intimately as anyone—it paints hearts black and walls red, steals men's minds and morals. And it had stolen her future.

I am the great whore of the Revolution, she realized. *If he is the master of terror, then I am its mistress.*

"You remind me of Edmond," she whispered, stepping away from the falsehoods on the canvas and the politician who believed them. "A man of iron will, a man with vision. Until those visions consumed him, and the people destroyed the rest." He hardly heard her, he was so engrossed in the painting of his own invention. Keeping him in her life posed the same risks as removing him from it. She and Gaspard could not depend on this deific madman. the tangled threads of his brilliant mind were too frayed.

"I cannot marry you," she finished. "I cannot marry a man who, under any other circumstance, would want to see me dead."

That caught his attention, and some clarity sparked in his eyes. "You are not *them*," he began. "One does not water a garden with champagne, Sylvie. I would never let them touch you."

"They *murdered* Lamballe!" she shouted. "Paraded her severed head on a pike. And her crime? Being born into nobility, befriending a queen people were determined to despise. Had I not been a mulatto bastard, I would've probably been one of her ladies' maids!" Sylvie shuddered. "I allied myself with you out of self-preservation. But I see myself in every one of those women sent to die on those scaffolds, and for their sakes and mine, I cannot wed you. I witnessed true slavery, true despots. Those you kill are not deserving of the Hell you call justice."

Robespierre did not respond at first and turned his slatelike stare on the painting. He reached out to touch Silvia's form, fingers brushing over the infants Romulus and Remus. Silvia's outstretched hand beckoned the viewer to admire the verdant fields behind her.

"You disappoint me," he said, though it appeared like he spoke to the portrait and not to her.

"Would you let me tie myself to you out of fear alone?"

He moved quickly, gripping the back of her neck in his broad palm. "We are bound together by more than earthly passions—"

"We are bound by nothing: you are neither my husband nor my

master." She pushed against his chest, but he didn't free her. "You do not possess me."

"Of course I do!" He pulled her face within inches of his. His spittle peppered her cheeks as he raged. "What were you before me? A spoiled child without purpose, without direction. Without my guidance you would've become just another Creole whore warming the beds of great men, instead of *this*." He turned her forcefully toward the damned canvas. "I made you the muse to genius. I made you immortal."

"I tried to be your Silvia," she sobbed. She meant it somewhere between an apology and an explanation, though she knew he deserved neither. He had no right to the secrets she kept. "But she isn't real, Maximilien. She's a fever dream."

Slowly, his hold loosened, and she lifted his hand off her nape as his eyes glazed over.

Sylvie wanted to ask for clemency, for assurances of protection, but he did not offer any more words. She supposed that Gaspard, with his connections and political savvy, might at least escape the wrath of Robespierre's fury.

But Robespierre no longer looked vengeful or spurned, just lost in the portrait—preferring the mythical Silvia to the real woman before him.

Cornélie's original portrait caught Sylvie's eye as she left the studio, standing out among the more expensive canvases and darker colors. She hugged the painting against her chest, shielding the art from the harsh afternoon sun as she walked home.

Chapter Thirty-One

Citizens, did you want a revolution without a revolution?
—*Maximilien Robespierre*

juin 1794

The future Sylvie killed, wept, and schemed for met its end by her own hand.

Sylvie couldn't foresee how Robespierre planned to react to her decision, but she hoped his affection prevented the temptation to seek revenge in the aftermath.

Days after their falling-out, the Convention voted to make Robespierre acting president—which he did not refuse—and Sylvie wondered if their liaison had restrained his desire for power. Or did their separation only unhinge his cowardice, leaving him unable to refuse this position when offered?

Regardless, only a fool did not consider the possibility of retribution. And Sylvie was no fool.

She kept the broken engagement from her brother so as to not increase his own distress, and it appeared Robespierre did as well. Gaspard said nothing about her choice, still assured by her promise that Sylvie's bond with the Incorruptible spared him from the guillotine. She wondered if the madness was their saving grace—if Robespierre was too obsessed with his delusions to organize a plot against them.

The Festival of the Supreme Being was upon them, and as Robespierre's secretary, Gaspard had no choice but to attend the debacle.

Gods had done nothing for Sylvie, and she did not need to endure hours of Robespierre playing one.

Sylvie clutched Cornélie's painting to her heart the next week, planning to use the art as a pretense to see her. They had not spoken intimately since the evening in David's studio, neither party reaching out to the other.

Alone in her torment, she sought the woman who, no matter Sylvie's crimes, showed love and forgiveness in spite of herself.

When the maid let her into Chez Duplay, a woman's scream greeted her.

In times like these, such a sound was not uncommon, though not in the Duplay house. "It's Lise," said Cornélie as she descended the stairs. "The baby comes."

My niece or nephew comes.

"Oh," Sylvie said. "That's . . . Congratulations." Lise's scream rang out again.

"Thank you," Cornélie said, wiping her hands on her apron. The scent of sour blood wafted over them. Sylvie's eyes must have widened, for she added, "Birth is a messy, bloody business."

As the youngest of three, Sylvie had never witnessed a birth. But as a woman, she understood the birthing bed to be a wife's greatest foe and sent silent words of encouragement.

"Most things are these days," Sylvie said.

"Why have you come?" Cornélie asked. Her tone meant to sound annoyed, but it came out pained to Sylvie's ears. "To ask for your beloved back?"

You? Sylvie wanted to ask. *Or Robespierre?*

She looked away, embarrassed that Cornélie knew of the estrangement. "Who told you?" she asked.

"You just did. Though I suspected something was amiss from his mutterings about Silvia." Cornélie tucked a wisp of black hair into her cap. "It's true, then."

Sylvie wanted to speak of her fears, her nightmares, and her disillusions. But she did not know where Cornélie's loyalties lay, so she only nodded.

"I brought you your painting," she said while holding it out toward its creator.

Cornélie made no move to grab it. "Leave it here. I will make sure it's put away. I don't want to get blood on the canvas."

There may as well be.

"I did not want it languishing in David's studio now that he no longer needs it," Sylvie said.

"Robespierre keeps your painting here; he does not want to reveal it without you beside him." For all her coldness, Cornélie could not keep the bitterness at bay.

Lise screamed again, this time less out of effort and more out of agony. "I must return to my sister," she said. "My mother has been up with her all night and needs to rest. We're nearing the end, and that's the hardest part."

"May I come? Perhaps I could be useful." Sylvie knew that the Duplays' *cat* would be more useful than her in a birthing room. But she wanted to be there.

Cornélie's expression betrayed her doubt, but she nodded and motioned for Sylvie to follow.

LA MERDE—SYLVIE did not expect so much *shit*.

Madame Duplay pulled soiled sheets out from under her daughter's writhing body, soiled by blood, fluid, and excrement. A battlefield in a bedroom.

Sylvie thanked the open windows.

Cornélie went to Lise's side when the contraction ended, pushing back her hair and blotting her sweaty skin. She shushed her sister while she whimpered and murmured encouragement in her ear.

"Sylvie?" Lise asked. Sylvie did not know a person's voice could sound so tired. "I'm glad you came. At least *you* can be here." Cornélie looked between them in confusion, but when another contraction came forth, the time for questions passed.

Lise sobbed as the pain seized her, pushing as her mother told her to.

"Help us move her back to the birthing chair," Cornélie said to Sylvie. Madame Duplay adjusted the arms of the chair for Lise's stature, while Cornélie and Sylvie held Lise's arms to support her weight.

"Thank you," Lise whispered to Sylvie, more out of exhaustion than secrecy. "'Tis like he's here with me."

She thought Lise absurd and pain addled, yet she couldn't help but feel touched by the sentiment.

Mother and daughter placed Lise's feet in the stirrups while contractions occurred with less time between them. Sylvie briefly wondered at the absence of a midwife, but she supposed Madame Duplay's obvious experience served them well.

"I'm going to speak with Cook about some herbs to move the labor along," Madame Duplay said. "Keep her calm and watch her progress." Lise whimpered, but her mother kissed her brow and promised to be quick.

Cornélie went to a basin of hot, scented water and dipped cloths into it. Lise groaned as another spasm came. Sylvie let her squeeze her hand, trying to contain a moan of pain herself.

Cornélie hurried over with the rags and placed one over Lise's head. "Sylvie, I need you to check her."

"Check her for what?"

Cornélie groaned in exasperation. "The babe's head, obviously. Her pains grow nearer and nearer."

Holding her breath, Sylvie lifted Lise's skirts and nearly screamed from fright. "Good God in Heaven!"

In a panic, Lise asked, "What? Is something wrong? Is the babe all right?"

Sylvie hesitated to even try to describe the horror she found between Lise's legs. She covered her mouth to keep from gagging. Cornélie pushed her aside and looked herself. "I see the babe! Lord, Sylvie, have you never seen a cunt before?" Cornélie's cheeks flushed scarlet when they both realized what she'd said. "*Never mind, just hold her hand.*"

Blessedly, Madame Duplay returned with her medicinal teas and herbs. Lise let out another piercing scream. Her pretty, fair skin was mottled with the agony of pushing for hours on end, and her auburn hair clung to the sweat on her cheeks and neck.

Madame crouched down beneath Lise's skirt. "Another push or two and that child will be ready to greet us," she said from below. "Remember how I said to push; we don't want you to tear."

"Oh God," Sylvie said, feeling her own nether regions clench. Lise screamed again, but this time a baby's cry followed.

Madame Duplay revealed a wailing infant in her blood-soaked hands, the cord connecting mother and babe still attached. Her face matched the teary smile of her daughter.

"A boy, my sister," said Cornélie, reaching out to touch the baby's downy tufts of hair. "A very loud one."

The baby, so pink and new to the volatile world in which he'd been born, frightened Sylvie, although she had endured horrors far more threatening than a squalling and wrinkled newborn. The babe itself did not scare her, but the power he wielded with one little cry did.

By all accounts, her only nominal connection to the babe was through his father. Logically, no one should feel beholden to a stranger out of a minimal relation.

And yet, the young stranger claimed a part of her raw and distrusting heart in mere seconds. She loved him, not because of what he could offer or out of obsession, but due to reasons devoid of sense. She bonded to him against her will, and so many threats could take him from this life despite all the love and protection his family could offer.

His life held the power to break her heart, and that potential was a terror unlike any she'd ever known.

In this wiggling, ugly little human being placed in Lise's arms, a bright spot emerged in an otherwise endless parade of death.

"Mama," Cornélie called. "Send for the physician—just to be cautious." Her mother kissed both her daughter's and grandson's brows before going downstairs.

Lise cooed at the now-nursing baby. He latched well and fed quietly as the trio watched him.

"Am I right that he is to call you 'aunt'?" asked Cornélie, looking at Sylvie. She said it without criticism, but Lise's face transformed from contentment to guilt.

"Forgive me," she said, lip trembling. "It was not planned—I could not help myself. Do you hate me?"

"You are my sister," Cornélie soothed. "I could never hate you. This Revolution seeks to break us, to pull us asunder. We have been forced to make choices, to commit sins in the name of a war no one sees we're fighting. France races toward a future I cannot foresee, but I know—I *know*—when we look back on the love and loss that led us there"—she looked into Sylvie's misty eyes—"this moment shan't be considered anything less than a triumph."

"We have all done what we must," Sylvie said, squeezing both sisters' hands. She meant those words more as a way of apology. "And if my brother's love gave you even a moment of happiness in this world, then I applaud you. Though you may spare me the specifics of your union."

Lise laughed through her tears, making the baby fuss at the disturbance.

"What shall you call him?" asked Sylvie. She ran her finger over his puckered mouth and soft skin.

"Philippe," said Lise. "My husband has always been good to me.

I do not mind giving my son his name—though you may judge me for it."

"I would never. It makes him no less my nephew," Sylvie replied.

The three moved to the bed, now covered in fresh linen, and huddled close despite the blood and sweat between them. Cornélie shared a look with Sylvie and for once she understood her.

They were regretful and hopeful all at once. The women must face the future their men had wrought, but they now had a bond unbreakable by time, distance, or guillotine.

THE NIGHT OF Philippe's birth, Sylvie and Cornélie held each other for the first time in over a year.

"I've missed you," Sylvie whispered. She dampened Cornélie's chemise with incessant tears, but the relief of her embrace brought a peace she hadn't known in months.

Cornélie smoothed Sylvie's hair, almost motherly in her tenderness. In silence they had cleaned each other—removing the traces of birth from their face and hands. Clean but exhausted, they lay together, entwined in each other's arms.

"And I've missed you."

"We are not engaged," Sylvie said abruptly. "I called off the betrothal."

Cornélie stared up at her, shock shining from her eyes at the rumor confirmed. "When did he end it? What reason did he give?"

"I ended it, not him. Whatever illness he had ruined the man I admired, or at least revealed his truer self. People languished in prison by the thousands while I served him tea—I could not allow the charade to continue."

Cornélie hung her head. "I should never have relinquished you in the first place."

"Had you tried to stop me"—Sylvie rested her head against

Cornélie's shoulder—"I would've resented you. The choice was mine, and I chose wrongly."

"And if you had the chance again?" Cornélie asked. A younger Sylvie might have begged to be his wife, but now, wiser and matured, she hesitated. "All of that effort to have him, and you throw him away?"

"I can't bear the weight of my own sins, let alone those of Robespierre. He has become bound to the whims of terror." Cornélie nodded and softly kissed Sylvie's mouth. "He wanted to consume me, and I feared he'd leave nothing behind."

Cornélie spoke from the crook of Sylvie's neck. "We're all gluttons—gluttons in love, in war, in our ambitions. Drink the wine but burn the vineyard."

Sylvie flinched. "There is more to love than destruction. I know there is."

Cornélie shrugged. "I have no wish to marry—besides, my bond with Robespierre was too public for another man to risk his life over an engagement."

She spoke truthfully, but Sylvie hated the defeat weighing on her shoulders. She took Cornélie's face in her hands and asked, "And what of me?"

Cornélie smiled sadly. "You have already broken my heart, so there is nothing more for me to fear."

Sylvie wished to take all of the pain she'd caused with her selfishness out of Cornélie's overburdened heart. "Don't say that."

"But," Cornélie said, rolling on top of Sylvie with a playful gleam in her eyes, "that does not mean I'm unwilling to let you try and put it back together."

Sylvie's love for her had not changed. But the mass graves grew deeper, and they approached a breaking point. When the Revolution ended, she couldn't fathom what world it would leave behind. She should not make assurances to last a lifetime when she hardly knew what tomorrow might bring. And yet, regardless of what loomed on the horizon, she wanted to be at Cornélie's side.

juillet 1794

From June to July, Sylvie watched the Purge of Paris destroy any hope for the redemption of Robespierre.

The prisons in Paris reached capacity, so the Convention discovered killing more quickly offered the most efficient solution. Trials happened back-to-back without witnesses or acquittals, with every new hour meaning another life lost. The Picpus Cemetery offered the final resting place for victims due to its proximity to the main guillotine; most executions occurred in the Place du Trône-Renversé, only a few minutes away.

The carts carried their headless bodies—old and young, rich and poor—and piled them high in the mass graves of the Picpus Cemetery garden beside Notre-Dame-de-la-Paix.

The area was blessedly far away, but the Place de la Révolution remained but a minute's walk from Chez Rohmer and Chez Duplay. Another notorious guillotine called the square home, taking the lives of some of the most notable victims of the Revolution while Sylvie played Mozart on her aunt's pianoforte to drown out the chaos.

The Place de la Révolution was the last thing Corday, Danton, Princess Élisabeth, and countless others saw before the blade fell.

Sylvie would never forget the roar of the crowd when the queen met her end just up the street; she had sobbed while screams of *whore* and *murderess* filled the neighborhood. Just like every other time a woman was executed. Sylvie awoke from many nightmares in which she stood on the same platform and heard the same words.

But instead of weeks separating such executions, the blade fell every day, if not hour—like a morbid bell chime.

Gaspard always returned home pale and resigned and drunk, the weight of condemned names he'd written heavy in his hand and heart. They rarely spoke, choosing to relish the rare silence night brought.

When Augustin returned to Paris that summer to serve as secretary to the Convention once more, Sylvie invited him to tea with her and Cornélie with the intention of trying to bring the killings to an end.

"There must be something you can do," Sylvie said.

Augustin, drawn and thin, kept his head low. "I assure you, there is not." He sank into Aunt Fifi's old chair and rested his head in his hands. "I've done what I could, but I failed. I failed you, and I failed France."

"You did not fail," she soothed. "Failing would've been to do nothing. The Convention failed *us*."

She held his shoulders as they shook with quiet sobs, seeing so little of the man she admired in his expression. The Revolution took him, too.

He dabbed his eyes and rested his hands on his knees. "An end approaches. The people are restless, their lives are no better, but the executions continue. They want bread, not blood. Maximilien had best learn that soon, for his sake, or the Convention will turn on him."

LISE STAYED AT Chez Duplay while she recuperated from the labor; Sylvie spent most days there to attend to her nephew and visit with Cornélie.

Now over a month old, *petit* Philippe was slightly more entertaining. He still slept an inordinate amount of time, in Sylvie's opinion, but when he woke, he now made noises beyond crying. He cooed and pursed his lips, waving his fists to show his pleasure when his aunts or mother smiled.

Sylvie held him more than before, as she deemed him sturdier looking, and baby Philippe enjoyed when she played lullabies while he watched from his mother's arms.

Lise surely noticed Sylvie and Cornélie's closeness during their afternoons, but she never mentioned their bond to either of them.

Gaspard visited once; he watched Lise tend to Philippe in pained silence, and she fell into hysterics the moment he left. Sylvie discouraged his visits after that, saying that Lise did not need her ex beau distressing her.

Augustin came to visit several times and teased Sylvie constantly for her sudden maternal nature.

"No one is immune to my charm," she teased back. "Even babies."

Those pleasurable weeks offered sanctuary against the rising tide of terror. Nonetheless, the end they spoke of came more quickly than either Sylvie or Gaspard had expected—but, unlike Saint-Domingue, Paris became a nightmare the Rosiers siblings could not escape.

The three ladies relaxed in the parlor on a humid day near the end of July. Cornélie sketched her sister and nephew in front of the window, while Sylvie read a British lady's magazine.

Monsieur Duplay rushed into the parlor, his wife sobbing behind him. Both of them had tears streaming down their cheeks and dread written in their eyes.

"Father, what's happened?" Lise asked, pulling Philippe closer.

He braced the mantel of the unlit hearth, staring into the ashes. "Robespierre's been arrested—so have Augustin, Le Bas, Gaspard— by order of the Convention."

Sylvie shot out of her chair, hand over her chest to steady her heart. "My brother?" she asked.

Maurice nodded solemnly. She fell back against the wall, her legs unable to support her weight alone. Lise sobbed with her mother, and only Cornélie kept her composure well enough to listen to Maurice.

"The Commune's troops went against the Convention and freed those imprisoned," he continued. So, Robespierre and his party escaped. The Convention, once their fortress, had become their enemy. "But since the Convention ordered Paul Barras's troops to assemble, hell has broken loose. Now they all hide in the Hôtel de Ville."

The Hôtel de Ville, an impressive symbol of French style and strength, now contained the last vestiges of the dying empire.

"And what of the Commune troops?" Cornélie asked. "Are they still loyal to Robespierre and his allies?"

"For now," he sighed. "The men won't stay loyal long. Barras's men are a formidable force; many deputies have already fled the Hôtel de Ville." The tide of power shifted, and self-preservation became the new law of the land.

A louder sob tore from Lise—she had more than one man to weep for.

"What will become of us?" Madame Duplay cried.

Sylvie moved to Cornélie's side while Maurice comforted his wife and daughter. "They'll come for us," said Cornélie. Her body went rigid with realization. "Not you. My entire family is suspect."

"You don't know that," said Sylvie. "I'm noble; my father was an émigré. I have a connection to both Robespierre and Gaspard. The Convention likes to convict mistresses." The Convention made their feelings clear over the course of their rule: the only good kind of woman was a headless one.

"We'll have to wait until tomorrow; nothing will be certain until then."

"I cannot stay here weeping with your mother while my brother awaits his death!" Sylvie hissed.

It was pure selfishness, she knew, to beg the Convention for mercy when Robespierre himself had given none. But she would convince Gus and Gaspard to reveal their allegiance to the moderates and the steps they took to bring down the Montagnards from within.

Sylvie reached for her hat and gloves. "I will go to the Hôtel de Ville and—"

Cornélie snatched her arm tightly enough to leave bruises, the calm gone from her eyes. "You will not. God knows what the troops would think if they found Robespierre's Creole betrothed sneaking into the Hôtel de Ville. I refuse to lose you to your own stupidity, not again."

Sylvie looked away, but Cornélie held her chin. "Promise me," she pleaded. "Without you, I am alone."

If Sylvie were to leave for the Hôtel de Ville, she'd have to do so in secret. She hated to deceive Cornélie, but she could not hide from this.

"I promise," she said, holding her close. A small lie to preserve the greater truth; Sylvie's very blood flowed through this Revolution, and she refused to let the Convention's perverted justice steal away what family she had left.

AT MIDNIGHT SHE untangled herself from Cornélie's embrace and went to Philippe's cradle, a small parcel wrapped up in her hand. Lise slept fitfully with her mother, and Sylvie avoided the creakier floorboards.

She unbound the package, revealing an ornate silver rattle. Sylvie had commissioned the gift in secret, designing it herself for the silversmith. Mother-of-pearl inlay coated the handle, and three little bells were attached around the head of the rattle. She had the smith make it in the form of an orchid.

Sylvie rested the toy beside Philippe's golden head and then followed the Seine to the bleeding heart of Paris.

Chapter Thirty-Two

He who builds on the people, builds on sand.
—*Niccolò Machiavelli,* Il Principe

The Hôtel de Ville took a half hour to reach by foot, twenty
minutes if you ran.

Sylvie did not know what awaited her at the heart of the coup, so she
tucked a small kitchen knife within the lining of her cloak. She could
and would murder again if needed, but she did not intend to linger near
an attacker long enough to kill—she'd lost enough time already.

The streets did not bustle with the hordes of Jacobin supporters as
she'd hoped; troops, police, and rioters ran to and away from the
Hôtel de Ville, but in small packs of two or three. Sylvie's presence
went unnoticed.

It stood out among the architecture of Paris, a Renaissance palace
rather than a simple city hall, though night gave the building a
haunting glow in the torchlight, the giant clockface watching over
Paris like an all-seeing eye.

Sylvie did not truly have a plan on how to enter City Hall; she'd
anticipated hundreds of troops and guards. Instead, she saw a few
dozen at most, scattered and nervous at their posts around the front
entrance. The people's allegiance had clearly shifted, which did not
bode well for the outlaws inside. Their castle had become their prison.

Sylvie considered the unfairness of it all. The Convention autho-rized the slaughter without hesitation—they made Robespierre their leader without hesitation. And now they called him dictator. They were all just as complicit in the evils of the Revolution as they were in the triumphs.

Yet when the people turned on the Convention's methods, the delegates served them the Montagnards on a gleaming platter. But to rue it now helped no one.

Breaching the hall, without the protection of loyal soldiers, re-quired little effort. Sylvie moved quickly and quietly, sneaking in through the rear entrance.

She'd been inside once before with Augustin, and the beauty never ceased to make her pause. Even in dim candlelight, the gold filigree brought life to every column and archway in the grand re-ception hall. But she did not have time to admire the art among the ghosts.

The hall had many private rooms and offices, and the clock chimed one by the time she found any of the deputies.

She did not wish to risk discovery by anyone other than Augustin and Gaspard, so she moved through the halls—ear to the doors—waiting to hear their voices.

A pair of double doors seemed promising; she didn't hear sev-eral shouting voices like she had behind others. She opened them as slowly as she could, the old hinges cooperatively not making any sound.

The doors led to a large salon or perhaps receiving room, a hand-somely furnished chamber that had been thrown into disarray. Arm-chairs rested on their sides, and the shattered remnants of a decanter littered the floor. Papers, ink, and books were splayed across a small writing desk in the corner.

Philippe Le Bas lay on the ground, blood still pouring from a fatal bullet wound in his temple. And Robespierre stood in front of the hearth, pointing a pistol to his own head.

"Stop!" she shouted.

She ran to him and grabbed his hand. She had come in time, and the gun did not fire between them. In Robespierre's shock, he released the weapon, and it fell by her feet.

She snatched the pistol out of his reach. Sylvie questioned his state of mind, his eyes bloodshot and wide. She instinctively kept the gun aimed toward him.

"Have you come to kill me?" he asked.

"After all you've done," she said, ignoring him. Her every muscle shook in fury. "You would take your own life? Your people hunger for blood; nothing will squelch their appetite but *your* head. But I would not take that joy from them," she said, lowering her weapon. "So, no," she sneered. "I've come for my brother." She decided to not mention her intention to save Augustin as well.

"Then you should not be here," he said. He sounded almost disappointed. "Give me the gun and leave."

She shook her head, raging and heartbroken over the pathetic creature before her.

"You could have done so much for France," she said through angry tears. "But instead you *killed* half of it! Are you mad? Are you mad like Marat?"

"Everything I've done," he said through gritted teeth, "was for France."

She strode toward him, fury raging in her face. "You told us we'd build a New Rome. You spoke of freedom, of virtue, of equality. Wrote me poems of Silvia, filling my head with promises of a utopia. And so we believed in you. We believed in all of you."

He pointed his finger toward the sky, and the veins in his temple pulsed. "What I built will shine eternal!" he shouted.

"You *betrayed* us! You became obsessed with terror—this precious fuel to revolution. I thought I understood what you meant—that freedom does not come quietly. Strong language, certainly, but I *understood*. Then you and the whole damned Convention paved the streets of Paris in hellfire—and called it *justice*."

He sneered, his face twisted in defeat and fury. "Do you think freedom comes easily? That intentions alone will disassemble the web of tyranny laced throughout our country? The Convention is full of cowards, weak men who suddenly whimper at the slightest obstacle. Terror exposes truth, and through terror we find *virtue*."

She pressed the mouth of the weapon to his chest.

"Do you feel that?" she asked. Robespierre inhaled sharply, still as stone. "Your heart is beating so hard that it hurts. All that blood pumping into every limb, but you can't move an inch." His pulse bounded beneath the pistol, the rhythm of his frantic heart betraying the truth of her words. "Raw and pure and alive—a cruel twilight between life and death. *That* is terror. I've seen it in the eyes of slaves, in my family, in my own reflection."

She exhaled and lowered the pistol once more. "Terror is a crueler tyrant than some spendthrift queen or hapless king could ever be. It's a monarch I wouldn't wish on anyone. Yet you wore terror like a crown."

She paused to let him explain, to beg forgiveness, to argue. But he said nothing, he just trembled before her, pale faced. The Revolution had taken much from him, too.

"But now I see it in your eyes." She pushed the mouth of the pistol deeper into his heart. "When they condemn you for your corruption," she said, "it saddens me to think you'll stand on the same platform, see the same crowds, be thrown in the same grave, as all the others you've condemned—so many who were better men with lesser crimes."

The musket shot outside startled them both. Several more bullets were fired throughout the hall, followed by the sound of broken glass. Muffled cries of "Barras's men!" could not be mistaken. She'd thought she had more time.

His capture now imminent, Robespierre lunged for the pistol.

Though not a burly man, he could outmatch Sylvie easily. But she'd grown up with two brothers with a penchant for filching her things, and she had wrested a gun away from a man before.

They battled on the salon floor, and challenging a man with death on his mind made it all the more difficult. She tried to cover the pistol by rolling onto her stomach, but Robespierre forced her onto her back.

"I will die by my own hand," he said, both of them panting and winded from their efforts. She tried to knee him in the groin but could not muster the momentum. His pockmarks looked more severe due to redness and sweat, and his wig had been pulled to the side during the scuffle.

"*Give me the—*"

The weapon fired.

In the tangle of their hands, they had managed to discharge the pistol. It had been aimed toward Robespierre's jaw. Sylvie could not see, as the spray of blood had gotten in her eyes.

He let out an agonized scream, rolling off his unintentional assailant. She rubbed her eyes to clear away the blood.

Robespierre huddled in pain—his jaw hanging by bits of frayed skin and muscle. The close range of the blast had caused some of his tissue to burn, which left an acrid smell of singed flesh.

Blood poured down his waistcoat and palms as he desperately tried to hold his jaw together. The window revealed Convention soldiers preparing to enter the hall, and the shouting of the other deputies confirmed it. Robespierre kept screaming, tears of pain streaming down his shattered jaw.

Another pistol went off somewhere else in the hall, bringing Sylvie out of her horrified shock.

Barras's soldiers began their unchallenged assault on the Hôtel de Ville, and she needed to escape the cross fire. She looked down at Robespierre's gruesome wounds, his cries not sounding human. He moaned and gurgled, clutching at the sinews of tissue dangling from his face. He did not look human, either. She dropped the pistol and bolted out of the salon.

Sylvie rounded the corner to the great staircase, only to see Couthon—a well-known and paralyzed Montagnard—lying at the foot of the steps, his wheelchair still on the third floor.

She ran past the unconscious man and around toward the back entrance just as the troops broke through the main doors.

The crowd had grown in size, though not in support. Several deputies already sat in a carriage bound in chains. As she ran, she looked for Gus or her brother, but the blur of red and blue made it difficult to see in the fray.

Onlookers crowded around several soldiers holding up a hollering deputy. His legs were bent in the wrong directions, with a pink bone tearing through one of his breeches. She concluded the deputy had attempted suicide, albeit unsuccessfully, by throwing himself from an open window several floors above. However, she knew Augustin's voice almost as well as her own, so she recognized his pained howl. Sylvie screamed for him.

Robespierre sat incapacitated in the Hôtel de Ville. Gaspard remained unaccounted for somewhere within City Hall. Now that Sylvie had discovered Augustin, yowling as they dragged him to a cart, his useless legs trailing behind him, she fell to the ground, her mouth open in a silent plea to make this torment end.

SYLVIE COULD NOT face the Duplays covered in their tenant's blood. Most of it had gotten on her face and cloak, though droplets from the bloody spray and residual gunpowder stained her dress and reticule. She needed to find a place to stay and wash before going out in broad daylight.

She let her feet take her toward home until she approached the sign of an open inn. Her dark cloak and the dim lighting obscured the stains, and she had used a public well to remove the blood. She'd brought enough money in her purse to afford a room.

Thankfully, the innkeeper was a hospitable widow. Seeing Sylvie's bourgeois gown and exhausted face, she had no qualms accepting her lie that she traveled alone, since her sister wouldn't arrive in Paris until tomorrow.

The small room served its purpose. Sylvie burned the bloody cloak in the fireplace using a lit candle before falling into bed.

SYLVIE SLEPT FROM that morning to the next, only waking for a few minutes at a time before succumbing to exhaustion.

When the sun became too bright to ignore, she re-dressed and washed her face in the water basin. Sylvie paid the innkeeper for the additional hours used and walked to Rue Saint-Honoré.

A part of her prayed Gaspard would be awaiting her return in Aunt Fifi's hideous yellow chair, but all of her hope did not spare her from returning to an empty house.

She did not inform the servants that she'd arrived, instead going over to Chez Duplay. Cornélie would be furious she'd broken her promise, but Sylvie needed Cornélie's strength. Sylvie had no idea when the convicts would be tried or if anything had changed in the day she'd been gone.

When she knocked on the Duplays' door, no one answered. The door's lock looked damaged—like someone had forced it open.

"Hello?" she asked. Her voice came out hoarse. "Cornélie? Lise?" No answer came from any part of the house.

She went to the sitting room only to find it torn apart. The end tables had missing legs, and teacups crunched underfoot.

"They've been arrested, Mademoiselle," said the Duplays' maid, entering the room at the sound of a voice. Her face glowed pink from a morning of tears. "All of them, even *petit* Philippe."

His silver rattle lay on the floor, broken in half.

août 1794

Gaspard was dead.

He and the other Montagnards died at the Place de la Révolution by guillotine.

Sylvie did not go to the execution. She could not stomach her brother's tearful blue eyes as he looked frantically for a savior that would not come. She could not endure the dragging of Gus's broken legs along the stage for the guillotine.

Still, she knew when the blade fell: the cheers from the crowd reached her sitting room on Rue Saint-Honoré easily. She thought little of Robespierre and his butchered jaw and his cowardice.

Only when Louise returned—having seen the guillotine fall on each and every neck—did Sylvie allow herself to feel the truth of his death. Louise approached her, ashen faced, and nodded her head.

Sylvie stared down at her empty teacup: she had never actually filled it. "Did he look frightened?" she asked.

Louise knelt and took her hands. "No, Mademoiselle. He was strong, so dignified—"

Sylvie started to sob, "Did he look for me? In the crowd? Should I have gone? Dear God," she wailed into Louise's arms. "God help me, I let him die alone. He needed me and I wasn't there."

Louise vigorously shook her head. "No one should witness such a death. He would not have wanted you there."

She imagined her brother's pretty blond curls matted with blood, and she fantasized about joining him wherever lost souls go.

She untangled herself from Louise's embrace and sat in Aunt Fifi's overstuffed chair, wondering when her aunt's perfume had finally faded from the pink velvet.

SOMETIME LATER, PERHAPS hours, perhaps days, Louise put a package in Sylvie's hands.

"This is from Monsieur Rosiers. He had it smuggled out." She waited for a response, but Sylvie said nothing. "He is buried at the mass grave in Errancis Cemetery; they all are."

Once Louise left, Sylvie unwrapped the crinkled paper to reveal Gaspard's favorite flask. She removed the top and could still smell gunfire. But tea stains were not the only thing in the flask—he had rolled a small letter inside.

She unfurled the note and read the trembling script.

Dearest Sylvie,

Forgive the lateness of this letter, but I doubt I will have another chance to write after today—I fear the Commune's forces will not hold for much longer.

The rioting outside the walls of the Hôtel de Ville torments me, but less than the silence of my fellow outlaws. I contemplate the sins of those trapped here tonight—a place once a Keep of Liberty that is now a self-made prison—and wonder what will be written in the years to follow us.

There were times I faltered, times when power looked alluring and duty did not. I had my triumphs, but it is the failures that haunt me as I share these chambers with doomed men.

I fear death, and I assume Maximilien contemplates the same as he stares at those long-cooled ashes. I shall think of what you've endured so I may endure as well. It is Gus who remains calm, and while his hands tremble too greatly to write, he asks that I tell you that you are his dearest friend.

I think of the unmarked grave I am destined for, and it is only fair that my end is the same as all the other people my father bought and bartered for out of greed. Death came quickly for Edmond, but it seemed it took more time with me.

I do not have the strength of mind to write to Lise, but please be a friend to her in widowhood. She has shown me more love in a few short years than most men can hope for in a lifetime.

Please do not come to see the execution; I do not want my last vision to be of your horror. And for God's sake, do not make some dreadful mausoleum from the flask—it ought to be full of gunfire, or gin in a pinch.

Your Loving Brother,
Gaspard

Crying and laughing, she called for Louise. "Could you bring me some tea and rum?"

Chapter Thirty-Three

Whoever did not live in the years neighboring 1789 does not know what the pleasure of living means.

—*Charles Maurice de Talleyrand-Périgord*

décembre 1794

Sylvie had sent a request to La Petite Force prison to visit the Duplays the week after their arrest. The conditions in prisons improved once the influx of "traitors" decreased and visiting requests had been honored for other prisoners. She did not receive her reply until October.

The prison administrators wrote back with approval and a time for the visit, filling her with a happiness unknown to her for months.

As much as Sylvie wanted to bring them a nourishing meal or a toy for Philippe, the prison allowed no outside contraband or food. She would have to be enough.

La Petite Force prison had not an ounce of beauty, unlike its older predecessor, the Hôtel de la Force. It served as an expansion of the previous prison, and the entire building was made of nothing but iron and stone—and the bleak December sky did little to improve the general atmosphere. But despite its austere exterior, imprisonment there offered a superior quality of life for those fortunate enough to be transferred.

The guards searched her person for weapons or smuggled goods and took her to a holding room where the sisters awaited her. The

Convention had acquitted Maurice Duplay earlier that month, despite his position as a judge in the Revolutionary Tribunal. His wife, Cornélie's mother, had killed herself days after her arrest, believing her family doomed to execution.

The sisters Duplay and *petit* Philippe Le Bas remained captives, their grieving father shut up in the house haunted by dead men on Rue Saint-Honoré.

The months of confinement indoors left the women ghostly pale, the color drained from their skin and eyes. But neither they nor the baby looked starved; Philippe had grown much since Sylvie had seen him last. The six-month-old sat in his mother's lap with little support, and Sylvie observed that his cloudy blue eyes from infancy had cleared into a truer blue like his father's.

She saw so much of Gaspard's face in his son, and both she and Lise teared up when Sylvie first entered.

"He's so grown," Sylvie said. "And *blond*."

The guard did not give them privacy, standing by the door instead.

Sylvie sat across from the Duplays; if she let her imagination take over, she could pretend they sat at a dinner table rather than in a prison.

Philippe looked at Sylvie curiously, no longer familiar with his aunt.

"I suspect it will darken as he gets older," said Cornélie. "Lise looked like a little blond cherub as a babe as well."

Prison had stolen Cornélie's healthy glow and paint-smudged fingers—instead, she had sallow cheeks and a weary soul.

"Tell me you're all right," Sylvie begged. "Tell me you're not suffering."

Cornélie reached for her hand, and they both shuddered at the touch. They had not felt each other's skin in months; the craving for intimacy was only barely soothed by the minimal contact.

"We are treated as well as one can expect," Cornélie said, her eyes flicking to the guard, whose back was to them. "*Petit* Philippe buoys our spirits; he is our sun when we long for the light."

"It is Cornélie whose courage keeps me strong," corrected Lise. "At first I wanted to die like Mama or my husband—to make the grieving stop. But she told me to live for Philippe if not myself." The baby babbled when he heard his name.

Sylvie adjusted a pin in Cornélie's hair, using her fingers to follow the line of Cornélie's ear and the curve of her jaw. "She has always been our strength when we had none," she said. "When I missed you most, I stared at your signature on my portrait, copying it over and over. The roses miss you as well," she added with a happier smile. "The garden has gone wild without your strict management."

"I long for my flowers," Cornélie said. "I had almost forgotten the color green until you came in with the floral print of your gown."

Another guard called from outside the door, and their current warden hurried out of the room. Sylvie did not know how long this spontaneous privacy might last; they would need to discuss any plans quickly.

"Do you think they will release you?" asked Sylvie.

"Papa does not know. He confers with his lawyer friends that survived the purge. Philippe would be spared, of course, and that's all that matters."

"Of course it's not," said Sylvie. She refused to let them throw their lives away. "You're as innocent as he—you've done nothing!" *Nothing that they know of.*

Philippe cooed—sweetly unaware that he'd spent his first months of life in a prison cell.

"Yes," said Cornélie as she stroked the babe's hair. "When Robespierre changed and began his campaign of terror, I did nothing. I loved the old Robespierre so much that I forgave the sins of the newer."

Sylvie let her nephew play with one of her rings. He hadn't seen anything beautiful for so long. "I of all people know what cruelties one forgives out of love. The Convention will acknowledge the 'influence of a husband.' There are benefits to indulging the idea we are empty-headed wombs."

Cornélie laughed. "You're the only person who could make me laugh in a prison cell."

Philippe reached out to Sylvie, and she eagerly held him. The weight of him in her arms was a tangible reminder of her duty to her brother.

"Do you think he remembers you?" asked Lise.

"Probably not," Sylvie said. The babe tried to grab her chin. "But this will not be the last time he sees me. My nephew will not celebrate his first birthday behind stone walls."

"I doubt Barras will agree with you," said Cornélie with a sneer. "I know him well through Robespierre; he's a man who allies himself with whoever can advance his career. As long as he controls the army of Paris and has a seat on the Committee of Public Safety, he controls our fate."

"Wait," Sylvie said. "Did Barras not serve with Augustin and Napoleon at Toulon?"

Augustin had mentioned Napoleon and Barras throughout his letters, singing the praises of the former like a proud parent. Both soldiers gained some fame under Augustin's tutelage, and she hoped their loyalty still endured.

"*Oui*, they did. But even if your connection to Augustin was known to him, there is no guarantee he'd even give you an audience."

"Would Barras accept a bribe?"

Cornélie did not look convinced. "The offer alone could get you arrested."

Sylvie scoffed. The very idea of mere bribery causing her downfall offended her. She'd murdered a man—it would take more than a petty bribe to defeat her. "The man *must* have a weakness. A mistress, perhaps? Someone close to him to whom I could plead my case?"

"Joséphine de Beauharnais," said Lise. Sylvie knew of the surname: Alexandre de Beauharnais died at the Place de la Révolution shortly before the coup. "They released her from Carmes prison right after the sentencing of Robespierre. The whole affair was rather suspicious because of how quickly she became Barras's mistress."

"She's from Martinique, the daughter of a planter," added Cornélie softly.

Mistress to a deputy and an island émigré: Joséphine sounded like Sylvie's mirror image, albeit a whiter one.

And her only hope.

JOSÉPHINE'S APARTMENTS BELONGING to Barras sat across the Seine, and the journey by carriage lasted only a few minutes. Sylvie decided to forgo the traditional route of requesting an audience with Joséphine and planned to arrive at her door with a simple note and the promise of a gift to gain entry.

Sylvie hoped to appeal to both Viscountess Joséphine's own losses to the Revolution and her birthplace: she had been arrested, her husband had been executed, and the tropical paradise she'd grown up in was thousands of miles away. Joséphine could not stay forever with her children at the Pentemont Abbey—apartments for wealthy women who sought separation from their husbands—once the Terror began. She needed support and, like Sylvie, secured a future for herself in a revolutionary's bed.

Barras had allied himself with Napoleon since Toulon, and Sylvie knew Joséphine and the Corsican general were at least acquainted. If Joséphine reasonably declined to risk her position for a stranger, then

Sylvie would simply ask that her request be passed along to Napoleon instead.

She dressed in a finer robe from her days on Saint-Domingue, a subtle reminder to Joséphine of their shared heritage. The gown was a little out of fashion, but then again, France had left their old worlds behind.

Unlike others in Sylvie's circle, the viscountess *had* grown up in a world full of mulattoes, slaves, and plantation society. Sylvie's race alone could be her downfall.

But the silk bag in her pocket contained what she hoped would balance the scales in her favor.

She presented the note to the steward of the household, who took her to a small receiving room to await Joséphine's response.

"She will see you, Mademoiselle," the steward said when he returned. "Do follow me."

Joséphine de Beauharnais relaxed in a velvet chaise, her gown cut fashionably high and a large brooch winking in the sunlight. With raven-black hair and an elegant pallor, Joséphine embodied the pinnacle of French beauty. But within a beautiful pair of dark eyes, Sylvie found a good deal of intelligence.

"You are very foolish to come here, Mademoiselle Rosiers," the lady said with a pinched mouth. "In your note, you apologize on Robespierre's behalf for murdering my husband, all the while confessing your connection. I could have the guard here momentarily and have you put in the same cell as the Duplays." Her manners reminded Sylvie of Cornélie—graceful and clever, but with a coldness that could cast a room in ice. "Why on earth would you come to me and ask for favors?"

Deference did not come easily to Sylvie, but she did her best to appear humble. "Love is a more powerful persuasive tool," she said. "And you have it. Also, I wanted to appeal to a woman whose losses are so similar to my own." Joséphine's husband had been guillotined at the Place de la Révolution only days before Robespierre's execution. The aristocrat turned away. "I worried the Tribunal would judge me for my connection to the Robespierres."

"And you thought I would not?"

"You are like me; your husband's death stranded you in the middle of war, and you allied with those who could ensure survival. The Convention spared your life, and I want them to spare the Duplays."

Sylvie was unsure if her candor would be admired or found offensive, but Joséphine's tone softened when she asked, "Why did you not go to Napoleon for aid? *He* was Augustin's protégé. Napoleon mourned him when he died."

She had only just become Barras's mistress, so her knowledge of Napoleon's friendship with Gus surprised Sylvie. In exchange for Joséphine's honesty, Sylvie offered hers once more.

"I've always put my protection in the hands of men, thinking that if I found the right one, I'd never know unhappiness again. All my life I've been attached, stained by the men who owned me. I am sure your Bonaparte is a great man, but great men cast wide shadows— and I've been out of the sun for too long."

Joséphine listened more attentively now, her eyes narrowed in interest. "You know my sad tale, though I don't know yours beyond what Barras and Napoleon have said. How did some runaway mulatta find herself in the bed of a radical?"

Sylvie recognized the distance and suspicion almost all women from the islands had of dark-skinned girls. "I'm also the daughter of a planter, though my mother's origins you can guess," Sylvie said. Joséphine's eyebrow quirked. "I may have been born free, but I had so many masters. Fear, lust, pride—I allowed myself to be governed by every weakness. When the rebellion broke on Saint-Domingue, I thought, I *hoped*, fighting for a noble cause would absolve me of my old sins.

"I was practically a mercenary for hire. I would have fought for anything; I only wanted purpose, worth. So, when they offered me a place in their mission, I gave them my heart."

"I have been in Mademoiselle Duplay's position," said Joséphine as she stared into her most unpleasant memories. "Imprisoned because of my husband's name and not my own, a criminal by association. Those were the worst days of my life." She stroked the diamonds dangling from her brooch.

Joséphine feared poverty most of all, that much was clear. And Sylvie came prepared.

She withdrew the silk pouch and poured the contents into her palm: two large pearl and sapphire earrings and a matching double-stranded necklace—her engagement gift from Julien. Those pearls had been anchors in her pocket on the voyage to Charleston, and now they could mean rescue.

Joséphine gaped at the bounty. The pearls looked even whiter in Sylvie's hand, and no doubt Joséphine noticed. "They are from Saint-Domingue. Each pearl is from an oyster fished from Saint-Domingue's sea."

Joséphine lifted a single earring into the afternoon light and said, "They are magnificent, as white as sugar. I can almost hear the ocean."

"They are yours . . ." said Sylvie. Let Joséphine have her white fantasies, as long as they ensured her agreement. ". . . if you convince Barras or Napoleon to free the Duplays. Philippe Le Bas has not seen his home since he was an infant."

Joséphine held a pearl to her ear with one hand and a mirror in another. "I make no promises," she said as she admired the movement of the pearl in her reflection. "But I shall try."

THE NEW YEAR came while France struggled to find its footing after the demise of its previous leaders. The unrest and unpopularity of Marat-esque methods could finally be discussed freely, and the military campaigns found success in the Netherlands.

But it was when a carriage pulled up to the Duplay house that Sylvie knew *her* war was over. And Sylvie suspected she had Joséphine de Beauharnais to thank.

Lise, Philippe, and Cornélie returned to Rue Saint-Honoré after their release from La Petite Force early in the morning; the fallen snow had not yet been soiled by horses or people. It required most of Sylvie's willpower not to go to them immediately; Maurice would need time with his children and grandchild as well.

After an hour passed, Sylvie trekked through the snowy street to unite with the liberated prisoners.

A piece of her worried whether captivity had changed Cornélie or hardened her heart beyond repair. The Revolution had stolen Sylvie's innocence, her brother, and a lover—she could not imagine a soul in France who had not lost something to the Terror. Though she prayed Cornélie's love was not lost to the Terror, too.

And when Cornélie ran into her arms the moment she entered, she knew the Terror had shown them mercy in that regard.

Lise joined their embrace, with *petit* Philippe wiggling in the middle. They remained fixed together for several minutes, with no one able to let go.

Later that week, Sylvie found Cornélie standing in Robespierre's old room after supper. "It's empty," she said.

"The Convention confiscated all of his belongings. Everything he touched belongs to them now."

Sylvie wrapped her arms around Cornélie's waist. "Not you."

"No," Cornélie said. "Not me."

In the time since their homecoming, she had regained her color and beauty. However, a few days after their return, she began dyeing her dresses and robes black. She wore one then, a robe that once boasted a beautiful floral print, now lost to the powerful dark pigment.

People mistakenly believed she wore black to mourn Robespierre, as did Sylvie for a time. But Cornélie mourned the man he used to be, as well as those he sent to an early grave.

"They did leave one thing behind," said Cornélie. "I kept it in my room."

She took Sylvie to a large chest at the foot of her bed, turning the lock and popping open the lid.

Under a linen sheet, David's *Silvia* looked up at them from her dark hiding place.

"We shouldn't keep it," said Sylvie. She could hear Gaspard sniggering that it was the most pretentious thing he'd ever seen.

Cornélie carefully removed the canvas from the chest and rested it against the bed frame.

"You must admit it's a very fair likeness," she said. "You're beautiful." She stroked Sylvie's cheek with winsome admiration.

The painting was burdened by so many memories and hopes Sylvie wished she could forget. Silvia mocked her, bloated with symbolism and grandiose morality. A beautiful dream she had murdered for.

And she did not want the world to see it. They had their *Death of Marat*. Let them soothe their hurts with *that* pretty lie.

"It's not me," Sylvie said. "I'm not the Madonna of the Revolution. The thing should be burned with the falsehoods it represents. Let the sins be forgotten."

Cornélie gave a dry chuckle. "We will be worm and rot before their sins are ever forgotten. But I see your point; the painting will only incriminate you further."

Using a pair of hair scissors from her vanity, Cornélie cut out the canvas from the wood framing and offered it to Sylvie.

They knelt before the hearth and tossed it in, the fire eating the edges of the canvas and working its way to the center. The flame reached Silvia's face last, and then the painting crumbled into ash—taking her connection with the Revolution, too.

"She did not survive the Revolution, Sylvie," said Cornélie as she stood, motioning to the woman sleeping in the ashes. "*You* did. It's time to put all your demons to bed."

Sylvie wished all of her memories could be so easily destroyed, that whole visions of horror and bloodshed and grief could be thrown to the flames and consumed.

She was now a Widow of Terror, a living reminder of those who did not survive their bloody sovereign. A childless mother, a living martyr, the widow who never married, the free slave. She lived as an impossible combination of fractions, a child of worlds separated by a vast ocean.

Cornélie kissed her temple, and Sylvie leaned into her embrace. Grieving, but with the flicker of a brighter future on the horizon, she could see her life without the bindings of her past. In her nephew, she found purpose; in Cornélie, she found love. Grief and peace, Sylvie discovered, might coexist in her heart.

She feared she hadn't done enough: for France, for Black people, for Nicole. The sands of Saint-Domingue would never be fully shaken from the fabric of her soul, and the little gold button of the dead Swiss Guard would be rubbed smooth by the end of Sylvie's life.

And she carried those burdens with greater wisdom and poise than when she was a girl, acknowledging their perpetual weight on her shoulders. But she had the love of a family she'd chosen, not defined by slave codes or tradition, and the fractions that had carved up her heart healed into something whole.

Author's Note

M*ademoiselle Revolution* was born on a sticky June day in Williamsburg, Virginia. As anyone who has visited—on either field trips or infamous family vacations—knows, Colonial Williamsburg is a tiny Virginia hamlet seemingly frozen in the eighteenth century.

I sat in the front of my American history class, one of maybe ten students, listening to my young professor explain the antebellum American South.

Up until that point, Western history courses hadn't offered anything new to my perspective or worldview, and that class began with much of the same information as my previous American history classes. But my professor was emotive, her red hair poorly held back with a clip, and she had a passion for her work that made American history feel novel and engaging.

"What made the Civil War inevitable?" she asked.

We provided many answers: the invention of the cotton gin, the first enslaved Africans being brought to Virginia, the Harpers Ferry slave revolt.

Her interpretation was one I had never heard of or even been taught about: the Haitian Revolution, which started in 1791. The slave revolt that incited the revolution was objectively gruesome and violent. As described in this novel, organized groups of once-enslaved people pushed from plantation to plantation to pillage and slaughter their previous masters.

There were immediate consequences: The revolution directly instigated significant American slave revolts, and the United States levied a brutal embargo against the new nation. And without Haiti, a cash-poor France offered up its North American territories, and Southern proponents of slavery enthusiastically lobbied for the Louisiana Purchase as a way to spread racial subjugation west.

But by choosing a more critical lens to interpret history through, we get a panoramic view of the American response: Slave owners considered the revolt as evidence of Black people's barbarism and, thus, their unfitness for freedom. They saw the Black democracy as a threat to their ideology of white supremacy and power, not to mention as a legitimization of their constant fear of revenge—given the methods the Haitians used to attain it. Northerners judged it as proof that enslaved people could not only be freed but they could establish a democracy in the image of the United States. Black people could and *should* become active citizens, and slavery as an institution was cruel, unnatural, and impossible to maintain indefinitely.

To oversimplify the matter, one could say the incongruence between Southern reactionary white supremacy and Northern abolitionist sentiment was caused by the Black success in what is now Haiti. Both factions felt vindicated by the events of the revolt, leading to a series of policies and cultural shifts that culminated in the Civil War.

But most importantly, my professor painted the American reaction with a human—and truthful—brush. I had never before been offered this kind of explanation. My prior education had consistently pointed the finger of blame from people to things: the cotton gin,

regional economic differences, geography. This new rationale offered me something greater. This examination of the Haitian Revolution as the flint and steel that sparked the Civil War restored the
human causes of American division.

Haiti sat at the epicenter of the Enlightenment, race theory, and
democracy—intertwining the threads of French and American history. This vital component of Black history was the keystone of my
own journey as a Black woman, and I knew this critically absent
piece of my childhood education needed an audience wider than my
little class of ten.

Thus began *Mademoiselle Revolution*.

As I wrote about protest, racism, and the vulnerabilities of tyrants, Americans elected a charismatic charlatan who championed a
population deeply tied to the bloody roots of the failed Confederacy.
But the shared grief over Black suffering at the hands of white institutions bubbled over into widespread protests in support of Black
Lives Matter (BLM).

Philadelphia bloomed with signs and chants as I walked the block
to city hall with the masses. The National Guard drove by my apart-
ment while I worked on law school outlines. I remember George
Floyd's face better than any court opinion from that semester.

But as BLM expanded in scope and intensity, conservatives decried the "rioting" and destruction of property by supposed protesters. The parallels to the slave revolt of 1791 brought the events in
Mademoiselle Revolution to the forefront of modern discourse.

In the eighteenth and nineteenth centuries, Southerners wielded
the same rhetoric of savagery to undermine the legitimacy of the Haitians' demands for freedom. They pointed to the carnage, the rapes, the
dismemberment, the thefts. This characterization of the movement
was correct, but that era of history, in all of its unpleasant but unalien-
able truth, requires acknowledgment of all the cruelties Black people
endured, not restricted to those deemed appropriate for a high school

student's textbook. Examining the weapons of white supremacy requires a broader picture.

In *Mademoiselle Revolution*, I offer historical anecdotes for the critical context of Black rage. For fun, French slave owners would force an enslaved person into a wooden box, fill it with nails, and push the box down a hill. Sometimes overseers would rub gunpowder into a slave's wounds and then set them on fire. Burying people alive was commonplace—enslavers would leave the head exposed and cover it in molasses to encourage insects to consume the person's face. Another pastime included putting people into the furnace with the bagasse (sugarcane waste). There are so many of these stories. So many.

This is not to excuse the violence of the revolt or to say it was justified—I am uninterested in weighing the atrocities of each side against the other. It's to retain the context of Black suffering, a suffering that, though eased with legislation and court cases, has yet to be fully addressed.

More than two centuries ago, the uprising and subsequent liberation of Haiti created a festering wound in the United States, one that would eventually turn gangrenous with racist dogma, fear, and capitalism. And modern conservative pundits sow white fear stemming from that same poison: Black people will terrorize white suburbs and cities, Black anger is undeserved, and white property is at risk of Black destruction. A response copied and pasted from 1791.

While the white reaction to Black freedom remains identical, the Black means of revolution have changed. BLM protesters did not adopt the same grim methods as the self-liberated Haitians. Kimberly L. Jones inadvertently summed up the critical difference between 1791 and 2020 in the viral video taken to counter conservative criticism of BLM: "They are lucky that what Black people are looking for is equality and not revenge."

So then what do the Haitian Revolution and all of its complexities teach us?

Slavery is bad. Racism is bad.

This is not an oversimplification; the enslavement of Black people and the racial justifications for that subjugation were the direct causes of the Haitian Revolution, just as they were the direct causes for the police violence preceding BLM.

I processed so much of BLM and the 2020 quarantine through *Mademoiselle Revolution*, using the framework of historical fiction to address modern questions. Sylvie struggles to embrace new worldviews with liberal hypocrisy, juxtaposing the characterization of the French (and white) Revolution with that of the Haitian, all while trying to mature in a time of immense terror.

And, like Sylvie, I struggled. I struggled through a pandemic and protests, mental illness, and the erosion of once-trusted institutions. But, as I experienced on that hot day in June, restoring history is a messy yet rewarding step in the long process of reconciling our past, our present, and ourselves.

Acknowledgments

My books, like the history they explore, are a product of many experiences and relationships. So, firstly, I must thank my mother, Mara, for making this novel a reality. It is her unconditional love for, and willingness to learn from, her Black daughters that gave me the strength and confidence to write about the privileges and struggles of a mixed identity. I owe my little sister, Zia, thanks as well, for joining me in the burdens and joys of a shared childhood the way only a sister can.

Additionally, I must thank Amanda Foody—to whom this book is dedicated—not only for being the best friend a woman could have but for expanding the limits on what I thought I could achieve. Her integrity and dedication to her craft were my compass on the journey to publication.

Of course, I have to highlight my incredible agent, Amy Bishop, and editor, Jen Monroe, for their infinite creativity, support, and patience. This book would not have been possible without the entire Berkley team, including Dache' Rogers, Lauren Burnstein, Jessica Plummer, Natalie Sellars, Claire Zion, Jeanne-Marie Hudson, Craig Burke, Candice Coote, and Christine Legon. I'd also love to thank

Vi-An Nguyen for creating a stunning book cover, and my wonderful production editor, Liz Gluck.

And finally, a huge thanks to Catherine Bakewell; Carrie Callaghan; Swati Teerdhala; Carli Segal; M. A. Guglielmo; Randall S. Simpson; Jason C. Lee; Alexis Castellanos; Frances Fok; Dystel, Goderich & Bourret; and the College of William & Mary.